"Last Flight Of The Electra"
By: Paul A Hinton
2014

Published in the United States of America
By Paul A Hinton

Printed in the United States of America
By Create Space
An Amazon Company
Charleston South Carolina

Cover Art I-Stock Photo
Vector Image
#4226035
Contributor Cyrup

Web: booksbyhinton.com
Email: paulhintonbooks@gmail

<u>Special Thanks</u>

To my beloved wife Cecily.

Thank you for supporting me in all that I dream.
Thank you for spending endless hours proofreading.
Thank you for loving me.

To my children
Jesse
Joshua
Melissa Jo

Thank you for letting me be the goofy dad,
and for not taking me too seriously.
Thank you for being my inspiration.

To my parents
Olen and Patricia Hinton
I love you.

To Janet Sauls
Thank you for all the hours, edits, and advice.

To Cathy

I hope you enjoy

LAST
FLIGHT
OF THE
ELECTRA

This story was inspired by a trip to the Marshall Islands in 2003. It was there, while visiting the island of Roi-Namur on the northern side of the Kwajalein atoll, among the ruins of the former Japanese base, that I first encountered the story you are about to read. Simply put, as I stood next to a jail cell that at one time may have held Amelia Earhart, in which a pen or broach with the initials AE was rumored to have been discovered, I felt a presence, something otherworldly, something that I cannot explain to this day.

Since that day, this story has brewed within. The main character Truc is a compilation of all the wonderful people of the Marshall Islands that I met while on my journey. In all my travels, I have never met a more kind and beautiful people. I want to thank the people of the Kwajalein Atoll for allowing me into their life, if but for a brief moment, and I want to thank Amelia Earhart and Commander Fred Noonan for being brave beyond measure.

I

Revelation

The sea is a creature best loved by the hands of men
Who will sing to her songs of peace in the morning
As if the world must not know they are lovers
For she is kind to those who penetrate her depth,
And desire no bounds but the salt of her womb

O tto was determined to grow old in a most
irresponsible manner, and to that end, his pride
and joy, the Sand Seeker, stood ten days out of Hawaii
and six months into their journey. Yet now, as he
stared at an oncoming storm, he began to feel as if he
may have traveled one mile too far. To make matters
worse, for the past half hour, as if warning that he
should not have come this way, deep within the
approaching squall a random wisp of light had begun
to pierce the storms dark face. The dance of light held
no course nor appeared twice in the same place. The
phenomenon, by its nature was erratic, yet it was there,
subconsciously pressing against his panic button. This
is how it all began, a wisp of light, a dreadful storm
and a weary sailor.

A white-knuckle grip on his binoculars was all that told of his inner turmoil as he surveyed the twisted skyline. He began to entertain the thought that a pensioner's home may have been the more reasonable pursuit as he observed lightning spit from the tempest's edge as if the Gates of Hell should have a rival. Perhaps his old mates would lift a toast in honor of his endeavor, he thought. Perhaps, they would even say that he was the best of them, but Otto knew, more likely than not, they would simply call him a damned fool.

They had done as much when he announced his intention to marry his beloved Catherine. Each had warned, Cat was a sharp tart with skinny legs and big tits after his pension. At the time, he wanted to believe they were simply jealous of his beautiful bride to be and his own brave life. His dogged determination, to circumnavigate the globe, had felt like a romantic endeavor, even cavalier on dry land. However, that was on dry land and there was little of that bravado left in him today. All he could do now was hope his old mates were wrong as he worried over his ill Catherine, for foul weather was not her cup of tea.

He decided to peer into the galley and reassure Cat that he was in control, however, as he flashed his famous broad smile, he found himself rewarded with a look of contempt. A look he had come to know all too well in the past few weeks. Her normally rosy complexion had grown to be pasty white below deck, like a rag doll left to fade in a windowsill and nothing he might offer could possibly suffice to alleviate her fear. He had fetched her away to this remote patch of ocean and he could not take that back now.

Otto cursed under his breath as he closed the hatch, then thought it best to pray as he attempted to start the engine one last time. The motor strained, in that strange metallic way mechanical things do when they are not going to cooperate but the effort was of no use. It seemed neither prayer, nor cursing would deliver the result he so desperately desired.

"Bloody Hell! Show me some love old girl," he snapped as he twisted the key once again in a vain effort to force a different result. Her engine had been out of commission for two days and every effort on his part to revive her had failed miserably. It would take a port and a good mechanic to bring her back into order and both of those were in short supply at the moment.

He considered hailing a mayday. However, they were not in distress at present and his pride would not allow him to abandon his beloved Sandy so easily. It would make no difference he told himself. It would take at least two days for the Coast Guard to come to their rescue and no another ship had appeared on his radar since the engine had died. All he knew for sure was that he would soon have a migraine if he could not light a cigarette. No amount of experience could solve that problem, he thought, as he fumbled with his last pack against the prevailing wind.

Sandy; a nickname Catherine had coined, as she accused the Sand Seeker of being Otto's mistress, was nearly as wide as she was long. A ketch of broad curves, highlighted by dark burgundy accents that followed her contours and his Sandy, like Catherine, was easy on the eye. Otto knew he had hit the jackpot in the arena of the two women to whom he had dedicated his life, and this was a good thing, since both had effectively consumed most of his life savings.

As he finished lashing the storm sails the flash of light issued forth once again, and then as quick, disappeared into the wall of rain before him.

"What the Bloody Hell are you?" he muttered, as he hefted his binoculars and peered into the brew. Highlighted with red streaks the storms edge was now seemingly supported by waves that looked to be lumbering giants arguing over who should swamp him first.

There would be no sailing around this storm and the objective, that had brought them to this point, now felt oddly unnecessary. The effort to convince Catherine, to seek a remote island known as Johnson, a detour from their original red pin plan, had required tact and several bottles of wine. The long romantic evening of steaks and liquor had ended with her approval and so he abandoned the tried and true northerly passage normally used by those who do such things as sail around the globe.

Having once housed a series of chemical warfare research labs, Johnson Island, had maintained during the Cold War a long string of multi-story buildings and a runway, which extended the length of the rocky outcrop. The runway remained for desperate pilots seeking a refuge over a vast ocean, but now, there was little to appreciate about America's dirty little secret. Proof the facilities existed was now no more than a few cracking slabs, as America, in an attempt right her wrongs, created the most expensive bird sanctuary known to man.

Otto began to survey his charts and quickly calculated the distance the beacon at Johnson should be visible, and with a huff, decided they were still too far away. Then, as if to remind him that he was on a collision course with a freak storm, a large wave swept across his bow and the Sand Seeker shuddered violently.

With the rising sun at his back, he decided the phenomenon had to be a trick of light against the gale wall. Until the wind shifted, and the flash of light descended into the least of his worries as he leaned into the wheel to correct course. His years of service in Her Majesties Royal Navy took over as he wrestled his Sandy into the next oncoming set of waves and he found the man he knew himself to be. Fear was no longer an option; Commander Otto Vonstreep would not go down without a fight.

"Cocked-up to Hell...you cheeky bugger!" he cursed the storm as he fought to find his footing. Then as if replying to his curse, a fierce rain band raced across the Sand Seekers deck, large drops that pinched exposed skin and found weary crevasses in rain gear.

Below deck, clinging to anything solid, Catherine decided that holding to the head and begging for baby Jesus during the storm would not do. She rallied her courage and cracked the hatch to survey the situation. The storm was still not upon them but it still looked rough she thought as she considered her options of remaining below and vomiting her guts out, or going top side to take a chance with lightning. The Sand Seeker shuddered once again from stem to stern and her decision was made. Lightning would be a quicker death, she thought to herself.

As she struggled to escape the confines of the cabin, Cat slipped on the steps, rolled across the deck, and immediately regretted her decision as a hard gust of wind and rain attempted to rip the hatch cover from her hands. Her ego bruised, she offered a weak but brave smile as Otto looked down upon her sprawled wet torso. She thought it odd that he was smiling was from ear to ear and she wondered what could possibly make him so happy at such a moment. That was until she realized that her bikini top had come undone. At least he knew what he wanted she thought, as she attempted to recover her dignity.

Otto tacked to gain a footing against the wind's sudden change in direction while Cat scrambled to take up post beside him at the wheel. The adrenaline of the moment left little to be said between the two doomed lovers. There was a comfort in knowing, no matter how the day ended, they would face it together.

Minutes became an eternity for Cat as the Sand Seeker crushed each wave beneath her bow with the force of a train crashing into a car, shivering violently with each volley. Finally, on a roll hard to starboard, Cat knew she would soon be sick, as the energy of each collision seemed to end in her teeth. It was then, as she leaned over the railing to vomit, that Catherine first witnessed a dark ominous shadow moving independently of the storm wall. Cat wiped the tears from her eyes to confirm it was not her imagination. The effort did little to help. Something large was heading toward them as sure as she was terrified. She grunted at first, then mumbled, and finally grabbed Otto's arm to gain his attention. As he turned to face his bride, the looming shadow within the storm wall emitted the signature flash of light that he had come to know all too well.

"What the bloody hell is that?" Cat snapped, as she looked to Otto then back at the looming shadow. "You said, this would be an unremarkable jaunt," she gasped.

Otto remained silent. For the first time in his nautical career, he did not have an answer.

A moment later, the dark object pierced the storm wall and a heavy mist peeled away from the specter. Immediately, the outline of a sail appeared. Yet the sail, or for that matter the vessel, was in no way common. Cat rubbed her eyes in an effort to believe what she was witnessing. Racing away from the storm and toward them, at a high rate of speed, the vessel looked to be powered by the wing of an aircraft, and it embraced the storm as if it did such a thing on a daily basis.

"That's an odd bird," Catherine remarked above the fray as she wiped spittle from her cheeks.

Otto chose not to reply as he attempted to clear his weary eyes once again. The boundless odd winged craft, leapt across the waves with little effort at a speed he had only witnessed on professional racing catamarans. Yet, this vessel was no playboy's toy. It was primitive; obviously hand built, and treating the storm as if it were a spring shower.

"Yes, it is odd," he finally replied. "I...I don't...what the...!"

Like a wound spring, the odd winged craft suddenly flexed as it entered the next set of waves, and revealed something Otto had not expected. Suspended by a control line, at the far tip of the vessel's opposing outrigger, an old man swayed like a marionette dancing to a song no one else could hear, and to Otto, he appeared to be dead.

"He's unconscious," Otto bellowed as he began evasive maneuvers. Nevertheless, to his horror, his beloved Sandy failed to respond as another strong gust forced her toward the oncoming vessel.

"Come about you sour old bitch," he cursed, as he attempted to swing the mast about.

He knew then, as the sea bred bitter waves and lightning snapped about him that they were doomed. For the odd vessel was far too fast and he had no tricks left in his bag.

"I'm sorry, luv...I...I," he began to mutter. Yet, as the words failed Otto, the old seafarer on the winged vessel suddenly awoke and initiated an emergency tack. The winged vessel moaned as if haunted by a thousand ghosts as wood and metal bound tight into a fist and tunneled deep into the next set of swells. The first set swallowed the main hull of the old man's vessel and the outrigger, from which he was suspended, swept up and away as if to protect him from their assault. He looked to Otto like a kid riding a bike downhill and the violent nature of all that was occurring, seemingly, had no effect on the old man. If anything, he was enjoying the experience Otto thought, as the old man's smile appeared to expand with each foot the outrigger raced toward the sky.

Otto howled for his Sandy to come about with renewed hope. Sandy moaned in her own odd way, as if in response to the winged vessel cry's, and in that precarious moment, when no other action could be undertook, Otto marveled at the magnificent vessel of wood and metal bearing down upon him. For never once, in all his years of sailing had he witnessed a vessel react as violently or as quickly as it crushed the last set of waves separating their two worlds.

Fighting to win the war of wind and momentum, the odd winged vessel, with only feet to spare began to swing about, which exposed a faded black call sign on her upright metallic wing. Jutting into the sky like a dagger, Otto found himself staring at the wing in awe. The large airplane wing and the mechanics involved to make her work were in his estimation a true a miracle of engineering.

Then, much to Otto and Cat's astonishment, the ancient sailor waved as if a long lost neighbor greeting them on the front lawn. Otto would later recall that it seemed as if the old man knew they would not collide.

With one last orgasmic moan, the winged vessel completed her course correction and her outrigger swung up and away once again, barely missing the railing of the Sand Seeker. With only feet to spare, the old man laughed aloud, leaned hard into his rigging, and held out his hand as if he wanted to touch his newfound friends.

Marked by caverns of time, wind and sun, his face told a story Catherine wanted to know. Moreover, she thought his smile to be the most pleasant she had ever encountered, and instinctively reached to know him, but inches failed, as the crush of boiling ocean between the two vessels forced the Sand Seeker over to starboard.

Then with the command of a master conductor, the old salt pulled a pin next to his torso and several ropes reeled away at his feet. A sail toward the bow burst forth with a loud snap and filled the sky. The sail, thick, brown, stiff, and resembling a large reed tablemat one rolls out for dinner guests, billowed twenty feet before the odd vessel and the old man returned to his original heading.

With the newfound sail the odd winged craft lurched forward, and the perch from which the old man was suspended, stole skyward once again. Otto could not help but to watch on as the old man worked furiously to make adjustments. The outrigger quickly dropped to within a few feet of the waves and the old man looked back, almost longingly, then waved one last time before he resumed his previous state of eyes closed, head leaned back and body limp.

To Otto, the old man looked to be dead once again, until, with no rhyme or reason, he reached to touch swells that passed beneath his fingertips as if they could speak to him.

Abruptly coming to life, Catherine snapped up a chart pen and Otto began a search for his camera. In an awkward dance of frustration and jubilation, she successfully wrestled the binoculars free of Otto's neck, while he snapped photos timed to the pitch of the swells.

"NR 16020," Catherine yelled aloud as she jotted the call sign down in her journal. She then began to draw the vessel as best she could under the circumstances for she knew no one would believe that they were nearly crushed by a vessel with an airplane wing for a sail.

Otto's endeavor to photograph the vessel only met with frustration. The camera lens coated with sea spray after only a few snapshots and he spun about to remedy the situation only freeze in his tracks as he witnessed what lay before him. Both he and Cat had unknowingly snubbed the storm in the midst of the near collision. He clutched Cat's shoulder, but she shook it off as she strained to focus on the odd craft sailing into the rising sun off their stern.

"Turn about luv...now," he grunted.

The change in Otto's tenor frayed Catherine's soul. The taste of bile began to fill the back of her throat as she gazed upon the sketch of the winged craft she had quickly etched. She thought the picture to be a good representation and her heart skipped a beat as the knot in her stomach returned. It seemed ashamed to die she thought, after witnessing such a miraculous vessel.

Cat mustered her bravery and turned about to face her deepest fear. Tears began to flow as a thin smile cracked her hardened exterior. The unimaginable was upon them. A passage of light had split the storm and blue sky began to pour forth as if a river through a dark jungle. God had heard her prayers and she began to dance about the Sand Seeker like a little girl as the fearsome storm dissipated before her eyes.

Otto asked his Sandy to follow the old man and his odd vessel, nevertheless, the bright metallic wing was no more than a dot on the horizon as he completed the tack. At that moment, as if a specter taking leave of a room, with one last flash of light, the old man and his odd winged vessel disappeared into the morning haze.

2

Acceptance

I denied this truth
As I longed for the taste of night to come
She touched my need, she called me home
Yet, I was but a rock on that far sandy shore
Whom neither believed nor hoped for more

The quiet nature of the Sand Seeker intensified as if by hushed words unheard by the human ear. The wind became a lover's caress upon her deck and the waves gently messaged her battered, sore hull, as if asking forgiveness. Moments like these had drawn Otto to the sea. As he opened the second bottle of wine and poured Cat another glass, he knew it was time to rethink his priorities.

"Are you trying to get laid, Sailor?" Catherine purred as she took the glass.

"Well, you can't blame a man for trying," Otto replied as he paused to consider the sea about them and his dream of circumnavigating the globe.

"I will take you home now Cat," he said abruptly. "I should not have made you come this far. We will return to Hawaii and book you a flight home. I'll stay with Sandy until I can sell her. If it is longer than a couple of weeks...I'll leave her with a broker."

Catherine remained silent; she had not expected an apology. She took a long sip as she absorbed the meaning of it all.

"Thank you," she finally replied, as she put her feet up on the wheel and playfully spun it back and forth. "That's a lovely gesture...but...who the bloody hell do you think you are to tell me I cannot complete what I set out to do? I chose to come on this trip as much as you, and I damn well mean to finish it...you cheeky bugger," Catherine snapped, as she punched him in the arm.

"I thought," Otto started.

"You best stop thinking. I will do the thinking...you will do the sailing. Do you understand me? And...you will be cooking a lot more!"

Otto, silenced, finally muttered, "Well then...I suppose that's settled."

No sooner had the words left his mouth than Cat's demeanor changed. She uncurled, swallowed the rest of her wine and began a thorough search of the Sand Seeker. A memory had begun to eat at her.

"Bugger it all, I've seen that number before," she announced, as she rummaged through a nearby locker. As if talking to anyone other than Otto, Cat carried on, "I was brushing up on the island chains. I know I have that book in here somewhere...it was in my hand yesterday."

Catherine fumbled about yet another locker, before declaring, "I am nearly positive I know what that number references Otto."

"It's an aircraft call sign," Otto replied, in his signature smug manner.

"I know...I know, you daft codger," she said with a huff, as Otto had a habit of telling her the obvious. With a great sigh of relief, she discovered the book and began leafing through the section regarding the Pacific island chains.

"Bugger me, there it is Otto!" she snapped, as she sat up and pointed.

"Take the piss out of me. It can't be," Otto mumbled, as he studied the picture.

"Well then, what the hell did we just see?" Cat asked as Otto glared at the page.

Otto snapped up Catherine's journal, on which she had copied the call sign, and studied each letter and number like a man confirming he had won the lottery.

"NR 16020...I know that is what I witnessed you old plonker. I am convinced of it," she demanded.

"It can't be," Otto mumbled once again as he scratched his head.

"Retrieve your photos. We can prove it!" she said as she tossed his precious camera into his lap.

The first photos were of their layover in Hawaii. A topless Cat, sunning top deck, appeared first and she punched Otto in the arm for the nerve. After a moment of verbal abuse for his indiscretion, Otto located the old sailor and his craft. The first photo was blurry, and the second not much better, but the third snapshot hit the jackpot. The call sign was as clear as day. Otto laughed aloud as he held the book and the camera close together in one last attempt to discredit his eyes.

"Holy mother of God...it is her," he bellowed as he bolted to the galley. He emerged with the satellite phone and a business card, and quickly dialed the number of Honolulu Coast Guard Base District 14.

"They are not going to believe us. She's been missing far too long," Catherine stated as fact.

"Bugger that; the world will know soon enough, if the old shite stays course," he replied.

3

Decision

Ache not Oh bones of despair
A champion rides the long distant swells
The song long lost matters no more
A new song is upon our shore

The base operator logged the call at 10:04 a.m. and offered the standard protocol questions. The British sailor on the far end grew frustrated and demanded to speak to an officer in charge before she could finish her questions. As fate would have it, Captain Steve Channing was to be that officer.

Captain Channing was in no mood for an irate sailor. His freshly discovered medical condition came with boredom-based migraines, and today's was a bad as any he had ever hoped to have. As the operator transferred the call, he laid his head on the desk and quietly asked God to kill him.

It would not have been a lie to call in sick, he thought as he stared at the phones' insistent flashing light.

"Another Monday, another idiot," He mumbled. "Please God" he said aloud this time, "kill me now."

As his eyeglasses advanced to Coke bottles, the rumor had it; he would be relieved on a medical discharge. A rare genetic disease would soon render Captain Channing legally blind, and along with that diagnosis, the dream of his own command had slipped away.

His fiancé ditched him a week after hearing the news, and to his horror, a week later was engaged to a more able-bodied officer; a man he had considered his best friend. To save face, the former friend transferred to the Gulf Coast and took his bride to be with him. The damage was irreversible. Captain Channing's failed life had become the talk of the base.

He loathed his peers who spoke in whispers when he passed them in the halls and he detested the fact that women treated him like a freak if he braved a night out. If only he could skip Monday, he thought as the light on the phone reminded him of his duty.

Life was quickly diminishing to a matter of measuring distances and staring at common objects for fear of forgetting what they looked like. He knew it would all fade and the reality of life in the dark had begun to fill a new set of dreams. Dreams he could not comprehend. The depression that followed his dreams was as debilitating as the loss of his sight, but it seemed he could stop neither. Counseling became fruitless as despair became harder to swallow, but swallow he did as he lived out his sentence in a condominium overlooking an ocean he could no longer enjoy.

Captain Channing had resigned all hope of a bright future only the week before, when he sold his car, put the local taxi company on speed dial and decided it best to know the bus schedule. It had to end today he told himself as he stared at the throbbing red light. The decision was made. He could not endure another Monday.

"Hello," he mumbled as he picked up the phone.

"To whom am I speaking?" the man on the far end asked with a thick British accent.

He cleared his throat and started over, "I'm Captain Channing. How may I help you?"

"My name is Otto Vonstreep," Otto began as if all should know who he was by now. "Two weeks ago my wife and I were at anchor in Hawaii. I was given a card from the officer who inspected my vessel and I want to report something of the utmost urgency?" Otto demanded more than requested.

"We are the Coast Guard; emergencies are the business we do best," Captain Channing replied as he remained bent over, running one hand through his dark shock of red hair. The man on the far end began his story and Steve began to doodle. He felt as if had become an excellent doodler the last few months. Perhaps he would become the world's first blind doodler, he thought as he half listened to story. There had to be other blind doodlers, he would not be the first he conceded to himself. Then he heard something he could not believe on the far end. As if, a ghost had pressed into his dark room of despair and forced him flee to the light. He broke the tip of his pencil, sat straight up and asked, "Did you say NR 16020?"

"NR 16020...that's correct," Otto replied, "Do a Google search and see for yourself."

It took only a moment to perform the search and Steve grimaced as the information lit up his screen.

"It can't be," he muttered.

"Are you still there Captain Channing?" Otto asked.

Steve cleared the frog from his throat and replied, "I'm still here. This must be an elaborate hoax."

"Bloody hell Captain, at the speed the old salt is traveling and the course he is taking, his vessel will be in Hawaiian waters within a week. If you do not believe me, ask him yourself when he arrives. He is coming your way Captain, as sure as I am a crusty old shite. You must see the vessel he is sailing to believe it. The damnedest thing I have ever witnessed I tell you."

Captain Channing balked. Of all the bizarre calls he had fielded, this was by far the craziest. He pondered his choices and found he liked not one of them. To believe the man on the other end would take a leap of faith he felt he could not muster.

Putting the man off felt like the right answer, he told himself. "I will have to take this under consideration Mr. Vonstreep," he finally replied. .

Otto knew a blow off when he heard one. He would have done the same; he decided to bring the big guns.

"Jesus, Mary and Joseph Captain...it is Captain?" Before Steve could answer Otto carried on, "The equivalent of the second coming is about to take place on your front door step...and I just told you the day he will arrive. Are you trying to tell me that you are going to shelve this news? Tell me that is not the case Captain?" Otto snapped as he intentionally forced his rising blood pressure across the line. "Check my service records with your intelligence service. I served thirty-three years in Her Majesty's Royal Navy. If you don't act...Hell, if you consider this too long, you will be remembered as a fool Captain."

If he were to believe him, Captain Channing knew he needed to bypass protocol and tell the Admiral personally...but how. He had only met the new Admiral once during his formal installment. He weighed the certainty that an officer of the watch does not interrupt a Vice Admiral with crazy stories.

Beyond his line of site, the Cutter Constance remained at rest. Light reflecting off the bay enveloped her but he could barely see the details of what he had hoped to be his cutter. It was then he calculated the consequences of getting it wrong. It only took a moment for him to determine that he was not every other officer. He had nothing left to lose.

After a quick overview of the Vonstreep's inspection log, he found the Sand Seeker to be flawless with no report of drugs or odd behavior. And, According to the officer who did the inspection, the Sand Seeker was in the best order. There was even a note on the hospitality of the Vonstreep's toward the crew. The report stated that Catherine had offered them food. He then confirmed Otto's claim that he was a former officer of the Royal Navy. As he read over Otto's accomplishments, he found himself impressed by Commander Vonstreep's illustrious career. A career he had hoped to have.

He decided that if he was going to pasture because of a delirious sailor, then this was as good a time as any. The United States Coast Guard would give him a medical discharge and the incident would die with his record of service if the story were a hoax. He could live with that, he thought.

"What if this is the truth?" he pondered aloud as he finished reviewing the records.

Otto heard the comment and snapped, "Why the hell do you think I am taking the time to call you on a satellite phone...at six pounds a minute?"

"Mr. Vonstreep, I believe you! I will take this to the Admiral. Call me back in two hours and I will let you know what to do," he said, as the fog of disbelief began to part.

"I've come about already Captain. Cat and I are returning to Hawaii. We wish to be on record for sighting him first. Make sure to put our names in your log. That is Otto and Catherine Vonstreep Captain. Do I need to spell them?" Otto ordered.

"So noted Commander Vonstreep! Your names are recorded in the original inspection log. You are now listed as first contact," Captain Channing replied with a chuckle as he hung up the phone and banged his head on the desk in disbelief for what he was about to do.

4

Fool's Errand

Tender she is beneath the strain
As time slips through her waves
And the bud of life traces her shores
Sing she will not, nor fain discourse
When mother wind begs a summer storm
Come now torrent and share the call
For we share no hope, within this lovers brawl

An hour later, Captain Channing waited outside the Admiral's office with briefcase in hand. Having printed the information and several period photos, he held the case next to his chest as if it were a box of dynamite. Each passing second began to feel as if an eternity as he second-guessed the decision to visit the Admiral unannounced. He quickly began to ponder an excuse to leave as he studied the military grey floor until the liaison returned from the Admiral's office. It was too late now. Whether he liked it or not, he was committed.

The liaison, a tall, lean Lieutenant with obvious Polynesian traits of dark brown eyes, bronze skin and long black hair was the talk of the base. Everyone knew she had transferred from the mainland with the Admiral. The positive rumor was that she had wanted to return home to the islands and the negative was that she was sleeping with the Admiral. Steve took little stock in the rumor, as the base was full of unnecessary gossip.

Immaculately dressed, he could tell she did everything by the book. Her grace and awareness of her unusual authority owned any room she entered, and for that reason most avoided her, afraid of the Admirals wrath. He had passed her in the halls, but never found the occasion or the nerve to speak for fear of making a fool of himself. He had not taken her into consideration when he planned to visit the Admiral, but now she was only a few feet away, and he could not take his failing eyes off her.

"Sir...I don't want to intrude, but what exactly is the nature of your business with the Admiral?" the liaison asked once again.

"It's a matter that I am not sure I can discuss with you Lieutenant. Nothing personal...I just don't know yet," he replied. He immediately hated his answer and wished he could take it back because if a blind man could dream...she would be his dream.

"There are many things I have no privilege to Captain. The Admiral however, does not like to be caught off guard." she warned. "As you can imagine, it is my job to be a filter if possible. Obviously, in this case it is not possible. He will be able to see you in a minute."

Captain Channing forced his eyes to the floor as pressure behind his temple began to build. Her questions had made him doubt and he could not help but look to the outer office door and dream of walking away. It would be the easiest thing to do he thought, even though the Lieutenants gentle smile reassured him that he would be OK.

"Captain, as you probably know, I recently transferred and...I do not know everyone. If you do not mind me asking, I heard a rumor that you are suffering from a growing disability. You know how rumors are on base. Would this be the reason you have requested the Admiral's time? Is it true you are losing your eyesight?"

Shocked at her candor, yet intrigued that she would broach the subject he replied, "Yes, it is true. I am going blind and no...my disability is not the reason I need to speak with the Admiral."

"I'm sorry...if I have said the wrong thing."

"No, please don't apologize. It's not like I can hide from the end result Lieutenant," he said, as he pointed to his glasses.

She was different and he found himself mesmerized by her perfume as it filled the ever-shrinking space. Her fragrance reminded him of a day at the beach and he wondered if it had been his mother's perfume of choice as the memory seemed far too strong. The diversion begged him to imagine the Lieutenant at the beach and the thought brought a smile to his face.

Abruptly, the daydream burst as the buzz of her phone snapped the silence. She quickly stood and motioned for him to follow. However, Steve remained frozen as he watched her walk toward the Admirals office. Finally, he had to order his legs to follow.

As she opened the door, he was grateful that his near vision was still adequate as she brushed against him. He imagined she enjoyed teasing the officers, who happened to pass through her domain, but then he noticed the look; a look he had come to know all too well. Captain Channing's heart sank as he realized she would only ever consider him the soon to be blind officer. He had little time to dwell on the subject however, as the cold reality of Admiral Simpson's office opened before him.

The Admiral, gruff, yet cordial chatted on the phone as he studied a map and rearranged objects on his desk. Short and black as night, with a spreading mid-section, Admiral

Simpson was beginning to grey about the temples as the stress of the job took effect. His face resembled that of a boxer who had seen one too many bouts in the ring, yet his piercing gaze surveyed the room as if looking for something else to explore. As the first black Admiral of the United States Coast Guard, he wore the badge with pride but in any other place, Simpson would be a man of no special interest to those about him.

The Admiral's demeanor caused Steve to fumble for a safe place to hide as Simpson motioned for him to sit in the corner. Barely able to discern the gesture, Steve felt a whip of panic as regret began to grow exponentially with each step he took.

The liaison watched on as Steve found his seat and he wondered if she were enjoying the fear, he was obviously displaying. She then closed the door and suddenly, he felt trapped.

As he listened to a female voice on the far end of the speakerphone, Simpson paid Captain Channing little attention. Suddenly he bellowed, "Don't give me cost overruns on the upgrades as the reason, Senator. Our cutters are old and need replacing. We have ships built in the 1970's, which deserved decommissioning twenty years ago. Cost overruns are to be expected when you are trying to hold rust together. How long do you think we can keep patching these old girls up, Senator?"

Simpson paused and waited for the Senator's reply. Steve listened in as she babbled on about state and federal cuts before the Admiral broke her train of logic, "I know you are doing the best that you can Senator, however we've needed two new frigates for five years. We patrol more ocean than any division of the Coast Guard and yet we have only two functional extreme condition cutters. Now, we have all the demands of Homeland Security to meet. We honestly cannot keep it up if we are not given the ships we need to patrol."

Simpson rotated about to confirm Steve was still waiting in the corner and then turned his attention to a large window overlooking the base. The second floor view took in all of Honolulu harbor and for a moment, the Admiral seemed satisfied as he listened to the Senator mumble on about pending budget cutbacks. Simpson finally had enough and spoke out of turn, "Thousands of ships pass through these waters and we are tasked with checking every single one of them for threats to our homeland. How do you suppose we do that Senator?"

Resigned to the fact that she was not getting anywhere with the Admiral, the call ended abruptly with the Senator telling the Admiral she would do her best. Simpson grunted, "Thank you Senator. I hope you have a good day," as she hung up.

Admiral Simpson turned his attention back to the charts, poked about in his desk, and produced a pipe. As he rolled it between his fingers Simpson peered over his glasses and asked, "You still here Captain?"

Steve seemingly did not know how to answer his Admiral and he fumbled about for his brief case.

"What is so important that you need to see me personally, Captain Channing?" Simpson asked, as he glared over his glasses and lit his pipe. He played with the pipe and his thoughts seemed to drift away as he adjusted his chair and pressed on, "You're my Captain with the failing eyesight? I remember reading your file. Are you here to ask for special consideration? Hell of a shame, we spent a lot of money on your training. I am sorry son; I know it must be disappointing."

With a wave of his hand, Simpson beckoned Captain Channing to the chair in front of his desk and said, "Come on Captain, show me what you have there. You bypassed a few levels to come here with this. I hope you have something worth my time."

It comforted Steve that the Admiral knew of his plight but his voice still trembled as he saluted and entered into what he knew to be his lynching.

"Sir, I have un-corroborated news that I believe needs to be...well...corroborated. It involves a vessel sailing toward our territorial waters that may be a week away from the islands," Captain Channing replied.

The Admiral remained completely dis-interested. It was obvious his mind was elsewhere when he asked, "What do you want from me Captain? Is it a cargo ship carrying a nuke or a drug runner? Why didn't you go through the normal chain and submit your request?"

Steve cleared his throat, as he knew then that his military career would soon end. It hit him as odd that he was hoping for a different outcome as he fumbled for his next statement, "Sir, it is a...well the description is that it is some type of homemade catamaran, sailing at a very high speed toward our territorial waters. Actually, the person reporting the vessel did not say catamaran. He said it was the best description he could give of the vessel. "

The Admiral, growing impatient glared at Steve and snapped, "What the hell are you getting to Captain Channing? I do not have all day. It obviously has some point of interest or you would not be bringing me this news. Long distance catamarans sail in and out of our waters every day. What the hell is so special about this one?"

Captain Channing could not help but imagine the Admiral as a dragon rearing to throw flames as the smoke from his pipe swirled about his head. He decided he had no choice but to fall on his sword as he pressed on, "Sir, this vessel was reported by the Sand Seeker, a large ketch that was in port two weeks ago. The owner thought the sighting important enough to call on their satellite phone. His name is Otto Vonstreep. He reported that this vessel happened upon them as they were preparing to enter a storm. According to Mr. Vonstreep, the vessel is sailed by one man and traveling at least thirty-five knots. He stated that it seemed to be made of wood, vines and pieces of metal. Mr. Vonstreep, by the way, happens to be a retired officer of the Royal Navy."

The Admiral's attention peeked at this bit of news, causing Steve to press on, "That's not the strange part, Sir.

Mr. Vonstreep reported that the main sail of the vessel could only have come from an airplane wing. Actually, Sir, he reported that they are convinced it is an airplane's wing."

The Admiral stole a deep drag from his pipe as he considered the news. "So you're reporting a sighting of a homemade Catamaran that is powered by the wing of an aircraft?"

Steve interrupted, "Sir, this catamaran was spotted over 800 miles out to sea. Sir, this begs the question as to who would take a homemade catamaran eight hundred miles out to sea," Steve said, then paused to allow the Admiral to think about that fact. "However, that is not why I came to you. I would have never come to you with only that information. I decided this needed to be your ears only because the sail, or wing, on the vessel has the call sign of the aircraft from which it must have come. The call sign is to say at the least...unusual, Sir."

Admiral Simpson peered at Steve through the cloud of smoke unmoved as the Captain barreled on, "The call sign is NR 16020."

Simpson's face seemingly disappeared behind the cloud of smoke as he rubbed his head and pondered his next question, "So I take it, Captain Channing, you ran the number through our data base and came up with something?"

Captain Channing began to pull papers from his brief case.

"Actually, Sir...I Googled the number. The aircraft in question...well, Sir...we have been looking for this particular aircraft for over seventy five years." Steve paused once again to watch the reaction of the Admiral. His Admiral remained a rock.

"If the reporting vessel is not delusional, then the wing of this mystery vessel bears the same number as a singularly unique L-10 Electra that disappeared on July 3rd, 1937. Admiral, the wing may be from Amelia Earhart's airplane," Captain Channing rallied as he placed his Google searches and his research on the validity of Vonstreep's rank on the Admiral's desk.

"This must be some kind of crack pot joke, Captain," the Admiral grunted.

"Sir, I considered that option. Then it hit me...what if the report is true? It is plausible that someone found the wing on a remote island. Sir, this old man could know where the Electra is located.

The Admiral's expression suddenly changed as Steve pressed, "Sir, this would solve one of the greatest mysteries of our time. I considered the options of letting it go. Then, I had to ask myself what would be the fallout, if this vessel sailed into port next week, and it turned out to be the real thing. If that were to happen, I believe it would be a hard pill for us to swallow; having known ahead of time it was coming. Then, I asked myself, what if the wing is real? On the other hand, I thought, what if the worst happened. What if it sank before arriving here and someone found out that we knew that it existed? Can you imagine the fallout," Steve pressed.

The Admiral took a long drag from his pipe as he considered all his Captain was telling him and the fragrant cloud billowed across the desk as if seeking Captain Channing.

The scales were tipping his way, Captain Channing decided it was time to die fighting as he stated, "Sir, I recommend we send a reconnaissance flight. I believe it should be the Coast Guard sharing this discovery and this vessel will be sailing near shipping lanes very soon. Sir, I do not have to remind you, that it was our ship, the Itasca, which Mrs. Earhart and Commander Noonan were searching for when they disappeared. I believe from a PR point of view that the worst-case scenario for us would be the Navy discovering the vessel before we do."

Sweat beaded across Captain Channing's forehead as he closed his argument, his pulse having doubled since meeting the Admiral. Simpson's face finally animated as he chewed on his pipe, and a sense of relief swept over Steve, as he could tell cogs were beginning to grind in the soul of his Admiral. The Admiral was working out the details.

Admiral Simpson suddenly stood and walked about his desk as he said, "It was gutsy of you to come in here with that bit of news. Nevertheless, you recognized the whole picture and that is rare. You are right Captain, we cannot let the Navy have this one. Even if it is a hoax, we need to know first."

The Admiral began to shuffle about his office as he thought out his next move then said, "The Rush can intercept the vessel at four to five hundred miles. I am going to turn it around if you can verify the claim," Simpson said, as he studied his charts, "I want you to be on that flight, son. Are you up to it?" he asked. Yet, before Captain Channing could answer, the Admiral slapped him on the back and escorted him to the door.

"Now, you do realize Channing, that if this is all a hoax, your days here will be numbered in the single digits," the Admiral said with a straight poker face, and then, he shut the door on Captain Channing, as if he were done with him permanently.

Steve found himself standing in the hall, dazed and confused, wondering what had just occurred, as the tall dark Lieutenant made her way toward him.

"Did I just get escorted from the building?" he mumbled to himself.

"Please come with me Captain," the liaison asked, as she pointed to her desk.

As she led him away, the Lieutenant's phone began to ring, and she pointed, forcing him to remain like a scolded dog. Steve watched on as the liaison rushed to her desk and he remembered that he thought she was beautiful only minutes before, but that seemed so long ago, as if in another life time. Now, she seemed to be all business and he didn't like the look on her face. It was time to leave he decided, but the Lieutenant raised her finger and pointed to his previous seat, as if an old school marm adjusting an unruly student. He obeyed without question.

He found himself doing as ordered, sitting in his original chair and holding his brief case next to his chest as the Lieutenant began to type. As the documents finished printing, she made her way to Captain Channing and sat beside him. He knew at that moment, the Admiral had ordered him to be released from duty. The story had been too much he thought, and the Admiral was going to let his liaison do the dirty work. It had to be less messy this way. Who could cuss out such a beautiful woman, he thought.

The lieutenant took her time and adjusted her uniform as she put the pages in order on the small table separating them. The epitome of perfection in full dress protocol, her graceful smile and refreshing demeanor did not help his sinking feeling. The brief case remained next to his chest in the hope that it would lessen the blow.

"Captain Channing, these are your orders. You are to move upon them with due diligence. My name is Lieutenant Clair Evans. As you know, I am the Admiral's Liaison. His orders are explicit. When you return, call me and I will work you back into his agenda. My cell and this office number are at the bottom of your orders. If you need anything else, call me and I will expedite the issue," she stated as if she were ordering a plebe about.

Still in a daze, Steve did not hear anything she said at first for he could not take his weak and failing eyes off her face her dark brown eyes. She was simply intoxicating he thought, and for a moment, his mind wandered to the beach he had imagined her upon only twenty minutes earlier.

"Captain Channing...do you not understand what I just told you. I can repeat it if you like," she pressed.

As if snapped from a state of shock, Steve took the papers from her, still expecting a release from duty order. Then his eyes widened as he read them. He was to proceed to the Coast Guard air command immediately.

Lieutenant Evans arose from her seat pleased to see his obvious relief. Unable to control his sense of euphoria, he leapt up and bear hugged her without thinking about the consequences. The Lieutenant stepped back immediately and peered at him as he suddenly glowed with embarrassment; he had just broke several dozen personal boundary protocols with no less than the Admiral's liaison.

"I'm sorry...I'm sorry. Please forgive me," he begged. "I was sure you were sending me home on a medical discharge."

"I wish everyone I gave the Admirals orders to was as excited as you. Most are stiff as a starched shirt. However, Captain...I would suggest, that what just happened, never happen again and yes...you are forgiven."

Steve bowed his head with a grateful gesture as he declared, "I promise, it will never happen again."

"Captain, it all sounds very exciting. Good luck!"

"I would be glad to take you with me if you like," he said, before he could stop himself from uttering the invitation.

"Who would keep the Admiral out of trouble?" she quipped.

The light banter was far more than he had expected and he blushed with the thought of actually knowing the prettiest woman on the base.

"You have a point there. Good luck yourself Lieutenant," he replied, as he spun about and bolted for the door before he said something else stupid.

The recon mission for the mystery vessel was underway.

5

Second Chances

Resist me cares for this mortal world
I am not the man I was once before
Take your time as I strive to know
How far these winds shall blow
Resist me cares for the mortal world
The man I was will be no more
The breath of dread shall
Flee this eternal shore

Two hours later, Captain Channing found himself in the belly of the Coast Guard's latest procurement bouncing with the evening thermals. Outfitted with the latest night surveillance, the large airplane flew west as the sun fell off the horizon. Night would soon be upon them.

The C-130, known more commonly in the Air force as a "Spooky", had found a second life in the United States Coast Guard. Designed to bring heavy firepower to a battlefield in the cover of the night, the large multi-engine aircraft commanded respect, and from the looks of her internal systems, Steve was positive she had been successful.

Like many pieces of equipment in the United States Coast Guard, she was well past her expected life span when apportioned to this assignment. As the property of the Coast Guard, the craft had been overhauled to meet the needs of search and rescue. In the process, her Howitzer and Gatling gun were removed to extend range and instead of the dark grey of the United States Air Force, she glowed like a beacon on a hill with bright white paint and a prominent orange stripe.

As a battle platform, she had been unstoppable at night. With microwave technology and thermal eyes she could locate the enemy in the thickest jungles. Now, the same equipment allowed her to save lives and monitor drug running activities.

It seemed fitting to Steve that she had found a new life after a career of delivering fear to a battlefield. Now she could find a floundering ship or lost sailors from the difference in heat signatures alone. As the best low-level recon platform the USCG operated when long distance or bad weather were involved she could deliver nearly anything a floating sailor or ailing ship needed.

He found hope rising up inside his heart along with his ride as it gained an altitude of eight thousand feet. It was odd to feel this way again...hopeful, he thought. As he studied the old airframe, he wondered if a second life apart from the one he had known awaited him. He decided to give himself permission to hope once again. It was all he had left.

Several hours later, Captain Channing found himself looming over the equipment operators as they scanned the horizon with their varied instruments. His confidence as a ranking officer once again found sea legs as he moved from station to station in an attempt to keep the men's spirits up. It had been easy to recognize the shipping lanes in the first few hours but, slowly, the sea became barren desert as they headed west into the vast expanse of night. Intermittently, an operator would discover the signature of a large tanker or a cruise liner but the hits had begun to fall away as the miles passed. This was the great expanse of ocean known as the Pacific, which he knew those who did not sail could never comprehend.

The massive nature of the task was more akin to finding a grain of sand on the beach than a needle in a haystack. However, the Spooky would be the great equalizer with her top-secret equipment. Before departing, Steve attained the last position of the Sand Seeker from the Vonstreeps and decided that was his best direct line. If the vessel maintained its last recorded course, he determined there would be a one in a thousand chance it could be located. These odds left Steve uncomfortable, as his career, which he thought must end only hours prior, now depended on the outcome.

At the seventh hour, the radar operator touched the thermal operator on the shoulder and Steve knew immediately that he had something, as a light dropped off the screen then reappeared. An object with an odd radar signature lay directly before them.

The thermal side scan technician barked that he might have something definite. The pilot adjusted course to give the thermal systems a better angle. From the growing image, it was obviously a sailboat but the distance was too great to make out any distinct attributes. It took twenty minutes for the Spooky to drop to a lower trajectory before the image found quality.

"It looks like an outrigger, like the tourists rent at Waikiki...except much larger," the tech said, as he studied the primary hull, which was far thicker and longer than the secondary.

As the Spooky settled in at three thousand feet, the vessel circled beneath, seemingly adrift. Suddenly, motion on the deck of the odd craft caught the crew off guard. Amazed by the clarity of the thermal systems, Steve could tell the person aboard the craft was fishing and that the vessel was as Vonstreep had described it to be. His heart began to pound through his chest as he ordered the crew to start collecting data.

The drone of the C-130's engines reached the sailor and he quickly began to climb to his outrigger. Steve watched on in fear that the man would take another course as the vessel cut through the chop slowly at first. Then, as if a jet pack took over, she raced away. As the thermal operator struggled to follow, Steve studied a compass reading on the back lit panel and sighed with relief. She was on course at least, he thought.

"Is there any way to tell if there are numbers on the sail?" Captain Channing begged the thermal operator.

"Sir, I can adjust the polarity to an extreme setting and if the letters are black they may have held more heat. It is a slim possibility that they are still visible," the operator replied as he studied his monitor

Steve ordered him to do so.

With that, the microwave technician shouted over the hum of the engines, "Sir...as far as I can tell there is not one functioning mechanical instrument on that vessel. He is sailing completely blind Sir."

"Or...he is sailing by the stars," Captain Channing responded. "And that means he is the real deal. Not many people can do such a thing."

The constant pitch of the vessel made it difficult for the thermal operator to focus his efforts. He called to the other operators to take stills of the vessel in case he could not make out the call sign. The C-130's night vision held no rival and with each shot, the vessel and her unique design became evident.

"I got it!" The thermal technician finally yelled.

Steve squinted at the image as it reluctantly solidified into the call sign NR 16020. His heart leapt, his palms became sweaty as if asking a girl on first date. He had the wing of Amelia Earhart's Electra.

"Save that, Ensign," Captain Channing ordered. He then proceeded to the communications pod and asked the operator to connect him to command.

"Can we send images to command in a secure manner? What I am asking is...can the Navy read our messages? "

"No, Sir! I will guarantee that. We have our own secure channels with our own encryption."

"Contact the Admiral's Liaison...Lieutenant Evans. Have her wake the Admiral and inform him that we have located the vessel and that it does contain the markings discussed," Captain Channing ordered with the newfound strength of an officer of the United States Coast Guard.

"Sir...may I ask, what is this all about?"

"At this point...that is classified information, Ensign," Steve replied as he returned to the thermal systems and watched on with an ever-growing slow grin, as the vessel raced across the open plains of a star covered ocean and restored his hope that life may still hold meaning.

6

Loose Ends

Lazy summer day of rain
Consuming the heat of time and pain
I lay before you prone
Trusting nothing but you alone
To bring me quietly away
Into the light of a far brighter day

Captain Channing tried to sleep on the return flight but the effort was fruitless as questions rattled about his head. Would they try to stop the vessel before it made port? Would they tell the media? Who was the old man? Who built the vessel? What happened to Amelia?

The next morning, the question regarding the involvement of media was determined for him, when a reporter from the local news station contacted the Admiral's office.

Steve arrived to deliver his report, unaware of the breach until Lieutenant Evans met him away from the Admiral's office and led him into a small conference room.

As she forced him into a corner, Steve found his blood pressure beginning to rise at her touch.

"Someone notified the press that the vessel is on its way. The Admiral is boiling. I hope to God it was not someone you know," she demanded without blinking an eye. "Tell me...you told no one?"

The close proximity of Lieutenant Evans' was disquieting and rousing at the same time. He tried to focus on her question but her familiar perfume and the passion in her voice where nearly more than he could stand. Nevertheless, slowly, the news sank in as he fought to separate the two competing emotions of fear and attraction.

"I don't know how that happened. I haven't told anyone, Lieutenant."

"I hope not, Captain. This is not good. I am doing damage control as best I can. You need to be ready when you walk in that office. Understand?"

"Yes ma'am."

"I hope you have thick skin."

Lieutenant Evans forced a smile and adjusted his collar. Then, with the determination of a drill sergeant, she marched down the hall towards Admiral Simpson's office.

Anger was visibly etched on Admiral Simpson's face and Captain Channing began to worry that he may never leave the room as he entered apprehensively. At the sight of his Captain, as if a pot boiling over, Admiral Simpson exploded.

"Who the hell called this into the media, Captain?" the Admiral bellowed.

Unable to give an answer, Steve gazed out the large window as he felt his heart sink. He could not focus on his Admiral; he needed to think through the problem. Positive no one on the Spooky would do such a thing, or even had the time too, the answer finally hit him between the eyes.

"Sir, it didn't occur to me that Mr. Vonstreep was a loose end. I guess he figured we would bury the story."

"Damn it! That makes sense. Damn it! Why didn't I think of that? I'm sorry, Captain. I'm just pissed...and you happened to be the only one who might have an answer. I needed more time to confirm your story."

Admiral Simpson slammed a drawer then looked about for direction as if he were confused. Then, as if a switch in his mind flipped, he forced a smile and straightened his back.

"Come with me Captain. We a have a news conference waiting for us downstairs."

• • •

Standing in front of a small podium behind the Admiral, Steve felt most uncomfortable. The Admiral, on the other hand, was in his element. The space normally used to announce search and rescue efforts seemed overburdened with reporters. At the most, two or three reporters ever attended briefs. Today, the energy was different as reporters forced their way in to see the Admiral.

"I know you are here because of a phone call. I want you to know that we have been working on this report. However, it would be remiss of me to give you the details since one of our finest Captains has been working on this issue from the beginning. I am going to give Captain Channing the podium to explain what may have been discovered."

With that, Admiral Simpson placed his hand on the back of Steve and whispered, "Son, I hope you got it in you."

Steve had not expected this change in events and gaped at the reporters in disbelief as he squinted through his thick glasses. As cameras flashed, searching deep, he found his courage and responded with an awkward smile. He could do this, he told himself.

"Yesterday...we were notified of a vessel...the report was that a single male of advanced years was operating the vessel approximately 800 miles due West. What makes the craft unique is the fact that it has an airplane wing as the main sail. Last night, I accompanied a reconnaissance team to discover if the report is true. After several hours of searching we were able to locate the craft. It seems to have no modern capabilities aboard such as radar or radio and I can confirm that one person operates the vessel."

Steve stopped to take a sip of water. He glanced at Clair who seemed relieved that he had met the moment with confidence.

"The wing bears the possible call signs of the aircraft to which it once belonged. I was able to confirm the existence of a call sign last night. If the call sign is not a hoax, and I stress, this may be a hoax," he said as perspiration began to pepper his forehead. He knew that what he was about to say could not be taken back.

"Let me say this, the historical relevance of the wing is what brought us all here today. If this is not a hoax, then this vessel is propelled by the wing of the LC-10 Electra that Amelia Earhart and Commander Noonan used in their attempt to circumnavigate the globe."

The pressroom burst into a flurry of questions as Captain Channing stepped back from the podium and nodded to the Admiral. Admiral Simpson merely pointed to the podium, ordering him to remain at post.

Steve regrouped, grabbed the side of the podium and regarded the nearest reporter on the first row.

"Are you saying that the wing of Amelia Earhart's plane is on a boat sailing toward Hawaii?"

"I think I said that already?"

With that question, he decided that he needed to do damage control. "Ok, let me make this clear. I am saying that this vessel has a wing on it. I am saying that the wing exhibits numbers consistent to a call sign. I am saying that those numbers correspond to the numbers of Amelia Earhart's airplane. An LC-10 Electra, if memory serves correct. I am saying that the wing matches the description in size to her plane. I also want to say that this may all be a grand hoax. There is no way to know until we make physical contact with the captain of the vessel."

As Captain Channing finished his statement, Admiral Simpson returned to the podium.

"Ladies and gentlemen, we currently have a cutter in route. It should make contact within the next twenty-four hours. I would warn you to be careful in making assumptions until we have made contact."

With that, Simpson grabbed Steve by the arm, as he said to the reporters, "We will keep you updated as we have more information. For now, that is all we have."

Once in the hall, Simpson popped Channing across the chest and barked, "Hell of a job, Son. I'm going to make an officer of you yet. I need to make a call to the Pentagon. Clair, make sure he is squared away."

The air in the room sucked away as Captain and Lieutenant stared at each other.

"I suppose I need to brief you on what we have discovered since daylight. Once you were able to locate the vessel the Admiral ordered a backup flight. They arrived at dawn and we have excellent footage if you would like to see it."

"I would. Where would we do that Lieutenant?"

"In the conference room, the one I pulled you into this morning."

"Yes...I remember. Thanks for the heads up."

"No problem. I consider you one of my pet projects now, Captain."

"Really! How so?"

"If the Admiral asks me a question regarding you and this mission, I figure it's my job to make sure that I have the answer. Therefore, Captain, we are going to be spending a few hours together...looking over this vessel. If it is a hoax, you and I need to figure it out. If it is not, then we need to be prepared for whatever that means."

"I suppose I should be flattered...never been a pet project before," he replied.

Lieutenant Evans rolled her eyes and said as she walked away.

"Consider it a professional courtesy, Captain. If this goes down the way I think it might...you're going to need my Admiral to have your back."

"My...Admiral?"

Lieutenant Evans stopped, looked him in the eye and replied, "Yes...he's a pet project too. Any questions?"

"No...I see how this works now."

"Good. Come with me then," she ordered as she headed to the conference room.

7

Entrusted

You cannot tell
Who brings this news so frail
Trust in me to share no more
Of the life I lived on that far distant shore
For one cannot tell
Who binds you to this present gale

By lunch, the news had spread across the globe. Admiral Simpson ordered extra flights to maintain a visual until the cutter could arrive. A private jet, that had tracked the Coast Guard flights, found and filmed the vessel for only a moment as cloud cover broke up the shot. The mariner's long grey hair, trailed in the wind and it only served to frustrate the networks hunger for more news as it hid his face like a blanket. He would remain a mystery to the world for yet another day.

The channel that paid for the footage recruited a naval expert, who babbled on that, by his calculations; the weight of the wing combined with wind force should have ripped the vessel apart long ago. An hour later, every network recruited a naval expert and each agreed the vessel should not be afloat.

To fill the story out, talking heads rehashed the history of Amelia Earhart and Fred Noonan and their attempt to circumnavigate the globe while experts in Polynesian culture attempted to explain the mysterious man sailing the odd vessel. Not one had a solid answer, nevertheless; T-shirts of the old man with his hair swept image and grand smile were on the market before sunset.

Admiral Simpson began to wonder how he was going to bring the vessel in without looking like a fool on national television. His window of opportunity would soon close as he learned from a good friend in the Pentagon that the Navy intended to intercept the vessel before his cutter could arrive. He had only one ace left to play. The Cutter Rush, although slower, was at least a day ahead of her pursuers. He knew he had to send someone he could trust not to scare the old man. With that thought, he decided to send the one who had brought him the news in the first place.

• • •

"Captain Channing, how long until you are legally blind?" Admiral Simpson pressed, as Steve entered his office.

Steve did not understand the reasoning behind the question and it showed.

"Sir, it is debatable. If I continue at the rate that I have been experiencing, I will be legally blind in less than a year...maybe as little as six months."

Admiral Simpson lowered his head and cursed under his breath, as he had not realized how quickly his Captain's life was changing. He lit a cigasr and studied his officer with the thick glasses and awkward smile. It was the glasses that made him look like an awkward teen, he thought as he studied the Captain's record, and found it to be flawless except for the one incident attributed to his loss of vision. He took note that Captain Channing had no living family and he knew the scuttlebutt regarding his fiancé. It had been he, who had approved the reassignment of Steve's former friend and colleague. He began to wonder how his Captain was even functioning as he studied the man sitting before him. The man needs one last chance to be an officer, he thought as he tossed his glasses on the desk and smiled.

Steve's stomach rolled as he feared the Admiral was about to release him. The breech with the reporter was too much, he thought. A problem he knew he should have foreseen. He suddenly felt odd. He should be prepared for the news he told himself. Nevertheless, something inside had changed within the last twenty-four hours. He did not want to leave now. He wanted to see Lieutenant Evans once again and he wanted to meet the old man.

Across the desk, Simpson took his time as he adjusted his seat and lit a cigar. Captain Channing could not hide his confusion, as he thought the Admiral a pipe man. What was Simpson's next surprise, he thought.

"Sir if you need to give me some bad news I am ready for whatever may come," Steve blurted as he could stand it no longer.

"Captain, don't get ahead of me. I am far from being done with you. We have too much invested in you to let a defense contractor reap all the benefit," Simpson replied as he peered over his glasses. "Hell, I'm offended by the insinuation that you think I might be that shallow."

Steve swallowed hard as he tried to reply but could not.

"I see by your record that you reenlisted prior to your little incident. The way I look at it Captain. I own your ass for at least three more years and you will do whatever I want you to do. Do I make myself clear?" Simpson snapped.

"Yes sir."

"Son, I want to send you to our cutter in route...the Rush...tonight. You will have to make a parachute drop into the drink to hitch a ride. I see you are a typical Coasty and have never been tossed from a perfectly good airplane. Consider this jump on the job training. Then, I want you to find a way to board that vessel...without causing harm to the vessel or scaring the hell out of the old man sailing it. He looks old...old men don't deal with strangers well. One more thing...you are to let no one else board that vessel. Do I make myself clear?" Simpson said, as he shuffled through his drawer, "If I was that old man, I would want to complete my journey. I'd bet a dollar to a dime that is his intention."

Channing, taken aback, took a deep breath to clear his head.

"Son, you signed up because you wanted adventure. Hell all of us do. It is the nature of the business. I believe you are a fine officer...are you up to it?" Simpson asked, as he gave up his search, turned to his window and studied Honolulu harbor.

"Yes sir, Admiral Sir," Steve barked as a frog filled his throat.

Admiral Simpson turned to find his subordinate at full attention with tears flowing behind thick Coke bottle glasses.

"Captain Channing, we don't have time for such nonsense. You need to be on that plane in less than an hour," Simpson ordered.

Captain Channing bellowed, "Sir, yes sir!"

"Bring that vessel and her old man here...safe and sound. Bring yourself home too! Don't be a hero but do everything you can to make contact," Simpson ordered, as Steve headed for the door.

He found Lieutenant Evans waiting outside the Admirals door and Steve knew then she had not known why the Admiral had called him.

"Are you ok?" she asked.

"Ok...Yes...you could say I am OK. I'm going to board the mystery vessel," he replied as he wiped his eyes.

Lieutenant Evans lit up with approval.

Steve returned her enthusiasm with a simple smile. "I would hug you but, I promised you I wouldn't do that again," Steve quipped, as the Lieutenant blushed and pointed down the hall.

"Good luck, Captain. I will keep you in my prayers tonight."

Steve spun about and replied, "Thanks Lieutenant. I'll take every one of them I can get tonight."

8

A Deep Blue Sea

Cold and blameless she meets me
Tasting my fear, she knows
I hold no hope but that she release me
By the dark of her grip, she bends my heart
Her finger's probe and I fail to start
Now, I taste her guile and shutter
For she is a cold blameless lover

An hour later, Captain Channing found himself in the belly of the same C-130 that had helped him discover the vessel only hours earlier. He tried to pay attention as the crew informed him of parachute protocol. All he was able to ascertain was that it was imperative that he release the parachute prior to entering the drink. He then had to locate the flares strapped to his leg and fire them so that the Rush might locate his position. It was not the idea of being lost Steve worried about; it was the idea of being overrun over by a cutter at full speed that had him most concerned.

As he hung from the open cargo door staring at the moonlit blur of ocean passing beneath, his knees began to buckle. This had all seemed like a good idea in the Admiral's office, he reminded himself.

"I wish I were going with you, Captain," the deck master yelled over the roar of the engines and Captain Channing knew, in that moment, that he might be the luckiest man in the world.

With that, the green light flashed and Steve bolted out the door as if he had done so a thousand times. The world rapidly changed from the blast of the open cargo door to utter silence as his parachute deployed. He looked up and smiled as the shadow of the parachute blocked the moon above. Relief began to fill his heart as the adrenaline rush wore off. Bright against the horizon, stars bathed in the light of a full moon. Everything seemed to shimmer, in that moment and he began to feel a sense of destiny deep in his soul.

The truth of the cold ocean arrived faster than he expected. Unable to judge distance, he mistakenly released the parachute far too soon and dropped the last twenty feet like a rock. It took a few moments of struggle to gain his bearing and then return topside. He broke the surface gasping, and realized in the same moment, he had somehow forgotten to secure his glasses before entering the drink.

His calm night of destiny quickly descended into a white blur as salt water stung his eyes. He knew he had a second pair of glasses in his leg pocket but dared not open it now. He quickly produced the waterproof flares and watched on as a blurred red stream of light spun away into the night sky.

To his relief the Rush arrived only minutes later but it had seemed like an eternity as he suddenly began to feel hypothermic. Having trained for each step of the process to come, he knew he should have felt at ease with this ordeal, but somehow, it felt different when he was the one needing rescue. He soon found himself swimming toward voices as a cargo net came over the side of the Rush. Minutes later, Steve was standing on the deck, fumbling for his last pair of glasses as shadowy figures surrounded him.

Captain Joshua Bearing studied the awkward officer with curiosity as the man fumbled through his pockets. He knew Captain Channing's reputation but their path had crossed little.

"This is who the Admiral sent to board a possible hostile vessel," he mumbled to himself.

Captain Channing discovered his glasses and reacted with a salute as he realized Bearing was standing next to him.

"Forgive me, Captain; I didn't know you were standing there." he said between gasps. "Permission to come aboard?"

"We are of the same rank, Captain; you don't have to salute me," Captain Bearing in his signature ice cold manner. "We need to get you out of these wet clothes. We are only a few miles behind our objective. However, at the speed the old man is maintaining...we are losing ground fast," Captain Bearing stated as he grabbed the officer next to him and ordered him to make full speed.

As he began his debrief, Bearing led Captain Channing to his personal stateroom.

"The clothes you will need are in that pack and you need to hurry. The Navy should arrive in a few hours and Admiral Simpson wants us to attempt the boarding tonight. We attempted to hail the vessel but the old man did not respond. He kept on sailing as if we were not there and you need to know that he is hauling ass."

"Tonight?" Captain Channing replied more out of relief than question.

"Can you think of a better time, Captain?" Bearing pressed.

"No, I understand the importance of us securing him first. It was my idea," he answered. "Just trying to adjust to how fast everything is happening."

"Well, this makes sense now. I was wondering why Simpson sent you," Bearing said as if a joke.

Steve chose not to reply and quickly became all business as he un-wrapped the packet of gear and Bearing's first impression of the man before him changed as he watched him prepare to board a racing vessel in the middle of the night. Captain Channing had the Admiral's respect and Bearing decided he would offer the same.

"I will take you to within a few hundred yards of the vessel. Then, I will light her up like a Christmas tree. Two of my finest are waiting for you in a rigid. I think you trained the ensign in charge. Anyhow, they will get you near. You will need to make the decision as to when and how to board. I can tell you now, that it is going to be one hell of a transfer at the speed he is traveling with the chop we have tonight. Do not hesitate when you make that decision. You may not get another chance Captain."

"I understand," Captain Channing replied with a bit more of a weak voice than he anticipated. He was still feeling hypothermic but he would never admit that to his counterpart.

"If you think we need to cut him off and stop him then just let me know. However, I don't believe he would stop. I would have forced the subject already but we can't chance a collision and losing that wing. He was hell bent on out sailing us when we first arrived. When you see him, you will know what I mean. In addition, the man is old...very old...but he does not look to be frightened by our presence. He seems determined however, not to stop. One more thing...the vessel, as you probably know, is unlike anything else on the planet. It is something to see in person."

"You said you hailed him? In what language did you make the attempt?" Captain Channing asked.

"We tried several dialects. I don't think he speaks any of them," Bearing answered, "You are not going to be able to tell him to pull over. Perhaps some form of sign language might work. However, he showed no sign of understanding anything we said.

"Well, this should make for an interesting night," Captain Channing replied.

"I want you to know, I have your back no matter what happens out there tonight," Bearing said, as he offered his hand.

"Thanks...I appreciate your confidence in me," Steve replied as he returned the gesture.

Bearing slapped Steve on the back and bellowed as he left the bunk, "Channing you have the entire United States Coast Guard at your side. Don't forget that in the morning, because, whether you want them or not...half the United States Navy will be here to stake a claim. Let's keep this in the family."

As Captain Bearing left the room, Steve took a deep breath and leaned against the bulkhead. Exhaustion was beginning to set in. He had not slept for the past thirty hours and his legs now felt heavy as the burst of adrenaline from the airdrop began to lock into his muscles. He closed his eyes and tried to pray but words escaped him.

9

Contact

Test this heart and find no fear
Break my spirit to make me clear
Chase my demons into the sea
Find no hate deep within me.
For I can no longer deny your call
Yes, I am given to the fall
Shape me now by this quest
Test me among these waves
Teach me now, how to rest
Shake me free of my silent grave

Thirty minutes later, the Rush closed the space between the mariner's winged vessel and Captain Channing's retrieval point. As he waited in the small pontoon craft known as a rigid, the ocean boiled below like a dark abyss waiting to swallow anyone who dared such a feat. Steve began to second-guess the plan to drop the rigid, with motor running, while the Rush maintained full speed but according to Captain Bearing, it would be the only way to catch the mystery vessel. Steve felt displaced as he thought about the implications. This was the one time, they could not get the landing wrong.

Captain Channing had trained the Ensign in charge of the rigid. He remembered that his name was Tucker and Channing remembered that the young man had scored high on his aptitude tests, and even higher on his skills adaptability test. According to Ensign Tucker, this new insertion method, with the cutter at full speed had succeeded three out of five times when recently tested.

A crazy smile swept across the young officer's face as he yelled over the cry of the waves below, "I was the one who made it three times. I got this down, like I was making love to your sister!"

"What happened to the other guy?" .

With a hearty laugh the ensign replied, "You don't want to know, Sir."

"So you know, Tucker...I don't have a sister, but if I did, you would be in the drink right now," Captain Channing popped off with a laugh while slapping the ensign across the back as if old football buddies.

"Yes Sir...I'll try and come up with a better analogy next time."

"I don't think there is going to be a next time Tucker...just make this time the best ever...Ok?" Steve yelled over the rush of wind and sea as the boom locked into place over the drop zone. And with a wave of Ensign Tucker's hand, the small rigid dropped like a lead weight, engine screaming at full speed. The rigid buried her nose into the first wave as she looked to be diving off the deck and the scream of the motors ended abruptly as the strain of the boiling sea crashed into the small vessel. Tucker backed off the twins to allow the nose of the rigid time to find the top of the next wave. Then, with a jerk of his wrist, the young man gunned the twins once again as the small rigid popped above the next set of waves, found her second wind, and sped away from the Rush into an uncertain night.

As the rigid made ground on the dark object ahead, the Rush brought her high beams to bear. As Captain Channing witnessed for the first time the winged vessel functioning in real time, his mouth fell agape. For the old man sailing her at near thirty-knots, was giving the Rush a run for her money.

Tucker cut the rigid hard to port to allow Captain Channing a healthy view of the craft. The vessel, an engineering miracle, seemed to be much larger in action than Steve had imagined. She cut through the waves as if she could predict the timing of the next volley while the sea broke beneath her bow and left a misty dense luminescent hallow about the wing. She was truly a magnificent creation, Steve thought, as he admired her simple, pure, raw power.

The mariner, as Tucker made up the yards, looked to be ancient as the bright lights exposed his creviced face. It was as Bearing had described for the old man looked to be at peace and Steve thought it odd that the arrival of a cutter and the bright lights had no effect upon him. Almost as if, the old mariner had expected their arrival.

The rigid raced to forty-five knots to overtake the modified catamaran and the old man, posted high on the far outrigger, waved to Steve as they approached the opposite side of his vessel. Tucker slowed to allow Captain Channing time to survey the situation and Steve returned the wave in his awkward manner, which brought a grand smile to the old mariner. He seemed genuinely delighted to see them, Steve thought.

Captain Channing attempted to yell over the roar of the engines that he wanted to board, but he soon discovered it was of little use. Ensign Tucker made another executive decision and drew up beside the large outrigger on the starboard side. The mariners long grey hair was course in the bright light and his arms rippled with muscle even though his skin looked to be loose with age. Obviously set by years of living in the elements, the lines about his eyes lent the old man a sense of wisdom, while his short rugged frame gave Steve reason to be hesitant. Yet, the old man's ever-present smile encouraged Steve to trust him.

Then, to every man's jack surprise, the mariner released a line at his feet and a large forward sail sprung to life as he tacked his vessel once again into the wind. The sail quickly filled and the odd craft left the rigid in its wake. It was apparent the old man thought this a good joke and laughed aloud as his little trick caught them off guard. Boarding was going to be a game of cat and mouse and suddenly Steve felt like a slow fat cat.

Ensign Tucker, caught off guard, cursed aloud as he tried to make up the lost yardage. Meanwhile the constant impact of wave after wave upon the rigid drove through Captain Channing and his knuckles turned white as he held a death grip of the rail. Ensign Tucker gunned the rigid once again and he informed Captain Channing that he wanted to force the old man to slow down. Steve nodded in agreement, as if the young man were actually asking for permission.

As they passed the odd winged vessel once again, Steve could pick out the airplane parts infused into the design. It all looked familiar and yet disconnected from the picture he held in his head of Amelia's L-10 Electra. What should have been the wheel well on most sailing vessels, supported a small shelter from the weather, but no wheel was present in area, for the craft seemed to be managed solely from the outrigger by a series of cables that jutted about the craft in no discernible manner.

Tucker pushed the rigid to her limit and with each hurdle; the prop left the ocean and screamed as it found, if but for a moment, freedom from the bond of earth and sea, only to have gravity win the duel and force the small craft into the crest of the next wave. Ensign Tucker would not to be outdone and Steve began to fear he would flip the small vessel in his fervor to win. And so it was, in a final act of defiance, Ensign Tucker positioned the rigid before the odd vessel and smiled at his Captain as the dance between the two vessels became comical. Steve began to wonder who qualified Tucker to slow down a vessel five times their size.

He soon discovered that Ensign Tucker had already formulated that plan. Without warning, his well-trained Ensign, who had passed all of his competency exams, abruptly let off the power to the twins and the rigid lurched hard to port as it slammed into the next set of oncoming waves. Captain Channing, in no way ready for such a maneuver, found himself flying through the air and cursing Tucker at the same time. His last coherent thought, to grab his glasses, paid off in aces as pain coursed his back upon the jolt of cold water slapped him hard.

Captain Channing struggled to understand his predicament as he reached to discover the top of the next wave. He then spun about to face his demise, as he knew he would soon be overrun by two trailing vessels but it was too late. The blurred hulll of the mystery vessel raced past his face with only inches to spare and the fleeting thought crossed his mind that this was not how he had planned to die. He began to dive to clear the vessels until a set of strong hands grabbed him by the collar. Steve instinctively snatched the arm of the one who had him, pulled, and in one incredible motion, popped from the water and landed on a hard wooden surface.

As if by a miracle, he was aboard the mystery vessel. The form of another human being danced before his sore eyes as he tried to collect himself. He scrambled to put on his glasses that had incredibly remained in his left hand. He thought it odd, that for the first time in his life he was grateful for his glasses. They were deformed and the right lens was cracked, yet he was grateful to see nonetheless.

He found the old man studying his catch, as if pleased with his fortune, and Steve returned the stare with his boyish awkward smile. Suddenly, the old man took him by the arm, put his forehead against Captain Channing's, and then mumbled something Steve did not understand. In the midst of the greeting, emotions began to overwhelm

Captain Channing as he slowly realized the old man was praying, thanking his God for him.

Steve wiped the salt from his eyes and found the old man to be peaceful and kind. Gently, the old man touched Steve's face, then leaned into his harness and adjusted his vessel. Effortless in his approach, he seemingly bent the vessel to the pressure of each wave as he asked her to find her inbred speed once again. Unlike the rigid, Steve felt little concussion against this vessel, as she seemingly absorbed each wave and gave them to the night as an offering.

A sense of peace flooded over Captain Channing as he listened to the vessel groan and pop, slowly regaining her forward momentum like an old steam engine finding traction, then suddenly, as if the wheels connected to the track, the outrigger from which they were perched stole skyward a half dozen feet. Captain Channing found himself holding to a long stay that ran to the wing and he could feel her energy coursing through his body. He knew then, this vessel was alive.

The moment soon passed as the rigid returned. Captain Channing waved Ensign Tucker off, hoping they would not scare the old man. Tucker gave thumbs up as he smiled sheepishly; obviously hoping that he would not be reprimanded upon the Captains return.

As the small rigid slipped away into the dark Captain Channing began to question how Tucker was going to return to a cutter sailing at full speed. He had never thought to ask the question in their preparations. Would they stop to pick them up, he thought? He decided if the Ensign could survive a return to the Rush that he had earned the right to one mistake.

Soaked and cold once again Steve suddenly felt lightheaded and stiff at the same time. His training told him that the second exposure to cold water and the near death experience had sucked most of his energy from his body. Knowledge was not going to overcome the sensation however. In an effort to stabilize his nerves, he leaned against the rigging and in doing so, he felt as if sea were singing a song that he had not heard for a long time. A lullaby, which only grew in strength as each muscle in his upper body began to lock up. He attempted once again to keep his eye on the old mariner, but that was of little help, as he found the old man hanging from his rigging with eyes closed.

Even in the haze of exhaustion, Steve noted how the old man stretched to touch the waves each time he lowered the outrigger. The up and down motion only served to compound his desire to sleep, as the ebb and flow of the vessel mimicked the old man's rhythmic need to touch each wave that passed his hand.

Captain Channing's body was no longer listening and he had so much to ask the old mariner, he thought. Yet, he could not stop his head from bobbing. Sleep would soon overtake him whether he wanted it to or not. Then, just as his eyes began to close, Steve felt a touch upon his shoulder and awoke to find the mariner pointing to the main hull. He knew the old man was telling him that he need to move to a safer location and he decided to give no argument.

Between the outrigger and the main hull, lay a maze of crossed lines and old netting, forming a loose mesh that crossed the span. The outrigger, little more than a canoe in width, seemed at the moment, light years away from the main hull, which was as large any ocean-going sailboat. He quickly scanned the wing that jutted into the night like a spire, and wondered how it had come to be. He quickly decided that the question would have to wait. It did not matter now. He had to make the crossing before he fell overboard.

As he searched for a path through the maze of ropes and netting, instinct told him that it would take more energy than he had available. To his relief, the old mariner maintained the craft on a steady course, and somewhere in the midst of his feeble attempt, the old man began to sing aloud in a language Steve did not understand. Captain Channing thought the song to be beautiful and decided if the old man was not worried that he should not be either. He crossed the last few strands of rope that attached to the main hull and with one last push; he located a secluded place, hidden from the brunt of the wind in what should have been the wheel well on most vessels.

As he tried to make himself small, he realized the Rush still had them in full beam. He cursed as he raised his half-frozen torso once again, waved to the Rush and fell to his knees as the light dimmed and the dark night fell about them. The full moon wrapped him in her blanket and he watched the stars dance with one another as he fought to remain conscious. He would sleep for only a few minutes, he told himself.

In the distance, the old mariner song remained in the air as Steve laid his head against the bulkhead. He was done for. Like a child, he curled into a fetal position as waves of exhaustion snatched him away to another world. In his final moments of consciousness, Captain Channing looked to the wing as it jutted into the dark night. A peace began to settle over him, which he had not felt since he was a child. He had done it. His mission was accomplished.

The hull tilted and timbers moaned as the mariner pressed his vessel into the night and within a few minutes, Captain Channing was sound asleep.

A vision of sailing with his father filled his dream world. The vision felt real, as he could hear the waves and taste the wind. The reverie was of a time before his father passed away; the last time life made sense. He attempted to focus on his father's face but no matter how hard he tried, his father remained turned to the sea, looking for something beyond the horizon.

There was something about this dream...a wisp of hope...something he needed to remember, something, he should know about life and of a child sailing with his father.

10

Speak English

A fear of presence cleaves to men
A poison deep within their soul
The past takes away their day
The future steals their way
For the constant truth may only be found
Among those who share the hope
Of a ship, inbound

Captain Channing could not figure out where he was when he awoke. He knew it was morning but for the life of him, he could not remember why he was in the bottom of a boat. He pried his eyes apart. The salt and sleep of the night before forced his gaze upward and there he discovered a dark figure standing directly above. Startled, Captain Channing banged his head against the hull as he tried to back away from the looming figure. And in the midst of his confusion; the dark figure broke into a hearty laugh.

"You...eat?" the old mariner asked in broken English, as he attempted to stop laughing.

Captain Channing sat up, put on his glasses and scanned his surroundings. To his chagrin, Navy destroyers surrounded him on either side and then he noticed the Rush at her post to his stern. His heart sank at the thought of them watching him sleep.

"Shit...nooooo!" was all he could muster.

The old mariner prodded once again, "You...eat?"

It took a moment for Steve to realize that he understood the old man.

"Do you speak English?" Steve asked, as he rubbed the growing knot on his forehead. It would take a few days for it to heal he thought, as he felt the skin begin to crack.

The old mariner ignored Steve, as he pulled rhythmically on a fishing line. Within a few minutes, the old man reeled in a small tuna, and as he attached the fish to the side of the vessel, Captain Channing noticed that the vessel was moving slowly in a large circle.

In the morning light, he could finally see the attention to detail, and that a master ship builder must have been involved in her creation. Everything about the vessel was unusual and the artisanship obvious.

The mariner carved the tuna using a sharpened shell into perfect squares and handed the meat to Steve. He demanded, more than asked, "You...eat!"

Steve, having never dinned on live fish, squirmed at the thought, but reluctantly took the piece of meat and ate it to please the old man. The fresh catch occupied his pallet with sweet relief, and he found himself genuinely shocked at how good it tasted, and a grand smile returned to the old mariner as Steve motioned for yet another.

"You speak English?" Steve asked, once again, as he consumed the next piece of tuna.

The old mariner shrugged, and then grunted as he maintained his vigil of fileting the live fish. He had an obvious ability to ignore and it was beginning to get on Steve's nerves. Meticulous in every effort, the old mariner

hung the strips of fresh tuna from guide wires supporting
the wing. This created a sort of fish jerky by the looks of
older filets nearby and then to Steve's horror, the old
mariner lifted the severed head of the young tuna, sucked
an eye out, and swallowed it whole. He handed the head to
Captain Channing who refused the offer. The old mariner,
nonplussed, shrugged his shoulders and sucked the
remaining eye out with obvious delight.

Somehow, the eating of the eye reminded Steve that he
had neglected the one thing he needed to accomplish the
night before. He quickly began to dig about for the small
radio as he motioned to let the Rush know he was about to
use it, then dropped his head as reality hit.

"They will know it's you, you idiot, when you hit send,"
he mumbled as he turned it on.

"Did you have a good nap, Captain?" Captain Bearing
asked, to Steve's surprise.

Steve grimaced at the thought. The ribbing he would
endure after this little event was over, would never end.

On the far end of the radio, Captain Bearing laughed
aloud. Then, as if turning off a switch, he informed
Captain Channing in a matter of fact tone, "the Admiral
wants me to relay to you that you did a fine job last
night...by establishing first contact. We were worried at
first; then we realized, that it must have been your plan all
along. That was a great idea, to feign sleep, so that the old
man would not throw you back. By the way...a few more
hours and our comrades in arms would have taken her
over," Bearing stated, knowing that the Navy would be
monitoring the channel.

Before Captain Channing could reply, the old mariner
ripped the radio from Steve's hand, glared as if he were
deeply hurt, then reared back and threw it as far as he
possibly could. Steve's eyes grew wide as the old man
walked away mumbling, "No Jeeps. They find...radio...it
bring Jeeps. Jeeps...they not come here."

"I suppose you do speak English," Steve quipped.

The mariner strapped into his harness, obviously frustrated with his guest, and began to adjust his control lines. Captain Channing looked to the Rush in complete disbelief as the odd vessel turned into the wind and sped away like a rocket. Still wobbly from his sleep, he worked his way across the netting as the outrigger stole skyward once again. There he found a perch against a stay and decided to wait for the old man to speak. He soon realized the old man intended to remain a rock of silence.

Finally, Steve broke the long silence. "I'm sorry. But I don't understand...why did you throw my radio away?" he asked as he bowed his head to express humility.

"Radio...Radio bring Jeeps. Jeeps...no good," the old mariner snapped.

Captain Channing had no idea what he meant by Jeeps and decided to broach the subject at another time. It was important to build trust and the radio was obviously a bad start, he told himself. He decided to secure his position against the stay and held on as the water passed beneath him in a rush of sound. He then decided that he no longer cared what his comrades thought as the scope of the odd vessel's simplicity won his heart.

Memories of his childhood sailboat resurfaced as he looked about her. Each part made of wood or old airplane felt pure and intended. She felt far too real...too visceral to be hoax, he thought. Amelia was part of this craft and her magnificent wing was going to tell a story few would forget for the vessel was a work of art in motion. In addition, as far as he could tell, there was neither navigational equipment nor maps to guide the old man. Guide wires and a rigging combination he had never witnessed before on any vessel held his attention for the next few hours.

Each line, terminated beside the old man in a coil and was clipped in place by large pegs, except for the one attached to his foot. Steve decided the line attached to the old man's food must be the rudder control, as he never seemed to let his leg rest. Moreover, other than the few wire cables, obviously taken from the plane itself, each cord looked to be meticulously handmade. It would take one a man a lifetime to make them, he thought.

Steve knew to sail such a complicated vessel required the highest attention, yet the old man focused on the task of sailing her as if asleep most of the time. It was the old man's trance that had Steve most curious for with every fifth or sixth swell that passed beneath, the mariner lowered the outrigger to within inches of the sea, and touched the next wave to pass. At other times, he waited much longer between touchdowns, and for the life of Captain Channing; he could not determine a logical order, or the difference from one wave to the next. There was no rhyme or logic to explain the system and he decided that he would have to accept the fact that there were mysteries regarding this vessel that he might never understand.

As the day passed, as fast as any day Steve had ever experienced, the old man began to sing once again in his native tongue,. Each melody, as mesmerizing as the night before caused Steve to worry that he would fall asleep once again. To combat the desire to curl up and call it a day, in unison with the old man, he began to hum rock ballads in return. It was in this way, that the odd couple passed the day with little else said.

Timing in sailing, like in life, is everything and the precision of each tack the old man undertook was that of a man with a compass. He maintained his trance and he worked his vessel eastward. Moreover, when his eyes did open, he focused only on the sky above and not at the sea before.

Sometime in the afternoon, the old man snapped out of his trance and yelled out a loud cry over the rush of wind. Steve, close to sleep, startled and nearly fell overboard.

"Big boat...make mess...mess sea bad," the old man shrieked as he waved his hands toward the Navy destroyers. Captain Channing found his bearing as the old man demanded more than asked, "You make go away...okeydokey?"

"Okeydokey?" Steve asked. Did he hear the old man correctly, he thought.

Captain Channing fumbled about for a few words that might express how the old man had ruined any hope of making the destroyers leave.

"That's why I needed the radio...do you understand...you threw away the only way I can tell them to move!"

"Okeydokey....you make move," the old man replied.

"Do you not understand...I needed that radio?"

"Okeydokey...you make move!"

It was of no use fighting with him Steve thought and he decided to use his rusty charades skills. He broke the old man's request into syllables and the harder he tried the more confused he was sure the crew of the Rush must be. Finally, he waved his hand in a large circular motion, pointed to each destroyer; then made a cutting motion across his throat, then waved his arms as if he were guiding an aircraft to park at a terminal.

"Is he seriously playing charades?" Captain Bearing asked his second in command.

"Sir, I think he wants those destroyers to get out of the way or...he wants us to sink them. My wife and I play charades with our neighbors often," the Lieutenant replied, as Captain Bearing looked on exasperated.

"Are you kidding me?" the Captain asked.

"No, Sir...I think he wants the destroyers to move."

"No...Are you telling me that you play charades with your neighbors? Have you told anyone else this before...God I hope not," Captain Bearing said as he watched Captain Channing jump up and down and press the same motions into effect.

"I do think he wants us to fire upon the Navy," the Captain said loud enough for the entire deck to hear.

"Sir, I concur. I think he wants us to sink them," the Second Lieutenant joked, trying to recover from his admission.

Bearing looked to his Second as if he had lost his mind and said, "You and I need to have a little talk after this is over, son. Get on the horn and politely ask the Navy escorts to drop back. Inform them that they are impeding our officer's ability to communicate with the Captain of the...foreign vessel."

The Lieutenant relayed the order to communications, and a moment later, the phone rang on the bridge. Captain Bearing watched on with a wry smile as his Second pulled the phone away from his ear. The Navy Commander, not feeling the need to be compliant had as Bearing expected, decided to express his concern in a visceral manner.

Captain Bearing snatched the phone from his subordinate and returned the barrage with a measured staccato. He maintained the assault of foul language, without raising his voice, until the other end fell quiet. As most on his deck knew, Captain Bearing considered this form of communication an art. The trick was to space each word with the expletive that best explained what he thought of their status without raising his voice. "It is not about communicating anger," he once told his officers, "it is about communicating your intent."

As he finished his reply, Bearing turned to his Second and ordered with the line still open, "Get ready in case those sorry ass sons of bitches don't move their fat asses."

Bearing returned to his conversation and pressed, "I don't think you understand, Captain...I am under explicit orders from my Admiral. We have a man aboard that vessel and he has the situation under control."

He then stared ahead as if looking for a dot on the horizon as he listened to the now muted officer on the other end. "I think you would find it to be a grave mistake to try and board that vessel, Captain." Bearing responded and then hung up while his second looked on with eyes as wide as saucers.

"Sir, are they going to move?"

"They're thinking it over. I think they will soon see things my way."

"Should I prepare to fire, Captain?"

Captain Bearing chose not reply as he let out a tremendous huff and stared forward once again.

The destroyers broke off and fell in behind the Rush, and a collective sigh swept across her bridge. In the awkward moment between, Captain Bearing never smiled and his gaze remained forward. He knew the crew needed to see his resolve and that the incident was just a pissing contest, but he was sure, he would pay for it one day.

"Give Captain Channing three strong blasts to let him know we've got his back," Captain Bearing ordered.

Aboard the odd winged vessel, the old man began to relax as the destroyers fell away and the ocean returned to normal.

"Okeydokey...you big man. You...stay now," the old man said to Steve as he grinned from ear to ear.

"I'm glad you think everything is okeydokey," Captain Channing replied. "You were planning on throwing me over board?" He waited for a reply to his quip, but the old man remained silent.

He began to wonder what the cost would be for losing the radio and he knew Bearing must have brought some big guns to the fight if the Navy gave up territory. Then the memory of waking up in the well returned and knew he must have looked like a fool to all. It did not matter, he told himself. He was the first aboard and he had their long lost airplane.

As the remainder of the day passed, Captain Channing studied the vessel and decided that it must have taken a dozen men at least three years to build the her. The central hull looked to be made of a wound cord stretched over metal plates that had to be the remaining skin and ribs of the Electra and with every fiber of his being, he wanted to open the hatch and explore below, but a small voice inside told him to wait. He would look no further until invited.

11

Steveee

Tender the night comes
To slay the foreign day
Which crawled upon my skin
As if uninterrupted tangles
Of memories seeking light
Yet, the fog of sleep will not relent
For giants live in our midst
And angels seek one last kiss

At sunset, Steve realized he was starving. The rushed plans to board had not included an extended stay. As he wondered, what he had thought might happen once aboard, he had to admit that he had given little thought to the subject, and felt foolish for not having a game plan. As best he could tell, they were heading in the right direction and he was confident that Captain Bearing would have signaled a change in course if they were heading away from the Hawaiian chain. At least the old man seemed steadfast, he thought as he watched him sail the vessel with little effort.

With the last few moments of day piercing the late evening sky, Steve gained the mariner's attention in the hopes that the man understood the international sign for hunger. To his great relief, the old mariner released the wind from the wing and set the vessel into a circle pattern. The old man then sprinted across the loose netting to the mainsail and released lines that forced a bag, hung high in the rigging, to open. The odd object was an ingenious water collection unit made of old rubber and reeds.

Fresh water poured forth as the old man popped a clip and drank deep. Captain Channing stumbled over the netting as if a child learning to walk, and except for the hint of old rubber, he was pleased to discover that the water was pure. He gulped like a man who had discovered an oasis until the old man suddenly took away the spout.

"You...drink much."

"Sorry, I'm used to having water available all the time."

"All time...that why...you fat."

"I'm not fat," Steve replied with indignation.

The old mariner grabbed him by the waist and pulled on the extra five pounds about his belt.

"You fat...okeydokey!"

"Okeydokey...ok....oh god...whatever," Captain Channing muttered under his breath. The term okeydokey was obviously popular with the old man, he thought.

"I'm glad you think I'm okeydokey!"

A large smile covered the old man's face as he slapped his chest and then Steve's chest.

"You... me...okeydokey?" he asked.

"Yes, we are okeydokey...I think."

With that, the old man returned to the task at hand as he put away the rain collection unit.

"May I ask...where are we going?" Captain Channing pressed.

The old mariner pointed into the coming eastern night sky.

"I go...to Amelia...home. She tell me...I go," he replied

Captain Channing found his knees beginning to buckle as the name of Amelia Earhart was mentioned for the first time. Suddenly, he felt ashamed of himself for having only believed the old man had discovered the wing and built a ship.

"Did you know Amelia?" he asked apprehensively.

"Ms. Amelia...she my friend. I know her...long time," the old man replied as he placed his hand on Captain Channing's shoulder in a fatherly manner.

Steve found himself looking to the Rush for guidance as he fought the urge to hug the old man. He took off his glasses and cleaned them in a nervous fit of energy. He wanted to enjoy the embracing smile of the old mariner who was obviously finding pleasure in letting him in on his little secret.

"Do you want to go to America?" Steve finally asked. "Is that where she told you to go?"

"Yes, Amerrrica...Amelia want I go...to her home. You... Amerrrrica? You Okeydokie?"

"Yes, I am American!" Steve replied as he felt his heart begin to pound through his shirt. "I was sent to help you get back to America."

"You look...like Mr. Fred."

"You knew Fred Noonan?"

The old man's smile was confirmation enough.

"I will get you to America. I promise!" Steve exclaimed.

"Alluluei, he show me...you come."

"Who?" Steve asked, confused.

"Alluluei," the old man replied.

"You mean...okeydokey?"

"No...you okeydokey. Me...okeydokey," he said as he pointed to himself. "Alluluei, he...show me...you come. Tell me wait for you," he replied as he pointed to the sea deliberately.

"It sure as hell didn't look like you were waiting for me," Steve replied.

"Alluluei know. He tell me wait...I wait for you."

Captain Channing decided that he needed to sit down and contemplated the news before his legs gave way. It would take some time to figure out Alluluei, he thought.

The sea suddenly fell calm, as if ordered to do so at sun set and the two shared a meal of dried fish and a paste the old man had retrieved from within the hull. The paste was bitter and yet consumable and it was an obvious carbohydrate source.

The evening breeze allowed the two men the first long quiet period of the day and Steve decided, only one more question needed to be asked.

"I don't know your name? My name is Steve Channing...they call me Captain Channing on the big boat behind us," he said as he pointed to the Rush.

The old mariner smiled and stuck out his hand.

"Steveeeeeeee," he said as if trying to see the word.

"No...It's Steve Channing."

"Steveeeee...Cannin."

"Just, Steve will do."

"Steveeeee...Willllldooo Cannin. I like...Okeydokey," the old man understood with a sense of accomplishment.

"No...not okeydokey...not willllldooo...my name is Steve. Not Steveeeee. My dad called me Stevie; but I haven't been called that name since I was a child."

The old man's smile only grew as Steve tried to explain himself.

"Steveee...Willdoooo..Cannin...my name...Truc," the old man replied as he attempted a weak handshake.

"Like...pickup Truck?" Steve asked as he decided not to push the point of the correct pronunciation of his name.

The old man regarded him somewhat bewildered.

"Oh...Ok...Truc. I like the name Truc. That's a very strong name where I'm from," Steve replied. Now he had something to report he thought other than the sleeping conditions.

"Stevee Willldooo Canninn...you okeydokey."

"Well, if you say so...Truc."

"I say yes," Truc responded as he patted Steve like a father welcoming his child home from college.

Steve, taking his cue from the old man, pulled Truc's head to his, and said aloud, "Thank you, God, for letting me meet my friend, Truc."

To his surprise, the old man hugged him until it became uncomfortable.

"You...me...friend?" Truc asked as he let go.

"Yes...Truc...I would like nothing more than to be your friend."

"Like...Amelia...my friend?" he asked.

"Oh...I hope so, Truc," Captain Channing replied.

"Alluluei...he say...I make friend. He say...you need me."

With these words, peace swept over Captain Channing once again as Truc held his hand and smiled. Steve knew then, Alluluei must be his God, and the fact that Truc's God had told him he was coming made Steve shutter as he considered the implications of such a truth.

"Did Alluluei tell you anything else, Truc?" he asked.

"Yes...he speak all time," Truc replied.

"Anything, specific?"

Truc looked to him confused. He did not understand the word specific."

"Don't worry...it's okeydokey Truc...you just tell me when Alluluei speaks again so that I can be sure to listen with you," Steve joked.

"He never stop...he speak now...you not hear?" Truc replied confused by Steve's lack of faith.

"Well...no, I cannot hear him," Steve replied, ashamed by his lack of ability.

"You like Amelia...she not hear Alluluei...for long time," Truc said as he squatted next to the wing and looked up at the coming night sky.

"Ms. Amelia...she could hear...him?" Captain Channing asked.

"She hear...and see Alluluei," Truc replied.

"So...Ms. Amelia is dead?" Steve asked, unsure if he should be treading in these waters.

"Ms. Amelia...she safe now," Truc replied, as he pulled the clip on the water collection unit and took a long drink.

Captain Channing took that for a yes and decided not to ask any more questions for Truc seemed to be finished with the conversation as he moved onto his next project.

Within the hour, Truc had his vessel racing into the coming night as he quickly fell into the trance. He never stirred when the winds changed and yet, he made adjustments, as if he were fully aware of his surroundings. Truc was doing something far deeper than sleeping, as he would moan at odd intervals and the vessel would moan in return like two whales letting each other know where they were in the dark sea.

As Steve knew was now his custom, often, the outrigger dropped and Truc would touch the next set of waves, as if seeking something only he could only feel. And as the night passed, and the stars filled the sky above, Captain Channing finally understood, that he was witnessing an artist at work, whose canvas was the sea and his odd vessel, the brush.

Several hours before dawn, Captain Channing made his way to the stern. Sleep came swift, and the dreams returned. He called out to his father, but he would not turn his face away from a storm building in Steve's dream horizon. The coming weather event bothered Steve, yet somehow he knew he was safe, as he was confident that his father had command of their vessel.

12

Close To Home

Among the machines of men
Hope drowns
As if to clog the mind and erode the soul
The will is bent to serve the cold
Oh,
If but grace should abound
As we taste the salt
Smell the sea
And in that moment know, we are as near
As we shall ever be

As the sun arose the next morning, several aircraft greeted the odd flotilla. As special reports with live coverage from Hawaii filled the air and Captain Channing's presence on the vessel was a development none had expected.

Truc had a goal in mind and, as the morning bore forth and more strangers entered the picture, Steve determined he would do everything in his power to help Truc meet that goal. He just needed to figure out what the goal might be.

"Jeeps?" Truc asked, as he pointed skyward to several private jets circling like buzzards waiting for the wounded to die.

Steve scratched his head wondering what Truc meant by jeeps and replied, "Airplanes....not Jeeps. Those are airplanes."

Truc breathed a deep sigh of relief as he released the forward sail once again. Though Truc could not know, as the sail billowed, viewer ratings doubled as hastily acquired experts attempted to explain the presence of the second sail.

As the day passed, Captain Bearing sent over M.R.E's and bottled water with Captain Channing's favorite Ensign Tucker. Steve exchanged an odd smile with Tucker and the transfer occurred flawlessly as Truc slowed to allow the hand off. Steve tunneled through the package expecting to find another radio and was shocked to discover Bearing had decided not to press the issue.

The reoccurring dream made Steve glad to see the next morning and, to his surprise, Truc seemed unaffected by the night of sailing. He, on the other hand, began to feel weather worn. The desk job had made him soft, he thought. He felt as if he should have his sea legs by now but that was not the case and to make matters worse, his blistering sunburn was beyond any he had ever experienced.

As lunch approached, an armada of charter boats and larger luxury yachts greeted Truc. He had become a spectator's sport and Captain Bearing became concerned as the weekend boaters pressed in closer with each passing hour. Bearing finally had enough, and within a few minutes of a well-placed call, the two destroyers leap frogged past the Rush to intercept anyone who might interfere.

Truc quickly became agitated by the wake they created and snapped, "You make...stop. Okeydokey!"

Steve felt they must be close if Bearing had allowed them to change position and he begged Truc to remain patient. His answer would come soon enough as the peaks of Hawaii slipped over the horizon.

"Like Amelia, tell. Like Amelia tell," Truc yelled aloud, as he released from the harness and danced on the webbing. He then fell back into the netting and stared at the sky with relief while Steve looked on in wonder, for he himself could not see the islands.

He squinted to focus on what Truc was making the fuss over, but it was fruitless.

"You...eyes...bad?" Truc asked, as he pointed forward.

"I will be blind soon," Steve replied, as he took his glasses off.

Sadness overcame Truc, as if he had missed something very important about his friend.

"I have a disease. A disease they cannot fix with glasses."

"Steveee...I see island...island see you too," Truc replied, as a comforting grandfather would.

Captain Channing could not believe that Truc was attempting to comfort him. He had come to help Truc and, so far, it had been the complete opposite. Truc had saved him, fed him, and comforted him. What had he brought to the picture, Captain Channing wondered.

"It's going to be OK Truc. I have made my peace with it...I think."

"You are be brave...like Ms. Amelia...you are Steveee Willdooo Cannin."

Steve chose not to answer. Time for personal issues could come later he thought. Right now, he had to make Truc go to the Coast Guard base at Sand Island in Honolulu Harbor. The Navy would expect Truc to follow them to Pearl but his orders were to return to base and that was what he was going to accomplish. Then it hit him, as to why Captain Bearing had not sent a radio. Orders, could not be changed if he could not receive them. In that case, the last order was the only order.

The perimeter before them was set, and he knew the destroyers would soon turn for Pearl.

"We need to go to Honolulu. I have friends who can help you there," he pressed Truc.

Truc studied his friend for a long moment then looked ahead, as if he wanted to head to the island he could see.

"The island I want you to go too, is north of that big island. I need you to go north to that island. Do you know which way is north?"

Truc remained silent, as he studied the peaks before him, then, without hesitation, he tacked to the Northeast.

Steve was finally able to relax. Truc trusted him, and that was worth more than a small celebration. They were headed for the west side of Oahu and, he could taste the burger he was going to order when his feet hit dry land.

It took several minutes for the destroyers to realize Truc had tacked hard North. He cut through the first layer of small craft like if a racecar driver at Indy and Steve did his best to maintain a heading within his own head as the day was fast fading. Several hours later, Captain Channing felt it more than he knew it. He believed that they were directly West of the port of Honolulu but he could not be sure without visual references, so he looked to the Rush for any clues as to his next move.

"Give him three short bursts on the horn," Captain Bearing ordered, as he knew what peer needed.

"Hell yes! Do it now...Channing...make him turn," Captain Bearing barked, as he watched Captain Channing climb the outrigger. Truc tacked once again toward Honolulu and the Rush followed her in unison and then, fell in close behind.

Aboard the Rush, the radio lit up with a barrage of curses and Captain Bearing, ever the professional, did not respond. The channel remained open and no order came for the speaker to be silenced, as the symphony of foul language hit a crescendo.

Finally, Captain Bearing picked up the radio and replied, "Sorry gentlemen, I have orders to escort our Captain...and the vessel he is inspecting to our base for debrief. I would suggest you bring up any disagreement you may have with my Admiral. I am sure he will be glad to address your issues over coffee next week."

With that, both destroyers came to an all stop as they awaited orders.

"Those pukes honestly believed we were going to let them take him to their house," Captain Bearing snarled for the edification of his entire bridge.

Truc cut through the next layer of onlookers that surrounded the harbor with great agility, as Captain Bearing brought the Rush in as close as he dare.

With the final hour of daylight falling off the horizon, Steve could not help but feel proud and as the harbor came into sight and two rigids from the Rush sped past. Tucker led a salute as he came near. His small flotilla and rigids from the base created a protective circle about the odd winged craft, and together they triumphantly entered Honolulu Harbor.

As they passed the cruise ship moorings, the Rush came about to face the entourage of vessels who were attempting to keep up. In a single flawless maneuver, the Rush swung about, and cut off all who wished to follow while even more rigids from the base plugged holes.

Captain Channing guided Truc by memory, more than sight, as he wanted Truc to moor behind the Constance, which was still awaiting her sea trials. He felt as if they were coming in much too fast and began to worry they would plow into the dock until, Truc released a handmade sea brake and the odd winged vessel glided next to the dock, as if it had completed the maneuver a thousand times.

Standing at post with clipboard in hand, Lieutenant Evans waited patiently. Her hair in a tight bun with her regulation dress cap neatly atop, Lieutenant Evans was a stark contrast to Admiral Simpson as he paced the pier, giving orders, and causing enlisted to stumble as he barked.

The ordeal was over and Truc seemingly deflated before Steve eyes, as he fell limp into his harness and passed out. Steve rushed to his side, worried Truc had suddenly passed away as he quickly felt for a pulse. To his great relief, Truc was in a deep sleep, a commodity he had enjoyed little during the journey.

With all the commotion to tie off the vessel, Truc never moved a muscle. Captain Channing raised his hand, as he made his way across the vessel, to silence the group.

"He is sleeping," he ordered more than announced.

In the state of sleep, Truc seemed to be far older than he did while at sea. The energy he had displayed would have been an amazing feat for a young man, Steve thought as he looked to the sky and said a soft, "Thank you." Moreover, for the first time, he could tell that sleep, and navigating, looked nothing alike.

"No one boards this ship without Captain Channing's permission," Lieutenant Evans ordered, as she snatched an Ensign who was about to attempt the feat.

Admiral Simpson, taken aback at the insistency of his aid asked, "What about me Lieutenant?"

"Sir, I'm sorry, sir. I'm simply trying to protect the historical integrity of the vessel," Lieutenant Evans said, as if stumbling for an out.

"Don't worry about it Evans. That's why you're my assistant. You get things done."

"You heard the lady. Stay off!" her bellowed.

Admiral Simpson offered Captain Channing an arm to dry land. His legs wobbled, as his equilibrium tried to find the next wave and Steve found himself falling into his Admiral's arms. Admiral Simpson held him by the shoulders as he had experienced the effect many times, and his face told Steve all he needed to know. His Admiral was pleased.

"You look like you've been sleeping in the bottom of a canoe," Admiral Simpson teased, as he dusted the Captain's shoulders with both hands.

"I'm sorry sir. I fell in," Steve muttered.

"That was genius Son...pure genius. Lieutenant Evans had to tell me it was all part of your plan and then she had to convince Bearing that you knew what you were doing.

As you can imagine, he came a bit unglued when you fell asleep. When she handed him to me, I told him that the old man could not throw someone off who was asleep. Moreover, here you are in less than a week; you, this boat and that old man. Son, you have done more for the Coast Guard than ten senators in my back pocket," Simpson supposed, as he slapped Captain Channing across the back.

"Yes sir," was all Steve could muster.

"Did you get a name?"

"Oh, yes sir. His name is Truc. You say it with a slight click at the end."

"That's a fine name," the Admiral added. "Anything else we need to know before he wakes up."

"Sir...you are not going to believe this. I think he knew Amelia, I mean, Mrs. Earhart personally."

Lieutenant Evans took both men by the arm and led them away from bystanders as she overheard Captain Channing's declaration and neither seemed to notice. Admiral Simpson stepped back and stared at his Captain as if he had lost his mind.

"Sir, he said he was going to Amelia's home. He told me...she was his best friend."

"He said what?" Lieutenant Evans questioned.

"He told me, Amelia was his best friend."

Admiral Simpson gripped Captain Channing by the arm and asked, "Son, do you think this is a hoax?'

"Look at that boat sir. Does that look like a hoax to you? It would take true ship builders years to build such a vessel, and a true set designer to make her look that convincing.

The Admiral's eyes began to dart about as Steve had witnessed in his office. He was thinking and the process, to the untrained eye, looked a bit maddening. Suddenly, he bellowed, "Everyone on deck! I want all of you back to your posts. Now! Have you never witnessed a man sleeping in his rack?"

He then turned to Lieutenant Evans and ordered, "Clair, get my command group in here. Seal this place off and get me several patrol boats around that vessel. Tell them to be very quiet. Make them use paddles if necessary. Tell them, if anybody wakes the old man, they will answer to me. Then call air command and have them force away those news choppers. As a matter of a fact, release the Constance off the dock and have it block the view from shore. Block that vessel as much as possible from view. I don't care if you have to drag another ship over here from the scrap heap! One more thing, tell every officer to inspect phones and remove any close ups. No pictures leave this base. Then to make double sure, have the gate check them again."

Lieutenant Evans began to initiate the calls and Steve could not help but watch her as she walked away. It would not be long and he would not be able to enjoy such a sight, he thought. As she disappeared behind a building, he turned to admire the winged vessel with his Admiral.

Admiral and Captain shared the moment like two children admiring a sandcastle, both keenly aware, the tide would eventually come and wash it way.

13

An Ocean View

Time lays waste
Consumes the gentle dream
While fools dances upon her edge
Prophets tell of her sorrows
Ah, but you
Sing aloud child of hope
For there may be no tomorrow

Truc's snoring had ceased yet his exhaustion was still present. Steve wanted to believe the old man needed him, but somehow, he knew that was not true. Truc's story was all that mattered now and Steve hoped time would be kind enough for him to share it as he chose.

As he surveyed the base, a sense of destiny pressed upon him; a sense that life was moving forward, and that this was his last chance to grab ahold. It would be these memories he would take into the dark night, he thought as he studied the vessel. He heard someone cough and turned to find Lieutenant Evans standing on the far side of the dock. To his surprise, she had been ordered to escort him to his condominium. At the gate, news trucks had begun to take over every square inch roadside. Then, and after stopping to buy him a hamburger, Lieutenant Evans delivered Captain Channing, as ordered, to his front door.

"I will wait for you in the car," the Lieutenant informed Captain Channing.

"No...please...come inside. I insist. It would be stupid for you to sit out here."

She hesitated then said, "Yes sir," as she hesitantly opened her car door.

She found the condominium to be dark with the shades drawn and a single dusty lamp in the living room. His home was sparse, as if he had recently moved in and the furniture had not yet arrived. He noticed her discomfort and pulled the curtains back to reveal a moonlit ocean view, then scrambled to turn on the lamp and one other hall light.

In an apparent effort to seem normal Clair began to study his pictures and awards as he attempted to pick up his clothing scattered about. He disappeared into the kitchen and found the fridge to be spoiled. The light had burned out and he hit the side of the fridge to see if it would come back on. His fridge was dead.

"I'm sorry...I don't have anything to offer you...it seems my fridge died while I was at sea and I apologize for the mess...I didn't expect to have visitors"

"I don't need anything, Captain," Clair mumbled as she picked up a picture and began to study it. "Do you like it here?" she asked as if she had been waiting for the answer for some time.

"Well...it used to feel like home. I cannot say that I care anymore. The view is nice...I suppose. When my fiancé left, the mortgage was in my name and I could see no reason to move. It's convenient to the base and I have only one bus transfer," he replied, while he attempted to water the one living plant in his kitchen window.

"Do you miss driving?" she asked as she picked up a photo from the TV hutch. The picture was of Steve as a boy with a man she assumed to be his father. She thought him to be cute as a kid, and his father, tall gaunt and unassuming, with a shock of wild red hair, looked exactly like his son.

"I try not to think about it. I do dream...of flying down the road on my motor bike...but those days are over," he replied while he opened cabinets and searched for something to put on the table. They were as bare as the fridge for the most part. It had been easier to eat out.

"I hope you don't mind me asking questions? I can't imagine what you must be going through."

Clair studied the solitary sofa sitting in the middle of the large living room as if a lost child. She suddenly felt sad for him, as she realized his fiancé had left only the one piece of furniture.

"I'm slowly growing use to the idea now. Well...sort of. The past few days, I believe have changed my perspective. I don't know if I should tell you this, but I was about to resign my commission the day I met you. I only asked the Admiral to let me find Truc, because I was half hoping he would release me. I didn't expect him to say yes."

"Is this your father in the picture?" Clair asked as she tilted the picture toward him. "Where are you? Tthe place looks familiar."

Steve dumped the spoiled goods of the fridge in the garbage and carried it to the breezeway as he replied, "That's my father. I did not know my mom. She passed when I was a baby. It's at a dock near San Francisco. My father and I would go every other weekend for a sail. I believe it was his way of compensating after my mother's death."

"Where does he live now?" she asked, before she remembered that she had read his file.

"He passed three years after that photo."

"I'm sorry...I didn't mean to pry. Please forgive me," Clair pleaded, as she set the picture down and watched him return to the kitchen with the empty can.

"I invited you into my house. It's OK. I'm not offended. Actually, I am glad to know you care enough to ask," he replied, as he took the photo from Clair. The picture was beginning to blur, but the memory was not. He turned to Clair and asked, "So, how did you become the Admiral's liaison?"

"I was valedictorian at the University of Hawaii. I signed up for the reserves to pay for college and after I finished officer training, at the top of my class I might add, one of my teachers recommended me to Simpson. I have been with him since my first day. He knew he was going to be an Admiral and he wanted to hand pick his staff. He assigned me to his command after officer training and I have been with him since. He has been like a father to me. Very protective...but he means well. As you know, he is a bit gruff, but I believe, he has a good soul."

"Wow...I knew you were smart. I didn't know you were that smart."

"It's a curse," Clair quipped.

Steve said, as he headed for his bedroom, "If you don't mind, I'm going to take a quick shower. Please feel free to look about or watch TV. Go outside if you like. The balcony is nice at night."

"I'll be fine," she replied. He seemed small in this house, she thought, as if he were being robbed by simply living here. Steve closed the door and headed for the shower.

As she thumbed through a photo album, she discovered pictures of him on the swim team and the basketball team in high school. Then she discovered his Academy photos and was shocked to see a man she would not have noticed as the same man living in this house the week before. At the Academy, he was handsome, strong and filled with hope, she thought. The man who had left on a crazy mission a few days before was not the man in the photos. The man who returned with Truc in hand, that was the man in the photos. She did not know what happened on Truc's vessel but whatever it was she liked the change.

Bored, Clair headed for the balcony to find some fresh air and reprieve from the sad living room. Below, rocks met the sea and she wondered if they were not the reason he had kept the condominium. She immediately cleared the thought from her head...who was she to assume his mental state. She turned to leave the porch but was stopped in her tracks as she could clearly see his naked torso in a mirror through the French doors leading to his bedroom. Clair blushed as a warm rush coursed through her at the sight of the man showering. His physical frame was strong, lean and cut and he had a farmers tan from a week at sea. She could not help but watch for a moment, as she hoped he could not see her.

Finally, her senses returned and she rushed back to the living room, turned on the TV and hoped he had not noticed her outside. As she flipped through the stations, she discovered that Truc and Captain Channing owned the airwaves. The job before her was going to be epic in nature if she were to maintain secrecy, she thought. It would be harder if he knew she was attracted to him.

Fifteen minutes later, Steve appeared with a mop of wet hair, dressed in BDU's. He turned to the TV as Clair flipped through the channels and for the first time, realized how important this story was going to be.

"You are a superstar...Sir. The press loves you," she teased as she stood and adjusted her uniform.

Steve noticed immediately that something was different about the Lieutenant. She seemed to be sizing him up and uncomfortable at the same time. All the while a pregnant pause remained between them.

"Well then, we best return to base before they decide to hate me," Captain Channing replied, as he headed for the front door with keys in hand.

"Yes...we best" she replied as she brushed past him.

14

What The Wind Brings

As if a leaf that falls
Upon a far distant shore
The wind lifts up
A fallow sail
To further see, how incomplete
To further taste, life so sweet
A constant move, ebb and flow
That wears on those
Who choose to never know
The endless bounds of a lover's soul

"Are you going to be ok tonight?" Clair asked, as she delivered Captain Channing to the parking lot next to the dock.

"I believe so. It's actually very comfortable. I would even venture to say the closest thing to a spiritual event I have ever experienced. Perhaps, Truc will take you sailing one day and you will see for yourself."

"I will put it on my bucket list. Good night Captain," she replied as she began to pull away.

"Where are you headed?"

"I will be nearby. If you need anything call me."

"Yes Ma'am," he said, as he stood smartly at attention.

"Stop calling me Ma'am. I'm not that old."

"Yes Ma'am."

Clair feigned disgust and drove away.

He located a blanket and pillow from base supply and curled up in the well as he had while at sea. He considered opening the cowling that covered the entry to the hold and he thought it odd, that he never once entered the vessel. Truc had done so only twice while in route but his relationship was not worth a sneak peak. As he settled into his favorite hard spot, before he knew it, the sway of the wing and the snap of the lines blowing in the wind sang him to sleep.

The dream of his father returned, of the sailboat and him as a child. As the hours passed aboard his father's boat, he longed for him to turn about and speak, but the dream would not allow it. The dream remained peaceful, of a kind moment that he treasured, and the storm that seemed to remain perpetually before them, never came to maturity.

Yet, he awoke in a cold sweat, heart racing and his complexion whitewashed. This was the last memory he had of his father and why it had returned, he could not imagine. He had not experienced the dream since a teen and it felt odd that it was with him once again. As he looked toward the sky and studied the blur of stars passing overhead, waiting for a voice that never came.

"Do you have something you need to tell me...Dad?" Steve whispered into the night. As a teen he remembered that the memory of his father would return in unexpected moments, in crowded rooms, the mall, and his car. It had been his father's voice to leave his memory first, and now, his face seemed to be fading away.

After only five hours of sleep, he decided it would be best that he get to work. Admiral Simpson would return well before daylight, he thought, as he looked over and found Truc sound asleep. He could not help but wonder how long it had been since Truc had truly rested.

• • •

Captain Channing discovered his favorite Lieutenant moving about the base, or rather, she found him searching for coffee in the mess hall with hair askew. She seemed neither tired nor inconvenienced. Did she wake up this early every morning, he thought as she took charge of his appearance.

With her by his side, he ordered the entry lounge of the main building to be rearranged and for maintenance to remove the TV's. He then ordered for the A/C system to be set at 80 degrees. He knew he could not chance Truc seeing himself on TV or catching cold. Food, drink and a cot were quickly delivered in case Truc needed to lie down or eat.

As the morning passed he began to understand why Admiral Simpson chose Clair to be by his side. Anything he could possibly conjure up, she made appear with a single phone call. He couldn't help but admire her knack of speaking with authority, never giving on that she was a Lieutenant, and her ability of taking on hard questions with little thought. Personnel began to move about base fulfilling her orders, long before they would have normally reported for duty. The sense of power had to be intoxicating, he thought as he watched her orchestrate their day.

Admiral Simpson appeared a little past daybreak and decided that all parties interested in the debriefing could watch the proceedings through closed circuit TV, as he was concerned that the presence of too many people might overwhelm their primitive guest. On his part, the Admiral had been dealing with requests from Homeland Security, the Department of the Interior, the State Department and various other entities, all of which, wanted to participate in the debrief. He began to worry that it was going to be a circus.

Admiral Frank Jackson of the United States Navy was the one whose request Admiral Simpson did not wish to deal with. However, he could do little to recuse Jackson. The two Admirals' had maintained a professional respect during Simpson's short stint as Admiral. Jackson was a serious player and respected among the Joint Chiefs at the Pentagon. Yet his hard nose demeanor was famous among his staff and those who served under him.

Admiral Simpson spent the rest of his morning in a video conference with the Joint Chiefs as Jackson made his case for the transfer of Truc and his craft to the Naval Ship Yard. Jackson, however, had not expected Admiral Simpson to be on the conference call, and the more he argued, the more he resembled a child tossing a fit. He finally conceded that Admiral Simpson could have his window to find the answers.

Truc remained busy with seemingly endless projects aboard his vessel and the grand smile returned upon seeing his friend once again as Steve came to collect him.

"I worry you...in trouble. Jeeps near?" he asked as he pointed about.

Captain Channing did not understand Truc's fear of Jeeps, and as far as he knew, there were no Jeeps on base. He decided it best to let it go.

"Several important people want to talk about your journey. Do you feel up to such a meeting this morning?

"I meet big man...Okeydokey? Amelia, she tell me trust you to .find big man. She say he called...cooomannndar"

Steve did not know what to do with that information either, and filed it away as a moment he would later need to remember. As he began to answer, Truc put up his finger, as if he suddenly remembered something. He removed the cowling and climbed into the hold that Steve had wanted to explore. After ten minutes, he returned topside carrying a handmade box, and as he placed it on the dock and stepped ashore, his legs buckled. Experienced in the things of the sea, Truc took hold of a pilling.

"Do you need my help?" Steve asked.

"I tell story now. I show cooomnanndar box...Okeydokey!"

"Okeydokey, Truc, that sounds like a plan," Steve replied, as he wondered if Truc had ever spent much time on dry land.

"Is... everything okeydokey Truc?"

Truc nodded yes in reply, then asked, "Who...here?"

Captain Channing thought that a good question, but he did not have time to explain the concept of command centers.

"The commander." Steve replied. This was somewhat true, he thought, as a commander in the Coast Guard was below his own rank.

As they approached the entrance to the main facility, Truc began to study himself in the storefront glass. It was apparent; he had never seen his full reflection.

"I...look old," he exclaimed, as he examined his frame in the glass.

"We all are growing old Truc," Steve replied.

"You not old...me...I...old."

All Captain Channing could do was nod in agreement, as he opened the door. The rush of cool air sent a shiver down Truc's spine, and goose bumps began to rise on his forearms.

"Truc...can I find you something warm? It is always colder in here than it is outside."

Truc decided he would not enter and he enacted his own plan.

"We meet cooommaandaar by tree...Okeydokey? Steveeee Willdooo Canninnn you tell...coooomandaarrrr. Okeydokey!"

He then spun about and marched toward a palm tree in the middle of base as if he were the king of the island.

"I need you to meet with the commander in here," Steve pleade, as he followed after. "And, my name is not Willdoooo."

"Tree is very good...Okeydokey!" Truc mumbled, as he squatted beside the bent palm. He then closed his eyes and Steve knew immediately, the conversation was over. Truc was going to play his cards as he saw fit, and who could blame him, Steve thought.

"Okeydokey...this will do."

Captain Channing glanced back toward the main facilities and there he could see the shadowed figures in a heated conversation. It could not be pleasant, he thought as Admiral Simpson burst out the door wearing his standard issue United States Coast Guard gear. His face was hard as he covered the distance but he quickly changed his demeanor as he approached the tree. Captain Channing was relieved to discover that Simpson's anger was not directed toward him. Rather, it was toward the one who followed close behind.

Adorned in full Navy dress, Admiral Jackson was the most impressive man Captain Channing had ever witnessed in uniform. A full six inches taller, he towered over Simpson, and his gate, twice that of a normal man, seemed to have an instructive purpose. His arms swayed, as if a general taking the field and his chest extended far beyond his waist. Captain Channing found himself hoping his Admiral was up to the challenge.

Following close behind, carrying a digital camera, Lieutenant Evans looked to be lost between the two men.

Admiral Simpson offered his hand to Truc first.

"Sir, it is my honor to meet you and to welcome you to our base. I am Admiral Simpson," he said softly.

Truc remained in his squat position as he took the Admiral's hand and held it, as if he did not know what to do with it.

"I happy...to...see you," he replied, as if a vague memory of etiquette training remained.

Admiral Jackson attempted an introduction, but it came across as awkward, as if he were annoyed that the old man had not stood to attention in his presence.

"Admiral Jackson...sir," he said in a gruff voice.

Truc studied the gaunt figure, took his hand much like Simpsons, and held it until the Admiral became uncomfortable with the salutation. It was obvious to all, that Jackson couldn't tell if the old man was measuring him up or simply afraid of him.

"Okeydokey, I...see...you," Truc replied as if confused. "Two?" he asked.

Each Admiral looked to the other, waiting for the other to answer a question they did not understand.

"Sir, Truc told me he is seeking a commander," Captain Channing interjected. "I should say he was told to look for a commander."

"Truc...we have different groups of men we that we manage. Admiral Jackson is with the Navy and he supplied the large grey boats that helped you on the last part of your journey. I supplied the big white ship with the orange stripe...the one that found you first," Admiral Simpson stated as if to rib Jackson.

"Big grey boat...make sea...bad," Truc coplained as he pointed to Jackson.

Admiral Jackson, for his part, did not know if he should laugh or apologize. His belief that the meeting was quickly becoming a sham was beginning to show.

"Steveee Willdoooo Canninnn...he my friend. He tell me...you speak. I sit...I talk."

He then swept his hands in a large welcoming motion as if he were the wise king of the island as he invited all to join him.

The Admirals looked to each other once again to see who would react first. Simpson decided fighting the situation was a waste of time, hiked up his pants and sat, as Jackson looked as if he were about to leave, then thought better of it.

As each made themselves comfortable, Truck broke the awkward silence.

"Amelia tell me...to tell you...her story."

Admiral Jackson mouth dropped with shock as he heard the name Amelia.

"You knew... Amelia Earhart?" he retorted.

A grand smile slipped across Truc's face, as if a faint wind had come to fill his sails, and it was obvious to all that he had wanted to share this news for some time.

"I know...Amelia," he replied while he played with the thick grass at his feet. "She...teach me...speak English."

"Are you filming this Lieutenant?" Admiral Simpson asked Lieutenant Evans.

She nodded in the affirmative and then adjusted her video camera, to seek a better angle.

As the trade winds swept gently across the base grounds and cooled odd group siting below the bent palm, the weight of the moment was lost to none. To those who had the privilege of passing nearby, the group appeared to be participating in a true Pow-Wow, and the last time a meeting of this type had occurred on American soil, the natives had been cheated of everything they owned Steve thought. He then determined in his heart that Truc would not receive the same treatment, if he had anything to do with it.

Admiral Jackson rubbed his forehead, as he tried to wrap his mind about the old man and his claim. It had to be a hoax, he told himself.

"Where is Mrs. Earhart now...Truc. Since you were the last one to see her alive, you should know?" Admiral Jackson asked.

"My Mila see...Amelia pass."

"Mila?" Steve asked.

"Ms. Amelia make Mila...she make Mila my wife...she say...we Okeydokey."

"What happened to Commander Fred Noonan?" Admiral Simpson asked, as if the whole event of Truc's marriage did not matter.

"Jeeps...kill...Mr. Fred," Truc replied with a growing sad look in his eyes.

Captain Channing clutched his forehead as it hit him what Truc had meant by the term Jeeps became painfully evident. Suddenly, he felt like and idiot for not figuring it out sooner.

"Truc, do you mean Japs...or...Japanese? We call them Japanese."

"Yes, Jeeps," Truc replied emphatically as he waved his arms about as if everyone should know about Jeeps.

Captain Channing decided he needed to explain himself to the Admirals.

"Truc asked me if Jeeps were on the base. I told him as far as I knew; no Jeeps were on the base, just Humvees. He also pointed to the sky when the planes were flying overhead and asked if any were Jeeps. I told him no, they were airplanes. How stupid could I have been...he was asking if any Japanese were on the island. I must tell you, he is from my experience...very afraid of the Japanese."

"Well hell yes there..." Jackson began until Admiral Simpson cut him off.

"Truc, there are no Japs on the island that you should fear. You are safe here," he pressed, as he stared at his counterpart in an effort to redirect his anger.

Jackson returned the glare as Simpson leaned over and whispered to him, "I don't think he knows the Japanese were defeated. I think...he thinks...we are still at war with them."

Jackson's demeanor immediately changed as he studied the old man sitting in front of him.

"Jeeps bad! Kill...my family," Truc alleged while large tears began to roll down his cheeks.

Simpson looked to Jackson and whispered, "He may not even know that we went to war with them."

Tears began to flow down Clair's face as she filmed the revelation. The realization that the man before her was a survivor hit her personally. Finally, she lowered the camera and looked to her Admiral. He knew immediately, she needed to stop.

Admiral Simpson pointed to an Ensign nearby and ordered, "Go get this young lady a chair and a camera stand."

He then made a quick call, "Tell the gentlemen waiting in the lounge that they may come out here if they can sit on the ground and remain quiet. Tell them to take off their jackets and ties and to bring blankets. We have a real story here."

Then, in an effort to reconnect, he took Truc by the hand and said, "Truc...I am sorry for your loss." As he studied the pain present on his guests face, he decided they still needed to press on.

"If you don't mind, there are others who would like to hear your story. Would it be OK if they sat with us around the circle and listened in?" asked Simpson.

"Amelia tell me...to tell her story. Okeydokey?" Truc replied as he wiped the tears from his eyes.

"Sir, when Truc say's okeydokey, he means "yes" or, he wants you to do something...it's kind of an all-purpose word," Captain Channing interjected.

A small group of officers and civilians quickly joined the circle, one with a chair for Clair, and yet another with a pitcher of water and cups.

"Truc...what...what is in the box?" Captain Channing asked as the group settled down.

Truc held the box close to his chest as he replied, "Book...Ms. Amelia's book...in box. She call it...journaaall. She say...you not believe me if I not bring book...so I bring book. Okeydokey?

"Yes, that is... Okeydokey!" Admiral Simpson replied ecstatically.

"May we see the journal?" Admiral Jackson asked in a far more pleasant voice.

As he thought how to go about the reading of his most prized possession, Truc studied the Admirals with uncertainty. The silence became awkward until, he looked to Clair. His eyes grew wide as his face attempted to hold in his broad grin. Caught off guard, and still wiping tears from her eyes, Lieutenant Evans recoiled as his gaze remained upon her.

"Amelia...picks her. She read! Okeydokey?" he said, as he held the box out toward the Lieutenant.

Her discomfort grew exponentially as Admiral Simpson's approval became evident for he could not have imagined a better outcome.

"Lieutenant, you may take the journal. It is most likely very fragile...so be careful."

Before Jackson could object, Admiral Simpson prodded Clair once again, "That's an order Lieutenant."

She forced a fake smile as her heart rate doubled. Slowly, she accepted the box, and her face flushed as her hands shook. She quickly pulled the box to her chest and protected it, much as she had witnessed Truc doing.

"You open...Ms...," Truc began and then a questioning look overcame him as he realized he did not know her name.

"My name is Lieutenant Clair Evans," she replied, soft as if her breath might damage the box.

He tried to repeat it, but the three words came out jumbled.

"Lieutenant, you wouldn't mind if he called you Clair?" Admiral Simpson asked.

She nodded in the affirmative and said, "My name is Clair...Mr. Truc. Clair...you can call me Clair."

"Okeydokey...Clairrrrr. My name...Truc...nooo Mrrr. Truc," he replied.

"Ok...Truc," she replied, as she attempted to steady her voice. "Truc is a very nice name."

"I'm glad that's settled," Jackson bristled as he was obviously upset about losing control of the journal.

Clair ignored him as she studied the simple box made of a dark wood, unadorned and held together by a simple binding, which acted as both a latch and hinge. As she began to open the box, she could not stop her hand from trembling. She decided it best to sit up straight and set the box in her lap for fear of dropping it. Then, with a slight twist of the latch, the box lid opened with ease.

Inside she discovered a bound leather journal, nearly a 1/4-inch thick, severely worn, covered with oil in patches and to the untrained eye, ancient. The book smelled of dried leather and deteriorating paper, yet it seemed to be intact and functional.

The truth was close and Steve wondered, if the world was ready. Clair suddenly pulled her hand back from the box and Captain Channing decided he needed to give her a moment by distracting the group.

"Can you start at the beginning Truc. Can you tell us about the day you first met Mrs. Earhart before we read the book? It will help us understand the journal...if you don't mind," he pressed.

Truc brimmed with delight as he replied, "Okeydokey."

He glanced to his vessel and then stared into a far off place as memories of his past flooded his conscious state. Captain Channing began to believe he could see the story come to life in the eyes of his friend.

"Amelia...she look...look like man...when first meet. She...not like woman...from my island. "

"How was Captain Noonan?" Steve asked.

"He okeydokey...mad...but not stay mad. He...not talk much...work on plane."

"Work on the plane? The plane was intact...not broken into pieces?" Steve asked to keep Truc in play.

"Her plane...stuck...when I see Ms. Amelia."

He then looked to Clair and said, "Open. Amelia tell you ...she tell good story...she write book for you...read...Ms. Clair."

With that, the Admirals and Captain Channing looked to the nervous Lieutenant. As she carefully removed the binding, sweat began to bead on her forehead, and her hands began to tremble once again. Suddenly, the journal fell open before her and she sat amazed at the neat handwriting before her. Clair poured over the first few pages, eyes wide, and silent. It soon became disconcerting to all involved that the Lieutenant was not reading aloud.

"Lieutenant," Captain Channing finally prodded.

A nervous smile returned, as she held to the journal, still silent. All the while, Truc seemed most pleased with himself for his choice, as the young Lieutenant leafed through the pages. She reached for permission to speak the words and cleared her throat but found that she was unable. Something felt wrong, she told herself, she suddenly felt as if she didn't deserve the honor.

"Amelia...she like you read...to Coomandaar," Truc prodded. "Trust Ms. Clair...Okeydokey."

Lieutenant Evans grew pale as she slowly lifted the pages, afraid they would disintegrate in her hands.

"Make sure you film this as she reads the journal," Admiral Simpson ordered the Ensign filming the event in the hope it would break her tension.

The Lieutenants flushed with anxiety as she stared into the lens.

Captain Channing could stand it no longer. "Lieutenant, please, Truc promise it will be ok."

Lieutenant Evans cleared her throat, and so began her journey into the mystery of Amelia Earhart.

The Journal of Amelia Earhart.

I believe it is July, 1942. It could be 1943. I am not sure.
If you have found this, then I hope it will bring a few answers as to our fate. This is a supplemental journal that I have written long

after the events it is to cover. My original journals regarding our passage were confiscated on July 5, 1937. This is my attempt to explain what happened since that day. I will tell you how my journals were confiscated in due time. I hope someday they are recovered for there are many details in them regarding our initial journey. I will not be able to share with you in these few short pages the initial flight plan. If my prior notes are discovered, I am sure they will prove most valuable. I am however, forced to start at the point in which we found ourselves lost. How we came to this place is a story I will try my best to recall in as short a manner as possible, because, this is the last blank journal I have at my disposal. I was lucky to find this notebook stuffed behind a rib of the Electra. I think Fred used it for calculations at some point. That is why many of the pages are missing. Also, I am not sure how long this pen will remain functional. So in the interest of getting the story told, I will be brief.

First, I must tell you that we will soon be attempting to leave our current location. If you have found this, then you must assume I did not complete the attempt. With this possibility in mind, I want to tell my husband that I love and miss him. I have often thought about what life might have been had given I up stunt flying and remained home with you. I remember telling you that I felt like I had one more in me. I am afraid it was one too many my beloved. I also want to tell my family that I miss them. I think about all those who enriched my life each night I am without you. Your memories have kept me alive.

I think it best to start on July 2nd and 3rd. Initially, everything seemed to be going as planned. Yes, we had our difficulties with each leg of the journey but nothing we could not handle.

I will tell you now that we were confident of our ability to find Howland Island. After having much time to think about it, I believe we were the victim of multiple circumstances beyond our control. A change in any one of them and I would not be writing this journal. Rather, I would be writing my book on our adventure. In retrospect, I realize we were truly looking for a needle in a haystack.

At what we calculated to be 200-miles from Howland, Fred and I finally concluded that our capability to receive radio signal was diminished at best. I now know we were deaf. This for the most part proved to be our downfall. We never considered the loss of our ability to receive a signal from the Itasca as a high-risk possibility.

The flight proved to be most uneventful until I tried to make contact with the Itasca. Without contact, this left me to believe that we were nowhere near our destination. To make matters worse the scattered cloud coverage cast shadows on the ocean that looked like islands upon the water's face. Fred confirmed his numbers repeatedly. I changed to multiple frequencies but could not find any way to make contact. Finally, we received a Morse code from the signal ship but our directional locator could not work in Morse code. It just could not lock onto the short signal. However, I kept up the attempt. I whistled to give the Itasca a longer signal so that they may locate our direction and send it back by Morse code but they did not reply in kind. To be honest, I am not sure that the Itasca even had a functional radiolocation system or the ability to speak with us since our radio system was so new. I have even wondered if the ship was at the rendezvous point.

We should have been nearing Howland and able to make contact. The thought that our lives depended on an under qualified radioman became a joke between Fred and me as we struggled to make sense of the situation. I have wondered many nights if the Itasca had adequate systems or if an electrical problem aboard her made her unable to communicate. These are questions for which I will never be able to know the answer. What I can tell you is that the feeling of helplessness was beyond comprehension. Hard decisions quickly became our only option and I began a grid search for Howland.

We had been lucky to that point in fuel use. I had experienced a strong head wind at first but I was able to overcome it by a change in altitude. I believe if the headwind had remained, I would have been forced to turn back. That is one of those circumstances that I spoke of earlier that I cannot change.

In our search for Howland, I broke from our eastward track to begin a north and south track for what seemed an eternity. We both knew each minute used searching meant we had fewer options. I informed the Itasca that I was low on fuel but this was due to nerves more than fact. At that point, Fred estimated our reserves to be slightly over 300 gallons. This was over twenty percent of our starting fuel. Upon telling the Itasca that we were low on fuel, I informed the

Itasca that we were switching radio frequency to *6210* from *3105*. Again, no reply came from the *Itasca*.

At this point, the tension was obvious between Fred and I. I had trusted him and he had trusted me. All we had left was trust. I recommended to Fred that we should turn back and head for the small chain to the west that we had crossed at 9,000 feet. Fred, ever the professional recommended we keep looking. He believed that it would be even harder to find an island in that small chain without a radio signal.

I did not see the situation at this point in the same light as Fred. Therefore, I asked him to find options as I searched for Howland. Fred spent five minutes thinking through the problem and then gave me his final option.

Fred made the assumption that perhaps the *Itasca* was damaged or unable to communicate. As we know, many things could go wrong with our radios since we had experienced them in earlier legs. However, the receiving problem did not involve the directional finder atop the Electra since it was a separate unit. We knew this because we were still picking up a weak signal to our north that we had tracked most of the trip.

Fred had located the Japanese commercial radio on the island of Jaluit of the Marshall Islands. He had been using the signal on his chart with the sun line to confirm our location. It was then he informed me that Pan Am used the signal to calibrate the Wake Island directional finder system and that he had used it when establishing the Clipper routes. Fred trusted this signal. The signal remained until we passed our directional systems range. Fred decided, that if we headed in its general direction, we would locate the signal once again with the directional system.

I still to this day do not know why our system could not lock onto the *Itasca*. My directional loop had no problem finding that signal. Fred calculated the distance and informed me that we would probably not make it to Jaluit but if luck held out, we could possibly cross the Milli Atoll. I thought that odd and a good omen since my nickname is Mili. He assured me that we would have a strong signal and a hope finding a place to land if we stayed true to the signal.

It did not take me long to make the decision. I adjusted course and headed for Jaluit. As we covered the distance, Fred and I did everything possible to feather the plane and stretch our fuel.

I believe at this point due to the length of time I had spent on the radio attempting to contact the Itasca that my radio over heated and blew a fuse. This had happened before on the flight. I smelled the tube blow before I could tell the Itasca where we were headed.

The flight to Milli was the longest of my life but Fred never gave up. He remained faithful to the plan as we pushed forward by telling jokes and making fun of the radio operators on the Itasca. He was amazing under stress.

Fred sited Milli Atoll first. A few minutes later, the port engine began to lose power. You can only imagine how good it felt to see an island. Now if I could only land on it without killing us. We did not have time to circle and decide on the best landing. Fred told me to make for the lagoon side of the island however, I was not sure that we would clear the trees. He told me that if we could save the plane that we could possibly salvage the radio system and attempt an S.O.S signal. I made for the lagoon side.

The landing did not go as I had hoped but in hindsight, we were lucky that the Electra did not flip. The beach was wide enough to put one gear on the ground. It took both of us to manage the wheel as we made our first skip on the water's edge. We managed to bleed most of our speed before the port gear caught in the water and spun us about ninety degrees. I can only imagine how it must have looked as far as landings go. It was horrifying experience is all I can tell you. Yet we had landed and hope returned as we looked about the island of our salvation. At this point, I knew we would be rescued.

15

Proof

Dine upon the foul stench of pride
Which is shared among thorns of desperation
Twisted tales of life so spun
Which sink deep into the cold night
Lost and broken upon the stones of old
I hear your whisper
I hear your call
I am center
I am one
I am

The odd group of Admirals and dignitaries dissected each word that dropped from Lieutenant Evans mouth as if being served honey from a spoon. The truth was far from anything they had ever imagined. Nevertheless, Clair could take no more. She took a deep breath and looked up from the page to her Admiral.

"You have brought to us a great gift, Truc," Steve mused, hoping to give Clair a break. "So she crash landed at Milli Atol. I wonder why we never found her plane there."

Truc looked to him confused until he realized Steve thought Amelia was still on Milli.

"Amelia...not on Milli long. I find Amelia...on Milli. We not stay long."

Admiral Jackson grunted, and then exclaimed, "Well this will all have to be verified. It sounds like more of the same speculation that dozens have promoted over the years. We cannot just accept this as truth Captain."

"Sir, with all due respect, I believe that boat sitting over there is verification if you ask me?" Captain Channing supposed before he could take back the words.

"I didn't ask you, Captain," Admiral Jackson fired back.

Admiral Simpson bristled but chose not address the pissing contest. He was obviously disappointed in his Captain for attempting to broadside Admiral Jackson, yet pleased that it had raised his counter parts ire.

Truc squirmed and grimaced as the two ranking officers returned frown with frown.

"I bring...proof," Truc interjected.

He collected the box from Clair and pulled a small board from the bottom.

"Mr. Fred. He give...me...this," he said, as he retrieved a gold pocket watch from within the box and handed it to Admiral Jackson.

"Open...you see," he pressed the Admiral.

Admiral Jackson flipped the toggle and the watch opened immediately. The gold casing looked worn and tired, but the watch was of the finest quality. He studied the watch for several seconds before Admiral Simpson asked, "What does it say Admiral?"

Jackson stammered, "It...It says...presented to Commander Fred Noonan. Job well done! Pan American Air Lines."

"It must have been given to him for his work establishing the Pan Am Clipper routes. That is why he was the best navigator for the trip. He knew that patch of

ocean as well as anyone. That is how he knew that the
Wake directional finder used the Jaluit signal for reference,"
Admiral Simpson said most excited.

"Did you witness her landing on Milli Atoll? Was
anyone else was with you?" Admiral Simpson asked Truc.

"Yes...Palau," he replied, and a gloom fell over him as
if a fog of despair had swept across the yard with the
prevailing wind.

"Who was Palau?" asked Clair.

Truc looked away. He could not hide his heart.

"Palau...Palau...my brother," he replied as tears began
to fill his tired eyes.

"So the two of you discovered Amelia and Commander
Noonan?" Jackson asked unmoved by Truc's show of
emotion.

Truc nodded in the affirmative.

"Truc, is it Ok, if Lieutenant Evans keeps on reading?"
Captain Channing asked.

Truc agreed but the smile that had marked his time on
the Coast Guard Base drifted away, as if stolen by a ghost.

Lieutenant Evans found her reference point and
began...

The Journal of Amelia Earhart

*The first day was eventful to say the least. Fred worked on the
radio situation and I began to explore the island. I found no fresh
water on my initial search but we had several days' supply on the
Electra along with our remaining food supplies. Fred's initial
inspection discovered that a transistor had blown as I had suspected.
There was one other obvious piece of damage to our radio system. We
could not tell if the under belly antenna wire had fallen off in flight or
upon our landing. We deduced that it must have been while in flight
since we had reception ability early.*

*We had a light dinner on the beach that night and if I had
known what was to come I would have enjoyed that evening more.
Fred was frustrated and grumpy and he began to question our decision*

to come so far off course. We should have been eating dinner with the Captain of the Itasca he told me. He was not blaming me. I think he was upset that we were not going to complete what we had worked so hard to accomplish. We had traveled so far and we were so very close. If we had made Howland, we could have easily made the states. Fred had not been negative until that night. I could not take it any longer and left to walk the beach. I had to believe we made the right decision.

I am sure I was supposed to get mad at Fred because the next thing to happen, I now know, was a miracle. Actually, I stumbled upon this miracle. In the dark, I spooked two boys who lay in the sand behind a piece of driftwood and my heart nearly stopped. I am not sure who was more frightened. In the rush of the moment, somehow, I grabbed the youngest one by the arm and held him as his brother ran for cover. I know now they had been watching us for some time. Fred came running as soon as he heard the boys scream and he found me with a wiggling adolescent in my arm. The boy was as strong as an ox however, and I nearly lost him before Fred closed ranks.

After everything calmed down we questioned the boy but it was obvious that he did not understand. What occurred next, I believe is one of the bravest things I have ever witnessed. The older brother returned without a drop of fear in his eyes. He pointed to his younger brother and motioned for him to come to him. The moment was most awkward to say the least, for the young man did not flinch in his demand. His eyes were hard like steel and I knew he would attack if need be. We had not come to make enemies and yet this young man was ready to fight for his brother as he held a sharp object in his hand.

Fred looked to me and I let the lad go. As the younger boy moved away, the older brother bent his head and smiled as if saying thank you. I will always remember that smile. It was as big as the moon. This is the first time I met my friend Truc.

The boys disappeared into the dark night. I was not sure where they would go because the island was so small. I was sure we would have known if there was a village. We started a fire in the hope that someone would see the signal and Fred worked for several more hours on the radio while I stowed gear. It was a good sign, we decided, that people must live nearby on one of the adjacent islands of the atoll.

Luck had been on our side during the crash landing in how the Electra had ended her landing. Both landing gears were on the beach and only the port side was damaged. The gear remained but it was bent. The tail lay in the water and looked to have no more than cosmetic damage. We were most lucky to have broken toward the shore. The Electra sat high enough that the tide did not take her that night or ruin her engines.

July 5th 1937
The next morning we attempted to crank the starboard engine. It started quickly and Fred and I attempted an S.O.S. call. He reminded me that no one would be looking for us at our current location. The plan was to start an engine every few hours, charge the batteries and make S.O.S. calls. On the second attempt on the second day, we could no longer make the starboard start. We were out of fuel. That was about two in the afternoon.

I prayed the boys would return. In an attempt to keep Fred positive, I told him that I believed they would return with their father and rescue us. He laughed at my optimism. Fred believed we had scared the boys and would not be surprised if they did not return with a head hunting party.

The boys did return late the afternoon of the second day. It took some time for us to break the ice. They were cautious yet curious and to our surprise they brought fish and fresh water.

I tried to ask the younger of the two what he thought of the plane. He did not understand me but I could tell he was impressed. The older brother, whom I assume was about thirteen, was not afraid of the Electra. I remember him walking around it and inspecting it. His smile set me at ease. Both boys were of the most pleasant spirit.

I offered to help the older of the two up the wing and he took the chance. His little brother, not to be left behind, soon joined. We spent the afternoon exploring the plane and the boys had a great time. Fred found all this very amusing and actually laughed as the boys explored our Electra. It gave us hope that someone else was out there. We just had to find them, I told myself. Rescue was most possible.

We made another attempt that evening to start the port engine after Fred had spent the day looking her over. For only a minute, we were able to run the port engine before it gave out. Both of the boys enjoyed the engine running more than I could ever have imagined as they held their ears and squealed with delight.

The boys left soon after the engine stopped. I tried to ask them to bring an adult back. I am sure they did not understand. They did not look to be orphans but I could not imagine where they went in the dark with their small boat. Fred felt like if they returned that we should go with them in the boat and find their village. It had to be on another island in the atoll he told me. As far as I could tell, there was nothing on our island but crabs and sea birds. We both knew survival was not going to be for long if we stayed there.

16

Electra

Wiles of light
Dance within the sight
Of fools and vagabonds
They sing songs of delight
Until the winter comes
And the cold dark night
Races to claim their tombs

Truc cringed as he reminisced, "We hide...onBagu. from Jeeps...Jeeps live on Jaluit. My Father tell me...go to Bagu. Jeeps bring boats...that fly."

Admiral Jackson interrupted, "We now know that Jap...Jeeps...were reinforcing their operational ability at this time. They built many facilities throughout the area long before the war. We also know they enslaved or abused many of the natives. There are many stories about their brutality on the indigenous. If Truc is a survivor of this time period, then he is a miracle."

"Glad to see you finally believe him," Admiral Simpson returned.

Clair squirmed at the jab.

"It was your people who lost contact with her," Jackson snapped.

"Everything possible was done to contact her. Every detail was documented during the enquiry. Now we know they couldn't hear us," Simpson replied.

"Was it because you didn't have the right equipment?" Jackson fired back.

"We were working of off leftovers. Hell, we still are," Simpson replied.

Steve cleared his throat, and both officers glared at him, until they realized the entire group was watching.

Jackson straightened himself and asked, "Truc do you mind if we take a break? My legs are going to sleep."

"Yes, we need to take a short timeout if you don't mind," Simpson pressed.

With that, the two Admirals headed for the office complex, side by side, chatting quietly.

"I keep book...on Electra...Okeydokey?" Truc said, as he retrieved the journal from Clair and put it in the box.

"Did you say the name of your boat is the Electra?" Captain Channing asked, shocked.

"Yes...Amelia say, Electra mean...bright light," he replied. Then without ceremony, he stood, headed for his vessel and disappeared into the hold.

"What the hell...I was on the boat a week and he never said the name once," Steve mumbled to himself.

He turned to find Clair staring across the harbor with tear filled eyes.

"Lieutenant...what's wrong?" he asked.

"She must have died without her friends or family nearby. How hard it must have been to know that no one knew what happened to them, and here I am reading her journal, for the first time, to a bunch of men who are acting like children," she said in disgust.

"Clair...we don't know that she died alone. Obviously, Truc was nearby," he replied, then immediately regretted calling her by her first name.

"Why is this so hard for you Lieutenant?" he decided to ask, in order to recover from the break in protocol.

"I don't know why. The story is sad, I suppose, if you have family and they don't know what happened to you. Moreover, it's sad that grown men can be so emotionally detached. This is not a history lesson Captain Channing. Hold the book yourself; you will see that she is a human being attempting to make contact. We are reading a miracle, and all I see before me, is political posturing. Why?" Clair asked, as she arose and straightened her dress.

He decided it best to leave the subject alone as Lieutenant Evans seemed ready to do anything other than discuss the subject any further.

"Do you want to go to the commissary?" he asked pensively.

"I would like that...sir. About time you invited me to lunch."

17

An Afternoon
With Amelia

The sun came too soon
To forgive our night
Time, wasted away
To inbound flights of shame
As if evil bleeds, dark grey
Along the shore of things
One should never say

Truc did not know what to do with it. Captain Channing tried to show him how to eat the sandwich, and watched on in amusement as Truc took his first bite of a BLT. A moment later, the sandwich was consumed. He then offered him a can of soda and a Twinkie. As Captain Channing feigned drinking the soda, the pop of the can made Truc laugh aloud. Truc looked to him as if he had lost his mind, but followed his teachers every instruction. Initially repelled, as the sweet syrup coated the back of his pallet, Truc quickly discovered his drink of choice. He smelled then devoured the Twinkie and followed it quickly with a soda chaser.

"Amelia...tell me, I like America food," Truc said, as he looked to be a one-year-old eating cake on his first birthday. Then, like a one year old, he asked if he could have another.

"You can have mine," Clair replied as she stood a few feet behind the two men watching their every move.

Steve spun about to find her sitting on the dock and holding out the soda. He could not help but stare, and wondered if she knew that as he was taken with her rare beauty.

"The Admiral wants us back at the palm in five," she stated as if an order.

Truc followed with box in hand and Captain Channing with half a Twinkie for neither man, would ever waste the invitation of Lieutenant Evans.

Strategically placed beneath the shade of the palm, a picnic table had suddenly appeared, and there they found the two Admirals sitting across from each other. It was obvious they were in a much better mood.

Steve grabbed Clair by the arm and asked, "I thought you said five minutes."

"That's five minutes in Admiral time...Captain," she replied.

He tried to force a smile as he approached the Admirals, but received no affirmation in return.

"Truc, do you mind if we use this table? We do not normally sit on the ground, and to be honest, it was making the two of us grumpy," Admiral Simpson stated.

"We have a chair for you at the end...if you don't mind. Admiral Jackson said in a far more cordial manner as he pointed to the seat.

"Lieutenant Evans, please sit to his left and Captain Channing, will sit to his right," Admiral Simpson ordered as he pointed.

Truc looked most uncomfortable in the chair, but it soon passed after several attempts to find the best position, he finally crossed his legs and waited for his friends to settle in.

"Truc, Admiral Jackson and I want to apologize for the fuss we made earlier. We are anxious to hear the rest of the story," Admiral Simpson stated as he looked to Jackson.

Jackson picked up where Simpson left off, "I fully agree with Admiral Simpson. I am most sorry for doubting you. You have conducted yourself magnificently."

"Amelia tell me...you act...such way," Truc replied.

Steve could not help but chuckle at the idea of Amelia preparing Truc.

"You have no idea Truc, no idea at all," he said with a hearty laugh as he looked to his Admiral fro approval.

"Truc, Ms. Amelia told you to come here...right?" Clair asked.

"She say come...when I ready," Truc replied, as the memory of their conversations returned. "I come...so, I ready."

Clair looked into his eyes and asked, "Truc, why did she tell you to come here?"

"She tell me...bring you book," he replied.

Clair was not satisfied but decided to drop the subject.

"Lieutenant could you please read the journal...so that we may hear Amelia tell her story," Admiral Simpson asked.

Truc took her by the hand, "Yes...Ms. Clair," he whispered, and then he reached into the box and gave her the journal.

With the book in hand, in an unexpected turn, Lieutenant Evans peered into the thick spectacles of Captain Channing. She suddenly she felt as if she could see him in a different light, as if she had never noticed him before. As he urged her on, she felt deep in her being that she could trust him, and she wanted to trust him. The moment broke as quick as it came and she quickly thumbed through the pages, found her place, and began...

The Journal of Amelia Earhart

The two boys returned the next day before noon. I was most glad to see them. Fred tried everything to communicate. He wanted them to take one of us back to their village but the boys only laughed at him and ran around as if he were a game to play. Fred finally gave up and began to play with the boys. It was the first time that I had enjoyed Fred's laugh since the accident. I treasure that memory. It is how I want to remember Fred; laughing with boys that could have been his own.

Two hours later, our world changed forever. The enormous weight of what occurred next still clouds my dreams. If I could take back that day, I would. We were discovered! I must tell you that for a moment hope sprung within us. We were walking with the boys on the ocean side of the island as a large ship came into view. I remember several smaller craft being dispatched from the ship. It took them some time to make their way through the reef.

We must have looked like fools as we jumped up and down and waved our hands. The boys thought it was a great game. However, as they came closer we soon realized that is was a Japanese contingent coming to our rescue. Fred and I had discussed the possibility of being found by the Japanese and had concluded they would most likely help us.

We had been warned by the State Department that the Japanese had become very odd in their behavior toward the territory. I have to admit that I became afraid. Fred kept his cool but I could tell he was upset and trying to calculate the best possible course of action. The truth is, we had only one course of action. It was not as if they did not know we were there.

The Japanese came ashore with rifles drawn and yelling instructions that we could not possibly understand. I grabbed both of the boys and held on to them as two sailors grabbed Fred from behind and forced him to the ground. The others quickly surrounded the boys and me.

The commander of the landing party focused on Fred and he spoke to Fred as if he should understand. The boys were crying in my arms and I held them as tightly as I could but it was of no use. It was then that one grabbed me by my hair and was shocked when he realized I was a woman.

The squad leader eventually told a group of his men to return to the ship with what I am sure was a message. He then returned to Fred and yelled at him yet again as if he could speak the language. Fred did not understand what the man desired as he tried desperately to speak with the man. Somehow, I knew what they wanted. I forced the man holding me to let go by pointing and began to walk across the island to our Electra. The jungle had hid her from a direct line of view but I knew they would find her anyway.

The commander studied the Electra thoroughly. Then he ordered his men to board and a few minutes later, they were throwing out much of our gear. Fred became very upset as they dug through our packs as he tried to tell the commander that we needed everything to survive.

I have nightmares about the next few minutes. It was then that Truc's younger brother found an opportunity and ran for his small boat. I remember him yelling for Truc to follow. Truc tried to pull away but it was too late. A shot rang out. I know his name now. I will never forget his name. Palau fell to the ground as the bullet ripped through his little body. I screamed as Truc ripped away and took off after his brother. I knew he would be shot if I did not intervene so I chased after him.

I could tell before I got to him that Palau was dead. I tried to stop the bleeding but it was a mortal wound to the head. It was then Fred tore away from his captor and began to yell at the commander that he was a coward for killing a boy.

It all seems like a bizarre dream now. Only a few minutes before we had been playing with the boys on the beach, confident we would be discovered. We had never felt alone or afraid once we discovered them. Fred had been laughing only a few minutes before. In our naïveté, we believed in a good world where people do the right thing. Those few minutes, I wish I could rewrite but they are forever written in blood.

I would soon learn that what I believed no longer mattered and that cruelty is a truth. The squad leader was that kind of cruel man who found pleasure in exacting his rule. The butt of his gun struck Fred in the side first. Then he struck Fred in the knee causing him to fall to one leg, and with the precision of a man who had done it before, *the officer smashed the butt of his gun into Fred's head. I could hear the blow crack his skull. The sound was unmistakable and harsh. I could not help but to vomit as I watched Fred's eyes roll back into his head. He began to twitch and moan immediately. He was suffering and there was nothing I could do to stop that fact.*

The rest is a dream that comes in pieces. I remember being dragged across the island with Truc in tow. I remember blood on my hands and clothes. I remember holding Truc to me as if he were my child. I could not let go as he screamed for his brother. All I knew was that I could not let him go. I knew they would kill him if he ran away. I vaguely remember being forced into that boat and at this point I believe Truc and I went into shock.

We were placed deep in the ship and I remember Fred being with me once again but he could not speak. His eyes searched for something but he could not focus. They remained dilated and his breath became labored as it speed up and then plummet. I remember being violently ill as the ship rolled from side to side. It was hot and damp with little light and mechanical sounds that quivered through her like a moan of pain. We were in the bottom of that ship for what seemed an eternity. The entire trip, Fred remained in what I believed to be a comma while Truc sat in the corner staring into nothing. We were a sad lot.

18

A Time To Cry

Tears claim us as true
They inflame our hue
They are waves that wish to force us down
Tears have come to drown

Clair looked up to find Truc crying. Setting the book aside, she hugged him.

"Palau want...go home...he...afraid. I fail," he mumbled through the sobs.

She held him as he sobbed as if the loss were only yesterday.

"Long ago. Long ago," he whimpered as he tried to compose himself.

She released him from her grip, and walked away as she did not like crying in front of the group and the pain was a real as any she had ever experienced. His story was personal now. Truc had experienced horrors they could only imagine and she felt sick for reminding him.

"Did you ever see your family again?" Captain Channing asked.

Truc nodded no.

"I'm sorry. We didn't know this was going to be part of the story." Steve said apprehensively.

Truc let out a deep sigh as he attempted to release the pain of the memory.

"Is there anything I can get you?" Admiral Simpson asked.

Truc did not reply.

"It must have been horrible for Amelia," Steve pressed.

"Amelia...she try to help...Mr. Fred. You read...you see," he replied.

Clair returned to the table, found her seat and gritted her teeth as she tried to smile for Truc. She would not let this defeat her, she thought.

The Journal of Amelia Earhart

I did not know this until much later but we were delivered to Jaluit Atoll. Truc and his brother had fled this place. The Japanese were busy building large docks and other facilities. I was very weak from a lack of food and seasickness. Fred slipped in and out of consciousness. I was able to feed him a bit of rice a cook brought to me one day. The gash on his head was black and filled with blood.

We were never brought ashore but for some reason I was allowed to walk above deck after a few days of sitting in the oven like hold. Crews of men were building what I believe to be seaplane docks. Two seaplanes were sitting on the shore next to the construction site and I wondered if Truc had family on the project.

Later that afternoon the commander of the base, whose name I cannot remember met us. He looked us over and spoke a broken English. He asked my name and I told him I was Amelia Earhart. Soon a medic came aboard. A very nice gentleman. He worked on Fred for over two hours trying to stabilize him and bandage his wounds. Fred did not respond to any of the treatment.

I noticed the commander scolding the squad leader of the landing party that attacked us. He was visibly upset with him. I never met the man who beat Fred again as he left the ship that afternoon with his detail.

The commander attempted to explain the situation but I honestly could not make out what he was trying to say. What I got was that we were to be transferred to another atoll but I did not understand much else. I asked him several times to contact our Navy. I told him that they would come and pick us up. I explained that we would be little trouble if they would leave us here to wait for our ship. He never responded and I never met him again.

On the trip to our next destination, Truc and I were allowed more freedom to move about the ship. I believe the base commander had ordered them to treat us better. I considered sneaking into the radio room and calling out an S.O.S but the radio shack was never unattended.

Truc had said nothing since our capture. Even though it was obvious that he was not mine, the crew treated him as if he were my child, as I always kept him under my arm.

Fred showed no sign of recovery. His days became a listless nightmare and it was painful to see him in such agony. I tried everything I could to comfort him.

19

Standard Protocol

The tempest knows the heart
It tests the soul
To see if we shall grow
Among wild flowers
Blooming in fields of white
For ours is not a battle
Without a light

"Amelia teach me...speak Englisssshh. But I not speak on jeep boat," Truc said, as the Clair took a break and his smile returned.

"Do you know the name of the ship that brought you to your next destination?" Admiral Simpson asked.

"No...boat hot all time," Truc responded.

"Did Commander Noonan speak to you any after the attack?" Jackson asked.

"He.speak...crazy," Truc replied.

"There has been speculation for years but no one ever took it as a serious option that she made it to the Marshall

Islands. The theory, although considered many times, the theory has always been discredited. She said her fuel was low. No one considered the Marshall Islands a viable option," Admiral Simpson pondered aloud.

Jackson interrupted, "Standard protocol for pilots is to declare low fuel when they near 20%. She had over 1000 gallons when she left Lea. It may have been as much as 1300 to 1400 gallons. She could have had 200 to 300 gallons left when she changed course for Jaluit, more, if the wind conditions were in her favor. I read over the records of the incident last night. She reported that she had a hard headwind but that may have lasted for only a short time because she never reported it again. I think it was wrong to assume she had a hard headwind the whole time. She would have turned, as she said in the journal. When she adjusted course for Jaluit, she most possibly had a tail wind. That would have increased her distance capability dramatically."

Simpson nodded in agreement as he offered, "I'm glad to see you're becoming a believer, Admiral."

Admiral Jackson chuckled. "As we discussed earlier, Admiral Simpson, were on the same side. Besides, at Annapolis we're taught that Admiral Nimitz believed the Japanese might have captured her. I mean "Jeeps." The records show that our ships never searched the Marshall Islands as some have speculated. The theory that she was a spy is ridiculous but the idea of her making it to the Marshalls is not. The Navy requested of the Japs...Jeeps...a search in their declared territorial waters. The Jeeps refused the search. I believe we know why...now. However, they did send ships and seaplanes to aid in the search. Of course, if this story proves true, then we know now why they found nothing because that is what they wanted us to believe. It was a smoke screen."

"So she really may have been taken to Saipan, as many have speculated?" Steve interrupted.

"It seems to have been very possible," Admiral Jackson replied.

"We stay... Kwajalein...long time," Truc said softly.

Channing was the first to speak after several long moments, "You never left the next place Truc? Where did you go next?"

"I not say we not leave. I say we stay long time," Truc answered.

"I think we need to hear the whole story before we decide what happened to Amelia," Clair interjected emphatically.

The Journal of Amelia Earhart

It took several days to sail to our next destination. This is when I began to believe that we might be in more trouble than I had initially realized. I had first hoped the cruel treatment was just a misunderstanding and that the punishment would meet the crime once I could speak to someone of authority.

I heard the crew speaking and I was sure I heard the word Kwajalein among them. I assumed we had reached the Kwajalein Atoll as we sailed past several islands. We finally arrived at what I believe to be the north end of the Kwajalein Atoll.

The islands were lush with palms and very flat. Fred was loaded on a boat and taken ashore first. I am not sure what happened to him in the hours we waited on the ship. I can only assume they tried to get information from him. I think they believed us to be spies. It must have been a useless interrogation because he could barely complete a sentence the hour before

In the early evening, I believe it was now late July, I was brought ashore with Truc. The island was a very busy air base with many planes. We were delivered to a command center next to the island's runway and I remember thinking it appeared to be extremely ornate. The island was crawling with workers and the runway was impressive for such a forward post.

I can tell you now, Roi is the name of the island on which we found ourselves. I remember the first time I met the commander of Roi because I will never forget how my stomach dropped when I saw what loomed behind his eyes. The man was hard and calculating and in my estimation a bitter person all around. I could tell he did not want to be bothered with unexpected problems and I knew immediately that I was an unexpected problem. I had hoped he would be understanding and attempt to fix the situation. My hope could not have been farther away from the truth.

He spoke in a broken English of which I could only understand a few words. He asked me if my name was Amelia Earhart and I told him I was. He pointed to Truc. I told him that Truc was mine. He waved to one of his men and spoke quickly. The next thing I knew, Truc was taken away and dragged outside. I watched on as they whipped him and yelled at him in what I now know to be Truc's native tongue. Then the officer pointed to the jungle and I watched on in disbelief as Truc ran off in that direction.

I must say I fell apart at that point. I tried to hit the commander but he stopped me with a quick backhand and I fell to the ground. He walked about the room as if he were a king and spoke as if I could understand Japanese. He was scolding me but not for my benefit. He wanted his men to witness his power because what he said did not matter since I was unable to understand.

He then grabbed me by the hair and dragged me to the front door, pointed to the runway and then the docks all the while yelling in Japanese. I suppose he was explaining to me what they meant to him or that I had somehow violated them. I wanted to die as his men stopped to watch the public humiliation.

Then with a short rod that he carried on his side, the man whipped me repeatedly as he held me by the hair. I could not help but scream. I tried to get away from him but he held fast to my hair and I was too weak to fight him properly. This beating must have lasted for several minutes as he drew blood and tore my clothing. His men watched on. Several even laughed. When he was finished, I had no fight left.

The beating ended with him kicking me off the front porch. I lay there as he strutted back and forth ranting about something. He then spat on me and headed back inside the command center. I was then dragged several hundred yards to a small concrete building. I did not know it, but this would become my residence for some time.

The building was enclosed on three sides while the open side had bars and a door. There were several cells there in this manner. They threw me into the cell and that is the last I remember of that day or, for that matter, several others.

20

The Secret Island

Secrets bind our truth
As if telling it all anew
This light shall not be found
Among untilled soil
Or thorny ground
Now shared as a secret, true

Admiral Simpson interrupted. "Where did you go Truc...why did they let you go?"

Truc was obviously tired. He sat watching the activity in the harbor as the distant day played on in his heart. He did not answer.

"It's ok Truc. You don't have to tell us," Steve said, as he eyed his superiors, hoping Simpson would not tear him apart for protecting Truc.

"Yes...it's OK," Admiral Simpson agreed.

"No...I tell. Soldier beat. Tell...go to my people. I not know island. Our men fish...to...Jeeps. Women cook...to... Jeeps. My people...fear."

"Where did you go?" Steve asked once again.

"I run. Soluu find Truc. She...old...she feed. Give...place to sleep.

"Did you know Ms. Soluu before that day?" Admiral Simpson asked.

"She say... she know my people...she not know me."

"Was she able to reach your family?" this was Clair.

"No," Truc replied.

Frustrated, Truc exhaled as if the memory was strong before he replied, "I tell Soluu of...Amelia. I tell her...I find her on Milli. I tell her...what Jeeps do...to my Palau...Mr. Fred."

"Who was this lady?" Clair asked.

"She...old mother."

"How long before you saw Amelia and Fred again?" Captain Channing asked.

"Not long time...Soluu go. Soluu find Amelia. She stay...but Jeeps mean to Soluu...she keep her head down...wait. Cooomandaarrr, he very angry...at Soluu...I not understand. He hit Soluu...but she stay. Soluu speak soft...keep head down. He spit...walk away."

A smile returned to Truc's face as he remembered the next part.

Soluu...she tell me cooommandaaar let...Soluu feed Amelia."

"She was a very brave lady!" Clair declared.

"She...old mother," Truc replied as if all should know the respect she deserved.

Clair asked, "They killed your brother. They beat Fred and Amelia. Why? What was so important that they did these things?"

"If you do not mind Truc, I think I can answer that question with a bit of history," Admiral Jackson interjected.

"If these are the islands of Roi and Namur, and it sounds like they were. They are definitely in the Kwajalein Atoll. What we know now, is that the Japanese built an airbase like the one Amelia is describing. The commander's headquarters are still standing. They managed to build many structures, especially bunkers. The structure that Amelia mentioned was one of the few that survived the bombing the Navy inflicted before our troops went ashore in World War II. These were some of the island chains we had to clean up before we could move on to Japan," Jackson stated, then looked to the group to make sure they were following.

"We believe the airbase was necessary to supply the island beside it. The next island was no more than a walk across a shallow reef as both islands were separated only by a small channel. Our engineers made them into one island after the war. Anyhow, the airbase provided an element of protection for the secret mission-taking place next door. I think we must assume this was a high priority base for the Japanese. It was obviously being built while Amelia was there. That would explain all the secrecy on their part. They didn't want the world to know they were beefing up. The fact that the Japs built the secret base next to the airbase was completely unknown to us until we invaded the island. The discovery of the second base was by accident and it cost us dearly. A Marine contingent lost a bunch of men when it was discovered."

Jackson stopped, took a drink, and carried on.

"When we invaded, a squad of marines was able to work its way inland and they came upon a bunker. After killing the machine gunner in the bunker, the marines realized that it led to a lower level. At this point, it becomes fuzzy as to what happened next. It is believed the assault group on the bunker took a backpack charge and tossed it in. As of today, what occurred next is considered the largest non-nuclear explosion to occur during World War II. Much of the second island blew up. There is a picture of the explosion taken by a naval surveillance plane at the Navy museum in Pearl.

The Marines had discovered the secret mini-submarine base the Japanese had been building for years. The mini-subs were man-driven torpedoes. They were a Kamikaze type unit long before Kamikazes filled the air. They were one time use weapons with a no return expected for the lone submariner. When the backpack bomb went off, it tripped off several dozen torpedoes stored in that underground bunker.

This mini-sub base was a sign of the serious nature of the Japanese before the war. We now know, they had been planning to use them heavily. The idea was to use the seaplane bases to discover allied shipping and then send the mini subs to their location and finish the job. The men who drove them were trained to be Kamikazes of a different sort."

Truc breathed out deeply. He was visibly upset as he said, "They make...work long in ground."

Admiral Jacksons eyes lit up, "Do you remember how it was constructed? Do you remember the floor plan? If you could remember these things, it could possibly answer how a backpack bomb could cause the whole place to go up."

Truc nodded in the affirmative.

"You may be the only person alive who can tell us what it was like. Everyone else who had anything to do with that base was killed when it exploded."

Truc nodded and replied, "Okeydokey...I tell."

Jackson could not help but chuckle as he realized he was about to reply with the odd term, "Okeydokey Truc...that would be incredible."

"Sir, it is getting late in the afternoon. May I suggest we take a break for the evening. I am sure our guest is tired," Captain Channing announced while he eyed his watch.

Jackson began to protest but checked himself as he realized it was his peer's decision. Simpson glanced at his watch. He had not considered the idea that the interview might take more than one day. It would be hard to explain to the Joint Chiefs why the interview had to end, he thought. If Truc were his father the conversation would have ended hours before, he decided.

"I suppose that would be wise. Truc, I would like to offer you my quarters this evening...if you like. They are most comfortable and I can have food delivered," Simpson asked.

"I stay...Electra."

Simpson looked to Channing for help. Then he realized what Truc had just said, "the Electra?"

"Yes sir," Captain Channing answered. "The ship is named after the airplane, Sir."

Simpson chuckled, the story was getting better every step of the way, he thought.

"Truc...Admiral Simpson wants to make sure you are safe. We have patrol craft keeping unwanted people away. Your arrival as you can see has drawn many who want to meet you. That is why he is offering you his quarters on base," Steve insisted.

"You stay...Electra. You...me," Truc replied, with his smile. "We make...safe...Okeydokey?"

Simpson conceded the argument and ordered Captain Channing to stay the night aboard the Electra.

"As I understand it, you sleep well on the Electra Captain Channing," Admiral Jackson Chided.

"Yes sir...it would seem that way," Captain Channing replied, embarrassed.

"I will see you gentlemen at ten in the morning. I have several items to attend to if you don't mind," Jackson seemingly ordered, as he stood to leave.

Truc stood before Jackson could and held out his hand. Admiral Jackson balked before he realized Truc was serious. Truc took him by the hand and held it as if holding a babes hand. The Admiral cleared his throat and bowed his head as he made his way to his waiting driver.

Simpson put out his hand before Truc could respond and engaged his subordinates, "Clair, I need you to come to the office. We have much to deal with tonight. I want security beefed up. Channing, I need you to come with me to the press area as soon as you get Truc back to his boat. Make sure he is fed and comfortable. I have a bus bringing news agencies for a press release in an hour. I expect you to make the statement."

Simpson then turned to the camera operator and ordered, "Secure the film you have at this moment and give it to Lieutenant Evans."

As the Admiral and his entourage headed to his office, Clair straightened herself and stood to leave. It was obvious to Channing that she was exhausted.

"You like Amelia...strong," Truc stated as Clair turned to leave.

Clair blushed as she processed the compliment. "I am honored, Truc...thank you," she mumbled, as she sped away with a tear in her eye.

Truc shrugged and asked, "I say wrong?"

Steve took Truc by the shoulder and said, as he began to lead him away, "She will be fine, would you like for me to take you to the place where we eat. It is a big room with lots of food. However...it will be cold in there."

"I eat...on Electra...okeydokey," Truc replied.

"Okeydokey, Truc...okeydokey."

21

Press Call

Evil men hold my days
As if my day were theirs to take
They call to gods
That I shall not know
Then they break their bonds
For they have no soul

Media outlets hired multiple marine engineers and professional sailors to supply commentary. Many compared the vessel to old photos of the Electra and supposed the whole thing to be a deliberate hoax.

Steve began to worry. He knew Truc could not handle the onslaught press and, as far as he knew, Truc had never watched TV or used a phone. He worried over these things until he arrived at the media center and in that moment, his fear was fully realized as he peeked through the door into the mass of faces waiting for him.

The Admiral arrived soon after and said, "You have done a magnificent job Captain. I could not be more proud of you. This is bigger than we could ever have imagined. The President wants to meet him. My God man...you just might meet the President."

Captain Channing, heavy with worry, mumbled, "Thank you"

Admiral Simpson noticed and asked, "What's wrong son?"

"There is no way he can take all of this attention. Truc has lived in relative isolation and I think we are going to find that his time under the Japanese was brief, Sir. The more I think about it the more I must conclude that somehow Amelia and Truc left Namur. They were not on Roi-Namur after the war. They had to be somewhere else... somewhere where they were isolated, alone," Steve said, as he pointed to the media room and pressed, "This sir...well it's a madhouse. I am afraid we may kill him if we are not careful."

Simpson thought for a moment before answering, "You think we need to protect him...to keep him away from his fans."

"Sir, I am not advocating that we lock him away. I am worried about the end game. You and I, to some extent, have a responsibility to guide how this materializes. That is all I am saying, Sir."

"I hear you Captain. I have begun to wonder how this will all play out too. All I know is...Truc wanted to come here. He wanted to bring us the journal and, he has made a great effort to tell us his story. He could have stayed wherever they were and disappeared into oblivion. Truc chose to sail across an ocean to share what happened to his friend. I think the least we can do is give him that chance. I promise you that I will do everything in my power to protect him when the time comes. I will put him on another remote island or one of our own that is sparsely inhabited. I will do this...if I have to sail him there myself. Now, the question is...do you believe me?"

Captain Channing's smile returned. "I'm sorry. Thank you for letting me vent."

"Captain, I didn't get this far by luck."

"I know Sir."

"OK, now that we have an understanding of how committed we both are to Truc. I suggest we handle that gaggle in there and set boundaries tonight."

Clair arrived frazzled as she reported, "Sir, I believe we have the area secure. We found a photographer trying to climb the fence. I have set up extra sentries around the base. The networks are able to attain glimpse shots of Truc's vessel but no more. I think we can control this for some time. However, we have a problem with the Rush blocking the channel. There are several freighters needing to make port and a cruise ship is arriving within the hour."

"Tell the Rush to escort each freighter into port. Inform them that no one is to be on deck but necessary personnel and that an officer will be aboard to guide the vessel. Bearing is a good Captain. Tell him to handle the situation as he sees fit," Simpson ordered.

"Is there anything I can do for you, Sir, to help with your stay on the Electra?" Clair asked.

Steve thought for a moment before answering. "Yes, do you think it might be possible to round up a couple of hammocks? I could rig a hammock but I can't have one for me and not for Truc."

"No problem, Sir. They will be here by the time you finish," Clair replied.

Admiral Simpson opened the door to the conference room and said, "This is your show Son, don't mess it up."

The room broke into a buzz as the two officers entered. Channing realized as he saw his reflection in a monitor that he should have taken a moment to fix himself up. He quickly ran his hand through his hair in an attempt to slick back the windblown look.

Cameras flashed as the Admiral stepped to the podium. He waited for the buzz to stop before he said, "Members of the press. I have a few comments I would like to make then I will give the podium to Captain Channing. He will explain to you the events as they have occurred in the last few days. However, first, I want to inform you that if any one of the press attempts to enter my base again. Without my express permission, I will treat that person as I would any threat to my base. Sentries are posted strategically around the base now and have ordered them to protect their base from all intruders. I hope I am making myself clear. You will be arrested and you will be charged in a military court. If you have someone you need to call, I would suggest you make that call now."

The room grew deathly silent as Simpson glared at them to make his point. "Second, at this moment, we are attempting to debrief our guest as to the nature of his craft and how he came to be in possession of the wing. We have not...repeat not...finished that job. Our guest is very old and it will take time to do a thorough investigation. I will tell you now that we are not under any false time constraint to find these answers. This could be a lengthy process that may take several days to accomplish," Simpson said, as he let that fact sink in. "Now, I would like to introduce you to an officer you have previously met. He is the lead officer in charge of this investigation. He is responsible for making first contact and subsequent safe passage of our guest. I give you Captain Steve Channing," Simpson said, as he turned and pointed Captain Channing to the podium.

Captain Channing inspected the room as he took his place. His heart began to race as he now had more information. He cleared his throat and began, "Hello, I am Captain Steve Channing. I suppose the best way to answer your questions is to open the floor and I will answer as best I can. I will decline to answer if I feel that I do not have a solid answer," Steve said, as he hesitated.

He immediately regretted his decision. He should have made a statement and left, he thought. Every hand in the room seemed to be raised at once as he struggled to make out anyone past the first two rows. Steve began by pointing to his far left and hoped no one noticed his squinting.

"Captain Channing, how did the Coast Guard discover the vessel?"

Channing smiled. The first question was easy enough, he thought. "As officer of the watch, I received a satellite call from the vessel Sand Seeker. She is registered in Great Britain by a husband and wife team who are currently circumnavigating the globe. Their names are Otto and Catherine Vonstreep. That is spelled V.o.n.s.t.r.e.e.p. I venture to say they are officially the first contact."

He pointed to the next person on his left.

"Captain, is this a hoax? And, if not, what made you believe the Vonstreeps?"

"Mr. Vonstreep is a retired Royal Navy officer and his wife made cookies for our inspection crew when they were in port," Steve said as jest and then hesitated as he got the response he had hoped for of the reporters laughing. The tension seemed to leave the room and suddenly he felt empowered

."Regarding this being a hoax, I can tell you that I have no reason to believe so far that this is a hoax. It will, however, require much research. We are working on that as fast as we possibly can. Remember, our subject is very old."

Steve pointed to the person next in line and it became painfully obvious to the group that this method was how the session would continue.

"Captain, can you tell us the name of the old man? Does he know where the wing came from?"

"His name is Truc. Like a pickup truck. He is a kind and gentle man whom I have come to find most pleasant. I believe he knows much more. We are currently looking into what we have of his story so far. You must understand that we cannot rush this process and therefore I ask everyone here to be patient. We are dealing with a man, who is extremely primitive. Nonetheless, he is smart and versed in a crude English...which has made the debrief much easier."

The next reporter in line asked his question before Captain Channing pointed.

"Captain Channing, does he have anything else other than the parts of the plane...other than the wing, Sir?"

"He has artifacts of interest. Again, it will require time to verify the authenticity of the material."

Steve took a drink of his water in an attempt to slow things down and the next reporter waited until he finished.

"Sir, can you tell us what those artifacts may be and do you think we will be able to meet Truc any time soon?"

"No. I will not discuss the artifacts until we can determine authenticity. As far as meeting with you, I believe that will be up to him. However, I can tell you that we are, at this time, protecting him from all interference until he has been fully debriefed. Again, I ask you to please respect the process."

Before Steve could finish the next in line shouted out, "Did Truc know Amelia or Fred?" This small, red headed reporter worked for a local station. She quickly realized she had cut Steve off and said, "I'm sorry...did you have something to add to the previous statement?"

Steve hesitated. Every second he waited gave away the truth.

"There is the possibility that he knew both of them," he finally responded.

The room exploded with hands in the air as a few reporters ran from the room to inform their news desks of the new development. The cat was out of the bag and Captain Channing, in a strange way, felt a sense of relief that the truth was out there.

Admiral Simpson quickly stepped to the podium and declared the briefing over as he clutched Channing by the arm and led him out the side door. Steve was surprised to see Clair waiting as Simpson ordered, "Get them off my base, Lieutenant! They have enough to swallow for one evening."

Channing braced for the tongue-lashing he was about to receive from Simpson. They had not discussed whether he should tell them that Truc knew Amelia. His face grew flush as the Admiral glared ahead. Steve tightened his stomach muscles to absorb the blow he knew was coming and was shocked when the Admiral broke into a deep laugh.

"Son, I wish you could have witnessed all their faces when you dropped that bomb. I think some of them shit themselves," he said, as his laugh would not be contained at the thought of the mayhem in the next room.

"You're not mad?"

"Hell no, if you hadn't have done it, I would have had done it simply to spite Jackson. That pompous ass plans to spill the beans in the morning before our next debrief. That's why I called the press in tonight," he said, as he mocked Jackson, "I will see you boys at ten in the morning. I hope that is OK with you. I have some things to tend to on my base...blah, blah, blah."

Captain Channing released a deep sigh.

"Captain, let me tell you something. I think this is the best gift ever. I am not about to let the Navy steal any of it. Now the press whores have their breaking news and we control the information in a manner that serves Truc best. You just gave the world a gift son and the world is going to love you for it."

Clair returned in time to watch Channing blush with the respect Simpson was gushing upon him. A slight smile spread across her face as she continued to pass orders over her cell phone. This awkward Captain was growing on her, she thought.

"Relax, Son. I got your back," Simpson said as a prod. "I'm not going to let you hang yourself."

Simpson then addressed Lieutenant Evans, "Take the Captain out to dinner nearby. I bet you're both famished. The meal is on me but remember Channing, she is my liaison."

Captain Channing blushed at the implication, "Sir, I would never have thought...."

"Enjoy you dinner tonight, Captain. You deserve a break from this place."

Captain Channing looked to Clair, but she was on the phone making reservations at a local place. He turned back and found Admiral Simpson heading for his office chuckling, shaking his head and mumbling, "There is a possibility..."

Lieutenant Evans took the Captain by the arm and spun him about as he stared after the Admiral. "Captain, the car is waiting outside. I hope you don't mind, but I requested that the driver leave it for us. I thought it might be better to not discuss anything of this day in front of subordinates."

"Yes, that makes perfect sense. Am I driving or you?"

"The car is checked out to me Captain. I'll be driving. I'm sorry, Sir."

Captain Channing realized that she was being polite as he changed the subject.

"I need to take Truc some water," he said.

"I've already taken care of that. I had a fruit tray sent to him as well. I thought he might enjoy a little of our natural foods. I wish we could take him, but...it will be a madhouse at the gate. He has been informed that you will return in a few hours."

"That was very considerate of you...Lieutenant Evans."

"You can call me Clair if you like, Captain, when other officers are not present. I believe we will be working on this project for a long time together. I was hoping we could get past the formalities, Sir."

"That would be fine with me...Clair. But, only if you call me Steve."

"That will only be in private...Sir," Clair replied with a smile.

22

Dinner With Mo Mo

I dine among the reeds
With the tides ebb and flow
Calling me home
Setting me still
The taste of love
Embraces my will

Captian Channing had never had an official chauffer and thought it odd that he had to duck as they passed the guard gate. After clearing the base, Clair drove for another hour.

"Where are we going?" he finally asked.

"I have a favorite place. It is very quiet. We will be able to keep you out of the lime light there. I know the owner very well."

Ten minutes later, Clair pulled up to a small restaurant hidden in a cove next to the shore. It was quaint and old. Only a local would know about the place, Steve thought, as there were barely any lights on the narrow road leading to the building. Clair immediately exited the car and headed for the front door as a large woman of Polynesian descent burst onto the porch. Steve's jaw draw dropped as Clair ran into her arms. They hugged for some time and the woman seemed genuinely pleased to see Clair. Finally, Clair introduced Steve as he slowly ascended the porch steps.

"Mo Mo, I would like you to meet Captain Steve Channing," Clair said with a bit pride in her voice.

The large woman shuffled over to Steve and put her hands on both sides of his face. She grinned with all she had as she pushed his cheeks together and said, "I know who this young man is...everyone knows this young man, Sissy. He's been on TV all day."

Steve's eyes darted about as he tried to make a connection between the old woman and Clair. Mo Mo then took him by the hand and led him into her small restaurant. "I am so happy Sissy brought you here. You honor me by coming here Captain Channing."

As she pulled him through the front door, and then the interior to the back porch, Steve looked about the odd restaurant with its old movie posters plastered about and large melted candles on each table. The place was empty and yet filled with memories, Steve thought. He soon discovered that it overlooked a small-secluded bay as she pointed out the scenery that made her buy the place thirty years prior.

"You can call me Steve," he said. He then turned his attention to Clair and raised his left brow as he pronounced, "Sissy?"

"We have called her Sissy since she was a baby. Her daddy named her Clair. I named her Sissy," MoMo said, as she seated Steve.

Clair began to reminisce, "I grew up working here with my Mo Mo. She is my grandmother. She raised me. Actually, I lived with my parents but I loved being here with her, so, I spent more nights here than I did in my own house as a kid."

Her thoughts ran away to her childhood as the smell of Mo Mo's kitchen refreshed her memory. "She is the best cook on the island. I asked her if she would prepare some of her favorite dishes for you tonight."

"I shoo all off when my Sissy called. I am so happy Sissy brought you to my place," Mo Mo repeated, as she bee-lined for the kitchen like a breeze looking for a place to settle. He noticed, that even with her great girth, she floated between the tables as a woman who had traveled among them many times.

"What is the name of Mo Mo's restaurant?"

Clair laughed, "Its Mo Mo's! Didn't you see the sign? Everyone knows my Mo Mo!"

"Thank you for sharing her with me. I am sure this is going to be a treat."

"You have no idea. My Mo Mo can cook. It is a miracle I am not as big as she. To tell you the truth, I believe she does not want to be any smaller. Its an old islander thing. She is the most beautiful person in my life," Clair said, as she trailed off and considered the recent events. "Well, that is, until today. I think Truc might be a close second. He is so pure...so gentle. I have embarrassed myself several times today because he reminded me of my Mo Mo so much. I could not help but feel his pain."

He absorbed the soft heart of Clair like a sponge needing water. He heart was that of an Islander, and with every word, she soon owned his.

"How did you ever get into the Coast Guard? You could have had all this. A safe place to live, good food, good neighbors, no pushy Admiral. Why the Coast Guard?" Steve pressed.

"My father was in the Coast Guard. He was a rescue swimmer. He died when I was twelve in a rescue attempt. He was a local and could swim like a fish...I did it to honor him. Now I couldn't imagine being anywhere else."

Steve listened carefully as realized that he had sized her up all wrong. Lieutenant Evans was far more than a pretty girl, he thought. She was solid people, grounded to earth by family, tradition and the sea. He suddenly felt like a fool for seeing her as every other man on the base had.

"How about you? What drove you to the Coast Guard?" she asked.

He remained quiet as he thought of his reasons. They did not compare to Clair's but they were his reasons. "I wanted to be a Captain. I wanted to be the man. I think I needed something to define me and I am sure the lack of parents had something to do with the decision. As you may know, I lost my father at a young age as well. One of my few memories is sailing with him. Captaining a cutter was a chance to be part of something bigger than me." He grew quiet. "I guess it doesn't matter now. I will never become what I wanted to be. I was...so close."

Clair could see the pain of his growing handicap on his face. However, there was something different about Steve now, a rediscovered inner strength, and it was something she wanted to know, so she decided to ask, "When did you first...you know...when did you first recognize that your eyes were failing?"

"Almost a year ago, I initially chalked it up to stress and being in the sun far too much. The deterioration was slow at first," he said as he voice grew soft. "You probably know about the incident. Everyone on base seems to know about the incident. The rumor mill is ever turning."

She did know the story but she wanted him to tell it from his perspective, "Tell me about it. I want to know the true story."

"The story you probably heard is true. I did not notice a small craft running beside the Cutter during a training exercise. I ran him over. Thank God, they survived. Now, in my defense, the craft was much too close and in what I consider the blindside of a cutter." He chuckled, as he thought about it. "As if the entire vessel isn't one large blind-side, but it doesn't matter now. The inquiry forced me to get an eye exam. The rest is history. I have been stuck to a desk ever since. I am surprised they have not relieved me. I suppose they are extending sympathy for my condition. I was exonerated for the incident because the approaching craft acted in an unsafe manner, but the simple truth is, I am going blind. I just didn't see him. Simpson's predecessor promoted me as his last act of kindness. He liked me, for some reason. He took it hard that I would fail out before my first cutter."

"Well it seems to me you have been given one last awesome mission."

"Yes...it does. I cannot tell you how alive I have felt the past few days. I want to feel this way the rest of my life. I was resigned to my situation. I was going to leave and hide in a hole because it was all I knew to do. I have decided that I am never feeling sorry for myself again, Clair," he said, with a newfound confidence.

Clair received his declaration and commended him by saying, "You have impressed many this week. I honestly cannot wait to see how this plays out for you. I think the best is yet to come."

"Really! Well...I'll accept that prediction. I think we both have been given a great gift in the past few days."

At that moment, Mo Mo broke through the kitchen door singing at the top of her lungs a Hawaiian ballad. She held in both hands, two plates filled with authentic Hawaiian cuisine and, as she laid them on the table she just as quick filled the glasses with her homemade pineapple tea, brimming with local fruit.

Mo Mo stepped back and waited for Steve to try the food. Knowing it was important, Steve took his time and breathed in the meal. The smell of each plate was exquisite and he wanted to dig in immediately but he knew an appropriate fuss was required before the act of consumption. Mo Mo shuffled back and forth as she became impatient with his theatrics. Steve finally took his first bite and grinned from ear to ear. Clair was right. This was the best food he had ever eaten and the expression on his face said everything MoMo wanted to hear. As he proceeded to devour the meal before him, with each bite he took, Mo Mo hugged her Sissy from behind with great pride.

"I like him Sissy. You must bring the Captain back," she whispered into Clair's ear.

"Mo Mo, will you sit with us and eat? I want to know more about you and Sissy. I think you should give me the inside scoop on our Lieutenant."

Clair retorted, "That's not fair. Your grandmother is not here for us to get the scoop on you."

Steve began to laugh as he replied, "Trust me...you wouldn't want to eat my grandmother's cooking."

The evening became a grand affair of dinning as the seemingly endless stories of Mo Mo were explored with each new dish. MoMo shared about her Sissy and the local area and Clair attempted to defend her dignity as she bristled at the gentle insinuations her grandmother made about boys and her teenage years.

After dinner, they returned to the porch to watch the moonrise above the ridge of the cove. Mo Mo loved Steve and he knew it. If Clair allowed him to return, Mo Mo and he would be friends for life.

23

Small Things

Waves of grace
Spent upon shores of haste
In your grip
I no longer know of remorse
There I wait with a knowing hunger
As I slip beneath
The tides of slumber

As Clair drove the long winding road back to the base, Steve could not help but believe that this may have been one of the best night of his life since his fiancé dumped him. As she dropped him off they shared an awkward smile as he exited the car. Before she pulled away, Steve opened the door and said, "I want to thank you for sharing your Mo Mo with me. I cannot remember the last time someone has been that nice to me. And thank you for seeing me as a human being and not as handicapped."

Clair glanced away quickly. She did not know how to answer. Her face began to flush and she felt a stab in her heart for a man she could not touch. How could she tell him that she had enjoyed the evening as much as he had? She chose not to respond and Steve watched on as Clair drove on to the motor pool. Once out of his sight, he broke rank and headed for the Electra. There he discovered Truc in the netting that linked the large outrigger to the main hull fast asleep. Beside him, the bowl of mixed fruit, lay half-empty and it looked to Steve, Truc, had enjoyed everything but the blueberries.

Two guards snapped to attention as he approached and there he found a sleeping bag and hammock waiting for him on the dock. He quickly decided the hammock would be too much effort and began to make a place for the night in the well.

"Gentlemen both of you can sit on the bench by the palm if you like?" he ordered the tired guards. To Steve's surprise neither man moved. He huffed, "That's an order gentleman."

One protested, "Sir, we were ordered to not leave our posts by the Admiral's liaison. She was very specific that the Admiral would have our asses if we should leave for any reason."

Frustrated, Captain Channing began to dress them down for their lack of respect, when he heard from out of the dark, "You should obey the Captain's orders!"

The young men snapped to attention as Lieutenant Evans entered into the light and ordered again, "I said you should obey the Captains orders."

With that, both men broke formation and headed for the bench.

"Thanks. I didn't know I could be out ordered by a Lieutenant," Steve mused.

"It helps if every order you give is directly from the Admiral," she replied. "It's a cause and effect thing."

"Was that order directly from the Admiral?"

"No, but they don't know that."

Even in the low light of the dock, her beauty seemingly radiated and he began to worry that his attraction to her may be far too evident.

"Captain, as I said earlier, if you need anything please feel free to call me. I will be in the office complex in my private bunk. I only wanted to make sure they had delivered the bedding...I see they have."

Steve glanced away toward the office complex as he said, "You have a private bunk in the office?"

"I am here most nights. The Admiral is a high need personality. Staying here is easier than going home late and coming back early. I can get a few extra hours of sleep if I stay here. I tend to only go home on weekends."

"Oh, I see. Well then, I will call you first," he replied. Both stood and quietly as if looking for something else to say but neither could come up with an excuse to carry on the conversation. She began to shuffle her feet as she looked to the sky as if she needed to take a star heading. His eyes followed hers to the sky for fear of saying something stupid.

"Good night, Captain," she finally offered.

"Good night, Lieutenant."

As Clair walked away, still looking to the stars, he cursed his eyesight as she faded into the dark. He looked on hoping she would return but the wait was in vain. He looked back to his bedding project and decided the well was too stiff, and spread his sleeping bag across the netting. He piled into it for the night. And as he thought about the Lieutenant and imagined the stars he could barely see, his eyes became heavy as if weighted by the sway of the Electra. He was nearly lost to the night when a familiar voice broke into his near catatonic state.

"She pretty girl...and she like you....she very pretty," Truc prodded.

Captain Channing rolled over to find Truc on his side peering at him. "I thought you were asleep," he said.

"How I sleep, you...talk much."

"Sorry Truc. I didn't know we were so loud."

"You...you like Ms. Clair?"

"Truc, she is a professional relationship."

A look of confusion swept across Truc's face, as he did not understand the concept.

"She and I work for the same people Truc. We are not allowed to have a relationship...because the rules state that we can only be friends...since I am her superior officer."

"I friend with Mila...before I love Mila."

"Mila?"

"Wife! Mila!"

Captain Channing sat up as he thought about Truc being married and said, "That's right. You told us that you had a wife and we just blew past that subject. How long were you married?"

"Long time! She live now...with Palulop. Mila, she sail...to Nakure," he replied as he looked to the sky as if to find an explanation. "She, live now...where food of spirit...grow."

"With Palulop? On Nakure?"

"Palulop...he great captain. Mila, she wait for me. Okeydokey!"

"I think I understand...okeydokey," Steve replied as he lay back into the netting. He had never thought of Truc as a married man, or for that matter, a man with a deity. Then another question hit him, "Did you have children?"

"Yes...he very strong boy. I name Palau."

"After your brother?"

"Yes."

"Where is he?"

"Palau, he leave...to find wife   Palulop he not show me...where Palau go."

"He left to find a wife?"

"He need wife...so he leave."

"I take it then, Mila passed away...went to see Palulop, not too long ago?"

"I tell Amelia...I bring her book, but Mila she want...we stay home. She hate...Jeeps. So, we stay long time...keep my Mila safe. "

"Is all this in the journal Truc?"

"Amelia on...Nakure long time now."

"I think I had better hear Ms. Amelia tell her story first. Is that okeydokey with you?"

"Okeydokey, Truc replied as he rolled over and closed his eyes.

Exhausted, Captain Channing fought to find sleep as he thought about what his conversation had brought to the surface. How did Amelia die? Did she escape? Truc knew the answer to every question and yet he was waiting for the story to be told by her. Why, he thought?

He dreamed of the open ocean once again but the dream had changed to Clair and him sailing on the Electra. He wanted desperately to hold her in the dream, if only but for a moment. After some time, the old dream returned and Clair turned into his father. Once again, he called out to his father, but no words of comfort would come. His father remained mute, and Steve, as desperately wanted to, could not understand why his father would be silent.

24

Rain On The Parade

I am among you
I never left
I called to you
I am within you
I gave you my final breath

Steve awoke to Revelry. As he rolled over, he noticed men standing watch on the Constance staring down at him, as if he were a freak show. He then looked over his other shoulder to find Truc moving about the Electra working diligently on a run of line.

"Damn it," he mumbled as he cleared his eyes.

"You...wake up. Get wet...if sleep. Storm come now...very soon." Truc insisted as he prodded Steve to move.

As far as Steve could tell, there were no clouds above. "How do you know a storm is coming? Did one of the men tell you?"

"I know rain come. Why you...not believe me?" Truc replied with a scowl.

Captain Channing quickly began to round up his gear and place it on the dock. Captain Channing then decided that he needed a shower and find a clean set of clothes before the debrief. He looked to his watch. It was only five a.m. and he was grateful Jackson had set the next meeting to ten o'clock.

"Captain Channing," he heard a female voice say at his back.

He spun about to find Lieutenant Evans wearing a pair of reading glasses. This was the second time she had startled him, he thought and he began to worry it was going to be a habit.

"You wear glasses?" he asked, surprised by the change it made in her appearance.

"I am out of contacts, Captain. I had to wear my glasses this morning," she replied, then cut her eyes as if embarrassed he had noticed her glasses.

"They are becoming of you, Lieutenant Evans," he said, as he wondered if she had worn them to make him feel comfortable around her.

"Thank you Captain Channing. The compliment is so noted."

"How blind are you?" he prodded.

"Let's just say, you would look much better if I took them off," she quipped, as she pointed to his hair and unkempt dress. "And by the way, they make a medicine for what you are trying to kill down there."

He visibly blushed, as he realized he had been caught scratching on the dock.

Without warning, she took him by the arm and ordered, "Come with me, Captain. We have a few things to discuss before the morning debrief."

"I will return for you in a bit," Steve said over his shoulder to Truc as she led him away.

Truc waved him on and then dove into the ocean for his morning bath.

"I have taken the privilege of having a fresh set of clothes delivered this morning. You looked to be a 32 waist / 34 legs. I know you do not have quarters on base...so I hope you don't mind. Your clean clothes are in my private bunk so that you can shower and change before we meet with the Admiral at o-seven hundred."

"Your private bunk? You're taking me to your private bunk!"

"Well, I couldn't exactly put you in the Admiral's private bunk. The only other option was with the enlisted quarters or aboard the Constance. I will not be in there if that is what you are worried about, Captain."

"No...Lieutenant, I am not worried about that at all."

A shy smile grew as she remembered him in the shower.

"Why are we meeting at o-seven hundred?" he asked.

"The Admiral wants to begin at o-eight hundred."

"What about Admiral Jackson?"

"His liaison was informed before I found you."

"What about the others?"

"They have been called. The Admiral feels that we should waste no time as he believes, Truc is a very delicate old man."

"Delicate? Truc? Are you kidding me?"

"The truth is the Admiral discovered Jackson had a press meeting set for this morning. We found out through back channels that he blew a gasket when he saw you on the news last night. Jackson, has since called in every favor that he has in Washington. He wants this debrief at the Navy yard. He is pissed to say the least and obviously does not appreciate being upstaged."

"How's our Admiral holding up?" Steve asked.

"What do you think? He is loving every minute. He had it all planned and cut Jackson off at the pass before he called in his favors. To say the least, Jackson's ego has been slightly bruised."

"Simpson's a salty son of a bitch wouldn't you say, Lieutenant?" he asked.

"Salty...hell, he is the Dead Sea when it comes to this kind of posturing. It doesn't hurt that he knows the President personally," she whispered.

"Does he really?"

"They played football together in high school," Clair said, as she winked. "I like to think of him as our ace in the hole."

"How are we going to meet outside if it's raining?" Steve asked.

"It's not going to rain. I checked," she responded with a bit of disdain.

"Truc seems to think different," he replied, as she opened the door and pointed him into the room.

As he studied the sparse quarters Clair called home during the week, he couldn't help but notice that it was personalized minimally. Only a single family photo, taken when she was eight or nine, adorned her wall. Her father, a true islander, stood with a woman he figured to be Clair's mother and a much younger MoMo. Mo Mo was as warm as he knew her to be in person and she had her arms about her Sissy much as she had done most of the night before.

Steve could see the awkward little girl in Clair now. Her father was handsome and her mother, a beauty in her own right, looked to be of mixed race. That explained Clair's unique features, he thought. Then he wondered why he had not asked about her mother at Mo Mo's and as he thought about it, he remembered she had never once mentioned her mother.

The shower smelled of her perfume and he could not help but take it in. At ten till seven, he returned to the hall and found her waiting in the reception area.

"I thought you would never get out of the shower. What took you so long?" she asked with a wicked little smile.

"I had to pry the barnacles from my ass," he replied curtly. He was beginning to enjoy the banter and he could give it as good as she could give he thought.

"Sounds like I may need to clean my shower."

"Yes you do...the hairspray was an inch thick on the floor. It stuck to my feet."

"It was not!" she demanded.

"Thank you for the courtesy Lieutenant. I needed the shower...hairspray and all."

"You're welcome...that will be last time," she snapped as she turned to her desk and buzzed Admiral Simpson. Steve brushed past her, much like the first time he visited the Admiral, but this time he did not feel awkward or sense pity on her part.

● ● ●

"Did you eat well last night, Captain Channing? Hell, did you sleep well?" Admiral Simpson asked through an unlit cigar protruding an inch from his mouth as if a growth he needed to have removed.

"I did both, Admiral. Thank you," Captain Channing answered.

Simpson locked eyes with his Captain; an inquisitive stare, something was different about his Captain. "Did you take him to Mo Mo's?" he asked Clair.

Lieutenant Evans stiffened and replied, "Yes sir, I felt it was the safest place that I could take him with all the press snooping about. Mo Mo closed down for him, Sir."

"You better tell no one about the place Channing. I don't want it flooded with tourists. If I weren't Clair's superior officer, I swear I would have kissed her for showing me the place," the Admiral quipped.

The searched for his lighter once again. Steve was beginning to believe it was a nervous habit of the Admirals.

"Sit down Channing. I appreciate you sleeping on that boat last night. I got up twice to check on you and there you were...the whole time. You seem to sleep well on her, Captain.

That old man is one sturdy piece of work. Can you imagine how much drive it must have taken for him to sail here? Absolute miracle, I tell you," he said as he walked from behind his desk.

Clair took up the chair opposite Steve as Admiral Simpson attempted to light his cigar. It was obvious that he was absolutely beside himself with pride.

"Sir, I think we may need to postpone the debrief for this morning," Captain Channing stated in a matter of fact manner.

"What for Captain? Truc's been up and moving about for hours," the Admiral replied as he pulled on his cigar with all his might. He became frustrated quickly as the old cigar refused to light. He found his cigar clip and cut the end off to start over and his smile returned as smoke filled the room.

"Sir, Truc informed me that it's going to rain this morning. I would request that we not force him inside if it does rain."

"I get the weather every hour on the hour. The best weathermen on the island have told me no rain is in the forecast for this morning. That is one thing those Navy boys do right. It's not going to rain today, Captain," he stated as he looked to Steve, as if he had lost his mind.

Captain Channing shrugged. "Truc seemed convinced, Sir."

"I know you think he's the next best thing since Jesus Christ but...I can tell you it is not going to rain today Captain."

"Yes sir," Steve replied with a confident grin.

"Captain, are you ready to finish this thing today? It can't be much longer until we find out what happened to Amelia," the Admiral asked.

"Sir, I found out last night that Truc had a son. He told us yesterday that he had a wife but we just blew past the point. From our conversation, I take it both have passed away. Well, at least his wife passed. Truc said he did not know what happened to his son. It seems the boy left to find a wife when he came of age. After the conversation, I feel as if Truc decided to come here soon after his wife passed away. He told me she didn't want to leave their safe place."

"How did his son pass?" Clair asked.

"Actually, he didn't say he passed. He said the boy left and never returned and that the sea would not tell him what happened to his son. I tried to keep the conversation short. I didn't want to upset him...his day had been long enough at that point."

The cigar finally took a flame and Simpson began to set the burn with heavy drags.

"Where the hell do you think they were living Captain?" the Admiral asked, as smoke swirled about his head.

"Sir, I have no idea. I find it hard to believe that it was a place inhabited by other people," Captain Channing replied.

"Ok, let's map out this morning's debrief then. Do we just start reading the journal? Do we take the time to question him on things we know like his wife and son?" Simpson asked.

"Sir, I believe we should proceed with the journal and I think we need to ask him if we can make a copy. I believe it can be done without harming the book," Clair interjected.

"That sounds like a plan, Lieutenant. Do you agree, Channing?"

"Sir, I would be cautious in attempting a copy. It is a great idea but I believe we are walking on thin ice now. This is a major historical document. Can you imagine the grief we would take if an archeologist were on site? They would never allow us to open the book without first taking measures to protect the pages. We are going to be severely criticized for hoarding the information as it is Admiral."

"Well, that's a bit of a problem, Captain. I called a few friends at the University last night. One has a Doctorate in Forensic Anthropology. I thought he would like to meet Truc, so I asked him to get a team together and listen in on our conversation. I did not tell him we have the journal. He delivered a group this morning from the university. They are in the front lobby waiting for us now. Should we send them home?"

Clair raised her hand, "Sir, if you do not mind, I think we need to have them sign a waiver that states they are privy to top secret information. That would relieve them of all rights, and allow us to keep a lid on information, until we want the can opened. If you declare this debrief top secret, that would make them unable to confiscate the journal, or the vessel, for that matter. The way I see it, this is an investigation regarding a missing person's claim and falls well within our purview. We have priority until we close the investigation."

"That's why I hired you, Lieutenant. Get me the documentation. I want all our people involved signing that thing...including you Channing. How long will it take to type it up Lieutenant?"

Clair reached into her brief, pulled out a copy, and handed it to the Admiral.

"Some days, I do not believe I am the one in charge," Admiral Simpson muttered

"I would never pull a string you didn't order me to pull...Sir," Clair replied.

Admiral Simpson read over the document and quickly signed it. He turned it over to Captain Channing who signed the next page as a knock occurred at the door.

"That must be Captain Bearing. He gave the Navy one hell of a tongue lashing out there for you Channing," the Admiral said as he opened the door.

"Permission to come aboard, Sir?" Captain Bearing snapped, as he saluted the Admiral smartly.

"Yes, Captain you may come aboard," Simpson replied, as he put his hand on his Captain's back and led him to the desk. "Captain, I want to thank you for the spirit of teamwork you showed out there. I take it you know Captain Channing?"

"Yes Sir. I like his style, Sir. My second in command was positive he wanted me to fire upon those Navy pukes at one point. I must say, it was tempting, Sir," Bearing answered.

"What does he mean by that?" Admiral Simpson asked Steve.

"I think he is referring to my attempt to communicate by jumping up and down, pointing to the destroyers and giving the international symbol of slitting my throat," Steve replied.

"That would be the incident sir. Thankfully, Admiral, I considered Captain Channing groggy at the time. I was positive he could not coherently make a decision after such a hard nap," Captain Bearing replied, still holding Captain Channing's hand. "I personally have a standing order to keep the trigger away from me until I've had my coffee."

Admiral Simpson slapped Captain Channing on the back hard as he said, "Son, you are going to be the talk of the Coast Guard for decades. I am afraid some unwanted bits will become the lore of your adventure. I would suggest you enjoy the digs. It's funny when you think about it."

"Yes sir...it is...funny if you say so, Sir," Captain Channing replied, as he pulled his hand from Bearings.

"Channing seems to believe it will rain this morning Captain Bearing. He said, Truc said so. How do you feel about that prediction?" the Admiral asked Captain Bearing.

"Our weather report was for sunny skies and a light wind from the west, but if Captain Channing believes it to be true, I will need to contact the Rush and order them to pull my laundry off the line."

"Well ladies and gentlemen; we have one old man with a great story to tell. I suggest we get on with the show," Admiral Simpson interjected as he laughed off Captain Bearing rib at Captain Channing.

As the group started for the door, a thunderclap rattled the office complex. Suddenly, the base disappeared behind a curtain of rain, as it grew dark outside. The Admiral and

Captain Bearing returned to the large frame window and stared at the yard before them as a squall swept over the base.

Below, they could see Truc as he darted to the main hull of the Electra. He looked up and regarded the Admiral standing in the large frame window, pointed to the black sky, as if to say...I told you so...before disappearing below deck.

"How the hell did he know it was coming!" Captain Bearing exclaimed.

"I hate to say, I told you so," Captain Channing quipped.

"I think it might be a bit late for your laundry, Bearing," Admiral Simpson quipped, as he slapped him on the back and laughed aloud at the sight before him

.

25

Singing In The Rain

The heat of the day consumes
The last vestige of my soul that remains untamed
So as I turn to the sky with dew in hand
Mourn for me
A stubborn man

Admiral Simpson waited near the main entry as watched the Electra bob within the storm for nearly three hours. Bearing circled nervously nearby; Admiral Jackson had arrived. Upon meeting Captain Bearing, who saluted smartly, Admiral Jackson pulled his hand back before he finalized his return salute.

"Are you the Captain of the Rush?" Admiral Jackson asked.

Captain Bearing decided to act dumbfounded by the question as he allowed Captain Channing break the ice, "Yes sir, he is the Captain who made first contact with the

Electra. I am sure it will earn him a place in the history books."

"I see," Admiral Jackson replied. "I've heard a few tales of inappropriate communication. Some would say...unbecoming."

"Sir, I am not sure what you are talking about. I only use Navy approved language, when communicating with my brothers in arms. My father was Navy so I tend to use the terms he taught me in my childhood. Very colorful terms...I might add," Captain Bearing replied, stone faced.

"So, how did your father feel about you becoming a Coasty?" Admiral Jackson said as a jab.

Captain Bearing's demeanor changed immediately and Jackson knew he had hit a nerve. He enjoyed his knack of finding a man's buttons and putting a Coast Guard Captain in his place was going to be good sport, he thought.

Captain Bearing saluted and spun about to walk away before he decided he could not stomach the insult. He turned about, snapped to attention and dug in, "Excuse me Admiral, may I have permission to speak candidly?"

Jackson smile grew as if a carnivore about to eat its prey. The Captain had taken the bait. "Yes you may Captain," he replied.

"Thank you, Sir," Captain Bearing replied with a growing bitter grin. "Sir, my father never witnessed my commission as an officer. He died a drunk in a ditch and I am not sure what he took away from the Navy, but self-respect was not in the mix. Therefore, in all due respect to you, Sir, I must inform you, that I never worried about what my father would have thought. As for my mother, on the other hand, what she thought, mattered. My commission was a gift to her since my Grandfather on her side was Coast Guard. My grandfather was the only man in my life who ever showed my mother respect. He was the only man in my life who believed in me. I decided to honor the only man who gave a damn by serving the branch to which he faithfully dedicated his life. I hope, Sir, that answers your question."

Admiral Jackson, taken aback by the outburst, stood erect and his demeanor became hard. His chest swelled yet he did not know how to reply. He had not expected a checkmate situation.

Captain Bearing excused himself and abruptly walked away. He wanted to punch Jackson. However, he knew he would die in the brig if he did so. Captain Channing decided it best he move away from the Admiral, as he pretended to need a drink. Admiral Simpson decided to do nothing to relieve the tension. He was proud of his officers for walking away.

Clair took the rainstorm as an opportunity to brief the scientists but not before making each sign the document of absolute silence. When she informed them of the journal, the group snapped to attention.

"This has to stop; we have to secure this document. Where is it now?" one of the scientists asked.

"The journal is aboard the Electra," Lieutenant Evans said, as she pointed and emphasized, "on that boat. It is in the care of the old man," she replied, with a curt tone.

The group, in unison, turned to stare at the bobbing vessel buried in the midst of a storm and Clair could swear she witnessed their hearts sink as one.

"The journal is on that wet boat, in this weather...what were you thinking?" one of the scientists demanded.

"It has nothing to do with us thinking. Truc is our guest. The document is his property until he decides to lend it to us. Truc has insisted that he keep the document. He has maintained this document and sailed a long distance to bring it to us. The journal arrived here dry and I am certain it will remain dry in his hands. No one has more determination to keep the document safe than Truc. If you feel otherwise, I expect you to keep those thoughts to yourself," she said, then stopped to let the facts sink in with her dumbfounded group of academics.

She then decided to soften her approach, "We are doing everything possible to make sure that he in no way feels threatened. We believe Truc is as valuable as that journal. You must remember he is extremely primitive. We believe Truc has never watched a TV, used a cell phone, or a blender for that matter. He is a living artifact and he knows ways that have long since disappeared. That vessel is proof of a boat building tradition long lost. You, my friends, will have the opportunity to study a man who has few worldly traits. If you jeopardize his willingness to communicate, I will lock you in the brig and throw the key away until such time as the Admiral sees fit to let you see daylight.

"You can't do that, we are U.S citizens. We have rights," a scientist argued.

Lieutenant Evans picked up the document each had signed and held them before the group. "Ladies and Gentlemen, this project has been declared a top secret operation by an Admiral of the United State Coast Guard. You, as a United States citizen, agreed to remain silent, until the Admiral removes the top-secret status. Yes we can, and we will," she stated in a most matter of fact manner.

A pleasant change was needed she told herself. These people were civilians and she needed them not to feel as if they were prisoners.

"I promise...you will not regret your decision to participate in this operation. As long as you play by the rules set out by the Admiral, you will be the first to write books about this project. You will be flying around the world one day soon, giving lectures on what you learn here today. Now...can we expect your support?"

26

A Break In
The Weather

I waited for the storm
Yet, the sea shared no wind as if to test by silence
The thunder's distant roar, shatters among the waves
No longer a shadow of the light that once it employed

The storm ended at noon. Captain Channing could hear Truc below deck as he approached and was caught off guard as Truc popped from the hatch as if a prairie dog.

"I tell you...rain come," Truc boasted.

"I will never doubt you again," Captain Channing replied as he boarded the vessel. "Would you mind meeting with the two Admirals once again Truc? We have more people who would like to sit in and listen. And, they are most interested in meeting you and hearing of your story."

Truc nodded in agreement, as he disappeared below deck. A moment later, he returned with the box in hand.

Truc greeted each scientist much like he had the Admiral's the day before by holding their hands, and without fail, he maintained his grand smile as each began to find their place in the growing circle. By the end of it all, the only person to remain standing was Captain Bearing.

"Truc, would you like to share the journal with us once again?" Lieutenant Evans asked.

"You read. Okeydokey!" he replied.

Clair blushed as the contingent of scientists began to take notes of her every move. And at the site of the journal, a collective sweat issued down their foreheads as Truc handed the journal most unceremoniously to Clair. Pencils' scribbling furiously was all that could be heard until Clair recovered the place she had last read.

The Journal of Amelia Earhart.

That is the last I remember of that day. I believe I was passed out for some time. I am not sure how long I remained unconscious but I remember an old woman trying to give me water and I remember Fred's moans of pain in the cell next to me. I tried to speak to him but I could not. The pain of the beating, I believe, had left me in shock.

I remember the old woman in flashes as she tried to make me eat. When I finally awoke from my nightmare, it was as if from all night bender. I remember being cold as it was dark outside when I gained full consciousness. I remember the wind never seemed to cease and I remember thinking it odd that I was cold. This is when I began to believe we would not be saved.

The next day the sun warmed my stiff bones. What was happening in the cell beside me was most horrible. Fred was dying and the sound of the pain he was enduring was unbearable. I tried to speak with him. I tried to tell him I was there but all he could manage was a mumble. For the life of me I could not understand a word he said.

That afternoon the old woman returned with water and food. I think she was surprised to find me conscious. She took her time and waited for me to eat. I asked her about Fred and I pointed toward him. She attempted to feed him but as best I could tell, he would not eat. I begged him to listen to me and eat. It was useless.

This nightmare went on for three days. On the third day, the mumbling stopped. I heard what I know now to be a death rattle. That was the darkest moment. I tried to tell myself to stop crying because I knew I was dehydrated. I knew every tear was lost energy but I could not so I begged God to take me with Fred.

It was the next afternoon before a guard realized Fred had passed. The guards were sporadic at best. I suppose they were not worried about an escape. The Commander came to inspect the situation and I could hear him kicking Fred. It sounded as if he were kicking wood.

My prison cell faced the water and I could see clearly what they did next. The action was taken without emotion or pity. They dragged Fred to the beach and tossed him into the ocean like cord wood. To them he was nothing more than trash. I couldn't help but watch on as he floated near the beach for some time then, as if by magic, he was gone. I suppose a shark took him because he disappeared below the water so quick.

This was supposed to be a day of victory. We should have been in the states having lunch with a member of congress and it all seemed so unfair. I have not slept another night without seeing Palau or Fred. They will always be in my dreams.

I began to think of the old woman as my angel. She soon recognized how broke I was without Fred. The day she finally said something I could understand I sat up and tried to make her say it again. I clearly heard her say the name...Truc. She put food to her mouth and repeated his name and I knew she was feeding him and I hoped he was nearby safe.

The cycle went on for weeks, months and I began to believe the commander had forgotten about me for he never came to visit.

Every now and again one of the troops would share the cell next to me. Officers never visited however, several from their unit would usually stop by and bring him food and water. They never fed me. I suppose they were only following orders.

A young man was placed in the cell next to me. He stayed for nearly a week and little food was brought to him. I knew this was not a good sign. He cried often, which was most unusual, for I never heard the others cry. If anything, they would taunt me but most remained quiet during their incarceration. This young man mumbled often and seemed most distressed. I tried to pick up words as I could but not being able to see what he was talking about made the language difficult to grasp. I tried to speak with him but it was of no use.

There was a moment, late one night, when I saw his hand reaching to my cell bars. I don't know why, but I felt he wanted someone to know he was still there. I took his hand and held it for the longest. I could hear him breathing on the other side and for a moment, I wanted to believe that we both would survive this ordeal. He never spoke and I held his hand until he fell asleep. He did not cry that night and for me, other than my angel, he was the first meaningful human contact I had known since the crash landing.

A few days later, the base commander arrived with a guard contingent and they dragged the young man out of his cell. He tried to fight them but he was weak from starvation and the fight was futile. I knew they were about to do something horrible because all of the other men had been released without fan fair.

The commander began to read a piece of paper while the guards tied the young man's hands to his feet in such a way as to leave him in a fetal position. He looked to me and I reached out. He began to beg, but it was of little use, in one swift motion, the commander pulled his sword from it scabbard and lopped off his head. I of course, screamed in horror at the sight.

The commander picked up the man's head, held it for me to see, and ranted about something I could not grasp. I am sure he was telling me that this would be my fate as I crawled to the far corner and I tried to hide my eyes. He was a most cruel man and tossed the soldiers head into the ocean as if throwing out the trash. The detail did the same with the young man's body and it was the same as with Fred. After an hour, he simply disappeared.

My angel did not come for several days after the beheading, and when she did return, I was famished. As best I could tell, her name was Soluu. However, I still like to call her my angel. She was old, gentle and hardly ever smiled. I asked her about Truc often as we returned to the waiting ritual. Without her, I am sure I would not have survived more than a week.

Several weeks after the beheading, my angel returned to the cell late in the day. The guard had disappeared. They came and went as they pleased. I think many times they were used for other details.

She finally smiled and in that moment, my Truc returned to me and I hugged him as if he were my own child. The reunion only lasted a few minutes before Truc had to go. That day I will never forget because that was the first day since my capture that I believed I could survive.

Truc began visiting me. I don't know why but eventually there were no guards near the cell. I suppose the commander decided it a waste of labor. You must understand, there was nowhere to run. Truc would come and spend hours with me at first in the dark. I think it became natural for him to be seen about the base with Soluu. Eventually, it was as if he were a ghost. He became bold and walked among them as many of his people were used in their details. To my benefit, he was able to locate food, which he most often brought to me in the night.

This is when I began the formal education of Truc for a selfish reason. The goal of teaching him English gave me a purpose. I challenged him to bring me items we could both see and touch. I must say this was very slow process. Not because Truc was a slow learner, quite the opposite. The situation forced everything to move at a snails pace.

Although I knew he could not understand most of what I was saying, I began to tell Truc stories. He was faithful to remain and listen and the stories helped me remember better days. They helped me to find enough courage to carry on and that courage was rewarded.

How do I tell you the next part? I did not believe it myself at the time. When I first saw it, I did not know I was looking at the first part of my salvation. She came early one morning as I lay there staring at the beach. A barge arrived and on its deck was my Electra. They had somehow rescued my plane from Milli Atoll and she was so beautiful. I have no idea how they removed her from the beach but I knew then why I was still alive. They wanted me to make sure she could fly.

The base commander returned that afternoon. This was the first time in months I had walked more than eight feet as he escorted me to the edge of the jungle and proudly showed me my beautiful Electra. They had placed her under camouflage netting, and as far as I could tell, she was in good condition. After a few minutes, he led me back to my cell without saying a word. This seemed most odd but now I am sure he did it just to make me hurt for her.

The next day my Truc did not return and when Soluu arrived, she was visibly upset. She tried to speak English and it was at this point that I realized I should have been learning her language. She let me know, with a crude sign language and the few words she understood that Truc had been taken away from her.

I did not see Truc for over two months. I did what I could to keep my spirits up by teaching Soluu and attempting to grasp her language. He did finally return and to me, he was visibly taller. We began working on his English immediately. He was able to meet with me for a week before he had to leave once again. I now know they were building something on the next island and had taken a break so that the islanders could supply for their families. I had a hard time during these periods. I had nothing to read, nothing to listen to but the sound of planes taking off and landing and the waves. Moreover, the wind...the wind never stopped blowing.

Very few soldiers found themselves jailed after the beheading. I suppose the young man was a lesson for the rest of the base and the lesson had stuck.

Months would pass before Truc would return. Sometimes he could come for only a few days and sometimes he could stay for a week or two. During this period, I lost all track of time. However, I was proud of my student because when he did visit, he seemed to have improved his language skills. He let me know he practiced his English while working. It was not long after that he was able to convey to me that they were building a large space underground. The work seemed most horrible as he described it.

27

When
Lightning Strikes

Oceans of lies cover me
Drowning the truth of hope
Begging a new jury
Demanding a new verdict
As the salt of truth reveals my way
Among those found within a better day

Clair hesitated before she asked, "Sir may we stop for a moment. I need to drink something other than coffee."

Simpson agreed and Clair handed the journal to Truc as she headed for the mess hall. Admiral Jackson stood to leave immediately without excusing himself, and returned to the office complex as his phone began to ring.

"Truc, I am sorry to hear about the passing of your wife. Captain Channing shared with me your recent conversation with him," Admiral Simpson said.

"She good...wife," Truc replied.

"I'm sure she was a fine woman."

Captain Channing noticed, as Jackson began to return, that he had suddenly turned about and headed back into the office complex with the phone still stuck to his ear. It was then that Captain Channing began to worry about Jackson. He was up to something, but the thought was interrupted as Truc passed gas loudly and said with a squeal, "Ohhhh..I like.wind! You see...I wait for.Clair leave."

"Well, I'm glad you learned some manners, Truc. I can't imagine if you had not," Admiral Simpson bellowed.

Lieutenant Evans noticed the men laughing aloud as she returned.

"What...What's so funny?" she asked, as the odd group immediately stopped laughing. "You three are up to something?" she snapped.

"No Lieutenant, we're just blowing off some steam," the Admiral replied.

She glared at the men then decided the conversation must be freshman in nature. A moment later, the scientist and film crew returned but Admiral Jackson remained missing in action.

"Truc, would you allow these ladies and gentlemen to ask you some questions while we wait on Admiral Jackson?" Simpson asked.

Truc nodded in the affirmative.

"Please make your questions brief, and try not to get ahead of what we have already covered," the Admiral admonished the group.

"Mr. Truc, may I ask, how long you have had the journal?"

"Since...Amelia die," he responded.

"How long ago did she die?"

Truc looked to be confused as he answered, "I not know."

A woman with short grey hair, frumpy glasses and a gravelly voice asked, "Do you know how long Mrs. Earhart was captive with the Japanese?"

Truc replied, "Long. I know wind...sea. I know... when wind change. "

"That is ahead of the story as we know it," Steve noted as he could see Admiral Jackson returning.

"Truc, how did you know it was going to rain this morning?" Admiral Simpson asked, at the last possible moment.

"It rain...soon. Not long now," Truc responded.

All looked up but there was not a cloud visible for miles.

"How do you know that, Truc?" Admiral Simpson pressed.

"I know...if sea happy...it rain. Fish jump...look," Truc said, as he pointed to the harbor. "When fish jump...to sun. It rain soon. Not big rain...like morning."

"He predicted this morning's storm and our weather advisor told us there would be no rain. So, if he tells you to head for the house ladies and gentlemen...I would suggest heading for the house," Simpson said half joking.

"Father teach me how...Aluluei...show me way. He teaches to...listen...okeydokey," Truc said as Admiral Jackson arrived.

Admiral Jackson demeanor was stern and his eyes burned with anger. Something had changed and Captain Channing suspected it had something to do with the phone call.

"Truc, not all of us are impressed with your parlor tricks!" Jackson snapped as he sat down. "I think it is time for you to tell everyone here the truth."

Truc looked to him dumbfounded and failed to reply as Admiral Jackson reloaded. "Let me tell the group what I think happened. I believe you found the wing on a beach and wrote this journal yourself. If you did not write the journal, then you had one of your kids write it? Come on Truc, tell everyone the truth. Tell them how you are a registered citizen of the Marshall Islands. Go ahead; tell them how you are using the old, debunked stories, about a crash landing at Milli. I think you are playing us, old man. Why...did you hope to get some kind of reward?"

Admiral Simpson's jaw went slack as Jackson fired at Truc once again, "You've made one mistake...old man...you should have used another name other than your real name. It was just confirmed to me, that you are Truc Benda of Ebai. You live next to our base at Kwajalein on Ebai and you were at one point a registered employee of the base for years. We have your pay files on record. I have your address on Ebai. So Mr. Truc Benda...please tell everyone the truth, Sir."

Truc's demeanor never changed. After several long moments he replied, "Who...Truc Benda?"

A smile spread across Jackson's face. He had Truc and he knew it.

"Did you find the wing or did some or your friends create it as a big joke? I bet you did not expect it would get this far. I bet...you were blown out to sea and couldn't find your way back to Ebai. I bet...you were lost and got lucky when Captain Channing found you. Truc...I promise...if you lie to me again, I will have you thrown in the deepest brig I can find. I will bury you for making a mockery of Mrs. Earhart and Commander Noonan."

Steel filled the eyes of Truc as his famous smile finally broke. "I not lie. I keep journal...for you...long time. I bring. Amelia she ask...I bring."

Captain Channing's mind began to race as he tried to find a way to save the situation. "Sir, how did you come up with this name?" he asked Admiral Jackson.

Clair felt her stomach twist and nearly threw up as she watched Captain Channing squirm. He had knowingly broken the cardinal rule of never asking an angry Admiral a question and weakness on his part opened the door.

Jackson began to burn a hole through Captain Channing as he snapped, "Son, you better be careful. Did you not think to run a check of his name? Did you not think to call the intelligence division of the USCG?" He then paused to let his question sink in. Then he raised both hands and slammed them on the table. "Oh, that's right, you don't have an intelligence division because you don't need one. That is why this investigation belonged at the Navy Yard...where real investigators could tear this fraud apart. Now, you are a part of the fraud, Captain Channing. For all we know, the people who called this in...the Vonstreeps...are part of this fraud."

Admiral Simpson had heard enough and slammed his fist on the table in return as he tore into Jackson. "Admiral you had better check your facts before you threaten one of my men, and for your information, we do have an intelligence arm. We like to call ours the C.I.A. My Captain has been busy building a relationship with our guest. For your information, I personally called the C.I.A, the moment I had Truc's name."

Simpson paused long enough to watch Jackson's ears turn red then pressed on. "Admiral, you know as well as I, that Admiral Nimitz believed Amelia was alive. You know that he believed she was in the Japanese controlled territories, and you know the monitored communications of the Japanese increased dramatically the days after she disappeared."

Jackson crossed his arms as if nothing Simpson was saying mattered.

"I have found proof that he is a registered citizen of the Republic of the Marshall Islands. I can have proof here in less than an hour if you like...Admiral. I have pictures of this man on their way here now," Admiral Jackson fired back.

Simpson huffed as if not impressed. "Do you really want to play this game, Admiral?" he said with a dark sneer.

"It seems to me, Admiral Simpson, it is you who have been playing a game. When all this comes out, I do not care who your friends may be. This little event will hurt everything the United States Coast Guard has worked to accomplish the last twenty years. All because of a little man, who played all of us like a fiddle. I am embarrassed that my name will in anyway be associated to this scam," Jackson snapped; a shot across Simpson's bow.

Admiral Simpson turned to engage Truc. "I am sorry...for the nature of this conversation, Truc. It would have been best played out behind closed doors. You must understand that the Admiral is only trying to get to the truth as I, but...Sir." He turned his gaze back to Jackson.

"You have chosen to play your cards in front of my subordinates and my guest. Admiral, you have made a conscious decision to demean my character and that of my officers; you have left me no choice."

"What Simpson? What are you going to do? This whole affair is a mockery of the armed services. I just called this old fool's bluff. If you have any cards that say otherwise, then play them. I have sat here long enough listening to drivel. Where's the proof that he is not a fraud?" Admiral Jackson railed.

"That's enough Admiral...Truc is a guest on this base and I believe you owe him an apology," Simpson shot back.

"I will not apologize to a liar and a fraud," Jackson replied as he returned Simpson's glare.

Admiral Simpson paused for what seemed an eternity to all else involved. A storm began to brew behind his eyes and Clair new; Admiral Simpson was about to fire all of his cannons. He reached under the picnic table, found his brief case, laid it on the table, and produced a file labeled Top Secret.

"Admiral Jackson...you contend that Truc is a registered citizen of the Republic of the Marshall Islands." He then placed a picture of a man resembling Truc before his peer. "I would suppose this is the picture of the man you are claiming to be our Truc. Yes, Admiral...this is Truc Benda. He is one of two Truc Benda's registered as a citizen of the Republic of the Marshalls. This Truc Benda in the picture, is 58 years of age, and yes, he was a laborer at Kwajalein."

Simpson pulled out yet another photo and pressed. "This is the second Truc Benda, is a current laborer on Kwajalein. He is the twenty one year old son of the previous Truc Benda. As you can see Admiral, these two men are near exact replicas of one another. That would make sense since they are father and son."

Admiral Simpson then retrieved yet another photo and laid it upside down on the table. A thin smile grew across his face as he flipped over the next photo. "This is the father of our 58 year old Truc Benda, the grandfather of the same Truc Benda who is 21. The father of Truc Benda...age 58...passed away five years ago. This is a copy of his death certificate. Our man, I am sorry Admiral. I mean, the C.I.A's man, stationed at the base in Kwajalein...well, he visited the 58-year-old Truc Benda last night. It seems the deceased Truc Benda, told a story of how he was named after his two brothers. Why was he named after them? It seems they went missing in 1937 after fleeing from the Japanese on Jaluit."

Admiral Simpson glanced about the table to make sure all were watching before he pressed on. "According to the deceased Truc Benda's account he had two older brothers. The brothers fled with the hope of meeting later at an uncle's fishing camp at the next atoll with the rest of the family. Suffice to say, these were brothers that he never met. This fish camp that the deceased Truc Benda spoke of...was at Milli Atoll. It seems it took several weeks for the family to follow them and when they conducted a search for the brother's they were not to be found.

Now, according to the 58-year-old Truc Benda, and according to the death certificate...his father's full name was Truc Palau Benda. It seems the family took the Sir name, Benda, after the war. Our Truc's brother served with the United States Administrator to the islands as a personal aid. Truc Palau Benda had a very distinguished record of service and eventually became part of the transition team that established the islands return to self-rule. Truc Palau Benda passed away at the ripe old age of seventy-three."

Jackson grew wide-eyed as he studied the pictures. His neck turned red and his cheeks went flush as embarrassment began to set in.

Admiral Simpson paused as if a lawyer making closing arguments.

"It seems our Truc, sitting here today, who according to his own story never saw his family again, did not know that his father and mother survived the Japanese brutalization. His parents assumed, as most would have, that Truc and Palau were killed. They did not believe that the two brothers were lost at sea according to their oral history because they found the boys small boat stranded on Milli and signs of a struggle, along with pieces of clothing they could not identify. The report states they also found many other strange items and the remains of what they assumed to be one of the brothers. The body was unidentifiable because the crabs had cleaned it to the bone. Their father kept up the search for several years. He even traveled to Kwajalein Atoll many years later to follow up on a report that the boys were on the island but he never made it North end of the Kwajalein Atoll, Roi-Namur."

Admiral Simpson turned to address Truc. "It was a very long distance to have sailed from one Atoll to another as a young teen. I must confess, I cannot imagine the skill you must possess to be able to sail such distances with no modern instruments."

Simpson then returned his gaze to Admiral Jackson, "The C.I.A. has come to the conclusion his parents had one last child whom they named Truc Palau, in honor of his lost brothers. I would be willing to say, he is the brother of our Truc sitting here today. His brother's death is documented with the base hospital in Kwajalein. He looks like Truc, but it is obvious he is not Truc, because of a birthmark on his face that you can just make out in the photo."

Simpson paused, and then pressed for a moment more, "There is only one conclusion Admiral. Our Truc is the real deal."

The wind began to leave Admiral Jackson as he studied the pictures of men who could have been Truc at different stages of his life.

"I'm sorry Admiral, but, as I said earlier, I think you owe Truc...our guest...an apology?" he asked once again.

Truc scooped up the pictures as tears began to stream down his face. All the while, Admiral Jackson tried to ignore the glare of Captain Channing.

"Truc, it seems I owe you an apology," he said pensively. "Obviously, I had incomplete intelligence; please forgive me for questioning your integrity."

Admiral Jackson then straightened himself as he tried to regain his dignity.

"Admiral Simpson, I owe you and Captain Channing an apology as well. I regret not having discussed my findings with you privately. I was a grave error on my part," he confessed. He finally looked to Captain Channing and found Captain Bearing, standing directly behind, doubling a look of disgust.

"Captain Channing, would you please forgive me for questioning your integrity, and in effect, that of the service you proudly uphold?" the Admiral asked nervously.

Admiral Simpson decided to break the deafening silence, "Captain Channing gladly accepts your apology. I for one am glad this is all behind us. I hope we can move forward now."

"Apology accepted Admiral. Anyone could have made the mistake," Captain Channing finally replied.

Truc gathered up the photos without asking permission, and then as if on cue, a light rain began to fall. He tucked the dossier under his arm and dashed for the Electra.

"You left the journal!" Lieutenant Evan yelled after Truc as he sprinted across the grounds.

"You keep!" he replied, then disappeared below deck.

Captain Channing took up a towel one of the Academics had brought and held it over Clair's head to protect the journal.

In the midst of the chaos, of rain and people seeking shelter, Admiral Jackson slowly strolled across the base toward his car in a daze. As if somehow, allowing the rain to soak him through and through, would bring to him a cleansing redemption.

28

Remember Your Shadow

Wash me clean from the wrath of my enemy
Restore my soul by the waters of redemption
Lead me to the table of peace
There, I shall dine
With the days that are left
The days that are mine

He listened to the rain as it bounced off the Electra's hull; the teen age Truc reminded him most of his brother Palau. He had Palau's eyes and Truc could not help but to cry as the memories returned of a brother he had hoped to protect. A knock on the hood of the Electra could not break through his grief. He remained quiet for he did not want visitors. The gentle knock came once again. Truc huffed aloud, wiped his eyes, and opened the cowling only to discover Captain Channing standing in the rain beneath an umbrella.

"May I visit with you Truc?" the Captain asked.

Truc gave him an affirmative nod. Truc seemed most at home outside Captain Channing thought and it felt odd that he had never considered where Truc went to hide.

The space hid two pilot's seats that were pinned against the walls and nets filled with food stores blocked any further forward view forward. Fred and Amelia had sat upon the seats and there was much more space than he had anticipated as he move to find his place next to Truc.

Captain Channing felt the seat as if he were inspecting a museum piece. He knew an archeologist would crucify him for even thinking of entering the Electra, much less sitting in Amelia's seat, he thought. The seats would most likely end up in the Smithsonian and he worried that he was making a grave mistake but his friend needed him and he would let the academics figure it all out later.

No personal pictures adorned the space, and Steve wondered if Truc had ever experienced a camera. Then he realized Truc may have never even viewed a photo until he touched the ones he now in his hands..

"I thought I would check on you," Steve said as he shook off the rain and settled in.

"I...okeydokey Stevveeeee."

"No you're not Truc. You can tell me the truth."

Truc lowered his head as tears began to roll down his face once again.

"I know the pictures must have been a real shock. But, if you think about it...this is a miracle, Truc," Steve said as he studied the picture firm in Truc's grip. The resemblance was amazing, he thought.

"Perhaps one day you will meet them," Captain Channing suggested to change Truc's mood.

As hard as he tried, Truc could not stop the tears.

"He...and Palau...look same. Eyes...just like Palau."

He then held up the black and white photo of his recently discovered brother. "Do I look like...him?" he asked.

Captain Channing considered it for a moment, and then nodded a confident yes.

"I... very ugly man."

Captain Channing held the picture next to Truc's face and compared the two. "You're much uglier than your brother," he quipped.

"You funny man. Funny man! Mila...she say, I pretty man.

"Of course she said you were pretty. She was your wife. She had to say that."

With that, Truc began to smile.

"I am not sure the world is ready for you Truc. I am afraid that we may have more incidents like today...because...there will always be those who do not believe you," Steve warned.

"Do...they," Truc said as he pointed to the pictures, "live on...island."

"It might be a good thing to visit them one day,' Steve replied.

"Ms. Amelia, she teach me," Truc said as he took Steve by the knee. "She say...I find you. She say...when I find you...trust you."

"Truc I'm not sure I'm the one she was talking about."

"I know...like I know rain," Truc replied as he tapped the ceiling of the Electra and listened.

"Rain...it stop soon," he supposed, and then, as if a spigot had been turned off, the storm stopped.

"I believe you think too highly of me. I can only help you so much. I am will be blind one day and you will be leading me around like a baby."

Truc placed his hand on Steve's forehead. "I teach you to see world...world you not see with eyes." He then removed his hand from Steve's forehead and a peace fell over Captain Channing that he had not known since he was a child.

"Wow...that's like a Vulcan mind meld?"

"Vullcannnn...?"

"No...No...What did you do to me Truc? I feel light headed." A sense well-being set upon him, as if he had been released from a tether. After several minutes, he opened his eyes to find Truc fast asleep. Sleep felt like the right thing to do he thought and he melted into his seat.

The dream returned. The small sailboat crested one wave after another as it sailed effortlessly in a light wind. Nevertheless, the face of his father remained hidden. He could hear his laugh and he remembered his smell, but his face would not come to him.

Waiting at the office complex nearby, the group of academics and officers had become restless. Admiral Simpson finally asked Lieutenant Evans to check on the Captain as the rain subsided. She had spent the morning protecting the box from the scientist with the full force of her glare and had grown tired of the exercise. The diversion was exactly what she needed.

As she climbed aboard the Electra, she could hear a low rumble from within. As soon as she lifted the cowling, she knew why. To her amusement, she discovered her two men snoring as if in a duel. She took a picture and cell phone to mark the moment. It would be fun to torture Captain Channing later; she thought, as she cleared her throat and forced a hearty false cough.

"Captain, you obviously like to sleep on this boat," she alleged as she snapped another shot.

Captain Channing awoke with a fright, banged his head against the low ceiling, as he glared into the light streaming in from above his head. As Lieutenant Evans stood above, the sun at her back enveloped her as he desperately tried to remember where he was and why an angel had come to visit. For a moment, he considered the option that he may have died as he stared up at Lieutenant Evans.

"You...keep Ms. Clair waiting...Steveeee," Truc scolded, as if he had not been asleep.

She stepped aside as Captain Channing extracated himself from the hold. He took a moment to fix his uniform and Truc remained next to him as if he were the little brother hiding behind his big brother. Clair first attempted to fix Truc's hair and he scowled as if a little boy made to dress for church.

She then turned her attention to Captain Channing who at first lifted a hand to stop her.

"Trust me, you look like hell. I cannot let the Admiral see you like this, Captain," she argued. As she attempted to straighten the Captain's mop, she ordered, "Ok boys; let's get on with this meeting. We should not keep the Admiral waiting."

Captain Channing thought the journey to the palm was far too short. Simpson looked to be angry but before he could speak Clair interjected, "It seems Admiral; the inside of the Electra is very damp place. I am sorry, but I had to fix them up for the camera and I think I interrupted a deep conversation," she said, with a flourish that could have won an Oscar.

"I apologize gentlemen. I didn't mean to interrupt your conversation," she said as she turned her attention to the two disheveled men. "I did the same thing to my Daddy as a girl. I have the gift of bad timing."

Admiral Simpson knew his liaison was covering but decided it was moot as he pointed to the seats that several enlisted had painstakingly dried.

To most everyone's surprise, a dry Admiral Jackson returned with a confident amble to his gait. He seemed to be in a far better mood.

"Please don't rise for me, I apologize for being late," he asked more than ordered. He then turned his attention to Admiral Simpson and asked, "I hope you will allow an old Navy puke like me to sit in on the rest of this fascinating story? I need to know what happens to Amelia," he asked as he snapped to attention and saluted smartly, "May I have permission to come aboard...Admiral?"

Admiral Simpson stood mouth agape, as he had not expected Jackson's return. He mustered his nerve, snapped to attention and returned the salute, but then, beyond normal protocol, he stuck out his other hand for a handshake.

"Permission granted, Admiral."

With a solid salute and a firm handshake, a new peace agreement was in effect and Admiral Simpson could not help but think he liked the new Admiral Jackson.

"Lieutenant, let's get on with this if you don't mind," he ordered.

The Journal of Amelia Earhart

My life became of no consequence on that island and I began to believe I would die in their cage, not that my condition did not improve over time. For some reason they began to let me out once or twice a week to clean my cage. I suppose the smell was a bit strong. This allowed time for short walks and I was grateful they continued to let Soluu bring me food and water. I honestly do not know how long this period was. I suppose it was at least a year but I don't know...It could have been longer. The whole experience became mind numbing as I could see no way out. Even though I was eating, I remained too weak to even attempt an escape. Even if I could, a nagging question remained. Where would I go? Nevertheless, it didn't matter, I knew I would never make it to the flight line.

I began to believe they could not fix my Electra. I never heard the start of her engines, nor to my surprise, did they ask me to help. Why they kept it at this point, I still could not tell you. I suppose they desired the latest American technology.

At some point I must admit that I started to think of ways of committing suicide as the periods of Truc's return were becoming longer and longer. I thought of running to the water and letting the sharks eat me. I would dream of a guard shooting me in the attempt but I could not do it. I felt like a coward because I could not end myself.

I slept most of the day and watched the stars at night. Lack of conversation, the constant noise of airplane engines and the constant hum of the sea caused me start talking to myself. I would spend days in conversations with those I loved. I remember having all-night conversations with Fred. He discussed flight plans and weather and told me all the same jokes I had listened to relentlessly in the Electra. We discussed the route I should take if I were to fly away from the island. Even as I write this today, I cannot tell you that he was not in there with me, urging me to live. If one could have a spiritual experience, I suppose that was as close to one as I could imagine.

I spoke with my parents and my high school friends and I imagined my high school classes and each teacher. The one person I could not speak with was my husband. I am sorry my love. For some reason I always ended the conversation. I could not breathe when I dreamed of my life with you and the stress of missing you would always snap me awake.

After several months, Truc finally returned. I am sure I looked different. I barely recognized him because he had become a man. I held his hand for the longest trying to understand why they were swollen and bruised. His eyes had aged and I cried the entire time as he waited with me. When he finally spoke, I understood much of what he said. I was thrilled to find he had been practicing. I must say it was most encouraging and before he left, Truc promised he would return the next day with a surprise.

Truc did return the next day with a surprise, a surprise I would have never imagined. He came with Soluu but she was not the surprise. In her tow, a beautiful young woman followed. She was scared and hid behind Truc and Soluu. I cannot blame the poor girl for being afraid. I must have looked like a monster. Truc seemed happy as he whispered to me, "I love Mila."

Somehow, the hope of love for Truc gave me courage. The young girl could not have been more than fourteen, yet I could tell she was smitten with Truc. They spent as long as they dared and left me in the early evening. I did not speak to myself that night. I dreamed of Truc and Mila. I dreamed of a wedding. Little did I know, the hand of Soluu had already bound them to each other? I found out later that both of Mila's parents had passed away fishing for the Japanese. Soluu had taken her in and quickly realized that she had a problem on her hand. Within a few months, she bound them together as one.

Truc was called upon to work once again and, while he was away, Soluu would visit with Mila in tow. At this point, I began to teach Soluu and Mila English and I tried my hardest to learn their language while doing so. This gave me a purpose if only but for a short while.

I knew now that any search and rescue efforts on our behalf must have ended long before. I wondered how long my husband kept up the search. I also wondered if he had already taken another wife. I tried to picture who it might be among our single friends. It made my heart sick to think about things like that but the mind will do what it will do.

The hand of God can only explain the next part of my story. The day started with a visit from an officer that I had never noticed before. If I had known what he would later mean to me, I would have been much nicer when we first met. No officers visited my cell. The commander came by rarely but only did so to ridicule me. This officer studied me like a science project for several minutes without a word. I hid in the corner afraid he was sizing me up for execution but then I noticed he was not glaring at me. He seemed to be sympathetic, which was most disconcerting.

He soon left and I did not see him for several days. This pattern maintained for several weeks. He would come and watch me and I would sit quietly waiting for something to happen. He never stayed but for a few minutes at a time then he would leave with no attempt at communicating. I felt like a monkey on display at a zoo.

I felt this way until he returned with a box to sit on one day. I decided that being afraid was a waste of time. This was a huge development for me personally. In a strange way, I had begun to hope he was there to end my agony.

I nearly passed away in shock when he spoke to me in perfect English. He asked me my name and waited for my reply. What I did next shocked me as it came out of my mouth. I told him only if he shared his name first. I suppose this was coming from my newfound desire to be defiant. He quickly obliged and told me his name was Ayumu. I am not sure but I believe that is how you would spell it in English. I found it to be a most pleasant name to say. So I was obliged to reply. I told him my name was Amelia Earhart if anyone cared to know. Ayumu did not respond for several moments which made me most uncomfortable. Then he told me he knew my name but wanted to hear me say it. I told him that I did not feel like playing any games with him and that if he came to annoy me that he needed to leave.

Ayumu studied me as if I was a textbook for the longest time. Then he asked me the strangest question. He wanted to know if I was capable of intelligent conversation or if the punishment had destroyed my mind. I know now that is why he asked me to say my name. I snapped, I told you if you are here to annoy me then leave. He told me that he was most pleased to see that not only was my mind working but that I still had strength to challenge him. Then he left.

I told Soluu about my visitor that evening when she came. I am not sure she understood. I could tell she was under much stress so I let it go.

The next day the officer returned with two guards and I knew at this point that he was there to execute me. He ordered the guards to open my cell and then he told me that it was ok if I wanted to come out. I had not walked for some time and I must have looked like a wet rat trying to be defiant.

Ayumu ordered the guards to enter my cell and to begin cleaning it. This did not take long since there was only a bucket for my refuse and a few blankets. They brought a small bed mat and placed it inside along with a new blanket but that was not the best part. I wept like a baby as they brought a small stool. I will never forget what he said next as long as I live. "I am sorry Ms. Earhart for the rude nature in which you have been treated. I promise you will be shown much more respect now." He then ordered his men to leave and said to me, "I hope this will make things slightly more comfortable until I can find better arrangments," he said to me in the kindest way. With that, he asked me to return to the cell.

For the first time in over a year, I slept on something other than the ground. I sat on my small stool and looked about as if I were seeing everything for the first time. When Soluu and Mila visited that afternoon, they were shocked to find me eating a bowl of rice from the base mess hall. I cannot tell you how human it made me feel to have a bed on which to sleep.

Ayumu returned the next day and opened the cell without a guard present. He asked me if I had slept any better. I noticed he *had with him a change of clothes that were those of a soldier. He asked me if I would walk with him. The walk was slow as I was not use to moving more than a few feet. I must have looked like my grandmother crossing those grounds. Ayumu took me to a small building near the officer's complex in which I was first beaten and I became afraid that I would see the commander. Ayumu assured me it would be ok. Men stopped to watch me as if I were a ghost. When we arrived, Ayumu handed me the set of clothes. He apologized and informed me that they were probably going to be too big. It seems they only had one size. He pointed to the door and said that I could take my time in the bath and that he would remain at guard outside.*

Why were they treating me so well, I asked myself? I didn't understand it. I could not help but feel that I did not deserve a break. I had come to a place where I had accepted my life in a box and the feeling of returning to normal was foreign. Even if normal was just being able to bathe.

After much hesitation and several nods from Ayumu, I went in and closed the door. In the middle of the room was a typical Japanese bath with a large barrel of water and a large dipping spoon. I laid my clothes on a bench and then I noticed it. A mirror! I was afraid to look but I made myself do so. I cried for ten minutes as I realized how disgusting I had become. I was a ghost in a bag of bones. Now I knew why the men stared at me so. Finally, I undressed from the rags that were mine. I was hideous to say the least. It took almost an hour to wash off the filth and never once did the Captain knock on the door.

When I finally came to the door in my clean clothes, he was waiting there looking away. He did not turn until I said his name. He did the kindest thing he could have possibly done for me. Ayumu smiled. I felt as if I was reborn.

On the return to my cell, I found the courage to ask Ayumu about the Commander. I wanted to know why he had allowed the shower and civil treatment. He told me a story of having arrived on base only a few weeks prior and that he had heard of my capture before coming to the island. He said the Commander had informed him that I was to be ignored.

Ayumu stopped short of the cell and told me something I could not have imagined in my wildest dreams. The Commander had died in a plane crash only a few days prior, leaving Ayumu as the senior officer in charge, until command saw fit to send a replacement. He imagined that this could be as short as two weeks to as long as several months. I have to admit that I found solace in the fact that the commander's brand of evil had found its reward. Ayumu then told me that as long as he was in charge, that he would make every effort to improve my condition.

To be clean and human once again was beyond description. Rice and soup were delivered and I worried that Soluu might stop coming if she did not need to bring food. When she arrived, I hid the bowl behind my bed mat. I also worried that the taste of humanity would be taken from me. That somehow it was all a cruel joke. Finally, I told myself that I had to enjoy whatever moments of peace came my way.

29

Slavery

You enslaved my heart to shame
You embraced me in days of pain
No longer do I know who we are
I only know of this space, of this scar

Truc began to look physically uncomfortable. Captain Channing decided it was time to act. "Do you believe, Sir; we could break for a few minutes? I personally could use a soda and I am sure the Lieutenant needs time to rest her voice."

Truc moved rather quickly toward the Electra upon Simpson's nod, as he did not wish to embarrass himself in front of Clair. Ten minutes later, the group found Truc waiting for them as they returned from their sabbatical. Captain Channing brought him a bottle of water, he took a sip and then pointed to a soda. "Drink it slowly," Steve warned.

As he took his first sip of a soda the look on his face made the entire group chuckle.

"I...tickle," he exclaimed.

"I suppose it does," Captain Channing replied.

"Did you work for a long time on the underground base?" Admiral Simpson prodded to change the subject.

"Some who work...they look like Jeep...but they not Jeep. We work long time."

"Do you remember hearing the word Korean?" Admiral Jackson asked.

"I not know...I no...speak Jeep."

"They did use Koreans as labor on many of those island projects...right?" Admiral Simpson asked Jackson.

"They used Korean women as prostitutes to keep their conscripts from going crazy. This may have been happening far earlier than we thought. The Koreans, like the Marshallese, were treated as slaves for the most part."

"Truc did you see other women on the island...women not of your people?" Admiral Simpson asked.

"Yes...sad, sad, girl."

"Did they try to take your women?" Admiral Simpson pressed.

"They come...to take my Mila but...Soluu hide Mila. You see."

With that, Clair opened the journal and regarded her Admiral for permission to begin once again.

The Journal of Amelia Earhart

Captain Ayumu came to visit most every day. He told me that he enjoyed speaking English once again and he pushed me to walk a bit further with every visit. I discovered that he had acquired English while at Stanford. His father was a staff member of the Japanese Ambassador and that he had traveled to America many times before college with his father.

One day, Ayumu took me to the edge of the jungle. A small hut had been erected hastily and he informed me that this was to be my new residence. It was no larger than a small shed but to me it was a palace. The hut came with one condition. I was to remain within fifty meters of the place and he asked me if I could respect him by not running away.

His men seemed most concerned as we walked about most evenings in deep conversation. I took it that many did not agree with him treating me kindly. I felt as if they believed that I should be a dog tied to a stake. Each week Ayumu had fresh clothes delivered and a bath became a regular event. I began to gain weight but I soon learned the rations for everyone on the island were meager as most on the island ate far less than they had been accustomed. Fish and rice were the staples and not much else.

I couldn't help but watch the base and it's coming and going. Most of the light aircraft were delivered by ship but every now and again, a seaplane would arrive. This time with Ayumu and Soluu was delightful! We would sit and practice English or groom one another and I decided that if this was the life I had to live, that I could live it.

One day I asked Ayumu about my Electra. I wanted to know what had caused them to save her. He informed me that they had considered it a spy plane and that they were impressed with its long-range capabilities. It seems several engineers had come to study the Electra during my incarceration. He told me they had stripped her of most of her electronics and sent them back to Japan for study. He then changed the subject and I decided not to press the matter.

Finally, Truc returned after being gone for several weeks. It was almost dark when he appeared. He was tired and thin. I asked him if they were feeding him but it was obvious they were not. This is when I found out that it was up to his people to feed themselves after working most of the day. Most did not feel like fishing or searching for roots and I felt as if something else was wrong but I knew he would not tell me.

I told him about the officer who had taken pity on me. I told him how the officer spoke English and liked talking to me to keep his English skills in order. Truc seemed pleased that I was no longer living like a dog. I told him that I would like to introduce him to the Captain but Truc became frightened; he did not think he would get the same treatment.

I asked Truc if Captain Ayumu was in charge of the business on the other island and to my relief, Truc had not heard the name. I discovered that upon the commander's death, another had taken command of the project. He told me the conditions had become much worse at the hands of the new command. Truc was changing before my eyes but his beautiful smile never left. I worried he would become hard and bitter or die of starvation.

Truc did not return the next day. After several days, I took it upon myself to ask the Captain Ayumu if he had visited the other island since taking over. He told me that he had at first but was not interested in the work and felt like the job was in the hands of a capable officer. I had to try to help Truc and I told him that I thought he should pay the job a visit. He was confused and asked me what I knew about the work on the other island. Then I became worried that I had compromised Truc but I had no way to back up from my previous request. I told Ayumu how Truc had saved me and I told him how he and Soluu had taken care of me. I asked if he could make sure, the islanders were fed properly after working all day. Ayumu became short with me and asked me to return to my hut. His change in demeanor was most upsetting.

I worried all that night as to the damage I may have done. The next day Ayumu did not return. Two days passed before Captain Ayumu returned. This time we walked a long way before he spoke. He had visited the other site and he informed me that conditions for the locals were less than ideal. He had removed the officer in charge and put another in charge with express orders to feed those who worked on the site even if they had to slow down the project.

Ayumu was very heavy and I asked him what was bothering him. The Captain again did not speak for some time. It was then he told me that he was afraid there were forces in motion that believed brutality was necessary to achieve their goals. I found it strange that a commander would tell me such things but the more I thought about it the more it made sense. He could talk to me because no one else understood what he was saying. I was his only safe outlet.

That day was most pleasant as we spent several hours speaking of things. He appreciated our culture and wondered when he would be able to visit again. He then informed me that he had Truc reassigned. I could not sleep that night with joy. It was the first time since my capture that I had been able to make a difference.

It was several days before Truc returned. I believe he was with Mila for those days.

Several weeks later, Captain Ayumu informed me that he had given the orders to have my Electra repaired. Ayumu said it would take some time but he had looked her over personally and he believed she could return to his homeland.

He also told me there had been complaints registered with command over his leadership and his treatment of me. He seemed unaffected by this development.

Truc's reassignment allowed me to keep an eye on him most days. His duties were to do keep the officers' quarters and command center clean. For some time things set into a routine that was acceptable. In the back of my heart, I knew things would change when Ayumu was finished repairing the Electra. It would mean a new Commander or worse yet, one of the previous commander's cronies. Each day I counted now as a blessing.

Our walks gave me hope. I tried to remember each moment, as I knew the walks would end. I could not help but believe I would be a dog again. We all knew that this season must end. As if a child in summer knowing school will begin in the fall, it was best not to talk about such things.

Captain Ayumu was deeply interested in my adventures. I took my time and told him of each flight. The good parts and bad parts and I grew to like him very much. If things had been different, I think I could have allowed myself to love him. In a strange way, I think I did love him if for nothing more than giving me the season of peace before the storm of his departure. Nevertheless, I dared not express these feelings. I was the captive and he was the captor. Yet, he was the only human contact I had beside Truc, Mila and Soluu. I did not want to ruin it.

Truc remained faithful to spend an hour with me each day. I know it was selfish of me to keep him from his young bride after his duties. Many days, she would come and sit but after Truc's return, she made little effort to learn English. It was odd seeing such a young man in love with such a young girl. Their love would have been most inappropriate in our society. However here, where life could end at any moment, it made perfect sense. It brought me much joy to know Truc was happy.

30

The Secret Mission

Take me away
To where I knew my future
Hide me among the thorns of your love
There, let me rest
Among the memory of hopes long lost
Among the life that would have been best

The sun hung low on the horizon as Clair asked Truc, "Is it about to rain again?"

Truc looked to her confused.

"I suggest we break for the evening. I slept on a boat last night and I'm feeling a bit tired," Captain Channing said, as he realized she wanted to stop.

"I suppose you are missing your bunk," Admiral Simpson teased.

"I don't know what you're talking about, Admiral," Captain Channing quipped.

"We will discuss your sleeping habits after this is over Captain Channing," Admiral Simpson chided. He looked to his peer and asked, "Admiral, do you suppose we have covered enough territory?"

"Yes," Jackson responded, "However, I believe we are going to have a hard time putting the Joint Chiefs off for another day."

"This does cause a dilemma," Simpson agreed.

"I think between the two of us, we can give them a reason to remain patient. I see nothing wrong with waiting one more day," Admiral Jackson said with confidence.

"So it shall be. Do you mind if we begin early in the morning?" Admiral Simpson asked Truc.

"Yes...I keep," he replied, as he snatched up the journal.

"Thank you for trusting me and letting me read it for you," Clair said, as she stood to leave.

Truc bowed to say good night to all involved then departed for his vessel.

To Channing's surprise as he watched Truc walk away, he felt Admiral Jackson standing beside him.

"Captain, you've done one hell of a fine job with Truc," Jackson said as he put his hand on Captain Channing shoulder. "I heard you might be looking at a medical discharge. I do have a few reliable sources. Anyhow, I wanted to let you know, if Simpson is stupid enough to let you go, you are welcome on my side of the island. You've shown major initiative Captain."

Captain Channing was shocked. He finally muttered, "Sir, I am flattered at the offer...I will keep it in mind if things don't work out here."

"Son, things have already worked out here," Jackson replied over his shoulder as he headed for his car, with brief case in hand and a smile on his face.

Lieutenant Evans returned to find Steve with tears filled eyes. He was embarrassed and she quickly took him by the arm and led him away.

"Sorry, Lieutenant, I'm a bit overwhelmed," he mumbled as he looked away.

"I understand. This is a lot to take in. The Electra, Truc, the journal; each piece is beautiful in its simplicity."

"Oh, no, Lieutenant, I'm not overwhelmed with Truc. Well ok, I might be. Right now, I am disappointed in myself. I would have quit if this had not occurred. Now, I cannot help but think about how much I have missed. I ran from everyone on this base...because I did not want to be judged. Truc...this whole situation, has allowed me to see what truly matters," he said, as he looked into her eyes and found great warmth.

"I'm sorry. I shouldn't bare my soul this way. It's inappropriate," he mumbled then turned away once again.

Lieutenant Evans mustered her courage up and said, "Captain Channing, I understand. Well, I think...I mean...I am not going blind, so I cannot honestly...share that trauma with you."

She took a moment, composed herself, then tried once again to explain herself. "I understand being angry. I understand being blind with pain...unable to appreciate life. I understand feeling as if you have no control over your situation. The whole world is hurt to some degree. Some more than others, but...I just want you to know...well...I that I understand."

"I appreciate you saying that," he replied while he watched Truc move about his vessel. Finally, Captain Channing began to fidget and said, "I need to go home, get a change of clothes, Lieutenant."

"Sir, we have a secret mission that we must accomplish first," Clair replied.

"A secret mission? How do you know about secret missions before I do?"

She tilted her head and batted her eyes, "It's not what you know Captain, it's...,"

"Who you know," he finished.

"Do you want to know about the secret mission or, do you want to go along and find out?" she asked bluntly.

"I think you should tell me. If Simpson wants us to egg Jackson's car, or fork his yard, I will need to change into black clothing."

"No. Nothing that daring, Captain! He wants me to break you in gently. We will save the toilet paper and forks for another night. By the way, you should know that forking is above your pay grade, Captain."

"OK! I get it. You have the Admiral wrapped around your finger."

"Oh...no Sir. I would sorely disagree."

"What is the secret mission, Clair?" he pressed, then paused, as he realized his faux pas. "I mean, Lieutenant Evans."

She wagged her finger as she playfully scolded. "I think you just broke protocol once again...Captain. You are going to have to do much better if we are going to work together on this secret missions. I will have to insist that we maintain our professional boundaries...Sir."

Now, he wanted to know what it was she had dreamed up, and huffed to let her know.

"The Admiral wants us to sneak Truc off the base tonight," she whispered.

"What," he snapped. "How do you propose we do that Lieutenant? The press is camped at the front gate and boats are circling the place as we speak."

"The Admiral is going home by driver tonight. He will stop at the front gate, and make a short statement about the how the investigation is going. He is leaving us his S.U.V. and has specifically ordered us to take Truc to Mo Mo's. He thinks she would relate well to Truc and...that he would like her food. He wants us to begin acclimating Truc. Mo Mo's is private and, she is closing the place down for us," she replied, sounding as if a schoolgirl who could not hide her excitement.

"How are we going to get him to the SUV without anyone noticing?"

"Captain, you are the senior officer. I would expect you to formulate our plan of attack."

He decided to concede the argument and walked away shaking his head. She was a handful, and he was beginning to love each and every moment that he was in her presence.

31

A Night
To Remember

I am the new day
I carry the sun on my shoulders
I hold the world in my depths
I will be loved
I will be hated
And from you
I will never be separated

They found Admiral's S.U.V parked on the far side of the administrative offices. Captain Channing's plan involved stowing away in the back of the vehicle and so he commandeered a tarp and a dark regulation t-shirt for Truc.

The mission kicked off with a fizzle. At first, Clair could not open the car doors, leaving the odd group exposed by the light of the parking lot. Clair quickly decided that she must have picked up the wrong set of keys and returned to her office to find the correct set obviously annoyed. In the meantime, two enlisted happened by, forcing Captain Channing to give orders that would keep them chasing rabbits for hours. Next, in their series of unfortunate events, try as he might, he could not make the back seats fold away.

As he waited in the front seat, Truc inspected the instrument panel with the curiosity of a child. He played with the dials and pushed buttons until Clair discovered the seat release, with that, Truc, was ordered to the back of the vehicle. Captain Channing explained that they needed to lie down and then pulled the tarp over their heads, only to realize, it was far too short.

As he struggled to make the tarp work, Clair became exasperated and she tapped on the wheel with a nervous rhythm. Steve finally snapped, "Just go, Lieutenant. If they see us, we will have to turn back and close the base."

It was the first real order he had truly expressed to Clair and she found it to be exhilarating to hear him speak with authority. There is a Captain in there, she thought.

"Yes Sir, Captain," she responded.

She called ahead and the M.P.'s at the gate cleared a dozen reporters away as the S.U.V passed. After a mile, Captain Channing began to sit up until Clair yelled, "Stay down! I think we are being tailed...he has made every turn I have. What do I do now?"

In the midst of the two officers panic, Truc, giggled with delight.

"Lieutenant, I want you to go to a well-lit gas station."

"Are you crazy!" she snapped, "I mean are you crazy...Sir!"

"Take us to the gas station Lieutenant, and once there, begin pumping gas. Keep pumping gas as long as the tail remains. Think about it, people who have something to hide, do not stop and fill up. You have nothing to hide, Lieutenant. It will look as right as rain...if you play it cool."

"You're devious, Sir...I like that about you. May I get a soda while we are there? You know the... natural looking thing. I'll buy both of you one if you like!"

"Don't push it, Lieutenant."

Clair found the next gas station, and as it happened, it looked to be the brightest on the island. A moment later, their tail entered the station, looking as if he were not interested, and for his benefit, she made a grand show of searching for her credit card and undoing the gas cap as if she had never done it before. She extended the task of filling the SUV by acting as if she had chipped a nail while checking her engine oil. Finally, the man returned to his car with a soda in hand and left. The plan had worked, she hoped.

"You owe me one hundred and five dollars. How the hell does he afford to drive this thing?" she asked as she returned to the driver's seat.

"Is he still there Lieutenant?"

"Oh no, that jerk left at about...ninety five dollars."

"Let's get out of here, before someone else comes to snoop around."

Captain Channing helped Truc to the front seat and he watched on with glee as the lights of the small towns flashed before him.

Luck, however, did not remain on their side. Two miles away from Mo Mo's, a state trooper pulled them over and Clair froze, as if a kid caught with her hand in the cookie jar. She rolled down her window, knowing that Captain Channing was not in a seat, or for that matter, buckled up. Her nerves remained on edge as the officer places his lights beam upon Truc, who was smiling from ear to ear. He then returned to Captain Channing, whom he could see was physically sweating. Suddenly, the officer exclaimed, "Is that you Sissy?"

"David, David Talonga? Wow, you look great in a uniform. I haven't seen you since high school," Lieutenant Evans exclaimed, obviously relieved.

\

"I heard you joined the Coast Guard like your old man," the officer said, all the while keeping his light on Captain Channing.

"Yeah, I did!" she replied.

"Sissy, is there something wrong with this picture? What...what is that box the old man is holding, and who is this gentleman in the back?" officer Talonga asked as he slowly unsnapped his holster.

"David, may I get out of the vehicle and speak with you privately...please?"

"Sure, Sissy, but tell these two to stay put."

"You heard the man, stay put, boys," she ordered as she stepped away from the car.

Lieutenant Evans took officer Talonga by the arm and spoke with him in a muted tone as she led him away. After five minutes, she gave the officer a kiss on his cheek and returned to the SUV. Without hesitation, she put on her seat belt and cranked the vehicle as Officer Talonga stepped up to her window, flashed the light in Captain Channing and said, "I'm sorry sir. I promise...no one will bother you the rest of the evening."

Captain Channing looked to him dumbfounded, with mouth agape, as he didn't know how to reply.

We will come back this way in a few hours. Keep an eye out please!" Clair exclaimed.

"I will Sissy," the officer responded timidly, causing Steve to wonder to what degree did he know her.

And with his promise in her hand, she gave the SUV a good punch and peeled off into the night.

"What did you tell him?" Steve asked.

"I told him, that you were the Admiral, and that Truc was...well...Truc."

"You said what! I could be busted for impersonating an officer of higher command. Are you crazy?" he replied.

"Calm down Captain. I told him the truth. He is good people. He is going to wait and make sure no one is following, and when we return, he has offered to escort us back to the base!"

"How do you know he's not going to call the press himself?"

"We dated in high school. I was a sophomore he was a junior. I broke it off with him, but...he still has a crush on me. Plus, he eats lunch at Mo Mo's all the time."

"Are we going to meet anymore boyfriends tonight Lieutenant?"

"He look...like nice man...Ms. Clair," Truc interjected.

"He is, Truc. He is a very nice man. These are good people around here. You would like most of them if you lived here. They love the sea almost as much as you," she replied.

"As far as your question, Captain...it's possible. This is my old stomping ground, and let's just say...I was very popular."

Captain Channing decided to fold his cards. He knew he was in way over his head with Clair and another question may bring an answer he did not wish to hear..

32

Hospitality

The caress of night
Among those who wait
Steal me home
Seal my fate
Racing toward the dark
Where shall I hide
Among the shadows of my heart

T he greeting was the same as the previous evening.
Clair ran to her beautiful Mo Mo as she called to
her tiny Sissy, and as if a repeat performance, Mo Mo took
her Sissy up in her signature bear hug.

"I see you came back for more, Captain. I knew you
would. No one ever eats only once at Mo Mo's," the gay
old woman said as she squeezed Steve's cheeks together.
She then looked over the odd little man standing beside
Captain Channing and forcefully held back tears.

"This is Truc, Mo Mo," Clair said as if introducing her
new fiancé. Having heard enough of the pleasantries, Mo

Mo swooped in like a mother bird and smothered Truc between her ample breasts in a monstrous hug. Truc, for a moment, seemed to disappear into the flower print dress that looked to have been worn more than it should have been. Covered in flower and sampling stains, Mo Mo smelled most inviting to Truc, and when she released him from her grip, his grand smile froze the moment in time.

"I have cooked the best food for you!" she exclaimed, as she took Truc by the hand and proceeded to the porch with him in tow. Immediately a TV caught his attention, and for the first time, Truc witnessed his Electra at sea and for that matter a TV. He looked to Steve for answers as he did not understand the strange devise hanging on the wall.

"Those are moving pictures...from an airplane in the sky," Steve explained. Truc remained confused and so Steve offered an option, "When we are through eating, we can watch the TV if you like."

Before he could reply, Mo Mo, pulled him through the next set of doors and onto the back porch. There, she placed him at the head of the table and fussed over him as if he were the Governor.

The night sky and the ocean below were calm and a gentle trade wind crossed the porch. It cooled the days sweltering heat but it had no effect on Mo Mo. Then, with a clap of her hands, as if summoning all her servants, Mo Mo began for the kitchen at a pace unnatural to her girth.

Truc was up and about before the door closed behind her, studying the workings of the place and the pictures on the walls. Captain Channing decided to turn off the TV as he attempted to explain the different items.

Clair watched on with great satisfaction for having brought them to her grandmothers. A sense of destiny swept over her as she watched the two men interact. Captain Channing caught her watching them and an awkward smile passed between the two officers as neither broke eye contact, until Truc asked, "What...this?"

"We call that a salt shaker, Truc. Tip it over your hand and shake it a few times. Salt will come out. Taste it," Steve said.

"Taste...like sea?" Truc responded. He made a long sour face and then wiped his tongue with both hands.

"It's for the food. You will see in a moment," Clair stated.

"She...was always...Mo Mo...Ms. Clair?" Truc asked.

"Yes, Truc, she has always been my Mo Mo."

"I like...her name."

"My father called her Mo Mo, when he was only a boy, because he could not say mama. So, Mo Mo, stuck."

At that moment, as if summoned, the generously proportioned Mo Mo burst through the kitchen doors supporting two trays of authentic Hawaiian fare in her two arms. She laid each on a large table in the center of the restaurant and motioned for all to come inside, only to speed off once again for two more dishes in her kitchen.

Truc surveyed the feast in awe as he had never viewed so much food in one place. Mo Mo made one last trip and returned once again with two large pitchers of her famous pineapple tea. She hovered about the table like a mother hen watching over her chicks, bristling with expectation.

Clair dutifully began to explain the ingredients of each dish and the proper way to eat them, and before he knew it, Truc's plate was full.

As if a child in preschool, Truc began to examine the utensils as he tried to find the one that looked most looked like Clair's.

"Amelia, she make...fork. It look like Ms. Clair...fork. She make it...from Electra," he said as he lifted his fork, seemingly practicing for the event.

Perspiration began to visibly race down Mo Mo's brow as she was afraid the feast would be too foreign for his pallet. Truc, ever the showman, embraced each dish as if it was his last, and with each big grin that followed, Mo Mo, clapped for joy.

"Slow down! We have all evening to eat," Steve insisted.

The pineapple tea turned out to be Truc's favorite and he consumed several glasses before pushing away from the table with a deep sigh of satisfaction.

Mo Mo, still unsatisfied with her masterpiece, asked if she could fetch more food him and was genuinely disappointed when he begged off by holding his belly and moaning as if he would pop. As if set up on a successful blind date, Truc and Mo Mo began to talk and tell each other stories. Finally, Mo Mo asked Truc if he would like to sit on the back porch with her. He agreed and followed her waddling as if he were pregnant. Soon, both carried on like long lost friends in what was to be a new experience for Truc, rocking chairs.

The two officers remained inside and watched on in amazement at the instant friendship blooming before them. Never a spoken word between as they enjoyed the moment and yet the silence was not awkward.

Clair began to pick up dishes and take them to the kitchen. Steve offered to help but she refused since he was a guest. Then after several trips, Clair could stand it no longer and decided it was time. "Would you like to go for a walk on the beach with me, Captain?" she asked pensively.

His heart leapt at the invitation. He barely swallowed his Pineapple tea as he said, "I would enjoy that very much...Lieutenant."

With that, she made for the side door that led to the beach and Steve watched on as if mesmerized by her way of walking.

Truc, completely unaware, carried on about turtle's, currents and waves. Mo Mo on the other hand, never missed anything that happened in her restaurant and winked at Steve as he looked back to her for permission.

He felt his way down the unlit steps and found Clair standing by the water. The cool sand beneath his feet felt foreign, as he had not stood on a beach since the news of his eyesight. A full moon framed Clair as she pulled Bobbie pins from her hair and allowed it to fall to her waist. She swept it from one side to the other to release the tangles of the day and then she pulled it into a loose ponytail.

"I've been waiting to do that all night. There is only one thing I hate about my job. The Bobby pins!" she announced as she ran her fingers through her long, thick black hair and breathed a deep sigh of relief.

Steve was convinced if she had chosen to become a model that she would have been famous for she was a rare beauty hidden in a package of United States Coast Guard regulation couture. He remained quietly beside Clair taking in her perfume as if a drowning man-seeking air, all the while hoping for something to break the tension. He knew she would never break the code and he dared not for fear of offending her.

Clair remained quiet as she stared ahead at the moons reflection upon the ocean. Steve knew deep within that he did not need to speak. He would stand here all night he told himself, if that was what she wanted but the gentle lap of the waves against the shoreline kept time for the two as if demanding a verdict. Moments became an eternity. The evening had been far too perfect he thought, to ruin it by saying something stupid at this point. He buried his feet deep into the black sand and stared up at the stars, asking for a sign, any sign.

Finally, Clair turned, looked deep into his eyes and asked, "So, how do we go about this?"

"What do you mean, Lieutenant?" he replied, obviously shaken by the fact that she had cut through the maze of regulations with one simple question.

"Captain, we are not at work. We are on my Mo Mo's beach. On Mo Mo's beach...my name is Clair."

"Oh...Ok, well then...Clair, my name is Steve on Mo Mo's beach," he said as if to parry, but somehow, his response felt like a clumsy reply.

Clair leaned in close, inches separating their two worlds, and asked once again, "Steve...how do we go about this?"

His eyes could not hide the fact that he wanted to know her intimately, so bad he could taste her, but how could he tell her that he thought? Was she truly asking what he thought she was asking? The tension that lay between them was undeniable, the night beckoned for an answer.

"I do want to go about this...if this is what I think this is, Clair. Can we go about this?" he finally asked, fumbling for a safe place to land.

Clair slowly took off his glasses, put them in his shirt pocket and placed her hand on his chest as she whispered, "Steve...please...don't make me ask again."

He did not need to be asked again. He took her into his arms and kissed her with a passion he did not know he had still and she responded in kind. She tasted far sweeter than he had imagined and he found his hands racing through her long dark hair uncontrollably. Perhaps, it was the pineapple tea, he thought, or perhaps, he was thirsty for love and no longer remembered the sweet taste of a woman. Either way, he consumed her gift as if a dry desert embracing its first rain in years. As she responded to his every touch, he soon found himself struggling to find a safe place for his hands. He could not stop, and to his relief, she returned his kiss ever more passionately as he touched her breasts for the first time.

"Wow...that was better than I expected," she gasped as she caught her breath and held his hand to her chest.

"I've wanted that kiss since the first day I met you," he admitted as he pulled her close once again.

She took him by the waist with both hands and initiated the next long kiss. For the first time in a year, he allowed his fear to follow the wind as he gave into her embrace. He needed to trust her. He needed to know her.

Clair suddenly stopped and looked the porch to confirm that Truc and Mo Mo were not watching. As she had hoped, she discovered Mo Mo and Truc fast asleep. The food, conversation, and rockers had accomplished the job. Her plan and its execution were perfect, she thought.

She then took Steve by the hand and led him around a rock outcrop with great care and gentle words. The exercise was one of trust for Steve and he gave himself to her leading completely. Clair then pulled him in tight once again as the porch fell out of view behind the outcrop of rock, and she began to kiss him as if she were as thirsty as he was for love.

The moon, the stars, the wind and the waves seemingly celebrated their union as he tried to take in all that was Clair. He felt his loin's begin to burn, and he knew she knew. His desire, for all of her, was a secret he could no longer hide.

A storm began to brew behind her dark brown eyes, a mischievous look he had never seen in her before. He knew then she was planning something he had not considered possible only minutes before. Clair pulled away from his grasp and stared at him, as if he were hers to do with, as she liked, as if he were hers to consume. She wanted him to look at her. She wanted him to see the prize for being patient and silent when it mattered. In one smooth motion, Clair took off her top and tossed it to a nearby rock. Her bra soon followed and his heart stopped at the sight of her dark olive breasts glistening in the moon light.

"Let's go for a swim," she teased with a wink as she unzipped her skirt and raced for the ocean.

33

Lovers Secrets

Swept away as if a wind
The salt of your breath still on my skin
Our hearts shared as hope
Embrace me now
On the sands of love

Clair found a towel stored on the lower deck and she took her time as she removed the sand from his naked torso. She could fall madly in love with Steve, she thought, as she did her best to tease him. For the first time in her life, she felt safe with man.

The full moon settled about them like a blanket as the two lovers dressed each other, and then settled into a large deck chair. Steve decided that he would allow her to tell him what was next. She had done a great job so far, he thought. However, as hard as he tried, his racing heart would not allow him kill the elephant in the room. He held her tight and hoped she would understand that he had to ask.

"Clair, I would understand if you decided that this was a mistake."

"Are you saying that you want this to be the last of it?" she replied with a deep sigh.

"Oh no - that's is not what I meant at all. It's just that...why would you want to have anything to do with me... I feel like broken goods."

"I know what that feels like. I've been smashed on the ground before," she answered as she ran her hand through his dark red hair and kissed him gently on the cheek. "I was angry; so angry that I could not see the forest for the trees. I've had a hard time trusting men ever since, it took me years to let my anger go."

Steve did not know how to reply or where she was going and decided it best to remain quiet.

She began to run her hands down his buttoned shirt and sighed as her mind trialed away for a moment.

"I have watched you fight for Truc. I have watched you stand up to Jackson and Admiral Simpson. Steve...a man with courage, is a very sexy man and you have a rare courage, a kind of courage that can only be found in someone who understands suffering."

"What about David. You must have a boyfriend on the island?" he asked through the press of her fingers on his lips.

"I dated a lot of guys in high school. I needed them to make me feel loved. They gave me value. David was no more than a high school fling. I haven't had time to have a serious relationship since I returned."

He held to Clair tightly and thanked God for the night, but he had to ask one more question.

"I've noticed that you and Mo Mo...well...I've noticed that you talk about your dad but I have never heard you once say anything about your mother."

Clair let out another deep sigh and dropped her eyes at the thought of explaining her mother.

"My mother married soon after my father passed away," she began. "I was a daddy's girl...and her decision to get married again, so soon, broke my heart. My father wasn't even cold...as they say."

"I'm sorry...I didn't mean to..."

"No, no...it's OK...I have made peace with the story. It's not pleasant but I feel like I should tell you. It wasn't that an ass married my mom. I would have hated the man if my mom had married him years later," she said before she paused and took another deep breath as if trying to process what to say next. "My stepfather...he was the worst type of man. He was a user...and when he finished using my mother...he would sometimes...use me."

Steve desperately wanted the right thing to say but nothing would land on his tongue as the horror what she endured hit him hard.. Clair knew this and put a finger on his lips to silence him. She didn't need him to say anything.

"Maybe, that was too much...too fast. I would understand if you," she started.

He quickly placed a finger to her lips as he whispered, "I'm not scared of the truth, Clair. I am amazed...that I am here with you. Everything there is to know about you, I want to know it. Everything...and I promise...everything you tell me will remain safe with me."

She looked away as her mind rushed to places she had tried hard to forget. Tears began to overtake her defenses as she decided she needed to tell him the entire story.

"This bad habit of his...me...went on for several months. He soon decided that he liked me more than he liked my mother and I am positive she knew what he was doing. That is what I mean when I say...I was angry. I will always hate that man...but my true anger...it comes from knowing that mother did nothing to stop him. She was responsible for bringing him into our house and that reality I can never change. My mother did drugs as her way of dealing with it. I have even wondered if she didn't encourage his behavior. All I remember of her was the drinking and the drugs now. And when she was passed out...he would come to me."

Steve felt her relax and he hoped the story was near its end.

"It was a messed up scene for a teenage girl. There was plenty of money from Daddy's insurance policy, so neither had to work, and I tried to stay away from the house by hanging out here with Mo Mo. I remember feeling lost. I remember feeling as if the darkness would never leave."

The sound of two old people snoring filled the night air above and she relaxed even further as she listened to the rhythmic sound of snoring, seemingly, timed to the waves as they crashed on the shoreline.

"Mo Mo, was the first to notice a change in me. I had become withdrawn and moody...I snapped at her several times. I even threatened to run away so, she began to ask questions. Of course, I didn't tell her, but she knew. I don't know how she knew...but she knew. I was about fourteen when all this happened."

She turned to study Steve's face and she wondered if she should tell him the rest of the story. It was time to tell someone, she thought, and hoped Steve would be able to handle the truth.

"One day, two of Mo Mo's older brothers asked my stepfather if he wanted to go spear fishing. My father's family is the best anglers on the island and my great uncles are a very superstitious group. They would never take a mainlander or even someone from the other side of the island. Fishing here is a family tradition, shared only with those you love and trust. My stepfather, as stupid as he was, thought nothing of it; that my two great uncles, who never once took an interest in him, suddenly wanted to spend time fishing with him. He was such a drunk; he had no clue what was coming."

"To this day, my great uncles claim, that a shark attacked my stepfather as they were spear fishing. The story would be humorous, if it was not so sad. According to my great uncles, the shark was so large that it cut him in half on the first strike, and then, according to them, it dragged his upper torso away on the second strike. The authorities never found any trace of him. They questioned my Mo Mo about the incident but nothing ever came of it. I believe the whole town knows what happened out there, but no one talks about it; that's the way it is around here. Family takes care of family and neighbors keep each other's secrets."

Clair had never told a man her story and the release was powerful. She pressed on, "I stayed away from my mother as much as possible by working for Mo Mo. I have never been able to forgive her for not stopping him. Not long after, my stepfather's unfortunate death, I moved in with my Mo Mo. As you can see, she is my safe place."

"What happened to your mother?"

"The last I heard she was a bank teller. I think she is afraid to come back here. She moved soon after I left to live with Mo Mo and she married again a few weeks later. I believe she has married four or five times since. She sends me an invitation each time."

"So how did you move past what happened?"

"When I was in college, I had another incident, with a fraternity brother. I beat the living hell out of him and he called the police on me. Something in me broke that night as I sat in jail for assault. I knew then that I would no longer be a victim, and that I have a power few can understand because of what happened to me. I can't tell you when...it was not long after the frat brother...I just knew that I was no longer angry."

"You beat the crap out of him?"

"Yeah buddy...with a baseball bat...so watch yourself," she quipped as she punched him in the arm.

"How did you get into officer training with a record?"

"Oh...the charges were dropped the next day. They found my cell phone at the frat house. Much to his surprise, I had the sense to record the incident."

"Clair, if we are going to be, whatever this is going to be...and I want us to be..."

He stopped and tried to find a way to say what was on his heart.

"You do understand that I will be completely blind in less than a year?" he asked. "How can I expect anyone to take on such a burden?"

Clair rolled over, kissed him once again, then pressed her pelvis into his as she whispered, "If I have learned anything in the last few days...it would be to live life, and go for what you want. I want you Steve...and I want to be brave like Amelia. I do not know why I want you. I believe we will work out the details as time allows, but for now, enjoy what is shared with you freely!

She began to roll her hips into hi, as she felt him fill with passion. Her wry smile returned as she ground hard against him. "Besides, you may not like me when you see how anal retentive I am," she quipped.

"I've seen a bit of that already...I think I can live with it, Sissy," he replied.

"I want to make a deal with you," she said ever so gently. "If you let me...I will try to be your eyes...as long you, remain true north to my compass. Is that a deal?"

Tears began to fall and he found that he could not speak as she forced him back into the chair, and kissed him with abandon. The deal was sealed.

34

Running With
The Law

Lost in the setting sun
I waited for your love
Lost in the setting son
You kept my heart above

Mo Mo and Truc waited like parents for their delinquent daughter to be returned from prom. Mo Mo raised an eye while Truc smiled like a coach whose quarterback had scored the winning touchdown as the two officers returned from the beach.

Clair attempted to restore her hair to the regulation bun with the few bobby pins that she had been able to rescue from the sand as she rushed to the restroom. She wore little makeup, but her amorous adventure would be obvious to anyone on base, she thought as she studied herself in the mirror.

A knock at the front door of the restaurant boomed in the midst of her makeover, causing her to smear her lipstick. As she peeked about the bathroom door, she found Mo Mo standing at the entrance talking to Officer Talonga. Panic set in as she made her way across the room. She immediately regretted the decision to leave the restroom as David physically reacted at the sight of her. She tried not to validate his assumptions but it was of little use as Talonga stared at her as if a memory had returned that he had long enjoyed.

"Sissy," he said, as he looked her up and down, "someone came along and he is definitely a reporter." He finally broke his gaze. "I told him he had to wait as I took my time setting up a roadblock. I hoped that he might turn around. Thirty minutes later...more arrived. I had to call in back up and I cannot keep the road closed forever. There are several dozen of them now and we are having a hard time convincing them that he is not here," Talonga said as he pointed to Truc.

Clair's face drew blank, she had been positive they had lost the tail. How, she thought, did they find her?

Captain Channing decided it was time to take over and asked, "Do you have an exit plan officer? They cannot know that Truc is here. They will never leave Mo Mo alone if they find out.

"No sir. There is only one-way out of here...other than the sea. We are prepared to give you an escort back to the base if necessary."

"Officer Talonga...I am right...it is Talonga?" Captain Channing asked. The officer nodded in the affirmative as Captain Channing decided that he needed to put himself between the officer and Clair. She took the opportunity he offered and returned to the bathroom.

"We will need that escort. Call your men and tell them to be ready to make a path through the reporters," Steve ordered as if on the deck of a cutter. Talonga snapped to attention and responded as if one of Captain Channing's men. A moment later, he was at his squad car giving orders by radio to half the officers in his district.

Steve looked to Mo Mo and said, "I am sorry. You will be hounded by them for weeks to come."

"I will not say a word...unless they buy lunch. I might tell them something then. Business has been slow lately. I could use the boost," she replied, amused by her own sarcasm. "I promise Captain, I will tell them nothing, until you say that it is OK," she finally responded. "But, you have to promise me one thing."

"What is that Mo Mo?" he asked.

"You better take good care of my Sissy...or for that matter...Mr. Truc. If you don't...I will come looking for you," she said as she put her hand on her hip.

Steve considered her brothers and nervously replied, "I will take good care of both. I promise."

● ● ●

Ten minutes later, officer Talonga's squad car barreled past the reporters with an SUV in close pursuit. Clair would later discover that she looked a little disheveled in the paper, as a dozen cameras' captured their escape.

Three squad cars fell in behind the S.U.V., and the small entourage passed through one small town after another. Officers began to leap frogged ahead in order to stop traffic before the convoy, all the while Truc was beside himself with joy. He held to the dash and whooped with excitement, as it was all Clair could do to keep up with officer Talonga.

Steve called ahead and a path through the gate cleared, at the last moment. The event would make the morning papers, but until then, their mission had been successful.

Clair hid the S.U.V. behind the administration office once again and thanked all involved. Truc shook each of the officer's hands and as he passed each, the officers removed their hats in respect for they each knew this would be a night to tell to their grandchildren.

"Thank you for helping us out of a very sticky situation...we are very grateful...however, I must ask that you leave the base because, technically, all of you are in violation of our Admiral's orders. I promise, we will be contacting your superiors and advising them of the excellent job you did tonight," Captain Channing said, before he made his way to officer Talonga personally.

"You better take care of my Sissy," Talonga whispered as Steve shook his hand thankfully.

"You're the second person to tell me that tonight," Steve quipped.

"I'm not joking, Captain. I know where you live now," Talonga pressed as he smiled a knowing smile.

As the police dissipated and the guard detail returned to post, Captain Channing put his arm about Truc's shoulders and led him away. Clair exchanged one last wink with her Captain and made like a bandit to her private bunk, before anyone else noticed her disheveled disposition.

"You...Okeydokey," Truc ribbed as they made their way across the dock.

"Yes I am...I am Okeydokey," Captain Channing replied. "Oh, soooo Okeydokey!"

35

Truc's Gift

A billion stars call my name
A billion stars chase this dream
A billion stars will wait for me
For a billion nights if but to see
One truth complete in me

Sleep came slowly to Captain Channing as he lay in the net and stared at the stars above. The adrenaline rush was over, yet his mind would not turn off. All the while, Truc remained busy beside him, working on a section of rope made from a thin vine, as if he knew, he needed to keep his friend company. The process of making rope looked to be meticulous and Steve knew the art had to be lost to the modern world as he watched on and listened to Truc hum one ancient tune after another. The song was graceful, gentle to the ear, and he wondered if the tune were a lullaby that had been sung to Truc as a child. As sweet as it was, the melody would not put him to sleep tonight as rapturous visions of his night with Clair filled his mind. Her gift had been more than he ever expected of her and he wondered once again what it was she saw in him. His confidence was returning and he knew that after tonight he would never be the same. Clair had made sure of that.

"How did you learn such things?" Steve asked.

"I learn...father...uncle," Truc replied.

"So they taught you how to make that type of rope?"

"Mila, she make...this new rope...when I wreck first time...with Amelia. Mila make this rope...a rope that will not break. My Electra...is very heavy...Electra break old rope I make...this is new Mila rope."

"You obviously loved her very much."

Truc never stopped wrapping the vine as he replied, "I love Mila...like you love...Ms. Clair."

"Is it that obvious, Truc?"

The old man only chuckled as he kept his hard dry hands working the grey strips of vine.

"Love...to .love okeydokey...Steveee. I...keep her secret...you not worry."

"Thank you. I am sure Ms. Clair will appreciate your discretion?"

Truc looked to Steve confused.

"Discretion...it means that you know how to keep a secret."

"Ohhh...I keep secret...long...long time," Truc replied, as if Steve had found a nerve filled with memories.

Captain Channing leaned against the hull satisfied that Truc would not sell him out. He would fall asleep fast if he could only remove the vision of Clair running to the ocean nude from his mind and that was not about to happen.

"I show you...how make rope."

"Not tonight Truc, how about another day. Today was a very long day...a very good day...but very long."

"I eat...too much. My tummy hurt." Truc added.

"Have you ever had so much food in your life!"

Truc once again did not answer; as if he did not wish to lose time on the subject of food.

"I show you...how make rope. You...learn make rope. I teach you," he pressed as he held out the piece he was working on.

"I'm sure I do...but not tonight, Truc, like I said, another day."

"May not be a new day," Truc replied with a whisper, in near perfect English

"Did you say there may not be another day?"

Truc did not answer. He took up another piece of vine and doubled his effort.

The thought suddenly crossed Captain Channing's heart, why is he still making rope. Had he failed to process all that Truc was saying to him?

"Did you just say that you built the Electra and that you wrecked her? Where is that boat, Truc?"

"This same boat."

"What did you mean...to bring Amelia? Was she alive the first time you tried to leave on this boat?"

Truc simply shrugged his shoulders. Captain Channing decided to try again and asked, "Are we going to find out tomorrow what happened to Amelia?"

Truc put the rope down and stared at Steve as if he were worried about his answer. He rubbed his head and looked to the stars.

"I will go soon...finish what Amelia...what Amelia ask me to finish. I make promise to Amelia...I will keep promise."

"Why would you want to leave here? The journal is safe. I am sure Amelia would want you to stay here, Truc. You finished the journey. You've made it," Steve exclaimed, as he looked to Truc exasperated.

Truc remained silent- his smile visibly hidden away.

"You have finished the journey...haven't you?"

Truc returned to making rope once again, as if determined the piece had to be completed.

Steve stood and began to move about the netted area, frustrated by the lack of conversation. He began to study the vessel once again. He felt that Truc was trying to tell him something...something he had missed. The vessel looked to be different but he could not put his finger on it. The details, the placement of the sail, the depth of artisan ship, all slowly began to tell a story he had not considered.

The realization of what Truc was intending to do came as if a rush, as he finally understood that the artisanship involved, that each control line, that every item aboard the Electra, must have been tested first. Nothing about the Electra was standard. She was a study in adaptation. He knew then, as he watched Truc take fifteen minutes to finish one inch of rope, that if he had accomplished her construction alone, it would have taken him decades to complete the work. He suddenly felt as if he had been trying to put the pieces of a puzzle together, without the picture on the box.

Steve sat next to Truc and asked, "You want to tell me...don't you, but you can't. You promised Amelia that you would not tell us everything and you...you keep your promises a long, long time."

Truc began to adjust the line of an outer stanchion. The work was tedious and he took his time as Captain Channing stood watch over him. It was then, that it hit Steve what was different about the Electra. Truc had repaired, replaced, or reinforced every binding on the Electra since their arrival. .

"You're still building the Electra. You're repairing her because your journey is not complete?" he said as he held his hands to his forehead.

"Truc, they will never let you leave with that journal. That journal...is a national treasure! This boat...is a national treasure," he snapped.

"I not take book. Amelia tell me...give commandaaar. I give to Ms, Clair...Ms,. Clair give you...you give commandaaar."

Then, as if finding a volume unnatural to his small frame, he exclaimed, "Electra, my boat...I build Electra...I go...soon."

Steve's head began to spin as he tried to imagine Amelia Earhart cooking up a plan with Truc to escape Hawaii. He looked to the stars above and tried to recall every conversation he had had with Truc. And now, what he believed to be the agenda, what Simpson and Jackson had thought to be the plan, did not matter now, as they had never once asked Truc if he had another agenda.

Before he could think of another question to ask, Truc sprung across the netting, like a trampoline toward the main hull. He lifted the cowling and began to wave to for his friend to follow.

"You bring...light," he ordered as he pointed to the inside of the Electra.

"You mean this flashlight?" Steve taunted as he flicked it off and on.

"Come Steveeee...you help me," Truc pressed.

Bewildered by Truc's sudden desire for him to enter the Electra, Captain Channing fixed his footing on the loose netting and wobbled across. Exhaustion had begun to set in, along with a headache that crawled up his spine with conviction. It was all too much for one evening, he thought as held on to a stay for dear life.

"Come...I show. You see...Okeydokey," Truc said to encourage Steve as he rubbed his shoulder like a father.

"I'm sorry, Truc; unless you have some good medicine down there, I don't think I could be any more tired," he mumbled.

"I have...very good medicine," Truc replied as he disappeared into the inner hull.

Steve turned on the flashlight and dutifully followed. The space below deck quickly began to feel small as they worked around netting that separated the bow from the stern. After several feet, yet another net separated what looked to be Truc's food stores. Finally, he found himself negotiating a large object in the midst of the hull. He determined the structure to be the mounting counterweight that connected the wing to rest of the vessel. He thought the design to be an ingenious use of raw materials and that it would take mechanical engineers years to figure it out the process.

The crawl space was cramped but dry, as compared to the living space and he felt as if he were spelunking as he worked past the wing mount. With one last effort, he pushed aside the last obstacle and was surprised to see yet another bulkhead fifteen feet beyond his hand. He planted his light on the bulkhead and he knew immediately that he was looking at the cabin door of the Electra. Truc tugged on a chord near his head and the door popped open with little effort. If not for the grin that spread from ear to ear on Truc, Steve would have thought Truc to be a carnie inviting children into a house of horrors as the light illuminated him from the chin up.

He pushed the door open and his eyes grew wide. Before him, lay the cockpit of Amelia's Electra with the twin rudder controls looking as if they had only been used yesterday. His heart began to pound, and his breath labored as he studied the space with his small light. Steve knew the cockpit was a time capsule of unimaginable worth, with each instrument locked into its final position. All the cockpit needed, were the two seats and her pilots, he thought.

"Oh my God Truc!"

Steve suddenly felt like Howard Carter opening King Tut's tomb as a light dust hung in the air. The space tasted stale, dark and bone dry. How Truc had preserved it he could not imagine. His exhaustion and stress headache fell away as his mind raced to remember the moment.

Truc waited patiently for his friend to embrace the scene. His exuberant heart present in his every move as he hovered over Steve.

"What is in the box...on the left side?" Steve asked.

Truc let out deep sigh as he had waited a long time to share the contents of the box.

"Open box. You see," he replied.

Steve crawled into the cockpit and searched for a safe place to sit. After several false starts he finally settled and began to study the box made of a rough-hewn lumber, bound by hand made joints of leather, which appeared to be as old as the plane.

"Open," Truc pressed Steve once again.

Sweat began to race across Steve's brow and he could barely breathe as he put the light in his mouth to free up a hand. As he bent over the box and ran his hands across the edge he discovered what he was looking for; a small latch. He focused the light by adjusting his head and he could see that the small peg was all that held the binding in place. His hands began to shake as he lifted the strap, laid it back, and slowly opened the box.

36

Step One

Come away my beloved
Come

Captain Channing burst from the Electra and leapt across the netting like an old pro toward the dock as he made for the office complex at top speed. Below deck, the rumbles of Truc laughing echoed into the night as Steve sprinted to the administration building, white as a ghost, searching for signs of life. He quickly wound through the maze of halls, turning on every light in the process, before he scaled the long flight of stairs that led to the executive offices. Once at Clair's door, he stopped, straightened himself and began to knock vigorously.

"What!" Clair snapped, as she cracked the door and squinted into the bright hall light. "You do know there are cameras on this hall? If you come in here the Admiral will know Steve."

"Clair...Clair!" he blurted uncontrollably.

"Yes Steve...are you OK?"

"Get dressed, call the Admiral, tell him to come as quick as possible...now! We have a major change in our situation!" he ordered between gasps.

"Could you repeat that...what...what has changed?" she asked as she tried to wipe sleep from her eyes.

"Trust me. Get the Admiral here before you dress. Tell him to be discreet and tell him that I will not tell you why he needs to be here. Please Clair!"

Lieutenant Evans, stunned did not move a muscle as she asked herself whom this man was standing before her.

He began to blink excessively as if he were having a fight with his nervous system, then leaned in close and said, "By the way...I think...I'm in love with you!"

Clair stepped back into the shadow of her room as if hit by a sudden shock. Steve, seeing an opportunity, leaned in beyond the view the camera and kissed her.

"I don't think the camera can see that!" he said as he pulled away. "Besides, what are they going to do...release me?"

"No! They will Court Martial you and release me...I need this job," she snapped.

"Trust me Clair. The Admiral will never release you. He is going to make you a Commander in short order after tonight."

What had she created, she thought she shook her head in disbelief. Yet Steve remained steadfast at her door, overly confident and filled with pride. Whatever he had...she wanted to see it now as she took in the man she had known intimately only hours before. She still wanted him and fought with all she had to not drag him into the room.

"Lieutenant, I think I gave you a direct order," he said, as he stared to the ceiling with faux disgust.

"Aye Sir!" she replied sarcastically, then put her hand on her hip and squinted as if to warn him he had crossed a line.

"Oh come on Clair. I was joking...not really...but I was joking. Please...just call the Admiral."

Clair stood with mouth agape. With that, Captain Channing spun about and sprinted down the hall before he did something he could not deny on camera.

37

Truc's Promise

Treasures hidden among friends of time
Come to me now all that I hope is mine
I shall not fail the gentle caress of life
You shared with me if but for one night
I will keep these whispers safe
Among the thorns of storms yet to be sailed
In the hope that, if but for little while
I should become a moment
In your journey tale.

Admiral Simpson arrived in his convertible Mustang at full speed, in no way discreet. All discretion was lost, but as luck would have it, the entourage of reporters waiting at the gate had fallen asleep or went home for the evening. As he ran across the damp grass, flip-flops flapping, Admiral Simpson looked to be an angry duck and at a distance, his scowl was visibly present as he huffed and sputtered toward his prey like a drunken alley cat.

Clair having never witnessed the Admiral in anything other than United States Coast Guard regulation gear, could not help but chuckle to herself at the sight before her. He was decidedly shorter without boots and his t-shirt imprint of a half-naked Polynesian girl, the mascot of a local bar, was much too tight, forcing the well-endowed young lady to jiggle with his belly as if she were designed to do exactly that.

"Captain, this better be good or we are both going to be keelhauled," Clair whispered to Steve.

For his part, Captain Channing looked to be a kid at Christmas waiting for his parents awake.

"He looks like a bear that had his crap in the woods interrupted," he observed casually.

"Must I remind you, that you have a lady in your presence," she replied as if offended. "However, Captain, I believe your description is lacking. I believe he looks more like a bear that wants to rip someone's head off, and then, crap down their throat."

Captain Channing stiffened but the smile remained as his Admiral crusaded the last fifty yards.

"What the hell has gotten into you Captain? Clair remarked as she looked to him one last time.

"Trust me...Clair...please...I need you to trust me."

She crossed her arms and gazed up to the sky, looking for strength.

As Admiral Simpson lighted upon his officer, steam lifted from his thick frame as he vigorously chewed on a tired cigar. His eyes fired daggers into his Captain and Lieutenant as if looking for a clue. In Captain Channing, he found no fear, and for moment, it rattled him the Captain remained cool and confident. He then looked to Lieutenant Evans. She squirmed with obvious discomfort and this unsettled him even more, as had never witnessed her seeming insecure before.

"Captain, what is this about?" he growled as he returned his attention to Captain Channing.

To his dismay, Captain Channing's grin remained front and center. The Admiral moved closer for effect and scowled once again, but it was of little use, the Captains grin would not wash away.

"What the hell are you grinning about, Captain?" Admiral Simpson bellowed.

Before Steve could answer, Simpson turned his attention to Clair and snapped, "What the hell is all this about Evans?"

"Sir...I am not sure. The Captain would not tell me," she muttered.

The Admirals disgust grew exponentially as he processed her answer and he crossed his arms as he looked to his Captain once again.

"I am sorry, Lieutenant. I should have answered the Admiral sooner," Steve said as he looked to Clair. "The problem is...I don't know where to begin, Sir."

Captain Channing paused and thought for a moment as he looked for a way to frame his news.

"Sir, I have discovered something...something that you will not believe."

"Captain, I am not playing this game with you again. Get on with it, son...if you don't want my boot up your ass."

"Sir...I cannot tell you."

"What the hell kind of game is this, Channing?"

"Sir, I have to show you."

The Admiral fixed his neck at a hard angle and stared at his subordinate as if he had lost his mind.

"Sir, we need to ask Truc for permission to board the Electra...Admiral...Sir."

Admiral Simpson turned to find Truc gazing at the stars above as he lay in the netting. In the strange light of the dock, Truc looked to be nearly angelic as he hummed a melody that seemingly rose and fell with the winds ebb and flow.

"This better be good Captain!"

The Admiral tossed his flip-flops to the side and made his way across the dock, all the while grumbling and pulling down his short t-shirt, as he seemed to be suddenly aware that his dress was inappropriate for the base.

"Truc, may I have permission to come aboard?" He asked with a decidedly different tone.

"Ms. Clair...she come too...Okeydokey!" Truc stated as he waved the Admiral aboard.

"What about me, may I come aboard?" Steve asked.

"You not ask ever...why you ask now?"

"He should have asked. It's a sign of respect to the commander of the vessel," the Admiral stated as he looked to Steve.

"I tell Steveee...he come anytime. Okeydokey?"

"Steveeee?" Admiral Simpson repeated.

"Steveee...he Steveee," Truc said as he pointed to Captain Channing.

"I see," Admiral Simpson said.

"Will you please show the Admiral what you showed me earlier Truc?" Steve asked as he climbed aboard in the hope of changing the subject.

With that, Truc lifted the cowling and pointed downward into the dark hull. The space below looked to be an uninviting black cavern.

"Oh!" Captain Channing declared, as he rummaged through his pockets and produced three standard issue flashlights.

"You will need these."

"What about Truc? Does he not get a flashlight?" Clair asked.

"He knows what's down there," Steve replied.

"I not...have light?" Truc asked, pouting as if filled with disappointment.

"Please lead the way?" Steve relented as he handed him the last light.

"Come, I show you...Okeydokey!" Truc exclaimed as he played with his newfound toy.

"Our host requests your presence Admiral," Captain Channing insisted as he pointed into the dark hold.

"Come," Truc, prompted once again.

"Are these...?" Admiral Simpson asked as he studied the two captain's seats near the entrance.

Captain Channing took Clair by the hand and forced her light to his face as he nodded in the affirmative.

"Gentlemen, let's get on with this. It's creepy down here," Clair remarked as she snatched her light away from Steve.

Truc took the lead and Admiral Simpson followed close behind as he worked his way forward on hands and knees. Clair followed the Admiral and Steve was pleased to find himself following her even though he did not possess a light because each time the Admiral stopped to clear an obstacle; he made double sure that he bumped into her.

"Captain!" she finally snapped.

"I'm sorry Lieutenant. I'm working in the dark back here and in my defense...I am going blind," he replied.

"Is everything kosher, Lieutenant?" the Admiral asked, as he pushed the next obstacle aside.

"The Captain fell on my leg...Sir."

"I'm sorry sir. I will try to be careful," Captain Channing replied defensively.

The center mass supporting the wing proved to be near impossible for the Admiral to negotiate. Soon his large frame wedged between the odd mechanism and the hull. After a short and pointless struggle, he was forced to ask Clair to push from behind. She grimaced at the thought, looked to Steve for support, and found none.

"Yes sir," she replied, as she placed her shoulder into his backside and shoved with all her might.

"I'm sorry Lieutenant," he responded, most embarrassed.

"Just helping a fellow officer in a moment of distress," she replied.

Clair accomplished the task of passing through the narrows with little effort.

"I see you needed no help Evans," the Admiral grunted as he adjusted himself on the far side. "At least, I hope there was no help involved, Captain," he barked into the dark space that now lay behind him.

"Oh no sir! I would never have imagined Lieutenant Evans needing my help," Captain Channing replied once he peered about the center mass.

Simpson began to search the space in which he found himself. Before him lay a bulkhead door that was obviously that of an airplane. To him, the entire scenario in which he found himself was an archeological nightmare. For he knew that forensic archeologists would discover his fingerprints, from one end of the vessel to other, and that would not bode well in an inquiry, he thought.

Captain Channing soon cleared the center mass, worked his way past the Admiral and pulled the door open, and then, watched on with glee as his Admiral and Clair peered inside for the first time.

"Is it!" Clair exclaimed.

"Yes it is Evans...yes it is," Admiral Simpson responded, as his light swept the cockpit.

"I think there is room enough for all of us to go in," Steve encouraged the Admiral in order to move them forward. "Just be careful, and watch out for the box on your left," he stated, as he pushed his head between the two of them and pointed to the left.

"What's in the box?" Simpson asked.

"Let's go inside first, Admiral. You have to experience the space. Think about it, Admiral, for over seventy years, we have believed that this was on the bottom of the Pacific. But, as you can tell, it should be hanging in the Smithsonian," he said with great pride.

"That's the problem, Captain...it should be in the Smithsonian...not here...not with us crawling around in it," the Admiral protested.

"Sir, Truc wants you to go inside. He has something he wants to show you. Besides...I've already been in there."

Simpson huffed, but entered the cockpit nonetheless and with his girth it helped that both pilot seats were in the stern.

Clair began to think of the journal and the range of emotions that must have occurred in the space she now inhabited. She began to feel the fear that must swept over Amelia and Fred, as they realized they would never find Howland. Then, as if a ghost appearing, Clair could see Amelia with the yoke hand and beside her, Commander Noonan calculating fuel consumption and watching his navigational aids.

As she moved past the bulkhead door, she found notations, quick calculations, on a side panel written in pencil, which if not for the dust, looked to have been written only the day before. As she studied the notes, she accidentally bumped the yoke and she snatched her hand back in fear as it fell forward and beat against the instrument panel.

"It okeydokey...you touch...it not break. Hold it Ms. Clair," Truc prodded.

Clair looked to her Admiral who nodded in agreement, as he wanted her to have the moment. And as she took the yoke in hand, images began to flash before her eyes, transporting her back in time, suddenly, the journal was alive. She felt a warmth sweep over her being, and there, if but for a brief moment, she knew that Amelia was with her in the cockpit of her Electra. Clair opened her eyes and looked over to where Commander Noonan would have been seated during the flight, but instead, found Steve's gaze intent upon her. Their eyes locked, and the space became far too small as each drank in the other. Then, as if kids caught on the playground kissing each looked away, but it was too late. Their Admiral knew he had a command problem on his hand. The gaze was unmistakable. His two officers were in love.

"Open...box," Truc, prompted Simpson, in an effort to distract to distract the Admiral and save his friend.

The Admirals gaze narrowed as he peered over his glasses at Captain Channing. He had no proof, but he knew, and what to do with the knowledge was most upsetting. He then decided it was not the time to deal with the matter, he had far greater pressing matters before him. He turned his attention to the box and for a moment, he felt all alone, as if caught in an alternate dimension. His palms began to perspire and his heart rate doubled as he imagined what might be in the box.

Only four feet long and two feet wide, he could tell someone had handled the box, as fingerprints marked the outer layer of dust. He looked to Captain Channing, who only shrugged in an attempt to lighten the moment. The gesture did not work.

"Open," Truc, prodded the Admiral once again.

"Sir, he told me to do the same thing," Steve interjected.

"Channing! What the hell have you done? We shouldn't be in here," the Admiral said in a pressed whisper, afraid that speaking loudly would damage the artifacts before him.

"Sir...Truc insisted," Captain Channing replied.

"Open...you see," Truc, pressed him once again.

"Sir, yes, the box has already been opened." Steve admitted. "Trust me. You want to open that box."

The Admirals breath became labored, filled with concern as he looked to the box before him. Somehow, he knew he was about to make the greatest mistake of his career. Yet he had to know. There would be no turning back he decided as he let his fingers grip the edge of the box. The lid felt heavy and cold as if it weighed a thousand pounds. Sweat began to appear on his shirt and the Polynesian girl's breasts swelled with each breath he took, and for a moment, he thought he would faint. It was time...he had to do now, he told himself. His fingers found the edge and slowly he lifted away the cover.

A look of absolute horror swept across Admiral Simpon's face. His hands betrayed him and he dropped the box lid on the floor. As much as he wanted, he could not stop his emotional response, his neck turned red, his stomach cramped and acid rushed the back of his throat. It was all too much to believe and he wondered if he would ever recover as he gazed upon what he knew to be the remains of Amelia Earhart.

"Oh... Holy Mother of God!" Simpson mumbled.

"No sir," Captain Channing whispered, "that is Amelia Earhart."

Amelia's face was taught, but recognizable and nearly perfect, as she rested in a mummified state before him. He thought it odd that her hair was unusually long, but the likeness was unmistakable. Her torso bore little clothing that might help identify her and her legs were pulled beneath her during the burial process. An ash covered her entire frame giving her a ghost like appearance in the box..

The Admiral quickly clutched his handkerchief and dabbed his face to prevent perspiration from falling on her mummified remains.

"What have I done?" he finally muttered. "What are we doing in here? We should not have opened this. You should have told me what was in the box Channing. We ...we...oh Holy Mother of God...what have we done?"

"I take Amelia home," Truc stated, matter of fact, as if giving the Admiral an order himself.

"Take her back...to where?" Simpson asked as he looked on in horror at the little old man in the dim light.

"I take...Amelia home. She make...me promise," Truc responded.

"Promise?" Clair asked. "What did Amelia make you promise?"

"I promise...take her back...to start," Truc insisted.

"To where she started? What do you mean by that, Truc?" Simpson asked.

"Admiral, he wants to take her back to Oakland California," Captain Channing intervened.

"I don't get it. Why Oakland, she wasn't from Oakland," the Admiral countered.

"Oakland is where she began the circumnavigation event. However, Amelia had little press until she arrived in Miami...but her journey, it officially began in Oakland. If she had made it to Oakland, she would have completed the circumnavigation in this plane," Steve alleged.

Admiral Simpson looked back to Amelia. Nothing his subordinate was saying seemed to make any sense at the moment, he felt light headed in the dark cramped space and worried he would soon be sick if he did not get out.

Clair placed her hand on Steve's arm to warn him that the Admiral was beyond any more shocking news. He did not need to be the one pointing out the gorilla in the room, but her effort was of little use; Steve could not keep the consequences to himself.

"Sir, if Truc delivers her on this vessel; Amelia will have successfully completed her circumnavigation of the globe. You cannot help but appreciate the beauty of the journey that Truc has undertaken for a friend. Sir, he has sacrificed everything to finish Amelia's story."

Admiral Simpson remained deathly silent. Then, as if he might blow away Amelia's remains, he said in a loud pressed hiss, "No way in hell will he leave this base with her on board. She is safe here...safe. That is what Amelia would have wanted. I am sure of it. If she is to finish the journey...then we will finish the job together...aboard a qualified cutter. Besides Captain, we cannot afford to lose her once again. You said so yourself."

Steve stiffened. He could not stop his mouth from saying the obvious. "It wouldn't be the same, Sir. The Electra must finish the journey...under her own power. Amelia wanted Truc to complete her journey. I think we need to honor that wish."

Truc, having seen enough, left the cabin with a huff and could be heard crawling through the tight space boisterously.

Simpson hissed once again, "What the hell do you people expect me to do? Just let him pack up and leave with her on board."

Captain Channing shrugged as he replied, "Sir, this is obviously your decision. All I know is that Truc is not planning to stay here. Yes, you have the power to stop him Admiral, but I think, the order would kill him. Think about it, Sir. Truc, has spent his entire adult life trying to accomplish this one goal and I believe that he has been building this vessel for this one purpose; possibly longer than you or I have been alive. Look at her, Sir...only one man built this vessel, and he did so, to bring Amelia home. Everything that is Truc and everything that is the spirit of Amelia is embodied in this vessel. Courage, commitment, navigational knowledge, and their friendship built this vessel. The Electra has one purpose, which is to bring Amelia home. Only one vessel deserves that honor, Sir, and we are inside her right now. I personally, will not be the one to tell Truc that he cannot finish the journey."

After his appeal, Captain Channing turned away without asking permission, and followed Truc to the stern. Clair forced herself to stop the tears, but they would not leave her be, as she remained with Amelia and her Admiral in the dim light of the cockpit. After several agonizing minutes of silence, she placed her hand on the Admiral's shoulder and asked, "Sir, may I have permission to leave."

Admiral Simpson nodded in agreement, as she extricated herself from the cockpit. For his part, Simpson remained alone with Amelia, keeping watch, hoping she might tell him what to do next. Finally, as his flashlight began to dim, he released every ounce of breath in his body, fell into a slump against the control panel, and moaned in anguish.

38

Aluluei

Let me race into the rising sun
Chasing dreams still undone
Let me laugh on the prow
Beneath a sky of blue
I will come to you my beloved
I will come to you

Simpson found Captain Channing, Clair and Truc laying against the outrigger in the netting. Sweat soaked his shirt as he crossed the main hull and ran his hands over the wing. The Electra was full of life that he had not noticed before, as if she were a living, breathing creature that Truc had created out of junk and vines. The miracle of being aboard her would be a memory he would always treasure in what he believed now would be a brief career as an Admiral.

It was two in the morning, and the base seemed to be exceptionally quiet, apart from for the guards standing several dozen yards away talking quietly among themselves.

Admiral Simpson cleared his throat and ordered, "Gentleman, take a break and get some coffee on me."

Each guard hesitated as they were not sure if this was a test.

"That's an order!" Simpson bellowed, and the men made double time as Captain Channing and Lieutenant Evans stood to face their Admiral.

The Admiral took his time and inspected the Electra as if she were one of his cutters. He thought her to be well constructed and how Truc had maintained her, in near perfect condition, in what must have been several thousand miles of sailing, he could not imagine.

"Truc, did Ms. Amelia teach you the names of the stars above?" he asked as if administering a test.

Truc looked to him, then rattled off in his broken English, "Pisceeees...Gemeennniiii...Caaancerr. I watch star...for long time."

"I take it that you know how to find your way by them at night...but, I want to know how you keep your line by day?" the Admiral prodded.

"Aluluei, he teach...way. Palulop...he with me...all day. Ocean tell me way...when star hide in cloud. Aluluei...Palulop both tell...storm come. Stars...tell good story....Aluluei...he tell true story."

Simpson looked to be utterly confused by the reference to Truc's god's. Lieutenant Evans stepped in with an explanation. "Admiral, sir...I have been studying his people the last few days. Those are his Gods if you will, or fathers of his people. I find it interesting that they consider these two gods to be father and son. It seems, that his people are not agreed upon, as to which one is the father and which one is the son. It is as if they are interchangeable, Sir. I believe the god Palulop is the one they call the great canoe captain. Aluluei is like...their patron saint of navigation. Alluluei is the great teacher of sailing to Truc's people. Am I right Truc?" she asked.

Truc was pleased to see Clair knew of his gods.

"So that is how you learned to sail...by the feel of the ocean? You know what is going to happen...long before it happens...don't you?" the Admiral asked.

"Father...he teach me...Palulop way.   He teach me...Aluluei and Palulop show me way home."

"Obviously your father taught you well. But, I'm still trying to process what would possess him to allow you as a young boy to sail to another atoll," Simpson said as he continued to examine the vessel.

"I go...many times," Truc replied. "We sail like...like you walk."

"Really, you were traversing the distance from one atoll to another when you were a boy?"

Simpson took his time as he walked about the main hull, in what looked to be an effort to touch as much of the Electra as possible.

"Truc, I believe I have never found a better maintained craft. You have taken excellent care of the Electra. I am sure Amelia would be proud of what you have accomplished," the Admiral said.

Simpson looked to his feet, then to the stars as if seeking permission. The weight of the world wore heavy on him and his liaison wanted to rescue him, but knew better than to speak. Finally, he turned to his subordinates and ordered, "Captain Channing, I want you to enter into the record that the Electra was personally inspected by me and that I found her to be of seaworthy condition," he said, then he hesitated before his next declaration. The strain on his face remained visible and his hands looked to be shaking as he gave an order he knew he would most likely regret, "I no longer find it necessary to keep this vessel in port, Captain.   Note in the log, that I have found the Captain of the Electra to be of the highest caliber, and note, that I would personally sail with him anywhere."

"Sir?" Captain Channing replied.

"Captain, I just ordered you to release this vessel from our customary inspection of foreign vessels and to inform the Captain of the Electra that he may precede as he sees fit. Was I not clear?"

"Sir, yes Sir!" Captain Channing yelped, as he popped back to attention. "You were most clear...Sir."

"As for you Captain, I order you to take medical leave for three weeks...effective immediately. I hereby order you to find whatever means you deem necessary to return to the mainland for a proper inspection of your eyesight. I want a full report, upon your return, of the prognosis."

Clair could not force down the lump in her throat, she wanted to be with Steve and Truc. She swallowed hard and blinked to clear her eyes. She would not cry, she told herself. Admiral Simpson studied her as her color faded. He knew he had a problem to deal with regarding his two officers but he also wanted the best for Clair.

"Truc, could you use a crew to help you complete your journey? It seems my Captain needs a ride to the States. Do you think you could use him?"

Truc's smile grew ever wider as he nodded in agreement. Admiral Simpson then turned his attention to his liaison.

"Lieutenant Evan's, I believe you have not had your sea trials. It seems you have been in the administrative pool for far too long. I think that it may be time for those sea trails to begin. I wonder if you would be willing to accept a multicultural exchange experience with Truc. We can register your time with Truc as a study in the ways of ancient sea faring. What do you think, Lieutenant? I know you can produce the paperwork in minutes...if you want to go then make it so."

Clair could not answer her Admiral. Tears could not be stopped as she stood at attention.

"Well...since you have no objection, I hereby order you to learn how this man sails this thing, and when you return, I expect a full report as well," he ordered, while holding to the wing column to support his ever weakening legs.

"Sir, yes Sir," Lieutenant Evan replied smartly.

"Ok ladies and gentlemen. I expect this craft to clear of my dock in one hour. It is now 0200 hour. You have until 0300 to load and clear this vessel. I think we have held it long enough for inspection," the Admiral ordered. He then stuck out his hand to Truc and said, "God's speed. I will not be far behind you. If you need anything...my officers will know exactly how to reach me...Okeydokey?"

"I leave...now?" Truc asked, confused.

"Yes Truc...you can finish what you promised Amelia but you need to do it now...before I change my mind," Admiral Simpson replied.

Truc took the Admiral's hand and shook it profusely in his odd manner. Simpson responded in kind then stepped off the Electra and called Lieutenant Evans to his side.

"Get the quartermaster on the phone. Whatever you need to ensure your safety, I want him to have it on this dock by 02:45 hour."

Clair hit the speed dial, and a moment later, a tired base quartermaster answered with a few prime curse words. She immediately handed the phone to Admiral Simpson.

"This is Simpson," he snapped, to let the man know who was in charge. "I am about to put my liaison back on this line. Whatever she deems necessary to complete her mission, I expect it to be on the dock in the next forty-five minutes. Do I make myself clear?"

He handed the phone to Clair and said, "Don't worry about typing up those orders. I will do them myself Lieutenant. The Electra needs to be well out to sea before the press gets wind of this. I will be following soon after aboard the Rush, but I need some time to make her ready."

Captain Channing saluted his Admiral and said boldly, "Sir, permission to speak...candidly?"

Simpson broke into a laugh, "Hell Channing, all you have ever done is speak candidly with me. I wouldn't expect any less now."

"Sir, this could cost you your carrier. Are you sure this is the best thing to do?" he choked out.

"Captain Channing, my career has been on the line since you walked into my office. I have taken more broadsides to control this event than you can imagine. I am depending on you, and the lieutenant, to finish this thing and make me look like a genius. I will be behind you the whole way. If you get in trouble, I will be there to pick up the pieces. That said; whatever the Sam Hell you do...do not lose the Electra. She has to make it Captain. Do I make myself clear?"

"Perfectly clear Admiral," he barked in reply.

The Admiral then pulled Captain Channing to him and whispered, "And by the way...I know you have a thing for my liaison and...I cannot say I blame you. Nevertheless, remember, I will be behind you watching your every move, as well as half the United States Navy by the time you arrive. I would suggest you keep those longing eyes to yourself and...If you so much as touch each other above deck, I will personally throw you overboard and drag you behind the Rush. Also, I expect you to bring my liaison back in one piece. She does not know the sea like you. You will keep her alive and well. If you drown, that will be your problem, but as for those two...well let's just say, I will come looking for you in hell, Captain, if anything happens to them."

"Top deck sir. I got it...stay off the top deck and kill myself if anything happens to Clair or Truc."

Nodding his head in disbelief, Admiral Simpson began the trek to his office. It was dark, but he knew he had to change before anyone else saw him in his t-shirt and shorts. Along the way, he met the returning guards, each carrying a handful of sandwiches and drinks. He asked for a sandwich from one and a Soda from the other. He lit his cigar, snapped about, saluted Captain Channing and headed off into the dark night.

"What do you want Captain. I've ordered several changes of clothing and swim trunks for you. I have M.R.E's, water and a heavy-duty first aid kit. Can you think of anything else?" she asked.

"Yes, I want a compass, a map of San Francisco Bay and two hand-held radios with extra battery packs. I want an ice chest with ice and a bunch of sodas. I don't want another caffeine headache like the last time...and toilet paper!"

Clair's face dropped as she realized she had nowhere to hide when using the restroom.

"Oh my God, I didn't think about that," she protested.

"Lieutenant, when they bring the toilet paper, order them to put all of it in two sealed five gallon container. We will take out the paper and cut a hole in the lid. However, do not expect me to wash out your bucket! You wanted ancient seafaring ways...well...you are going to have to flush your own toilet."

"That's brilliant," she said as she hit speed dial once again and relayed additional orders to the quartermaster.

39

Load Up

Send me into the deep
With only a hope of light

Thirty minutes later, the quartermaster arrived in his personal pickup truck with two sleep-deprived greenhorns. As Captain Channing inspected the lot, he was pleased to see the sodas. He then discovered Dramamine, caffeine pills, the medical kit and he wondered aloud what he had brought to the table but toilet paper and a bucket.

"You have...more?" Truc asked as he studied the growing pile.

"I don't know Truc. The question is do you think this will all fit? Three people will be hard to feed and water. I know we need the food and at all costs we must take these five gallon buckets!"

Truc motioned for him to hand it all over and as Steve tossed Truc the five-gallon bucket he said, "Keep these near the back where we can reach them easily. It is for Ms. Clair."

Truc shrugged his shoulders as if confused so Steve pinched his lips together and forced a strained face.

"Ohhhhh. We keep close," Truc replied.

"I see you find my need for privacy funny. Perhaps I should inform the Admiral of your insensitivity toward the opposite sex," Lieutenant Evans snapped as she tossed her duffle bag at a surprised Captain Channing.

"Sorry Lieutenant, I didn't know you were listening in behind me...just trying to lighten the mood around here. It's been all business since you left."

"Don't push it, Captain," she replied. "Remember, I have friends in high places."

"Don't worry Lieutenant; I have been informed that I am to kill myself if I should return without you or Truc by both the Admiral and your grandmother. Trust me; I know how important you are."

"So what have you got in here?" he remarked as he attempted to lift her bag.

"My makeup Captain...why do you need to know...stuff a woman needs to survive on the open sea. It's not that big!"

Truc looked on as the officers bantered back and forth, and then suddenly hugged both. The quartermaster thought it funny and began to laugh as Truc held on for an unusually long time.

"We go...Oakland!" He squealed as he let the two go.

This left Captain Channing and Lieutenant Evans standing far too close as they heard Admiral Simpson bellow from across the yard, "Quartermaster are we squared away here?"

"Sir, I believe we have everything as ordered," the quartermaster replied.

"Captain Channing, do you have everything you need to accomplish your mission?" he pressed as he ambled up to the dock in uniform.

"Yes, Sir" Captain Channing replied, while purposefully stepping away from Clair.

"Lieutenant, are you prepared for your training in advanced ancient sailing methods?" the Admiral asked with a sly grin.

"Yes, Sir!"

"Have you brought with you a means in which to record this study?" he asked.

"Yes, Sir!" she said and she presented a small digital recorder and several packs of batteries.

Admiral Simpson turned his attention to the quartermaster. "It seems you have done an excellent job. I will see to it that your record shows your diligence."

The quartermaster, stood grinning from ear to ear, until the Admiral ordered, "I need the Rush fully fueled and stocked for several weeks at sea in the next two hours."

"Sir?" the quartermaster asked.

"You heard me. Two hours!"

"Yes, Sir!" he replied, as he snatched both greenhorns by the ear and loaded them in his truck. Before the key hit the ignition, his cell phone was waking every able body on base.

40

The Great Escape

Chase after me oh stars of the night
Sing to me the song of lovers and light
Teach me the way home this day
For once more I shall enter the furious fray

aving changed into proper attire, Admiral Simpson began to pace the dock. For the first time in his life, he was going to let his heart decide and not his head. Once done, he could not take back the decision, however, he had never imagined that he would have to let go of the Electra.

"What the hell, it was good run," he quipped as he released the half hitch that held the Electra to the dock, tossed the line, and worked his way down to the last two lines. The Electra reluctantly slid along the dock, as if she were struggling to let go herself.

Truc, realizing he had forgotten to do something, leaped across the netting and landed on the dock with box in hand. He flung himself about the Admiral in a bear hug, and Admiral Simpson knew in that moment, that no matter what happened next, he had made the right decision. Truc unceremoniously handed him the box and returned to his Electra only moments before she cleared her moors. He then made his way to the outrigger and in his awkward manner; he saluted his newfound friend as he had witnessed Captain Channing do many times.

Several enlisted witnessed the awkward display of affection and in a gruff voice, the Admiral bellowed, "What...have you never seen two men hug?" Then he watched on as Truc skillfully maneuvered the Electra to escape the shadow of the Constance. Truc turned about and waved good-bye one last time. Admiral Simpson snapped to attention and returned the gesture with his best salute as he yelled out across the growing distance, "God's speed my friend."

Simpson then turned on his radio and ordered two waiting rigids to follow the Electra until she cleared the channel.

The base in the meantime had come to full power as officers and enlisted rushed about fulfilling the orders of the quartermaster as if he himself were the Admiral. Every light on the base had come to bear while every available vehicle seemed to be emptying the warehouses of supplies.

The Rush eagerly awaited the attention she was receiving, as fuel lines and forklifts spread about the base in a managed web of efficiency. Admiral Simpson placed himself in the midst of the mayhem until Commander Bearing could return from his first free night in months. For many, it was the first time they had dealt personally with the Admiral and all soon discovered why he had earned his rank.

As the Electra slipped away under the cover of dark, the managed insanity brewing on the base grew in scope, and Captain Channing knew it would not be long before the press realized something was up.

Nevertheless, luck was with them, the wind picked up and the Electra moaned like an old woman whose joints had grown tight from too little use. The wind gave her life and she soon found her sea legs. Her groans and consternations slowly slipped from the rigging as Truc began to dial her in. And except for two tired trawlers returning from a long week of fishing, the mission to escape the base went without incident.

Once clear of the harbor, Truc tacked hard south in an effort to round the island, then after another two hours, he turned east and headed for open water. He felt his way around the island as if he had done it a hundred times and the Electra's pace slowly increased as he continued to trim her for a life on the open sea.

The night remained cloudless and lights along the shoreline darted across the rolling sea. Steve would not be able to appreciate such a sight before long he thought, and took in every moment as if it were his last. The small crew remained quiet, and waited patiently for the Electra to fully embrace the wind and sea. They felt it was as if she knew she were about to be free and no one wanted to miss the moment. Her full stride arrived as the first ray of sun light slipped across the horizon like a key opening a door to the glory of the sea.

"This may be the last time we can hold hands," Clair whispered to Steve as she leaned in close.

"I was thinking Lieutenant, when we are done with this, would you like to go out to dinner...on a real date?" he asked as he took her by the hand.

"I would be honored but...it better be as good as Mo Mo's," she replied.

Truc adjusted his course to due east. This would lead them past the southern edge of the island and into the open Pacific. Now, all that lay before them, was a little over twenty three hundred miles of ocean as the night sky released her hard grip and the rising sun reached to know the eastern sky. Her crew filled with anticipation of the journey to come for each knew that from now on, their world would be forever different.

● ● ●

The restock of the Rush, as expected, drew unwanted attention. The shocked group of reporters awoke and called in for instructions as they watched enlisted scurry from one point to another, like ants building a mound. Across the harbor, one reporter and her camera operator discovered a perch atop the cruise ship terminal and with excellent camera work, were able to film between the Constance and the dock. The world would soon know that the Electra was missing.

Suddenly, smoke billowed from the Rush as deck hands struggled to release boomed fuel lines and cargo nets. Then, to the filming news crew's delight that had waited atop the cruise terminal, her mooring lines fell away, and in singular, radical broach move, the Rush slipped away from her moorings. Within seconds, she was at full speed, trailing a massive wake as she left the channel.

41

Into The Fray

Against these days
I shall sail into the fray
With no hope to return
Single in mind, single in heart
The tempest calls my life to sing
For I am undone by this season of tasteless wind

I shall sail into the fray
With no hope of return

The byline, "The Electra has flown her coop," broke at 4:00 a.m. Not long after, at a local TV station, a call from an officer of the Coast Guard to the stations night manager took place that would forever change the lives of two of its employees. It was an offer the manager could only dream of having come his way. A reporter and camera operator needed to meet a Coast Guard helicopter within a half hour if the station wanted the exclusive.

All the station manager had available was a young, unknown cub reporter, who worked the night shift and chased lost stories few would see. He decided to take the chance and send Kiki along with his best camera operator, who happened to be in house editing a story he had filmed at 1:00 a.m. of a local house fire. The grizzled veteran, George, could take care of the cub reporter he decided, and so, the manager ordered both to leave immediately for a local hospital helipad.

They found the chopper waiting at the helipad as instructed and were hurried aboard, strapped in, and, before Kiki could adjust to the thought of flying, the light duty chopper was airborne. The lights of Honolulu glistened against the dark waters of the Pacific as the helicopter gained altitude, and for a moment, Kiki was elated. That was until she realized they were heading to sea as the chopper suddenly banked and the lights below fell away. For Kiki hated boats, sea life, and the ocean in general.

"I thought we were going to the base?" she asked George pensively.

George remained at the task of cleaning a camera lens and never broke a smile as he simply grunted. The response was actually more than she had expected. She knew him to be aloof and had personally never had a meaningful conversation with the man. She sighed as she turned and looked to the fading lights of Oahu. It was going to be a long day.

Barely twenty-four, and with the station for only eight months, it was obvious to all that Kiki was easily overwhelmed when it came to stories involving danger. To her credit, she had been a local beauty queen and had studied communications at her community college. Her dark auburn hair and pale face worked well on camera, but she had a curse that most believed would one day end her career. In a most unbefitting manner, when stressed, Kiki's eyes would twitch and reveal her inner demons. Unbeknownst to her, an editor at the station had named her Crazy Eye Kiki and had even gone as far as to put together a montage of her worst moments. She was aware of the tendency and diligently worked on the problem for hours, but she never felt anxious when practicing in the bathroom mirror, and so, the problem remained.

As the island slipped away, Kiki knew she was in over her head and decided she could find solace in the fact that she had a great cinematographer at her side. Having overheard the station manager order George to watch over her and not allow her to hang herself, in a strange way had given Kiki a sense of comfort. With all his rumored personal failings, George, for a reason she could not explain, was the only camera operator in which she had confidence. She would have to ignore the stories of his less than desirable qualities and make friends with this man, she told herself as the chopper began to bounce upon the evening thermals.

For his part, George hated the terms camera operator, cameraman, the camera guy, and cursed those who said it unknowingly. Ever the southern eccentric, he would only accept the term cinematographer when professionally referenced. Kiki had made the mistake only once.

Having served as a front line war cinematographer, in Iraq and Afghanistan, he now lived a half-drunken life chasing women like Kiki for sport. His arsenal of stories had made him famous among the bars of Honolulu and worked more often than not among female tourist seeking a little risk in their vacation. George, naturally considered himself the most interesting person in the room, and for the most part, he was right, as he had witnessed nearly everything a man could see in a war zone.

As George realized they were leaving the shelter of the island, he felt in his bones that the trip would be longer than anticipated and he cursed himself for not watering his plants before leaving his apartment. Other than the death of his two house plants, to him, an extended stay did not matter for his duffle bag contained items most would not think to take unless they knew they were on assignment for several days. He had learned the hard way that small creature comforts go a long way when stuck somewhere you never intended to be in the first place.

Making use of the early morning light, George began to film stock footage of the sea passing beneath until the chopper suddenly shuddered while losing altitude as it banked. It was then he saw for the first time the Coast Guard Cutter Rush sailing at full speed below and he craned his neck to get a better shot of her from on high as the helicopter banked once again. He then took up his bag and held tight for George instinctively knew that it was going to be rough landing by the look on the young pilot's face.

The helicopter spun about to bleed off more speed as it attempted its first approach and George began to wonder aloud if the Rush would give them the courtesy of slowing down. He thought it odd that Rush seemed to be gaining speed as the helicopter forced its way forward against a wash of wind and sea spray. He had landed on ships many times in the past, in fare more desperate circumstances, but, never at full speed. The entire act seemed unnatural to him and he decided he would have a few words about professional courtesy with the Captain of the Rush if they made it on deck.

It was then he noticed that the pilots were cursing among themselves as their helicopter suddenly dropped to only a few feet above sea level. It was apparent that the Rush would not slow for their approach and that her wind wake was causing the chopper to shutter violently as if she were about to come apart. Then to their surprise, the Rush nearly stopped; as it crested a large wave. The helicopter's crew pulled back to adjust for the change in attitude and once again lost their approach.

Kiki grabbed George by his arm as the pilot forced his helicopter to bank hard as he sought yet another attempt to land and George unknowingly returned her embrace as the craft lurched to one side, then pulled up yet again.

"Why the hell are they not slowin down?" George railed the pilot in his signature deep southern drawl. "We ain't at war boys! Hell, I've landed under fire in better conditions than this."

The co-pilot turned to face George and snapped, "If I hear another word from you!"

This only served to tick George off, and he would have usually entered into a full-blown argument with the co-pilot, but suddenly he found that he had bigger fish to fry. Kiki had buried her face into his arm and her eyes had begun to show the tension for which she was famous for at the station. With yet another violent bounce, the two were tossed about in their seat as if shaking a soda can. Kiki looked to George pleadingly, and for the first time in a long time, he felt sorry for a cub reporter, for the ride was giving him a stomach ache and this was not his first rodeo.

He lifted her chin and tried to encourage Kiki, "Girl. This ain't nothin. I was just given em some hell for missing that first approach. It's a common thing to miss on first approach. Trust me!" he lied, but Kiki didn't need to know that he thought. "Those flyboys, they hate it when they have to come back round. They'll get it this time, I promise." he said, as he stroked her hair in an attempt to calm her down. He knew he would catch hell by his other comrades at the station if they knew he was acting like a concerned dad.

Upon the next bounce, Kiki's stomach rolled and the cabin filled with a vile smell as projectile vomit. George pulled back her hair and wiped her face, then yelled over the roar of the rotors, "Serves you right you somebitches. Now you gotta clean this up when you get back. Way to go girl...give em hell. Get all that crap out of ya girl!"

Kiki needed no prompt and flooded the far side of the helicopter with a breakfast burrito and a thirty- two ounce soda she had consumed on her way to the helipad. The Co-Pilot turned to see what was causing the stench and found George flipping him off and smiling with a most evil grin.

Another large wave crested the bow of the Rush as it plowed forward at full speed, causing the helicopter's windshield to be coated with seawater just as it was flared for the landing. The pilot decided he had enough drama as his windshield whited out and dropped the bird on the deck like a bag of bricks; all the while praying the deck crew could secure his landing gear before they blew over the side of the Rush.

As the deck crew opened the side door to remove her passengers, vomit sprayed the flight deck and all standing within thirty feet. The master chief found Kiki with her hand held out, crying like a baby, as if wanting her mother. A trained firefighter, he quickly slung her up over his shoulder and ran to escape the rotor wash. George maintained a barrage of curses toward the pilots and with a final huff, he grabbed his large duffle bag and flipped them off once again as his feet hit the flight deck. He began to walk away as a man who had walked away from helicopters his entire life, and for good measure, he flipped the crew off one last time as he made his way down a set of steps.

On the bridge of the Rush, the second in command reported that the light duty helicopter had dropped its package.

"Get that thing off my deck. I want our long range bird on board before it burns anymore fuel," the Captain bellowed.

"Sir the crew of the bird is reporting that it is full of vomit. They want to know if they can wash her out first," the second relayed.

Captain Bearing bore down on his second in command with hate-filled eyes to deliver a nonverbal answer.

"Get that bird off my deck!" the second yelled into the radio.

Captain Bearing turned his attention to the sun peaking over the horizon. To his port, lay Crater Rock. It would be the last of the island's grip and he could not believe they had not caught the Electra as he began his third cup of coffee.

"Where the Hell is that boat?" he mumbled.

Below deck, the master chief carried Kiki all the way to the mess hall as George followed close behind. Once there, George decided it was time to take charge and save her dignity.

"Don't you understand, the girl needs some privacy? Get us to a female head, son. I can't let her meet the Captain looking like this," he snapped.

The Chief changed directions and headed for the women's shower. He banged furiously on the door to the female head but George chose not wait and barged past the chief. "Man on deck," he yelled. With no reply, he took Kiki by the waist and ordered the Chief to find her a change of clothes.

"Come on girl, we gotta get you straight. This ain't any time to fall apart on me," he said as he turned on a shower and placed her under the water fully clothed.

Slowly, Kiki began to come to her senses as the warm water washed away her nightmare. To George's surprise, he found that she was far prettier wet than he could have imagined, and found himself caught off guard as she awoke from her daze. His first instinct, to close the shower curtain and walk away, only served to confirm his guilt and he cursed under his breath for not being more professional.

"Ok...I'm gonna stand over here...while you shower. I will watch the door and make sure no one disturbs you. You gotta get out of those clothes Kiki. I got one of them boys bringin you a fresh set," he said still embarrassed.

Kiki began to whimper. "Oh God...what the hell happened...I shouldn't have come," she said as she could finally see how covered she was in her own vomit.

"Girl don't beat yourself up. I pissed all over myself the first time I had a hard landing in Afghanistan. Nerves will do funny things to ya," George replied in an effort to lighten the moment.

"Is there any soap out there?" she asked with a still weak voice.

He scanned the space and found a bottle of leftover shampoo in the next shower.

"This will have to do," he said, as he handed the soap over the shower curtain. Discomfort with the situation began to take over and he decided to head for the door and give her privacy. He was nearly there when it unexpectedly opened. Before him, Captain Bearing stood with daggers for eyes. George knew immediately that this was the man in charge and that the shit had just hit the fan.

Unbeknownst to Kiki, she broke the silence between the two men as she yelled over the sound of the shower, "Thank you George for being such a sweet heart. I thought you would be a hard ass. I guess I was wrong."

George returned with great affect Captain Bearing's glare as he answered, "You would have done the same for me. I'm gonna step outside a minute...and wait for your clothes."

As if a dance, both men stepped into the hall, neither Captain Bearing nor George choosing to release the other from the mutual stare down. Each decided it would be a good fight as they sized each other up.

"Who the hell do you think you are barging into my female head?" Captain Bearing said with a measured reserve.

George leaned into Bearing and replied, "Who the hell do you think you are...scaring the ever livin shit out of my reporter. Why the Sam Hell, did you not slow this bucket of damn bolts down for a civil landing? Remember, you invited her...the least you could do is let the chopper land."

Captain Bearing stepped back, sized up the man before him, and then decided the pissing contest needed to end.

"I apologize for the situation in which we find ourselves. I realize the landing may have been rough. However, we cannot slow down if we want to have any hope of reestablishing contact with the Electra," Captain Bearing replied.

"Well then...I apologize for the situation in which you just found me. I was trying to reestablish the dignity of my reporter," George returned.

Bearing liked the man's spunk for standing up to him and broke the tension with a smile and an open hand.

"I suppose we have come to an understanding then...Sir. I am Captain James Bearing of the Rush. I have not been afforded the honor of your name by my subordinates," he pressed.

"I'm George Shavinoski, most just call me George. That is my reporter Kiki Evans of WKGI 6 Honolulu in the head," George said as he decided to return the handshake.

"Get him stowed away and make sure a female delivers the young lady a fresh set of clothes," Bearing ordered, as he sniffed the air about him. "You smell like Hell yourself, Mr. Shavinoski. Would you like a change?"

"I came prepared. I can live for weeks out of this," George said proudly as he hefted his camera bag.

"That's good. You may well be aboard a week or two."

"Why would we be here for a week? We were told nothing about a week," George bristled. "And, how the Hell did the old man steal his own boat from the base?"

"He didn't steal his own vessel. He was encouraged to finish what he began," Captain Bearing replied as he began to walk away.

"Woa..woa...where is the old man headed?" George pressed.

"I believe we are headed for Oakland California," Bearing said over his shoulder as he climbed a narrow ladder leading to the next deck.

Realizing he had been summarily dismissed, George turned to find yet another officer holding his nose and pointing in the opposite direction. He could smell the vomit now. It was time to change.

42

Sailing Lesson

Hold the line, not of your own making
For the swells of life singularly sing
Of shadows and mist, of mountains deep
In the hope that we may claim
A flash of an angels wings within our sleep
So away my slumber, tempt me no more
As I wish to remain on that far distant shore

As Clair sat precariously on the outrigger watching Truc work the control lines, she decided that he looked like a cowboy breaking a horse more than a sailor. He suddenly awoke and the Electra began to slow to only a few knots as he set the rudder to circle the craft. He then quickly released his harness and made his way to the main hull, filled with determination as he bounded across the netting like a teenager.

Steve, long holed up in the well area, was enjoying a novel for the first time since college as Truc approached. Clair had packed, "The Old Man and the Sea," in one of the boxes and he wondered why he could not remember reading the novel in high school.

Truc forced Steve to move away from the entry cowling and a few minutes he later returned with another harness in hand. It took him fifteen minutes to link it to the rigging as Steve wondered if Truc had made the harness while in Honolulu. Then it crossed his mind; that Truc had not offered the harness to him on their lone journey.

As Truc finished the set-up, he held out the harness for Clair to take. Clair thought the harness looked to be most uncomfortable, but she was not about to turn down the opportunity and decided it best not to take the time to change or ask questions.

"Lean...back...Ms. Clair," he instructed as he settled into his own harness.

Captain Channing found that he could not take his eyes off Clair as he struggled with the fact that he was a bit jealous that Truc had trusted her first with the harness first. Truc, unaware of Steve and his competing emotions, took up several lines, hooked another around his foot and snapped the lot as if prodding a mule team to pull. The Electra reared into the wind at his command and the outrigger snatched from the sea to compensate for the sudden pressure change against the large wing. He then trimmed the Electra, all the while prodding Clair to lean out as far as she could. Suddenly the outrigger fell to within a few feet of the waves as he made another adjustment. The extra weight of Clair against the wing allowed him to pull it in hard against the wind and his Electra responded in kind with speed.

As Clair finally relaxed and trusted the harness, Truc handed her a single control line. The outrigger bucked up and down at first as she tried to understand the mechanics of the line. Like a father, he placed his hand on hers in an effort to show her the way, and ever so slowly, she grew to be confident as they finally sailed the Electra as team.

Stuck on the main hull, Captain Channing decided he had best stop gawking at Clair's ample curves and returned to reading Hemmingway. The story seemed to have a greater significance aboard the Electra, but the night before had been long, and the sway of the vessel was fast inviting him to find rest. And so it was, as the old man in the novel fought off the shark in a vain attempt to protect his greatest catch, Captain Channing fell fast asleep.

The dream returned, much as it had before. The sailing was intense, the ocean alive, the sky a bright blue and as his father's hand warm against his as they guided the tiller together.

43

Tell The Story

An honest story is among us
A noble adventure of truth
Who shall be her voice
Who shall sing her song
Among the waves of soulless chatter
Who is the valiant
Who will tell the tale that must be told

George had finished changing into dry clothes when a bang came at the door.

"Sir, I have been ordered to escort you to the landing pad...with your camera. The Admiral will be arriving soon and the Captain thought you might want to get a shot of the Admiral boarding," he yelled through the solid metal door.

"Why, is General MacArthur returning to the Philippines?" George replied.

The officer, as he tried to think of an answer, sounded stressed as he mumbled something George could not understand.

"Ok, let me put on a better shirt," George replied as he opened the door. "Are shorts appropriate? That's all I have in my bag?" he asked.

Ten minutes later they were waiting in an area that the officer told George would catch the least amount of prop wash. The helicopter was far more substantial than the one George had endured earlier and to his chagrin, this pilot had no problem touching down with the Rush at full speed.

Admiral Simpson exited the chopper and was escorted from the deck by the same chief who had rescued Kiki. Captain Bearing greeted Admiral Simpson then gave thumbs up to the pilots as his helicopter blazed ahead of the Rush. Captain and Admiral spent a moment away from the prying ears of their crew. It was obvious that things were serious but cordial between the two as Admiral Simpson found his way to the same level as George. To Georges surprise the Admiral immediately stuck out his hand for an official greeting as he approached.

"I hear you had a bad landing, son. I want you to know, I ordered that both pilots be recertified. I am deeply sorry for the discomfort suffered by you and your reporter. It will never happen again...I assure you!" the Admiral said above the rush of wind.

As he thought of the pilots, and their plight, it brought great pleasure to George; in all his years of covering the military, a senior officer had never apologized to him. He knew immediately he was going to like Admiral Simpson.

"Thank you, Sir," he responded as he returned the Admirals handshake vigorously.

He had covered Admiral Simpson's change of command ceremony and had considered him to be another stuffed shirt during the event. However, aboard the Rush, the Admiral seemed much more human, someone that he would like to have a beer with.

"Come with me...what's your name?" the Admiral ordered, more than asked, as he made for the closest hatch.

"It's George, Sir. George Shavinoski."

"Ok, George...let's find the bridge."

Simpson barreled through the long maze of halls and ladders like a pro. George remembered something about him commanding several cutters from his induction ceremony, which explained his ability to navigate the maze with little effort. Following along close behind, Captain Bearing ordered a master chief to bring Kiki to the bridge. George grimaced at the thought. She would meet the Captain and the Admiral at the same time and he wondered if he had any valium in his bag that he might slip her.

The bridge of the Rush opened before George and the crew snapped to attention at the sight of the Admiral. The Admiral headed immediately to the Captains seat, placed the odd box he had under his arm on a panel and then propped his feet up. Ever the professional, Captain Bearing, never flinched at the takeover of his ship by an Admiral. If he were upset, the Captain's poker face never gave it away and George found that he could not help but to admire a man who knew his place.

"George," the Admiral pressed, "I need you to pick the best camera angle...one with someone sitting in the Captains seat. I want the shot to convey that we are on the bridge, but not show the commotion of the crew actually driving the cutter. It needs to be a place that you won't be in the way, but at the same time, in the middle of the action."

"What is your best side Admiral?" George asked, half expecting a laugh from the crew. Not one person offered him the coveted response.

"Oh...no George...you're not going to film me. Well... you may for the back-story...later...but for now, you need to plan on your reporter telling the story. Did we get Kiki; I like her...she is always on when I am up. She's the pretty redhead right?" the Admiral asked.

George wondered, if the Admiral was Kiki's only fan and had he ever noticed the crazy eyes. He knew then, he had to find a way to film Kiki without allowing her to look directly into the camera.

"Admiral, forgive me for asking, but what exactly...is Kiki going to be reporting?"

"She will be reporting what I tell her to report and she will be reading a prepared text,"

"So...you have a script for her to read?" George parried.

"Yes...something like that."

George looked about the bridge, searching for the best shot, all the while taking into account that Kiki would most likely suffer a major panic attack upon meeting the Admiral. As he thought through the problem, he wondered if he could just film the back of her head.

"Mr. Shavinoski, did you bring a remote microphone? It might help overcome the hum of the ship," the Admiral suggested.

"Yes sir. I have a lapel microphone. I will get the shot and record the sound on a separate track. That will allow a better edit. I may need a man to help hold a boom microphone if the lapel is not picking everything up. Trust me sir...I am very good at what I do."

"I am sure you are," the Admiral replied as he watched George begin to move about the bridge. "I heard you worked in Afghanistan, Pakistan and Iraq. Have you been to any other war zones?"

"Most would call the other places conflicts. I have a few stories to tell if you want to chat over drinks one evening Admiral," he replied as he tried to lend his hand to humor once again. Once again, no one responded.

"We will have to do that this week George. I commend you for your service. It takes a special breed to go into a war zone for the story. I am glad we have you on board," the Admiral replied as if he genuinely cared.

"Are we going to be at sea for a week? No one told our manager that we would be gone for a week," George pressed.

Admiral Simpson chose not answer and George quickly realized it was time to stop asking questions as the bridge door opened. In the midst of the near hurricane beyond the hatch, Kiki stood with hair askew and mouth agape. She was befuddled as she glanced about the bridge like a lost puppy until George appeared on her radar. Dressed in standard USCG jumpers complete with orange stripes, Kiki looked like a clown. This only served to make George cringe all the more for her. To his great relief, the Admiral quickly made his way across the bridge, took her by the shoulder and led her away from the wind beyond the door as if asking a child to follow him.

"Kiki...I am Admiral Simpson and this is Captain Bearing. Thank you for volunteering to do this story," he said as he escorted her past George and skillfully placed her in the Captain's seat. Kiki, having no idea that she was sitting in a seat that no one else on board would dare stand near, quickly placed her hands under her legs and generated a vacant smile.

George decided it was time to come to her rescue, "Kiki, this is going to be a straight up shot. For the most part, you will be reading a script. We do this all the time. It's not a big deal...OK!"

Admiral Simpson did not appreciate the interruption and with a glare, he let George know as he pressed, "Kiki, dear, first I want to tell you that I am a big fan. I have seen several of your late night pieces. I tend to be awake most of the night." He paused, then took her by the arm as if her father and said, "I need your help. I need to catch you up with what is happening and why we are chasing Truc, and then, I want you to tell the world. That will be the first part or our relationship. I hope we can shoot that in a few minutes. George has assured me that he could make this work. You don't need to worry. You will not be working off a script at first, but I promise, you will be fine after I explain everything to you."

Kiki held firmly to her fake smile as she looked to George for assurance. He decided at that moment that a side shot would serve her best as her left eyes slowly twitched.

"Are you ok, Kiki?" the Admiral asked.

She nodded in the affirmative and never stopped smiling.

"OK, I'm set up," George announced. "Now, I need to get Kiki straight."

He began to dig about his bag and produced a makeup kit, brush and hair spray. He took her by the face with his free hand and told her in his best gay southern voice, "Girl, you need some love. The wind tore you up!"

The crew watched on, a little bemused, as the apparently straight man began to apply makeup and use hair spray like a professional hairdresser. He ran his fingers through her hair and stepped back several times to review his handiwork and with each adjustment; he gave her a reassuring smile in the hopes of calming her down. To his relief, Kiki slowly began to relax. For the moment his plan was working.

"I never noticed how strong your features are. You're going to look like a movie star when I finish with you," he said and this forced a true smile from Kiki. With the smile, he knew he had her firmly in his control and decided to press the Admiral for more information.

"So, Admiral, what exactly is Kiki going to be telling our news audience? It would help me set up the sequences and plan edits...that is if I know the intended story."

"She won't be telling your news audience, George. We are going to be sending her news briefs to the Pentagon by satellite. The Pentagon in turn, will make sure that every major news organization in America receives her report. You're going national, Kiki!"

George maintained his grip and attempted to lock eyes with her once again. "Well Kiki, let's show the world how we do it in Honolulu." His words did not help. The crazy Kiki eye began to manifest.

"Girl, there is nothing you can do that I can't fix in the edit. I have been national more times, than you can imagine. We will not be live. We will have plenty of time to fix whatever is wrong," George said, desperately trying to rescue his cub reporter.

"We're not going to be live?" she asked the Admiral as if she did not believe George.

"Oh no, we will have the ability to do several takes if necessary," Admiral Simpson replied.

"Ok...go gently with her Admiral," George ordered as he looked away from his creation. "Remember she is new to all this and this clown suit your guys supplied...after tossing us about...it ain't gonna work on screen, Admiral. Your boys should have found something a bit more appropriate for a national shoot."

"I know how to make her look far more in charge. I have a great idea...trust me, George," the Admiral said as he put his hand on Kiki's shoulder. "The good thing is Kiki; we have several days to release the information. We will do all of it in controlled bursts and we will take breaks, as you need them. Kiki...I take care of my people, and right now...both you and George, are my people."

She was not sure if it was his gentle eyes or the kind way in which he spoke to her, she liked Admiral Simpson; for he reminded her of her own father.

"I promise...I will not disappoint you," she replied with a returning courage.

"I never expected anything less," the Admiral said as he offered her his hand. "Will you, do me the honor of letting me escort you to the chart room. You and I need to talk privately."

Kiki took him by the arm, and with a tip of his hat to George, the Admiral led her away to the chart room and shut the door behind them.

"I see you have honed your beauty school skills...George. Did those come in handy with Afghani rebels? I can't imagine what they must have looked like before you fixed them up," Captain Bearing ribbed George as he slapped him on the back.

"Why, would you like a makeover Captain? It looks to me like it's been awhile since you had one," George returned as if in a duel.

Captain Bearing's crew fought to suppress a smile and George knew they would be talking about his dig at the Captain privately for weeks.

"Checkmate...George. Checkmate," the Captain replied, as he lifted his binoculars and studied the sea before him once again.

"No hard feelings Captain, just trying to relieve some of the stress around this place," George said as he offered his hand in peace. Before Captain Bearing could respond in kind, an Ensign broke the silence that had held the bridge since the Admirals arrival.

"Sir, the helicopter located the Electra. They are about 70 miles ahead. He reported that the Electra seemed to be circling at the time; however, the vessel left the area before they could make contact. They are having to return for fuel and can't maintain contact, Sir."

"Sounds like they decided to give you a chance...to catch up...Captain," George joked.

"Yes it does sound that way," Captain Bearing replied as he snatched the intercom, "Engine room, if you got anything left, I want it now!"

Captain Bearing then turned his attention to George. "We have been running on only one gas turbine and two diesels. We have two gas turbines," he informed George as if it might explain how a sailing vessel was staying ahead of a Coast Guard Cutter. "We need all of them to catch her."

"This thing can go faster?"

"Just wait and see Mr. Shavinoski. Just wait and see," Captain Bearing replied through clinched teeth.

44

The Trance

Melt away oh days of sorrow
Bent to the dark of lost things
Come no more
Come no more

Her confidence grew as she managed the one
control Truc had allowed play with, to the point
that she could finally look about. She found herself often,
glancing over at Steve who was asleep in the well. She
thought it odd that both men looked to be asleep while she
was awake at the wheel. Clair had grown accustomed to his
trance like state and would have assumed him asleep, if not
for the outriggers methodical dip which allowed Truc to
touch the sea. She was sure the act had something to do
with his sailing method, but what, she could not imagine.

Keeping on course and in balance had put Clair's every
last nerve on edge, and to make matters worse, she
desperately needed to use the restroom. Finally, she could
stand it no longer and shook Truc from his trance. He

responded as if knew her need and released the Electra into a stall. He then removed his harness and helped Clair from hers. As she quickly made her way to the main hull she yelled at first to gain Steve's attention, but finally resorted to shaking him in order to wake him up.

"I need that bathroom, tell me you put it together while the rest of us were contributing to the journey," she asked with a suppressed grin of pain.

Steve rolled over, lifted the cowling, and to her relief there sat her improvised restroom, complete with a roll of toilet paper dangling from a cable. She grabbed him by the cheeks and said, "I would kiss you...if I didn't think we were being watched."

Steve for his part decided it was time to visit Truc as she completed her business below deck. A minute later, she opened the cowling to peek about and found both men relieving themselves overboard.

"Show offs," she snapped as she came topside to wash out her bucket.

"Don't worry gentlemen. I will wash my hands, of which, I am sure you did not!" she prodded as she witnessed them smile between themselves.

As the afternoon passed, they shared a lunch of cold MRE's. Truc devoured the crackers and sweets first then dug into the Twinkie supply. Feeling like a mother of a teenager Clair warned, "If you eat too much of that...you will get sick...Truc!"

The warning did little good. The Twinkie smile remained from ear to ear, and she couldn't help but laugh at him, as he forced the next one into his mouth and grinned a gooey grin.

45

Kiki's Day

Do not waste the tune
Sing the song while the dark days still roam
Lest you be the last to know of the song of hope
For the light will come to break these bonds
Of shadows that choose to wander on

Admiral Simpson and Kiki returned after thirty minutes. Lit up with excitement, she made her way to the Captain's chair and Captain Bearing handed it over without a fuss. George decided it best to reset his camera due to the change in light and then he pointed to Kiki's jumpsuit to remind the Admiral of his promise.

"Oh...yes, I told you that have an idea for that problem," he said, as he took off his jacket and held it out for Kiki to try on. George thought he heard a collective gasp from the bridge crew. The Admiral's jacket screamed of authority and it immediately made Kiki feel as if she were important, and even more so, it made her feel safe.

"I think that will do," the Admiral said as she adjusted the jacket and he admired his handy work.

It was a good look; George had to admit as he connected the microphone and repaired her hair one last time.

"Are you ready?" George asked Kiki.

"I think I am. I have my notes. I may have to look at them every now and again. Is that OK, or will I need to stop each time...you know...for an edit?"

"I think it would be best for you to just keep going if you can. It will look as if we are shooting it live with fewer edits...if you can pull that off. However, if you have to stop...don't worry about it. Just give it your best."

"Do I need to order complete silence on the bridge?" Captain Bearing asked George.

"No, I think the idea of a busy bridge will be best received."

"You heard the man ladies and gentlemen. Be normal," Captain Bearing, ordered his crew as if the demand would actually work.

With that, George raised his left hand and gave Kiki a silent count.

"This is Kiki Evans from WPGI 6 Honolulu, reporting aboard the Coast Guard Cutter Rush. I am the guest of Admiral Simpson and Captain Bearing...and we are currently in pursuit of the vessel bearing the wing of Amelia Earhart's aircraft. As you can probably tell, I am sitting on the bridge...surrounded by America's finest, as they go about their duties. If you hear orders being given, or...if I have to stop for a moment, you must remember that I am on a working cutter at full steam," Kiki said, as she released her gaze into the camera.

"George...why don't you pan to your left and show everyone the bridge?" she pressed. George dropped his head with the break in protocol but obeyed nonetheless. As each of the bridge personnel came into view, not one lost their forward observation of the sea ahead. George then spun about and pointed for her to take back the shot.

"As we were informed by...Captain Steve Channing in our last press conference...the old sailor's name is Truc. I can officially report, that Truc and his vessel did depart before sunrise this morning. There has been some speculation that Truc may be attempting an escape. I can tell you at this point that Truc was allowed to leave."

Kiki looked away and studied her notes. She then smiled and returned to the camera and George found himself impressed, that she had made it so far, without one crazy eye.

She took a moment more to brush her hair away from her eyes, and then pressed on, "I can also confirm that Truc did have information concerning the whereabouts of Mrs. Amelia Earhart and Commander Fred Noonan. This was alluded to in the earlier press conference with Captain Channing, but...now, I can confirm it. This news is...well...," she looked up from her notes to allow the news time to sink in.

Admiral Simpson looked to Kiki as if to order her to carry on.

"Ladies and Gentlemen...this next bit of news is exciting. If you are not seated, I would suggest you do so now. It seems...Truc brought with him what is believed to be the final journal of Mrs. Earhart."

She stopped once again, a long pregnant pause, to allow the news time to simmer once again.

"Admiral Simpson and his staff have shared with me that Truc is very protective of the journal and that it has been in his possession for some time. Due to Truc's old age, the Coast Guard, in cooperation with the United States Navy, felt it best to allow Truc time to release the information as he saw fit. The Coast Guard took deliberate steps to make him feel comfortable. These included such measures as, not meeting in buildings, and keeping the press away until they could confirm or deny his story. Their concern for his welfare is why there has been a press black out. This is the best part...it would seem that Truc has had no contact with the outside world for most of his adult life."

Suddenly, Kiki turned to Admiral Simpson and asked, "Admiral would you please come close, so I might ask you a few questions? I think the people would like to hear this straight from the man in charge of this whole operation."

Admiral Simpson frowned at first, and then decided he had better cooperate. He had not expected her to begin controlling the story so early and it showed on his face. George panned to create a wider view, as Admiral Simpson entered the frame a bit uneasy.

"Admiral, this journal is a most interesting development. Is the book real?" she asked.

Simpson cleared his throat and replied, "Yes Kiki it is a huge development."

Kiki gave him her best clueless smile, and then touched his forearm. George nearly came unglued as the Admiral squirmed in the midst of the affectionate gesture. He knew it would look to the world, as if father and daughter were having quality time.

"Admiral...would you say that you have come to the conclusion that the journal is authentic?"

"I am most sure that the journal is authentic, Kiki," he replied.

"Sir, what makes you so sure this journal is authentic?"

"Well...when you hear the story, you will begin to believe that it could not be a hoax. Also, we have corroborating evidence...but I cannot discuss that at this time."

"Ok...I guess that means...that the topic is off limits."

"Yes. We still have some things to accomplish regarding the evidence."

"Admiral, have you made any attempt to confirm the nationality and background of Truc?"

"We are confident that we have confirmed the family line of Truc. We were very lucky to discover relatives that Truc did not know existed. It seems, he is originally from the Marshall Islands."

"Could you please tell us a bit about Truc?"

"He is of Micronesian descent. He is...in our estimation...over ninety years old and he is in excellent physical condition. He speaks a broken English...that we believe he learned from Amelia and, we are most sure he built the vessel that he calls the Electra."

"So you are saying that Truc actually spent enough time with Mrs. Earhart, to learn a language?

"Yes."

"How he was able to spend so much time with Mrs. Earhart?"

"I am not going to tell you...as of yet," the Admiral replied with a slight grin.

"Ok...Admiral, you called the craft the Electra. How did you come to that name?"

"Truc called it the Electra...in honor of the plane from which it was built?"

"So you are confirming that the wing on his boat is from Amelia's airplane, once again?"

"Yes...as best we can tell."

"Sir, what will we find in the journal?"

"I am glad you asked that."

The Admiral was beginning to find his wind and he liked the questioning far more than his plan to have her tell the entire story.

"The journal is sitting in front of you in that box. The same box that Truc used as storage for God knows how long. Nevertheless, to ask me what is in the journal...that would be inadequate. I think it best we let Mrs. Earhart tell her own story."

"Admiral...you're confirming that the journal tells a different story than the official declaration from over seventy five years ago. Are you saying that this journal tells a story...a story that does not have Mrs. Earhart crash landing in the ocean on July 3, 1937.

"She crash landed Kiki...but not in the open ocean. I suggest we let the journal tell the story."

"How would you propose we do that Admiral?" Kiki pressed.

"We have two officers who have been involved with this story from the beginning. They are currently sailing with Truc on the Electra. Captain Steve Channing, whom you have all met and my liaison Lieutenant Clair Evans are on board the Electra. Both have worked tirelessly with Truc.

In our debrief of Truc, he asked Lieutenant Evans to read the journal. He felt it best that a woman read the journal and I think he was wise in the decision. Lieutenant Evans has been instrumental in Truc's transition to our culture. Therefore, what I propose is that we watch footage of Lieutenant Evans reading the journal for the first time. I think the world will find it most powerful."

Kiki remained quiet for a moment as if she were absorbing the story herself.

"You have this footage and you're willing to share it to the world?"

"Yes."

"How long is the journal?"

"It's is not very long. We believe it was the only means available to Amelia. In an attempt to make sure all was said, Mrs. Earhart kept it brief."

"How will this take place, Admiral?"

"We are ready to share this information," Admiral Simpson said, with a pressed smile, as he relented to the next statement.

"I am going to release twenty minute intervals, or thereabout, for the next few days. I think, if we try to hear the story in one sitting...it would be too much. In addition, I think most people like a good mystery."

"Captain, we have a visual of the Electra at eleven o'clock," an ensign bellowed.

Kiki turned to find Captain Bearing desperately studying the sea ahead with his binoculars.

"Admiral, I confirm the sighting at eleven o'clock," Captain Bearing barked.

Kiki watched on helplessly as the bridge suddenly became all business. She bent over toward the Admiral and asked, "So, why have we been chasing the Electra?"

"Kiki, I will share that with you later," he replied, and with that, he left her side and grabbed another pair of binoculars.

Ever the professional, Kiki returned to the camera and pressed on, "As you can see the events are unfolding as I speak. I will make every effort to follow this story as it develops. This is Kiki Evans, reporting from the bridge of the Rush for WKGI 6 Honolulu."

She remained still for the edit count, until George gave her the all clear, then broke into a nervous laugh as he reached to hug her.

"How did I do, George?" she asked.

"You were the prettiest girl at the prom, Kiki," he answered like a proud father.

Admiral Simpson waved for George to come beside him as he asked, "Do you have a long range lens for that thing?"

George reached into his bag and held one up.

"Do you have a good stiff drink in that bag?" the Admiral asked, half joking.

"Do you really want to know?"

"Should we have inspected that bag for contraband, George?"

"I would hope not Admiral."

Captain Bearing turned to study the bag warily as George shrugged his shoulders and changed lenses.

"See if you can get a good shot of the Electra at sea," the Admiral requested.

George stabilized the camera and pulled the dot in his viewfinder up to full scale. Suddenly, he could see people moving about the Electra.

"Can you plug that into the bridge monitor?" Captain Bearing asked.

George held up a wire and replied, "If you can find a place to stick that then we might be in business."

Bearing snagged the cord from George and fumbled behind a mounted monitor. And as the monitor came to life, the Electra became a show the entire bridge wanted to watch.

"What are they doing, Captain?" Kiki asked.

"It seems they are cleaning up after lunch and preparing to sail," he replied as they watched Captain Channing drop a bag into the main hull and secure the cowling. Truc, made quick business of Clair's harness and then set himself into his own, as Steve leaned against the cowling and waved energetically toward the Rush.

"I see they stopped and waited for you once again, Captain," George jabbed.

Bearing's return scowl was damning, counter to that of the large smile lighting across the Admiral's face at the audacity of George.

"Did you not give them radios before they left?" George asked defensively.

"Yes we did. It seems that in the excitement of the mission, they forgot to turn them on," the Admiral admitted. "I would appreciate it if that bit of information remained on the bridge, Kiki."

"Well, like I said, they were kind enough to wait for us," George pressed once again.

"They had a significant head start. They won't get away from us again," Bearing said confidently.

At that moment, Truc reigned in the control lines and nudged the Electra to find her course. Clair leaned away from the outrigger and allowed her long hair to drag in the ocean. Truc then pulled a pin and the forward sail deployed. Within seconds, the Electra went from all slow to jet powered. Truc and Clair, as a team leaned out as far as they possibly could, forcing the Electra to press into the wind and waves. She left the Rush behind her like a racecar leaving a large truck.

Bearing slammed his fist on a console and cursed aloud as he snatched up the communications head and dialed in his intended mark.

"Master Chief. I would suggest you figure out why my turbine is still not running. You have ten minutes."

He then returned to his binoculars in an effort to ignore his new nemesis. George, and his camera, had a better line of sight, but for some reason, it felt like cheating to Captain Bearing.

"George, do you have enough footage of the Electra under sail?" the Admiral asked.

George nodded in the affirmative.

"Well then, I would suggest you get out the laptop I know you have in that bag of yours, and get busy editing Kiki's intro. With any luck, we might make the evening news if those pukes at the Pentagon can up-load a file," Admiral Simpson ordered.

George took Kiki by the hand and headed toward the mess hall, as he knew, another sarcastic word, could have him thrown overboard.

● ● ●

Two hours later, George handed the Admiral his edited copy with extra footage of the Electra at full sail and his chopper landing. He included the entire interview without cut.

"I love it...perfect George! I think this is going to be a great partnership," the admiral rallied.

George handed his jump drive to the Admiral and asked, "Do I need to find the guy who can upload this to the Pentagon or should I trust it to your hands?"

"I will make sure it moves forward from here. Go eat and get some rest. I would like to meet with you after dinner to review the footage that I have from the Truc interviews. I would love to see if you could improve the quality and possibly add some edits this evening."

George snapped to attention, saluted and said, "Aye, aye, Sir."

"If you're not careful, George, Bearing is going to put you in the brig, and I wouldn't half blame him," the Admiral warned.

"I'm sorry sir. It would be my honor to review the footage. I have a great editing suite and I will be glad to clean it up."

"1900 hours?"

"Sir?" George replied as he shrugged his shoulders.

"Oh, that would be seven p.m. your time."

"Yes, Sir. I remember from Afghanistan. Where is the video I need?"

"Oh, in my bunk," the admiral replied.

"Sir, I hardly know you."

The Admiral began to laugh at the off color jab as George got up to leave.

"By the way George, tell Kiki, she hit a home run. This is going to be a game changer for her."

"I don't think she ever wanted a game changer Admiral. That is what makes her genuine. She never planned on more than covering local news."

Simpson nodded in agreement, as George shut the door and headed to the fly bridge to film the Electra in the last hour of daylight. He could eat later, he told himself.

The wind was fierce as the Rush plowed ahead at full steam with her final turbine on line. George felt alive, as if on a foreign assignment. His rhythm was returning.

As the sun began to burn a hole into the horizon, Captain Bearing stepped to the fly bridge for a smoke and discovered George filming.

"Captain," George said politely.

"Mr. Shavinoski," the Captain replied, as he tipped his head in a polite response.

"I see you got your turbine on line."

"Yes...it seems we have."

"This is something we are going to tell our grandkids about, Captain," George said in an effort to generate a conversation.

"I know. It is all very exciting. This could not have happened to a better man than Captain Channing. He has been through hell the last year. I have to admit, he is a goofy sun of gun...but I tell you, he would have made one hell of a cutter driver."

"Do you know him well?"

"Not as well as I would like. I am few years ahead and we never served on the same cutter. However, I have several good men who have served under him and I tell you. To a person, they would give their life for him. You can tell how good a Captain is by how well his people are trained. His are some of the best on my ship."

George adjusted his camera to keep the Electra in view as the fading evening light rippled off the wing. It looked to be winking at him, George thought, as he framed the shot.

"I am sorry Captain...if I was an embarrassment in any way on the bridge this afternoon," he offered.

"Don't go soft on me George. I enjoyed the banter. Everyone else on board is scared shitless of me. I think when we get back, it would be nice to have a few drinks and swap stories. But until then, remember, I am not averted to having you keelhauled."

"Yes, Sir," George replied.

At that moment, George noticed a change in the attitude of the Electra as it went into its signature circling stall. Lieutenant Evans was about to give up the reigns.

Bearing stuck his head in the bridge and ordered, "Maintain our distance. All slow."

George was able to catch Captain Channing and Clair high-five as they passed each other. She then opened the cowling and disappeared below. All the while, Truc walked about, eating a Twinkie and drinking bottled water.

"I wish I could sail her for a few hours. I have never witnessed anything like her. It's a shame...once she gets to dry land...she will end up in a museum," Bearing lamented.

"Why are we going to Oakland?"

Bearing only smiled.

"Makes sense! That's where the Electra began her journey. Truc is trying to finish the last leg of the flight, isn't he? That's why you guys are backing off and letting him go on," George mused.

"You would be wise to keep that to yourself for a few days."

"The networks will start figuring it out soon enough. They will probably speculate that much tonight when the interview airs with Kiki," George replied.

"They will be speculating, George. You will report."

"I like the way you think, Captain."

Clair appeared above deck with a white bucket, dipped it in the ocean and washed it out. George looked to Bearing and asked, "What is she doing?"

"It's not what she is doing. It is what she did. Think about it, George."

"Oh. I never thought of that. I guess I believed Truc had a bathroom aboard."

"You have a lot to learn, George," Captain Bearing replied, as he turned, entered the bridge and shut the door abruptly as if to let his crew know he still hated George.

46

To Feel
The Hand

To taste her wet kiss
Shall only cause pain
For time will bring to her no shame
She must not live among the waters of our youth
Nor shall she be spilled on the shore of loves open arms
For she hid among the depths of our night
Taste my wet kiss she will cry
In her grip we all shall die
Run from her lie
Embrace the child of eternal light

Captain Channing remained in his utilities as he
strapped into the harness that Truc had prepared
earlier for Clair. In the well, Clair quickly found comfort
with a lamp and a book. She then looked about as if
something was wrong but she could not put her finger on

what was wrong. Then it hit her...she really could not put her hand on the problem. She flung the cowling open and dove below deck only to appear a minute later with the two-way radio in hand.

"Tell me you checked in sometime today!" she yelled across the divide as she held the radio out for Steve to see.

"I guess that falls to you now. Tell them we were maintaining radio silence, so as to not attract attention," he returned with a blank look as if it were not his problem now.

"The Admiral is going to have my ass," she mumbled to herself. "We are so screwed."

"Clair, they would have found some way to gain our attention if they felt it necessary. They have been holding back all day as well. So, just put your big girl panties on and call them."

Clair dropped to her knees and covered her face. She had only witnessed the Admiral seriously mad once before, and in that incident, a Commander exited the Admiral's office in tears.

She switched on the radio, "Electra to the Rush. Do you copy?"

"This is the Rush. We copy?"

"I need to give our first report."

"Lieutenant, please hold while I find the Admiral. He gave me orders to locate him as soon as you realized you had radios on board."

Clair dropped her head and replied, "Copy."

As Truc began to adjust lines, Clair wondered if they could make a getaway and claim signal loss.

"I am glad to see you and the Captain are doing well in your sailing lessons. I hope this was not too much of an inconvenience to check in, Lieutenant?" Admiral Simpson crackled over the radio.

Clair hated it when the Admiral was sarcastic.

"Sir, I am sorry. We were caught up in the moment, and, well...there is no excuse."

The radio's silence was deafening as Clair waited for the barrage of expletives to come.

"What do you mean, Lieutenant? I specifically remember ordering you to maintain radio silent...until dark. I see you have been training all day in the methods of primitive sailing. I believe this may confirm that it was the Polynesians who discovered the Americas first. By the way, you looked like a pro driving her today, Lieutenant," the Admiral replied.

Clair began to hyperventilate with relief. Her Admiral had her back.

"Yes, Sir. He allowed me to control a single element for the day. It was very demanding, and I believe it will take several more days before I learn how it all works together. I am not sure it is possible to understand this vessel. She is unusually complicated, Sir."

"I see he is going to give Captain Channing a turn."

"Yes, Sir. Truc said something about teaching him to see the ocean. He said, the Captain needed to sail in the dark."

"Do you need anything, Lieutenant, of personal effect?"

"No Sir, we are well stocked for the journey."

"Lieutenant, I expect consistent radio contact at 0600, 1200 and 1800 hours from here on out."

"Yes, Sir," she replied.

"We are going to be playing the footage of you reading the journal to America...while this little journey takes place. I believe, you will be a superstar after tomorrows airing of the footage, Lieutenant. How do you feel about that?"

"Sir, I am content to be an officer of the Coast Guard."

"Well said, Lieutenant. OK, I'm going to let you go now. If you need anything don't be afraid to call."

"Yes, Sir."

"God's speed, Lieutenant!"

"Thank you, Sir," Clair offered as she fell like a ragdoll into the well with relief.

Truc dropped the hammer and the growing night soon overtook all that Steve could see and so he leaned into his harness and felt for the first time the full measure of the Electra's power.

"How come you never showed me this harness?" he asked Truc.

"You...not ask?" Truc replied over the howling wind.

"Oh," Steve replied a bit bemused by the answer he had received. "I suppose you are going to teach me the same thing you taught Clair today?"

"No," Truc replied.

Shocked once again, Steve did not know what to make of Truc's reply.

"Do you just want me to dangle here...as ballast?"

It was obvious that Truc was choosing not reply as he stared into the coming dark. As the Electra cut across the waves and the stars above broke through the coming dark, Steve decided he simply needed to relax and enjoy the ride. He could not help but feel like a baby, rocked to sleep in his snug harness, as he swayed to the light chop that passed only inches beneath his feet.

Truc paid Steve little attention as the final moments of the day slipped away,. He tacked often to work the head wind that they had experienced for most of the day, but to watch Truc, one would soon realize that a head wind was of no consequence to him.

In an effort to remain awake, Steve began to imagine the things Truc would see for the first time; San Francisco, the Golden Gate Bridge, Alcatraz, and he pondered how he would explain the Golden Gate or Alcatraz.

Two hours passed before Truc stirred from his trance. He released the Electra from his command and she immediately circled to bleed off speed.

Truc ran to the bow, grabbed a fishing line, and threw it several dozen feet overboard. He quickly snagged a fish and tied off the line to tire out the creature. He then bobbled back to the hold. Clair remained asleep in her sleeping bag and awoke startled by his presence and they exchanged a knowing smile as he returned with several bottles of water and Twinkies. Clair opened them for him and he made quick work the Twinkies as he returned to the bow and pulled in his catch.

After several awkward attempts, Steve finally released himself from his harness and took the opportunity to take care of his bodily functions while Truc wrestled with the small tuna. He offered a peace of the fish to Steve, who consumed it with the same delight, but upon offering the fare to Clair.

"That's just gross."

"Clair, trust me. Do you like Sushi?"

"Yes, but I have never eaten it while it was still wiggling."

Truc held out the piece of fish once again.

"Take a bite Clair. It's the best," Steve pressed.

Reluctantly Clair took the piece and was ready to gag until she realized it tasted good and fresh. They dined and laughed for an hour as Truc, with Clair's flashlight, made funny faces.

After they cleaned up and grabbed a couple bottles of water, Steve began to put on his rigging once again. Truc stopped him.

"You wear...mine," he ordered.

"Truc, I can't sail this thing. I could flip it."

"I show...make you...go straight."

"I could run us into another vessel."

"Yes. Two come...close."

Steve suddenly wondered if the Navy had come along for the show as he had learned to trust Truc's instincts.

"You...put on," Truc prodded once again.

"Truc...Amelia is on board!"

Truc held out the harness. Steve finally took it and fitted it to himself.

"You wrap...around foot," Truc said as he pointed to the line heading toward the rudder.

Steve connected himself to the rudder line as ordered, Truc snapped the lines like a wagoner telling his horses to pull once again, and the Electra plowed forth dutifully.

"You go," Truc yelled over the rush of wind as he pointed in an eastward direction. Suddenly, the Electra began to swerve, back and forth, as if driven by a drunk.

Steve began to feel desperate as the fear of tipping the Electra and losing Amelia raged within him. He fought with every muscle to discover how much tension he should apply to the rudder. And as he expected, the Electra responded to the jerk of his foot as if complaining to Truc that he did not belong here.

"Truc...are you sure?" Steve asked as the Electra bucked him once again.

"You make...go straight," Truc ordered.

"How do I know that I am going straight? What star am I sailing toward?"

"You not see star. Steveeee....you blind!" Truc replied rather sarcastically.

"Well...exactly...why are you making me do this?" Steve pleaded as they careened hard to port.

"Alleluia tell me...you see...soon," Truc replied.

"You've told me that before but I'm not sure you can teach this old dog a new trick?"

"What dog?

Steve began to curse under his breath as the slightest motion on his part caused her to veer. The stress only compounded and he knew the crew aboard the Rush was trying to follow his lead. With each over adjustment of the rudder, the Electra plowed deep into the next swell and he cringed at the thought of Amelia below.

"Truc, I don't know where the hell I am going. I can't do this!"

"Stop talk...you make...go straight."

"I don't know where straight is Truc," Steve snapped as he released the rudder from his foot.

"Put on...now!"

"I can't do this. I am blind. I can't tell if I am going in the right direction. I'm trying to tell you Truc...this is crazy."

Truc abruptly slapped Steve across the face.

"You...feel?" Truc asked with a growing fire behind his eyes.

"Hell yes!"

Truc poked Steve hard in the ribs.

"You...feel?"

"Truc, if you hit me again, I swear I will knock the crap out of you."

"You...own anger, now?"

"Hell, yes! I do now!"

"You love...Ms. Clair?" Truc asked with a wry smile.

Steve became pale.

"That is personal. What are you getting at?"

"You...feel love...Ms. Clair love?"

"Yes, I think so. Why are you asking me this now?"

"You love Ms. Clair...then you fight...to save Ms. Clair?"

"I would if I had to Truc. What does this have to do with anything?"

"You love...sea?" Truc pressed, as he pointed to the ocean.

"I did, when I could see and appreciate her. I can barely make out the ocean anymore, Truc," Steve replied with bitterness in his voice.

"Sooooo, you stop love...Ms. Clair...if... you not see Ms. Clair?"

"No, Truc, I think I could love her blind."

"You must love sea...same as you love Ms. Clair... Steveeeee...Okeydokey?"

Steve hung his head; Truc was pushing against the wounds of his anger.

"You must learn...trust sea. When eye not see...Alleluia, he speak. You trust...you will see," Truc said as he slapped Steve on the head once again. "You must feel...you must hear...you must love...Okeydokey."

He then patted Steve on the chest.

"Palulop...live here." He then rubbed Steve's head. "Alleluia...live here. You make...them one," he said as he touched the water. "Aluluei...he teach us to sail. You listen...you hear Alluluei...you sail Electra."

"I feel like the Karate kid."

"Who...this kid?"

"Never mind, Truc. I think I get what you are saying."

"You...hear..."

Truc thought for moment trying to remember the word, "Wh..Whisper. You hear...whisper...Okeydokey?"

"OK, Truc, I get it."

"You make...Electra go straight," Truc encouraged him once again as he pressed Steve into action by handing him the lines.

Steve began his search for the elusive process once again and the Electra reacted like a pair of scissors ruining a dress. He quickly let out a sigh and was about to give up when Truc slapped his chest, then his head, and said, "Here...Here. Palulop...Aluluei...you make one...okeydokey Steveeeee!"

The Admiral and Captain Bearing watched in horror as the Electra bucked Captain Channing like a stallion trying to toss him off. Finally, Simpson ordered that Lieutenant Evans be contacted immediately.

"What the hell is happening, Lieutenant?" Simpson bellowed.

"Sir, this was Truc's decision. He wants to teach him how to pilot the vessel. Truc is forcing him to do it. Steve has tried several times to stop...Truc will not let him. He keeps telling Steve he must learn how to see," Clair replied, then flushed at the mistake she had just committed of calling the Captain by his first name.

"He's nearly blind, Lieutenant. Does Truc understand this fact?"

"Yes Sir! I am sure he is aware of Captain Channing's disability."

"If you feel like they are about to wreck the vessel, I order you to take over, Lieutenant," the Admiral snapped.

"Yes, Sir."

Clair grimaced at the thought of telling Steve to stop. She could never do what her Admiral had just ordered her to do.

As the Electra continued to buck, Steve began to hate her as he was convinced she was an unruly beast in the wrong hands. Finally, in a fit of desperation, he looked toward the sky, put his glasses in his shirt pocket and consciously decided to not to trust what remained of his eyesight. He would imagine the stars he needed to navigate, he told himself.

At first, all he could hear was his heart racing. He exhaled to release the stress present in his body, and then, as if piercing through a thick fog, the star systems began to form in his mind's eye. Then suddenly he was sure that he could hear voices all about him. People he had known in his past. The sound brought with it a sense of peace and as he relaxed further and listened, the relentless fight with the rudder began to subside.

Steve leaned into his harness and listened to the water as it passed beneath his feet. The waves began to sound like a chorus against the hull and he thought it odd that he had never noticed the musical rhythms they produced. Moreover, as their ballad filled his heart, he found himself feeling as if a child at the beach, with waves at his feet, sand between his toes and scurrying fiddler crabs all about. The memory remained strong as the two spheres of his present and his past began to collide. He could see the beach he knew as a child, yet he was still aware of his present need to sail the Electra. All the while the voices grew within his soul and he suddenly became overwhelmed by an acute awareness of his lesser used senses.

As the two separate worlds of his past and present expanded before him, the Electra jolted hard once again to remind him that she needed his attention, forcing him to fight for the vision. At that moment, as if hearing from an unknown whisper, he corrected her course and she responded nudge in kind.

Abruptly, the vision changed, and he found himself on a dock, walking toward the family sailboat. The memory was vivid; he knew the rattle of the stays and the smell of the wind, the feel of the roughhewn dock on his feet, each having been long lost to his past was now alive in his soul. He adjusted her rudder by the sound of the waves against the pilings alone in this new vision and the Electra responded once again to his lead as if a he had always been her captain. Her constant bucking began to cease and his heart leapt at the sense of peace surrounding his every nerve as she gave into his hand willingly.

It was then in his vision, as he neared the end of the dock, Steve felt his father's hand upon his head. He looked up but could not make out his face. A jolt of energy released through his father hand. The sensation was deafening and he felt as if he were being filled from the top down with untold energy and suddenly, the sun charged over the horizon and broke into blocks of a different reality, cascading orbs of light falling about him like snow. Emotions and senses began to connect to his mind and body. The edges of his reality bled into the vision as the orbs surrounded him. He could finally feel, he could finally breathe and could finally see the ocean as if it were one with him.

Yet, try as he might, he remained unable to see his father's face. A sense of desperation began to take over for he did not want to be left behind once again. He called out as his father climbed over the railing.

"Please stay with me!"

Decades seemed to pass as his father paused. He did not look back to Steve and in a fit of desperation; Captain Channing called out to his father once again.

"Daddy...please...take me with you!"

Time and space came to a crawl. The orbs stopped their pulsing but his father did not move toward him, nor did he speak. Instead, he held to the mast of their small sailboat looking away and Steve was sure that this would be how the dream would end, as it had a hundred times before. Moreover, as Steve's hope began sway his control over the Electra slowly slipped away. His heart sank and all his childhood fears welled up once again. He called out one last time.

"Daddy...please!"

His father turned about and there for the first time since his death Steve could see the face he had longed to touch for so long. The man he remembered his father to be as a child. The man he had always wanted to be.

Truc watched on with a broad grin as he knew what was happening to his friend.

Tears raced down Steve's face while the world below and the stars above became a liquid motion of events. He and his father left the safe harbor in their small sailboat for deep water. The peace that had long been missing had returned. He felt complete.

The harbor fell quickly away and the ocean was wild and free. The wind filled their sails and the sun beat down upon their small world with a brilliant aura. Then suddenly, four pillars of light lifted from the sea, as if Titans rising to fight the sky. The captain in him knew immediately that they were the four points of a compass. His technical mind came to life and he could finally measure how the waves and the sun aligned to the pillars. He corrected his calculations to the star map that had suddenly begun to spin above pillars of light; then pulled hard against the rudder and forced the Electra into the head wind. She gave no resistance to his command.

Truc instinctively released tension from the wing and as the outrigger dropped to within inches to the passing waves; he guided Steve's hand to skim the top of each passing swell like a father teaching his son how to ride a bike. All of a sudden, Steve somehow knew that all ahead was well, but, he had no idea how he knew this to be a fact. He decided it did not matter and with that, the connection to a living world he had never experienced filled every fiber of his being.

On vigil aboard the Rush, Simpson and Bearing watched on amazed as Captain Channing caressed the waves. They watched on as the Electra listened to her new master without hesitation. They watched on as he executed a tack to the Northeast, then, fifteen minutes later to the Southeast. The maneuvers were deliberate and perfect in timing. He executed each by the strike of his newfound internal clock and the pillars of light that he could so clearly see now. Admiral and Captain looked to each other and a knowing smile rested between them. They were witnessing a miracle and nothing more need be said.

Truc adjusted the wing as if a proud father.

"See...I tell you. I tell you...Steveeee. You...you... Okeydokey!"

Clair could not resist the urge but to howl aloud as she realized he was in full control. Her man would never be the same and she picked up the radio and dialed in the Rush to celebrate the moment.

"Sir, he's got it. He's figured it out!"

"I see that, Lieutenant...I don't think I could be any more proud of the two of you."

"Thank you, Sir...but, I'm just along for the ride at this point. It's Captain Channing you need tell that too, Sir."

"I will, Lieutenant. I will. Get some sleep now. You have to take over tomorrow."

"Yes, Sir! Electra out," Clair replied as she fell to the bottom of the well and bawled like a baby for joy. In her life, she had never experienced such joy for another person and his or her success. This was a feeling she wanted to keep the rest of her life.

Truc forced the wing hard into the wind and Steve could feel that the Electra wanted to break free of her bonds and fly. He could tell that she was holding back and he wanted more. Truc bent the wing to meet his desire but like a drug demanding more, Steve would not be satisfied with half speed. And without a word between them, Truc pulled the pin holding the forward sail at bay and the Electra leapt to full speed in an instant as the dark sail billowed before them. The Electra writhed and moaned beneath Steve as if a woman making love to him by the pulse of the ocean. Truc released the tension in the wing once again and the outrigger fell to within inches of the ocean swells. He touched each swell as if shaking an old friend's hand and once again, all ahead was perfect.

As the hour passed, Truc systematically released his control over to Steve. Each line felt like a tendril connected to Captain Channing's cerebral cortex. Once he had full control of her every resource, the vast connected nature of all things became apparent to him as the Electra snatched each wave and forced them beneath her bow as if a cougar chasing her prey. It was not enough for Steve. He asked her to give him every ounce of energy she could conjure. The Electra rallied to his call. She would not disappoint her new master.

Daybreak would come too soon.

47

Breaking News

Unfurl my soul
Stretch beyond my control
Find purchase within the prevailing wind
Let me begin again
Where once, I was at my end
Unfurl my soul
For today remains yet to be untold

WPGI Honolulu broke the news first by request of Admiral Simpson, as the Pentagon released the news to the major networks. Kiki became a household name in a matter of minutes. An hour later, WPGI's network inquired if she was available to work the national market. For the news team at WPGI, it was all very flattering and yet, desperately exhausting to be in control of a story in which they had no input.

The next morning, Kiki landed a report in prime time detailing life aboard a United States Coast Guard Cutter. The piece was delivered with a short clip regarding the current state of the Electra. It was the best George could pull off after meeting with the Admiral and watching the debrief most of the night. He made copious notes of locations that best suited a place to cut away as he knew he needed to offer commercial breaks. He then decided to film a cameo of Kiki saying, "We will return after this commercial break."

He then planned on her opening with, "This is Kiki Evans of WPGI Honolulu bringing you the first reading of Amelia Earhart's journal."

This was the plan until George realized Lieutenant Evans had never finished the story. He checked his equipment to make sure it was working properly and searched the case Simpson had supplied. Had Simpson held out on him, he thought. George decided at four in the morning to edit the first section and wait to speak with the Admiral after his morning coffee.

He finished the edits at five a.m. then broke into Kiki's bunk ordering, "Put on your Coast Guard cap and the Admiral's jacket, then meet me on the bridge in fifteen minutes. We have to catch the sun rise, Kiki."

Kiki cursed George for his lack of sensitivity, but George held his ground.

"Kiki, you are a professional. This is no longer a dog and pony show. Meet me in fifteen," he said as he barreled out of her room towards the bridge. He desperately wanted to film the Electra at sunrise.

George was not surprised to find Captain Bearing and Admiral Simpson enjoying coffee together. Both seemed genuinely pleased with each other, as if they were an old couple enjoying the morning newspaper. A moment later, George knew why the two were so pleased. To each side of the Rush, in a tight formation, lay two United States Navy destroyers.

"So when did company arrive?" George asked.

"About two hours ago," Bearing replied, as he sipped his coffee.

"Were they invited to the party?"

"They asked to join in formation, as part of a Joint Forces support team. They were sent by a friend of mine," Simpson replied as he lit his pipe.

Obviously, this development gave the crew of the Rush a charge as not one person could be found without a smile.

"Sir, I need to set up a morning promo for today's debrief. I need Kiki to perform a few lines to set up commercial breaks."

Bearing moved from his chair and pointed to his seat.

"My pleasure."

"Captain, I was thinking it would be a better shot...if you remained in your seat...while Kiki stood beside you."

Admiral Simpson loved the idea and it was plain Bearing wanted him to turn down the request.

"Sir, I don't wish to garner any publicity from this event," Bearing stated.

"It's not you garnering publicity Captain; it is the United States Coast Guard. I would hope that you would be willing to promote our branch of service?" Simpson said as he took another long drag from his pipe.

"Yes, Sir," the Captain conceded as he glared at George for promoting the idea.

Kiki arrived and George set up the shot with little fuss. He gave Kiki her script and then decided the shot would have more action with a Navy Destroyer in the background.

"This is Kiki Evans reporting from the bridge of United States Coast Guard Cutter Rush and I am the guest of Captain James Bearing." She placed her hand on his shoulder and to George's relief he attempted a smile. "We will soon return with the journal of Amelia Earhart," she said boldly, then after a short count from George, continued.

"This is Kiki Evans of WPGI Honolulu, live from the United States Coast Guard Cutter Rush. We will now return to the journal of Mrs. Amelia Earhart."

George gave her the thumbs up. Then, Kiki did something no one on the bridge expected. She hugged Captain Bearing.

"Thank you for working with us this morning," she said as she blushing like a little girl.

Bearing shifted in his seat uncomfortably and returned a nervous smile.

Ahead, the Electra sailed into the morning sun in full glory as she skipped from wave to wave. George, ever looking for filler footage asked if he could plug into the bridge monitor. Bearing nodded in agreement and a moment later, the Electra owned the screen.

"Is that Captain Channing driving the Electra?" Kiki asked.

"Yes it is. It seems his training paid off. He sailed her all night long," Captain Bearing replied.

George worked hard to stabilize the shot and cursed as the Electra suddenly disappeared from his view.

"All, stop!" Bearing suddenly ordered as he jumped to his feet and clutched his binoculars.

The Electra had begun to circle. The footage would be some of Georges best, however, the shot soon soured as Truc and Captain Channing took the opportunity to urinate.

After his morning constitutional, Steve lay down in the netting and George nearly turned off the camera. That was until Lieutenant Evans appeared topside, and three bridge crews found themselves severely distracted by her choice of uniform for the day.

Silhouetted by the morning light, Clair revealed her decision to change into something more appropriate for wet conditions by adorning a dark orange one-piece swimsuit that proudly displayed the Coast Guards signature orange stripe on white. The swimsuit exposed every inch of her long dark physique as she seemingly glistened in the morning sun. Her hair was now in two long ponytails and each swung from side to side like a little girls. A pair Ray Bans finished the ensemble and only made her smile seem the brighter.

Aboard the Rush, silence swept across the bridge until a young Ensign was heard to say, "Damn!"

Certain, the same sentiment was repeated multiple times aboard the other vessels, Simpson stared down the Ensign who looked away from the monitor in a desperate attempt to disappear into the console at his back.

Clair collected a few items from the well and the tension aboard the Rush became palpable as she climbed across the netting and stood above Captain Channing who looked to be fast asleep.

"Captain...would you like some breakfast?" Clair asked.

Steve squinted and then shaded his eyes as he tried to make sure that he was not in a dream. He could not help but to sit straight up and stare with mouth agape. The sight before him had to be supernatural he thought, as the rising sun surrounded her long smooth torso. He was sure an angel had come to visit him wearing a tight swimsuit.

"What did you say?" he stammered.

"Stick your tongue in your mouth, Captain. We have company," she quipped.

"You should have given me some warning, Lieutenant," he returned.

"What...because I am wearing a swimsuit. This old thing...its regulation swimwear Captain," she stated as she pointed to the Coast Guard logo plastered above her ample breasts.

"Well, I must say, I see why they approved."

"For some reason, I thought you would."

She tossed him a bottle of water and dropped the radio in his lap as she began for Truc.

"It's your turn to report in, Captain. And, you're ten minutes late."

Truc sat up and smiled as he enjoyed watching Steve's reaction to Clair. Clair returned his smile as she asked, "Did you sleep last night or did you have to stay awake and babysit Steveeeee?"

"I sleep like...baby, Ms. Clair," Truc replied. "Steveeee do good....very good!"

"Are you hungry?" she asked.

"Twinkie?"

Clair handed Truc two Twinkies and a bottle of water and he quickly devoured them. He then began to inspect the Electra as Clair returned to her Captain.

"I made you a fresh bed in the well."

She hesitated, as if unsure. She needed to tell him something, but wondered if she should.

"You surprised me last night," Clair said in a soft voice, afraid the Rush was somehow listening in.

"I surprised myself."

"That's twice you've surprised me, Captain," she teased as she gave him a quick wink.

The private moment between the two lovers broke as Truc yelled, "We go now!"

Clair leaned over to give Steve a better view, and in a near whisper said, "When you are sailing her, Captain...I just want to...well, let's just say you're going to be a very happy man if you can sail her all the way back to the states."

Steve glowed with the thought of the two of them in each other's arms once again. Life had suddenly improved.

As she headed for the outrigger, he watched her every move even though he knew Simpson was watching him. How they could hold it against a soon to be blind man he could not imagine. He then remembered her last instruction and dialed in the Rush as Clair and Truc, connected into their harnesses, and within minutes, they were leading the Electra away from the fleet.

"I see you mastered the art of sailing Captain," the Admiral said as he snatched the radio away from Captain Bearing.

"Yes, Sir. I think I have figured out how he does it. You're not going to believe when I tell you. "

"Captain, does Lieutenant Evans realize that she has three crews watching her every move?"

"I would have to report Admiral, that the Lieutenant is very aware of her surroundings and that she is wearing standard Coast Guard approved swimwear, complete with logo. You know Lieutenant Evans...Admiral. A stickler when it comes to protocol," he replied.

"I see...thank you, Captain, for being attentive to such things as compliance with the dress code...and logos," the Admiral responded a bit flummoxed. He glanced about the bridge and realized he had an unusually large number of binoculars trained on the horizon to deal with.

"Get some sleep, Captain. You have a long trip before you."

"Yes, Sir. Electra out."

Kiki suppressed a smile but the Admiral did not miss the fact that George had took the opportunity to zoom in on Clair while he was on the radio.

"George!" he bellowed as an order.

With that, George pulled the cable from behind the monitor, grabbed Kiki by the hand, and headed for the mess hall.

48

Kiki's Turn

The sand beneath my feet grows weak
The stars above hide, lost to the night
My soul seeks to discover
As waves consume all about me
That my heart is as if an uprooted tree
So, let the wind test this child of woe
For there is no crown for a lost soul
Test me now
I have nowhere left to go

The first reading of the journal by Lieutenant Evans was released at 11:00 a.m. Eastern Standard Time. George had broken the story into several 15-minute excerpts, and enjoyed the fact that the network had no say in how he chose to make it all work. He could only imagine the meetings taking place at the network offices, as they pondered their predicament.

America stopped to watch the story unfold. Coffee shops and bars flooded with people drawn to the story. Schools ran Truc's debrief directly to each classroom so that they might learn of Mrs. Amelia Earhart and Commander Fred Noonan. Congress called a recess and the President met with his staff in the Oval Office as Lieutenant Clair Evans read the first installation. News agencies flooded the command centers of every United States Coast Guard station in an attempt to attain personal information regarding Lieutenant Evans and Captain Channing.

Meanwhile, Kiki and George filmed introductions and smaller segments on the inner workings of a United States Coast Guard Cutter. Kiki dug in and wrote much of the dialogue, which made the pieces feel more natural and they dropped each block, as fast as George could edit.

The routine remained the same for four days as the Electra plowed a path toward the mainland. The two began to work as a team, searching for new and interesting shot locations as if they had been together for years. Kiki started each segment by giving a short synopsis of the previous segments. George took creative license and used the footage of Lieutenant Evans in her swimsuit in the hope of running up the ratings.

Kiki worked the crew, searching out special interest stories, when not maintaining a vigil on the bridge beside Captain Bearing or Admiral Simpson. Soon, she was able to find her way to near any section of the cutter with little effort, but most important, she made friends with many of the female crew. This proved to be an invaluable link in understanding the role of women in the Coast Guard. And so it was, Kiki asked George if she could do a piece on the subject of women in the military and he agreed. The piece took most of the day to shoot and half the night to edit. Little did they know that the piece would win awards for their effort; even though to them it felt like a rushed endeavor.

The day before Lieutenant Evans segments ended, George and Kiki were summoned to the bridge. As they entered, Admiral Simpson lit a cigar which had been strictly forbidden on other cutters.

"Kiki...has George shown you the last segment by Lieutenant Evans?" the Admiral asked.

"No, Sir. He has kept it all to himself."

"He has, has he...well, that is most reassuring," Simpson said as he gave George a knowing grin. "That's because George knows that after tomorrow morning, there will be no more segments by Lieutenant Evans."

"Will we find out in the final segment of what happened to Amelia?" she asked.

"No Kiki...there are no more segments," the Admiral replied.

"Are you telling me, the story is over...and we never find out what happened to her?" she pressed.

"The story is not over Kiki. The Electra is still creating the story with each mile that she sails closer to the West Coast. We are out of segments simply because Lieutenant Evans did not finish reading the journal before the Electra left port," he replied as the thick smoke swirled about his head.

"Do you have the journal in the box?" George asked.

"Yes we do. I think you know what needs to happen next George," the Admiral insinuated.

"What's going to happen next?" Kiki asked of both men, obviously concerned.

"You're going to finish reading the journal, Kiki," George said in a direct manner.

Her weak eye began a search for different corners of the bridge as she paled at the thought.

"Isn't there someone a bit more qualified?" she mumbled.

"No. You're the real deal Kiki," the Admiral responded. "Truc, would choose you...if he knew you," Admiral Simpson added.

"Why?" she asked.

"I think he likes a pretty face," Captain Bearing interjected.

With that, Kiki turned to watch the Electra as it skipped across the waves. The morning was glorious and the energy of the bridge filled her soul. She knew she was up to this if the Admiral believed in her. A determined look grew from within, and she said with a newfound authority, "OK, let's get on with this. We have good light now, and I don't want to waste it. In addition, Admiral, you are going to have to put that cigar out if you want me reading the Journal. Open a window...the smoke needs to be pulled out of here."

"I think we could make an officer out of you," Admiral Simpson quipped as he stubbed out his cigar and opened the outside hatch.

"I have to say one more thing, Admiral. After watching Lieutenant Evans, handle that...boat out there. I believe, Truc chose Lieutenant Evans for a few more qualities than her pretty face. Wouldn't you agree, Admiral?" she asked as she glared at Captain Bearing.

"Lieutenant Evans will take over my job one day, Kiki," Admiral Simpson responded, obviously filled with pride. "She is the real deal!"

"Where do you want me George?" Kiki ordered more than requested as she looked about the bridge with her hands on her hips.

"I think that the Captain's seat would be best Kiki. But, only if you think so," George replied as he playfully cowered to her demands.

Feeling empowered, Kiki railed, "Admiral! You need more women on this bridge. There is far too much testosterone up here."

"Hell yeah!" the lone female Ensign on the bridge grunted.

Admiral Simpson looked toward her but chose not reply. His newfound confident reporter bemused him. He put his hand on her shoulder and said, "We are now two days away from Oakland California. Truc is taking the

Electra to Oakland because he wants to complete the circumnavigation attempt of Amelia. Amelia began her attempt in Oakland. If he arrives with the Electra, by July 4th, he will have completed the journey seventy five years...nearly to the day, on which Amelia should have returned," the Admiral stated as fact.

"Amelia would have arrived on the Fourth?" George interrupted.

"Most likely not, but she could have made Hawaii. If they had landed at Howland, refueled, and the Electra had no mechanical issues, the two of them could have pulled off landing on the Fourth of July in Hawaii. Amelia would have landed in Hawaii none less, which is still in my opinion, America. It does not matter...at the speed Truc is maintaining, he will arrive on the Fourth of July. He will pass beneath the Golden Gate, and then he will pass Alcatraz as he makes his way to Oakland, California. Nonetheless, it doesn't matter if he actually lands in Oakland...he simply needs to make the West Coast," Simpson stated.

"So we need to finish this journal before then? Is that possible?" Kiki asked.

"I looked it over before I came aboard. We can accomplish the task in the next few days. I was hoping we could time the final entry as he passes through the Golden Gate," the Admiral replied.

"You got a bit of a stage director in you, Admiral," George pressed.

Kiki took hold of the box as the Admiral handed it to her and held it much like Clair had before.

"I have one more thing I need to tell you," Simpson said, then paused. "I need to tell...all of you, the reason why I let Truc leave the base with the Electra. The reason involve far more than the completion of the circumnavigation attempt."

He looked about the bridge. Then with a bit of bravado he said, "Truc has the mummified remains of Amelia aboard the Electra. He is taking her home."

Bearing dropped a pair of reading glasses. Kiki held to a railing to find her balance and George felt his knees buckle. A silence swept over the bridge as the Admiral smiled on like the Cheshire Cat. Truc's secret was out of the bag.

Captain Bearing finally broke the deafening silence with, "Ok. That was unexpected."

The Journal of Amelia Earhart

I only have a few pages remaining. If you have discovered this journal and read this far, then I suppose you want to know how it all ends. Well for me it will end on these pages. I must tell you that I am dying. I am concerned that I may not finish and I feel like I need to tell you how this will end. My health has been failing dramatically since the accident. I am not telling Truc what I know to be happening. He blames himself for the failure of the Electra. I have tried to tell him that he is too hard on himself. I was asking for a miracle that he could not accomplish with the materials he had to work with. He tried so hard to please me and it has become apparent to me that I will never leave here alive.

I am bleeding internally and I can do nothing to stop the end result. I was going to leave this journal here in case we did not make it. It seems I will be leaving my journal with Truc and Mila to do with as they please. I began this journal because Truc was going to take me away to another island. Truc studies the water like a professor and I have never known him to be wrong. However, I wanted there to be a record in case we did not complete the trip.

For the past few years, Truc has worked when not fishing for food or bringing water on the most ingenious creations. We were testing the largest by far made from parts of the Electra. My current injuries were caused when the wing collapsed on this new sailing vessel he has been building. It pinned me as we attempted to test the design in open water. As I lie here thinking about it, I suppose no other outcome was ever possible. For some strange reason, I am at peace with the fact that I will never leave this place. However, I do want the world to know what happened.

Since this will be my final destination, I want to tell you about it before I carry on. This island is volcanic and very beautiful. It is the largest of three. I have no charts so I cannot supply a name. We have made a wonderful camp here next to the lagoon. There are wild creatures here that frighten Mila. She never interacted with such things and she is very much like a child. In many ways, I feel as if I am in Eden with Adam and Eve. The two of them are so innocent and uncorrupted.

I want to tell you the best part of this story. Mila is pregnant. If I will regret anything, it will be that I will never see their child.

As you can tell, I am no longer on the Kwajalein Atoll. I will tell you how in a bit. I know that I should not waste these pages and ink with the small things. This however has been a beautiful experience. I wish I could fill volumes telling the adventure of it all. When we first arrived, we spent months exploring our new home. At first, I had hoped for other inhabitants. Once I realized that no one else lived here, I found that I was not disappointed.

Mila feels safe for the first time in her short life. She believes the Japanese are everywhere else but here. It is her greatest fear that they might discover us. I am sure we are well beyond their realm of influence but how can I explain this to her. Mila and Truc are safe and that is what matters now. They have suffered enough.

Mila and I have turned into a team of root and fruit hunters. Mila has picked up some English and I am semi fluent with their tongue. I have learned to live as natural as any human could possibly be. I think of how others would judge my appearance back home. They would think me most odd now with my long hair and bits of clothing. To tell the truth it is all very liberating. I have even wondered if I could return and live a normal life.

I am so different from the girl who left the States with hopes of being the first. I always wanted to be the first in everything. I told my George before I left that I had one more stunt flight in me. This however, is no longer a stunt. People have paid for my ambition. I wonder many days how Truc and Mila would have turned out if I had *not met them. I wonder if they would have met. I also wonder what has happened to Soluu for taking care of me. I wonder what Fred would be doing now if I had not pushed him to come with me. I wonder if I would have grown old in a small town and had a fine funeral for the old woman who once did stunts.*

These things fill my heart at night as I look at the millions of stars. Fate is a funny thing. I cannot help but ask myself if everything was decided long before I came along or does it just happen through circumstance upon circumstance? As my final hour draws near, I know now that I cannot choose my end, but I can choose how to greet it. I have decided I will shake fate's hand bravely and welcome the end as if a friend.

I have one more conclusion and it took living here to make me realize it. Truc and Mila do not consider themselves stranded on an uninhabited island. They are at home as if a newlywed couple with a new place to decorate. They would be most content to spend their days here and live a life of peace. I see them as if they are Adam and Eve.

Truc knows I miss my home and he tries to cheer me up. He has worked so hard to take care of us. He is relentless and never loses faith that things will work out. I believe I could have lived a long life here if I had not pushed Truc to do the impossible. I am amazed by his tenacity. How do you grasp the physics of such things as wind load and lift when you do not understand math or have a scientific method? Nevertheless, I tell you, Truc is a genius. He understands things that would take many scientists a lifetime to figure out.

I believe if I had not pushed him to take me home, he would have figured out every detail and another form of the Electra would have taken me home. He built several small vessels to work around the island for fishing and foraging; each an improvement upon the other. A professor would spend a lifetime teaching his students what Truc knows about the ocean and sailing. I believe he breathes in the world around him and then he processes it to his advantage

I will tell you that I do not think it was his design that failed. Rather, he did not have the means to bond such massive forces. I asked him to use the wing of the Electra. It took us forever to remove it from the Electra with the few tools we had aboard her. I thought it might be the perfect sail. As it turned out, it will be my undoing.

Thank God, we left Mila on the island for the test run. Not all was lost and Truc was able to bring most of the vessel ashore after rescuing me. I am heartbroken that he had to cut the wing free to save me. He is devastated at the outcome. No matter how much I tell him that it was not his fault .he still will not forgive himself for the failure.

I must move on. I have so much more I need to say.

I suppose I need to tell you how we arrived at this paradise. It all seems so unbelievable now. As I told you before the accident, I was living better by the hand of Ayumu. He was a faithful friend and I must say that I miss him deeply. He was intelligent and kind. He was the best of people and he sacrificed so much to make this possible.

49

Deep Below

I waited for you
Yours to embrace
Face me now and rest
This shall not be the final test

Clair lay beside the wing in the tangled netting and watched on with deep interest as Steve entered into his trance. He had taken over for the evening as Truc uncharacteristically left his post. For the first time, Truc had looked tired to Clair, his age apparent, as he handed the controls over to Steve. She took it as a good sign that he trusted Steve with his Electra, and hoped he would rest awhile below.

Steve began his first leg without the safety net of his mentor; yet, the evening run became near flawless within minutes. Clair and Steve had exchanged one last glance before he departed into his newfound magical realm and she could no longer imagine a future without her Captain.

As the last vestiges of day departed, the first flights searching for them from the mainland became apparent. Steve thought it odd to hear the sounds of civilization after a week at sea. He knew the morning would be a mad house of onlookers by both air and sea and he hoped they were still far enough out that he would not come across someone at anchor in the midst of the night. He pushed the thought aside. He had to believe that the Rush would find a way to warn him if he could not sense another ships presence.

He set his focus on the pillars of light and the star map in his head, his heart rate lowered, and the sea began to lead him home. It took only a moment to clear his present consciousness stream future concerns. Things he knew he could not determine nor change. Moreover, as he did so, his senses quickly expanded beyond his known limitations. Every sense but his eyesight was alive, breathing, communicating to his mind and his soul that all that lay before him good.

The Electra answered him in kind then suddenly, the connection broke away. Something was wrong with the ocean. The waves were falling away in the wrong direction. He awoke and looked to the Rush to confirm that the two Navy escorts at her side. All three remained well beyond any interference, yet, his sense of smell was telling him that something unnatural was presently below him. He returned to his trance and listened, and then he felt the problem, more than he heard it. He knew immediately what he was dealing with and wondered how long it had been nearby, as he released the Electra into a circling stall.

He quickly released the harness and returned to Clair visibly upset and unable to speak. She dared not interfere and waited patiently as he paced the well.

"Do you have the radio?" he finally asked.

"What's wrong Steve? Is it something I can fix?"

"No, I have to fix this problem...and they are going to think I have lost my mind."

"Are you sure you want to call it in then?"

"Yes...or we will spend the rest of the night here until Truc is rested. I don't want to do that."

Admiral Simpson happened to be on the bridge to enjoy the sunset and oversee the changing of the guard aboard the Electra when the radio crackled.

"Admiral, I have a request," Captain Channing said forcefully.

"Yes, Captain, what can I do for you?"

"I need you to ask the submarine that is below us to fall back. It is causing a swell and messing up our navigational abilities."

"Are you serious, Captain?"

"Sir...is there a submarine below me?" Steve asked.

A long silenced remained.

Clair took Steve by the arm and asked, "Are you kidding me? You can tell that a submarine is below us?"

"Yes...I can."

"Oh my god they will never let you out of the service now. You will be at sea the rest of your life smelling out Russian subs!" she exclaimed as she fell back into the net and laughed aloud at the revelation.

Simpson, was taking far too long to respond, Steve thought. Finally, Captain Bearing returned to the radio.

"Captain, I have been ordered to inform you that no submarines are in the area...and... Moreover, it would be a breach in national security, if we were to reveal the location of our fleet, intentionally, or by accident. I believe you will discover that you have been mistaken once you return to your duties. Rush out."

"Oh my God it is there. How did you know?" Clair asked.

He held up his hand to let her know he was about to answer the Rush, "Thank you for correcting my false assumption. Electra out."

With that, he tossed the radio to the safety of the well and he could not help but pull Clair up from the netting as he passed. It was the first time in days that they had made any meaningful contact and he held her hand for what he knew to be far too long.

"I would suggest you get this vessel to the States. I have a date with an up and coming Captain upon our arrival and I would hate to be late?" she said as she pulled her hand back from his grip.

"Well then...about that subject. Where exactly do you want go on our first date?" he replied.

"Who said it was with you, Captain?" she teased as she helped him with the harness.

The Journal of Amelia Earhart.

As read by Kiki Evans.

So how did I ever leave Kwajalein? I suppose I should have told you that story by now but it seemed best to tell you why I am writing this. So I will keep this brief for it pains me much to think of the sacrifice paid for my survival.

Ayumu and I were on one of our long walks when his superior arrived. I will refer to his replacement as nothing more than the bastard from this point on. Ayumu noticed his plane circling first and that it was a command aircraft. By the time we returned, the new base commander was already inspecting the headquarters. The bastard came off like an emperor, brash and immediately unkind to those about him. He was confident and ugly at the same time. He was truly evil and I knew immediately that my time of peace had ended.

I will never forget the look Ayumu received when the bastard noticed me. His anger was apparent as he began to attack Ayumu verbally. Ayumu tried to answer the man's questions but it was of no use and before I knew it, a security detail surrounded me and returned me to my original cell. The nightmare had returned.

I cannot imagine what Ayumu must have been experiencing. I am sure he was grilled over his decisions and actions regarding me. I will never know but I believe to this day that I could hear the bastard yelling at him for most of the evening. If he was not yelling at Ayumu then he was giving the entire base hell.

Later that afternoon, things took another turn for the worse. Guards arrived with Truc and Mila. They were beaten and Mila's clothing was torn. Mila cried so hard. I could not take it that they were mistreated for being my friends. After several hours, I could hear Truc singing to her gently. It was comforting to hear him as the sun set that day with no food or water. In the back of my mind, I knew it was all over. The calm before the storm had come and gone and now I regretted ever having known the calm. I just knew we were going to be fed to the sharks the next day.

One can only stay up so long when emotionally exhausted. All I remember is that I awoke to Ayumu whispering. I thought it was a dream at first until I realized he was holding his hand over my mouth to stop me from making a scene. He was calm and deliberate as he opened Truc and Mila's cell and brought them to me. He explained that he was ordered to return home with the Electra in the morning and that she had been moved to the far end of the runway and fueled.

Ayumu planned to take us with him and he believed if he could get us back to his home that cooler heads would prevail. He then told us that he had learned that our execution was scheduled to happen soon after he left. The plan was simple. He figured that they would focus on him leaving and would not think of us if we could get aboard before daylight.

Here began the second longest day of my life. We started for the far end of the runway by working through jungle cover. Truc knew the way but it took some time to work around the base. Finally, we made the jungle nearest the Electra and waited as Ayumu checked things out. Several other aircraft were parked nearby and we could see two men working on one of the planes as the sun began to rise. Ayumu walked from the jungle and startled both men. I do not know what he told them but both began the long walk to the command center at the far end of the runway.

As we boarded the Electra I cannot describe the joy I felt upon the returning to my plane. She was beautiful and strong but I soon noticed that she was different. Both of my radios were missing and many other flight instrumentations, including my compass. I suppose they had removed them to see if we had technology, they did not. They had begun to rewire, but as best I could tell, what little was there was not functional. I was however able to check the battery charge and found that they were strong enough to attempt a start without an outside source.

That is when I heard the morning call to inspection. The men who had once been posted near the Electra had nearly returned to the command center when the bastard stepped out on to the porch of the officers' quarters. I could tell it was him by his walk alone. He looked about for officers and noticed that he was missing Ayumu. I told Ayumu that he had to go and meet with the bastard if he hoped to get away without suspicion. He then quickly left the Electra and ran toward the command post. As the bastard looked him over I could tell Ayumu was talking quickly and I could not help but to shake like a leaf for him.

Before I knew it, both men bowed to each other and Ayumu began the long walk back. He was committed at this point and I never doubted his resolve but his return seemed to take forever since he did not want to give us away. I could see the sweat running across his brow as he neared the Electra. It was then one of the sentry's ran from the command post calling his name and Ayumu stopped. I will never forget the look on his face as he turned about to meet the man half way. To my relief, they spoke for a moment and then the sentry handed Ayumu a piece of paper and saluted smartly.

Again, Ayumu began his walk back. Now he could not hide from the fact he was helping us to escape.

As he boarded, I glanced back to Truc and Mila. There was little space for them with the extra fuel tanks in the back. Mila was overcome with fear. I cannot imagine having never been in anything like the Electra. How horrifying the experience must have been. It was time to attempt the engines and I raced through everything that I could avoid in the preflight checklist. I primed the port engine and was relieved to see the remaining instrumentation lights came on line.

I lit the first engine and she sputtered and spat like a kid with a cold. The batteries seemed weak to me. I was certain they had robbed several sets from other aircraft.

I believe it was at that point the bastard received the report that I was not to be found in my cell.

I fired her off once again and the same thing happened. I knew I only had one more attempt left in her as weak as the batteries were now. If she did not fire, we would not be able to charge the batteries for the starboard engine. I reset everything and fired her again. She sputtered and spat as she tried to clear out built up carbon. Then she hit. That was the most beautiful sound in the entire world. I brought her to full power and held the brake as I primed the next engine. It only took two attempts with the batteries receiving full charge from the running engine.

I was so engrossed in getting her fired off that I had lost contact with what was occurring several hundred yards ahead at the command center. When I looked up, I noticed dozens of men scrambling for a bunker and the bastard walking down the runway toward us with his pistols drawn. I released the brakes as I brought the engines to full power. I could tell she was heavy with fuel and I began to wonder if she could take off before the end of the runway. I began to regret that I had never taken the time to measure the runway in all my walks. It did not matter now; we had to go, because at that moment a bullet pierced my windshield and hit a control panel behind me.

Ayumu helped me taxi to the end of the runway and there I brought her about only to face the bastard still walking our way. I laid into the controls, released the brakes and said a prayer. I thank God now they only seemed to have pistols, which were very inaccurate from a distance.

As I barreled down the runway, the bastard's clip ran out and he had to jump aside as we would have hit him. As best I could tell, only a few men made it back from the weapons bunker with rifles. I will never know to this day how a fuel tank was not punctured. I can only call it a miracle.

I must say that I was most impressed with my Electra as the runway started to disappear. I could tell she wanted to escape as much as I did. I pulled up on the yoke at the last moment and she responded by giving me a few feet over the water, and for the first time in what seemed an eternity I was free.

50

Storm

Pressed by the folds of time
Called to be free, called to shine
I race toward to that far starry shore
For I see an end
I see the door

Clair bundled up in the well and read a book by flashlight, as Steve pushed the Electra to full speed. The early evening passed peacefully and the stars above were brilliant. She decided to check in on Truc before she settled down for the night herself and discovered him curled up under a sleeping bag with a bottle of water in his hand. He seemed to be at peace, and so, she decided not to wake him, as she was sure he needed the rest.

Upon returning topside, she noticed that Steve was beginning to stir in his harness.

"What's wrong?" she yelled over the distance of the passing ocean.

"I believe we have a storm coming. It's the only thing that makes sense to me. I can feel it...and it's coming quick."

Clair peered ahead at the dark horizon. At first, it looked no different from any other evening, until a crack of heat lightning in the far distance revealed the truth, and at that very moment, the radio in her hand snapped to life.

"Electra, this is the Rush," a young voice crackled, that Clair did not recognize. "We seem to have a storm on the radar that has popped up rather quickly and, it seems to be gaining speed. The best we can tell is that we have two colliding systems. It's developing at an alarming rate and it looks to have high winds Lieutenant," the young man sounded wary as if not wanting to cause fear, but in so doing, only generated the more. "I have requested that the Captain be informed immediately."

"Copy, we will discuss this development and see what our options are. Electra out," Lieutenant Evans replied.

"I'm glad you are here with me," Steve said, as Clair finished covering the span between them.

"I'm glad to be here with you too," she replied as she pulled hair from her eyes.

"No, Clair...I mean...I need to tell you something," he said nervously. "I don't know how long all of this will last and I don't want to risk not telling you. So...I'm just going to say it...I think I love you."

Clair did not know how to answer. She wanted to respond in kind, but everything was happening so fast and to her relief, Steve released her from the pressure of an answer.

"Please don't answer. I just wanted you to know...Ok?"

"Ok."

"Now, I need you to check on Truc. I can feel him...something is wrong...very wrong."

"How do you know that? Only a moment ago...he looked fine."

"Something is wrong, Clair. I just know it. Please check on him."

"What's wrong...is it the storm? Truc will know what to do, Steve. He must have survived dozens of them."

"It may be nothing more than nerves. I do need him to tell me what to do next. Neither you nor I have sailed the Electra in a storm. I'm pretty sure however, that we cannot head for the Rush. I need him."

"It will be OK. I promise," Clair encouraged.

"I know," he replied.

"No...I mean you and me. Give me time...I think I can meet you half way...if you will give me some time."

He took her by the hand and his smile reassured her that he could wait.

She reluctantly pulled away to check on Truc as Steve leaned into his harness and fell into the trance once again. With every fiber of his being, he soon knew the weather system was going to be bad and then he sensed something else and shuddered at the thought of it.

The journal of Amelia Earhart

It was a miracle to clear the beach, and then the ocean. I flew for several miles barely a dozen feet above the water before I could gain altitude. I wanted to cheer for having made a most magnificent escape until I noticed Ayumu. He sat perfectly erect and somehow I knew. Blood began to soak his uniform yet he maintained a calm demeanor. He was growing pale, yet he still smiled. If I had noticed his condition, when only a few feet above the water, I believe we would have crashed.

I remember how he told me to remain calm but I yelled for Truc to come all the same. When Truc did not answer, I began to worry that they had been hit too. However, Truc finally appeared and began to pull Ayumu from the seat but Ayumu would not let him. It was all too painful to watch but Ayumu never lost his composure.

He told me to stay in close to the water because he knew they would follow. I asked him where he thought we should go and I remember him smiling but not answering. It did not take long for me to discover three planes several miles behind, as I broke hard to port. I then broke southwest and dove for the water. I decided if they were going to follow me, they were going to have to be good pilots.

They were making time on us but I knew my Electra could handle bad weather and before me was a strong squall line. It was our only hope. There would be no instrumentation to guide me once in the storm but I felt that I had no other choice. Somehow, I just knew they would not follow me into it at sea level.

I am not sure what happened to our pursuers because I never saw them again. Once firmly in the storm I pulled up to what I believed to be five or six hundred feet. I could see nothing for the longest and wondered many times if I were flying level. I finally decided to gain altitude in hopes of not crashing into the water. It took nearly an hour for me to fly through that storm and as it ended, I banked south by my reckoning and took us to what I believed to be 6000 feet.

51

At The Gates
Of Hell, Trust

Let me dance among the fruit of life
Let me sing in the wind of grace
Let me stand within your presence
Let me touch this holy place

Clair gently called his name. When Truc did not respond, she entered the hold, switched on her flashlight and gasped as she found him shivering and pale.

"Oh Truc...what are you doing...why did you not tell me you were sick?" she pleaded as she felt his forehead. Truc did not stir at her words and she knew his fever had to be well over 100 degrees. When he finally awoke, as he reached to touch her face his eyes filled with pain and tears ran down his cheeks.

"Ms. Clair...no worry...I okeydokey," he whispered.

"No you're not okeydokey?"

A lump began to grow deep in Clair's throat.

"You have a very high fever Truc. We were so stupid, we never thought about your immunity to our diseases. We just assumed you were bulletproof," she said as she rubbed his head like a mother comforting her child.

"I Okeydokey...Ms. Clair."

"You don't have to be strong all the time. You should let others help you," she insisted.

"Amelia, she say...same," he replied.

"We have to get you help now."

At that moment a rogue wave crashed over the deck upper deck and the violent impact forced her to remember that she had come to fetch Truc.

"Truc...we have a problem," she said as she slipped in beside him.

"Storm...come now...Ms. Clair," Truc replied as he lifted his arm and pointed toward the sky.

"Yes, it's here."

"Tell Steveee...no stop...Okeydokey? Electra...good...in bad storm...if Steveee...trust Electra," he mumbled.

"He will want to make sure that you are treated first Truc. We will have to turn back and take you to the Rush," she replied.

"No...No...must go straight...no...no turn...no stop. Electra...must not turn in storm...she go straight. You trust Steveeee...when storm bad. Trust...Steveeeee."

She attempted to force upon him water until another large wave slapped the hull once again. Clair cracked the cowling to look about and discovered a driving rain, powered by strong gusts and lightning. Moreover, as she looked to their stern, suddenly, the lights of the Rush and her escort of Navy Destroyers disappeared behind a curtain of black rain.

Clair forced the cowling to open, snatched the radio and ducked as lightning snapped nearby. Then, as if letting all aboard know this would be a serious weather event, a deep rumble rolled across the ocean; it vibrated deep in her bones and caused her hair to stand on end. She decided to ignore the warning and clambered toward the outrigger as the growing waves attempted to knock her free.

Steve hung by his harness and swayed with the outrigger as he fought to maintain control of the Electra. The look on Clair face told him more than he wanted to know. He reached out and took her by the hand as she stumbled the last few feet toward him. Clair wore her fear like a garment, as lightning split the expanse between sea and sky and he knew that instant that his premonition was correct.

"Truc is sick...a high fever," she yelled over the growing melee.

With this news, Steve released tension from the wing and the Electra began to slow dramatically.

"He has a virus...I suppose from us. He is not immune to our world," he replied.

"How did you know?" she asked as she fought back tears.

Steve remained quiet for a long moment, his heart searching for his next move. He suddenly felt disconnected from the living world he had only recently come to know.

"I need to check on him!" he finally said.

"No! He is resting now. I forced him drink some water. He wants you to stay with the Electra. To keep sailing her," she replied.

"I think we need to turn about and take him to the Rush!" Steve exclaimed holding Clair as if to protect her from the next bolt of lightning.

"Truc told me that we must not stop. He told me, the Electra was not built to turn about in a storm. He also said that I need to let you and the Electra find the way when the hard part hits," Clair yelled over a strong gust of wind.

"The hard part! What the hell do you think this is Clair?" he replied as he wrestled a control line.

"I think we may break apart if we try to come beside the Rush in this weather," she returned.

"I know. I know...I don't think we have a choice at this point either. If we turnabout now...we might just sail right into the Rush at full speed," he replied.

Clair retrieved the radio from her pocket and dialed in the Rush, but no one answered. She attempted several times and checked her settings with each attempt, but to no avail.

"Go back inside and see if you can reach them there. I cannot be worried for the both of you. As long as you are out here, I will worry," he whispered in her ear as he pulled her head close to his.

Clair kissed him passionately as the lightning poured down about the vessel. And as she broke away, a loud clap of thunder shook the Electra and with that natural display of power, Clair decided it best to run the gauntlet and dive into the well before the next set of waves hit. She returned much as she had witnessed Truc do a hundred times, skipping from one line to the next, suddenly she stopped mid-point and began to work her way back to the outrigger. She took Steve by the harness and kissed deeply once again.

"I love you too!" she said as she released him from the bond.

"I know!" he replied as he pulled her close once again.

"Remember, when this gets bad, you must trust the Electra. Those were Truc's orders. He said you would know how to do this," Clair encouraged him. She then let go of his hand and raced the next set of swells for the relative safety of the well.

Below, Clair discovered Truc fast asleep upon her return. She switched on her small pocket light and searched for a focal point as the hull bounced violently into the crush of waves upon her hull. She quickly scavenged her duffle bag for dry clothes and changed in the dark. With that completed, she then turned her attention to the first aid kit. Working with the light in her mouth, she filled two syringes, wiped Truc's arm with an alcohol swab and hit him with a shot of antibiotics and then a B-12.

He did not awake for either shot and so she began to force fluid upon him, but it was of no use, and her frustration only grew as her small flash light began to flicker. Buried in a box, somewhere deep in the hull, was another set of batteries, but now was not the time to start digging for them, she told herself.

The Electra rocked violently and moaned under the pressure against as she cut through the next set of waves. More for her own comfort she decided to lie down beside Truc and hold him. As she did so, she began to hum a song, her father taught her as a child, to comfort herself more than Truc. Then, as the Electra fought the elements with great moans of pain, she began to sing each verse as if she were a little girl singing to her father. Somehow, it helped, and so she continued for the next hour to hold tight to Truc and sing her song of years long lost.

The light flickered once again and Truc awoke as she finished a verse. The grand smile swept across his face as he took her by the hand and Clair cried the more as she realized he was beginning to hallucinate. As if finding the perfect note, Truc called out, "Mila" and then closed his eyes, satisfied that she was with him as he looked at Clair.

Clair laid her head on his chest and prayed as the Electra plummeted down the face of another rogue wave, wailing as if the storm would rip her apart. Clair held tight to the old man she had come to love nearly as much as her own father, and with each crushing wave upon the hull, the little pocket light flickered, as if it knew it must hold on for one more moment. Then, in a weak final gasp, the light seemed to sparkle as it offered up the last of its strength and died. The long dark night had begun.

52

The Tempest
Of Time

Life breaks upon our bow
For the world is but a moment
I am but a spot upon the clouds
A fold of dust in the wind

Captain Bearing ordered the armada to a complete stop, as he watched in horror, the Electra disappearing into the storm. Seconds later, radar reported that they could no longer follow the Electra. To hold position in the midst of a storm with a missing craft was not how the Rush normally functioned. They attempted to hail the Electra, but no signal returned and the Rush began to roll with the ever-increasing waves. Captain Bearing began to sweat his next move, as lightning filled the sky about him. A wrong decision and all could be lost.

Admiral Simpson arrived on the bridge with daggers for eyes and quickly ordered his Captain to the chart room.

"What the hell is happening?" he snapped once the door closed. "Why are we at all stop?"

"We lost them, Sir. They drove headfirst into that storm and we cannot find them by radar. We heard a short sentence or two from their radio, which tells me they have it on, but it was not a distress call. I ordered an all stop for fear of running them over."

"What do you mean the radar can't see them? Did you check the systems and run a diagnostic?"

"Yes Sir, we did...there is something about this storm that is blinding our radar. It's not just us Sir, the Navy lost theirs as well, and they have run a complete diagnostic."

The Rush rolled hard to port as she now lay broadside to the storm. Captain Bearing knew he could not remain in this attitude if he wanted a functional crew, and he found himself most unsettled, that Admiral Simpson looked like man who had just witnessed a ghost.

If Captain Bearing had only known the half of it, he would have worried the more, as his Admiral had been experiencing nightmares of losing the Electra since the first night of their journey. As his dreaded dream became reality, Admiral Simpson turned to Bearing and ordered, "Get us underway Captain."

"Yes, Sir," Captain Bearing replied as the Rush rolled into the next broadside, forcing him to grab a control panel for stability.

Admiral Simpson slammed the door shut as Bearing exited. He began to sling charts about the room in frustration and he fought the urge to break something, but his emotions were taking over and he found himself throwing everything on the chart table across the room. After a few moments of staring at the floor, he regained his composure, picked up the mess, and returned to the bridge. He had to remain the Admiral, he told himself.

"Tell the Navy escorts to fall back two miles and to put look outs on their deck. Also, tell them that they need to turn on every light they own." Knowing they had most likely done all he had just ordered. "Post five men on our bow and let's begin a search grid ladies and gentlemen," Bearing ordered, as Simpson looked about to the crew. To a person, the look was of defeat. He needed to rally the troops.

"Let's not assume the worst. If anyone can get through this storm...it will be, Truc," he said with as much confidence as he could muster.

Kiki and George entered the bridge, as Simpson gave his rally call, and noticed that the mood was ominous. Kiki made her way through the maze of instruments and boldly stood post next to Captain Bearing. For Bearing's part, he did not hesitate to offer her a pair of binoculars as she looked to him with tear-filled eyes and forced a smile. He returned the smile and then ordered the bridge to go to dark.

As Captain Bearing managed his well-trained crew through the heart of the storm, Simpson remained silent. If anyone were to locate the Electra, it would be this crew and this Captain, he told himself. For his entire life, he had been a practicing agnostic, but he decidedly took a moment, and sent up a prayer for his missing crew. He reminded himself, that the Electra was first spotted sprinting away from a storm as he took post next to the radar operator and held a firm grip on the young woman's shoulder to maintain his balance. As he watched her, the radar screen told a story he did not want to hear. The night was going to be long and dark.

The journal of Amelia Earhart.

There are days I would like to forget. I would like to forget the day we did not make Howland. I would like to forget the day the Japanese found us on Milli Atoll and beat Fred senseless. I would like to forget how they murdered Palau and Fred. I would like to forget the day Fred passed away. I would like to forget the day I watched the young man's execution in the cell beside me and I cannot help but wonder if Soluu fell to the same fate as the price of knowing me.

However, I know I must never forget those days for that would be a dishonor to those who died to help me. I can only thank them by remembering them. That is why I have written this journal. My journey is no longer my story. Their journey and their sacrifice is what matters. My story is nothing without them.

Ayumu passed a few hours after we broke free of the storm. He left peacefully as a bird from a cage. As I lie here today in my final hours, I know that I will see them all again. I am sure they are waiting for me. Fred will ask me why it took so long for me to find the place. He always made fun of my navigational skills. Palau will want to play. I will tell him how brave his brother has been. I will tell him how Truc has missed him and if I find Soluu there I will feed her as she fed me.

I think however, I will most enjoy getting to know Ayumu. If God is as generous with me in death as he has been with me in life then I know he will let me fly with my friend. I want to do another stunt with Ayumu and Fred. I want Palau and Soluu to show me the wonderful land beyond my understanding. I like to believe they will all be waiting for me, ready to fly away to other worlds. I have to believe that. I also wonder whom I will meet that I did not expect to meet. I wonder if any from my family that were alive when I left will be there.

How we got to this island is a mystery that I will never be able to explain. I tried to return to New Guinea. All I know is that I burned all but a few last gallons of fuel when we found this paradise. I must believe that God or the universe wanted us to find it.

As I watch Truc and Mila make a life, I now believe the universe conspired to save them. I was only the ferryman. This place was made for Truc and Mila. They are the reason I am here. This is the perfect place for a young couple who knows nothing of the modern world. I have spent hours telling Truc of the things he would see if he were to leave and I have told him of my desire to complete my journey. All that matters not. I have concluded that this entire journey was never about me. I believe, I was supposed to get lost so that Truc might find me.

53

To See As In
A Fogged Mirror

Oh shadow, lift away
Living light, come this way
Upon these seas, I shall roam
As they call me forever home

The blip appeared an hour before daylight, on the outmost ring of the radar's effective range. As the sun cracked the sky before them, it became obvious that the vessel on the radar was moving at the same speed the Electra normally traveled. If the unknown vessel stayed the course, it would pass beneath Golden Gate Bridge at sunset. The timing was not lost on Admiral Simpson. It had to be the Electra, he told himself.

A thick fog had moved in after the storm, like a shroud covering a body, forcing the Rush to proceed forward at half speed, still in fear of running over her prey. Nevertheless, the Admiral gripped his binoculars, desperately searching as he had throughout the night, white knuckled and shaking with anticipation. The fog had forced his helicopter to remain grounded and, yet, for the first time since the Electra had disappeared a knowing smile had returned. Everything within, told him it had to be her for he did not allow a single soul to speak a dire prediction on the bridge of the Rush throughout the long dark night.

All the while, Kiki remained on watch beside Captain Bearing, scanning the seemingly impenetrable wall of fog, while George worked his camera's best long-range lens in hope of spotting her first. The Rush was ready for a miracle.

The journal of Amelia Earhart

I hope you have the opportunity to know my friends, Truc and Mila. They have things to teach the world. Truc has a way about him that I cannot describe. A sense of life, I cannot fully comprehend. He tells me I don't understand, because I trust my knowledge more than my heart. I think I am just beginning to understand that now. The simple truth is, facts will not take me to where I am heading now. Only what I believe in my heart matters now.

Truc told me of his heaven recently. It seems he believes that he and Mila will one day live on an island called Nako. He tells me that Nako is a place where the spirit food is everlasting. This makes me think of how we all see heaven through our own lenses. It makes sense, that heaven is an Island to Truc, filled with rare food. To me it sounds like a lovely place to visit. I was hoping for streets and a few stores. Either way, I pray the winds find me worthy of such a journey.

54

Where Is Faith?

We shall race upon the tempest
We shall hold the makers hand
We shall break the mortal coil
And say, this was the plan
A testament of life I share
A testament of grace
A testament we all shall pay
To the one, who gave us the way

A brisk wind came up from the south; a clean wind, offering life after a long season of dark storms. For some reason, it reminded Captain Bearing of fly-fishing with his grandfather and he could not imagine why the memory had returned. He decided to take it as a good omen.

As the rising sun began to break the fog into ever smaller patches, his vigil remained intent. He wanted nothing more than to locate the Electra for his Admiral.

He closed his eyes and mumbled his first prayer; "Please God...let it be her."

To his surprise, God heard his prayer, and at that moment, the thick fog parted and the Electra sprung forth from its grip like a lost child running to a parent.

"Eleven o'clock. I have her at Eleven o'clock!" Captain Bearing shouted.

Sailing at full speed, the Electra was a beautiful sight to the tired eyes aboard the Rush. Moreover, to their great relief she looked to be in near-perfect condition. Captain Channing was in command, seemingly lifeless; swinging from side to side in a rhythm that matched the pulse of the sea.

"Is he alive?" Kiki yelled above the passing wind of the fly bridge.

Captain Channing looked to be as limp as a wet rag, and fear gripped the crew of the Rush, until the outrigger dropped a half dozen feet and he systematically touched the waves that passed beneath. In one accord, the bridge of the Rush celebrated with a loud chorus of cheers as Captain Channing snapped from his trance, raised his right hand, and saluted smartly. To a person, the crew of the Rush returned the honor.

In the midst of the moment, Kiki hugged Captain Bearing by the neck and he did not protest as George took the opportunity to grab two female technicians and bear hug each. Admiral Simpson simply lay over the railing of the fly bridge, exhausted, relieved, and listened on the chorus of praise as their destroyer escort discharged their horns in celebration. He lifted his binoculars that felt like they weighed a thousand pounds and he studied the Electra. Captain Channing was noticeably different, as if he had climbed the mount of God and returned with the Ten Commandments. He looked old about the eyes to the Admiral and yet his smile was far more inviting. Captain Channing leaned into the harness and asked the Electra give him more speed. It was then the Admiral realized something was wrong. Something he could not define.

The journal of Amelia Earhart

If you find this journal, I hope you stop doing and start being, as Truc has tried to teach me. The world is larger through his eyes. I believe he must pass these gifts on to others, and I believe he will not remain on this island. Truc was created to sail to far away places, and I cannot imagine his God wasting that gift. In the hope that he does one day leave, I have told him all I could about where I am from. I have shared with him everything I can think of in the hope that he might find you. However, I have told him that he must only go if Mila approves.

I pray for others to find the vast expanse of life as he sees it. The universe will not let Truc pass without giving away what he has to share. It has invested far too much in him.

55

Broken

I shall wait for you
But never alone
For the sea knows my name
It holds me without shame
And there, in the midst of its bosom
I shall wait for you
But never alone

As the Electra tacked to avoid the oncoming armada following the Rush, the crew of the Rush was finally able to see Clair, seated awkwardly between the opposing forces of hull and outrigger. As she sat up to investigate the sound of ships, Admiral Simpson leaned into his binocular to see if she might be injured and his smile quickly faded as he thought she looked to be forlorn. Then, as if lost in a dream, Clair slowly raised her hand and waved to the ships in a most defeated manner.

The journal of Amelia Earhart

I have asked Truc to bury me next to Captain Ayumu, on the ridge overlooking the lagoon. Who knows, maybe one day I will go home, but until then, I will be content to wait with my friends. The ridge is a beautiful place. I go often and tell Ayumu about our day, and I think. I owe him that much, for walking with me, for rescuing me, for being my friend. The wind always blows across it and I cannot help but imagine flying when I am there. I hope the wind will help me take wing to my Nako, wherever that may be.

56

The Sea's Desire

Cry not for me, Oh mortal world
I came to you with no hold
I will return with no other gold
Other than the love we shared among the sea
And the gift of hope given freely

Clair remained motionless, her eyes obviously swollen from crying. After several long minutes she finally picked up the radio and held it close to her chest. She said not a word as she thought about the night she had just experienced. A night in which she feared she would surely die. A long night with Truc in her arms as if she were holding her own father. The universe had created a space for Truc and Clair. There, in the final hours of the storm, as he lay in her arms speaking to his beloved Mila, Clair decided she would never again talk about things she could not change or love, ever again, with half a heart.

The radio remained heavy in her hand as it beckoned her to say something. Yet the weight seemed to double again as she lifted it to her lips and pressed send.

"Electra...to the Rush," she mumbled more than spoke.

Admiral Simpson, having watched her every move, was waiting for her with radio in hand.

"Lieutenant, are you Ok? What happened to you last night?" he begged.

Clair looked to be a limp rag doll tangled in the Electra's netting and so she held the radio close to her chest.

"Lieutenant?" the Admiral asked, "Where is Truc? Is he ok?"

The question hit Clair as if a slap across the face, and with the radio link open, in front of God and the world, she laid her head in her hands and began to cry aloud. Her grief swept across the bridge of the Rush and her pain told a story none could accept. Admiral Simpson looked to Captain Bearing, dropped the radio handset to the floor and buried his head in a nearby instrument panel. Nothing more needed to be said. Truc's journey was now in the hands of his God.

The final journal entry of Amelia Earhart

I only have a few hours now. I have become numb from the waist down. The good news is that I am no longer in pain. This will be the end of it. I want to say something profound, but for the life of me, all I can think of is the next journey. I keep trying to imagine what is before me. Truc of course tells me, Aluluei and Palulop will be with me as I cross the great channel. I can only hope so. I know one thing is for certain, I have one more stunt flight left in me.

Amelia.

57

Homecoming

The sea is a creature best loved by the hands of men
Who sing to her songs of peace in the morning
As if the world must not know they are lovers
For she is kind to those who penetrate her depths
And desire no bounds but the salt of her womb

The final installment of the last journal entry, broadcast nearly two hours before the Electra entered the channel of San Francisco Bay. Enough time for those who could, to see for themselves the miracle of the Electra as it passed beneath the Golden Gate Bridge.

The final leg did not turn out to be the chaos Admiral Simpson had imagined, as hundreds of private vessels lined the final mile, as if standing at attention. George made every effort to record the event, as the channel looked to be a super highway, in which the traffic had been properly separated for a Presidential motorcade. And to a vessel, each onlooker remained at attention as the Electra sliced past their vantage point. Then, as if ordered to do so, each fell in behind the Electra's entourage, unknowingly forming a funeral procession of unimagined magnitude.

As the evening lights of San Francisco covered the horizon, Clair decided to strap into the second harness and settled in beside Steve. With Clair at his side, Captain Channing reigned the wing in tight to gain speed, and asked the Electra to dance once again as she tackled the light chop of the bay. Both knew as they looked to each other and leaned out as far as they could, this would probably be the last time she would be free to fly.

The Electra and her crew passed beneath the Golden Gate with the sun setting at her back, and the bay cities rallying their Fourth of July fireworks in her honor. Tens of thousands lined the Golden Gate Bridge to see for themselves the Electra as she passed beneath in all her glory, but to Steve, it was all a blur of light and motion. To him, the spectacle paled in comparison to his new view of the natural world. He embraced the unexplored realm, a place that was now his to discover, knowing that Truc would be at his side in this place of ever-growing revelation.

The spectacle above the Golden Gate hit a crescendo. The view was more than Clair could have imagined, and she knew then, she would spend the rest of her life trying to define this moment. Although her heart was broken, she could not help but smile, as pride filled her heart for what they had accomplished together. She decided she no longer cared what Simpson might think or do and she hugged Steve with all her might, as the Golden Gate fell to their stern. A secret would no longer serve the love she felt for him.

"You did it...you brought them home!" Clair exclaimed as the bay reflected the spectacle of fireworks against the wing. A cheer echoed across the water, adding a human voice to the symphony of fireworks as dusk began to settle into dark. Steve instinctively dropped the outrigger to skim the swell, he leaned into his rigging, and skipped his hand across the waves, as was now his habit. To his surprise, the cheer hit a crescendo once again, as Clair's hand joined his.

"I think Truc would have liked the Golden Gate. He would have said it was...okeydokey," Captain Channing proclaimed as he adjusted the wing and forced the outrigger to reach for the sky.

"Truc was here long before we arrived," Clair replied as she wiped the tears away from her lovers face.

"Yes he was...yes he was," Steve conceded as he leaned into the strain of wind and wing and asked the Electra to fly one last time.

Epilog

One Year Later

The Journal of Commander Clair E E Channing

After much prompting from Catherine Vonstreep, I have decided that I need to journal the events of this day, and all those that are to follow. How we are watching the most beautiful sunset, that I have ever witnessed, began with a phone call five months ago.

I will have to take this back a bit for everything to make sense. I still laugh to this day, as I think about the face the Admiral made when he heard the voice on the far end of the telephone. First, he became white as a ghost, and then he nearly had a stroke. Truc was on the other end. At least, he sounded like Truc.

As it turns out, Truc's son, Palau Jr had finally heard about his father's story, and our journey. He was himself living in a very remote location with his family. We know now, that it was at his father's insistence, at seventeen or eighteen, when he left to find his own life. I cannot tell you how excited we all were when we learned Palau Jr. had survived. He has been able to fill in so much that we did not know.

Now, let me jump back a bit further. Steve and I married three months after we delivered the Electra to Oakland. After the Golden Gate, it was hard for us to hide our feelings from the Admiral. I kid Steve, that he only asked me to marry him because he was afraid that Simpson was about to have him flogged.

A month later, my Steve was offered a radical surgical experiment to save his eyesight. The surgery was only able to save one eye, but he can read with it, and make out my face. To tell the truth, his eyesight is not much better than it was before the surgery, however, it is no longer deteriorating.

Cat and Otto flew to the states and watched us arrive at the Golden gate. We met them soon after in Oakland as news crews put us together. We have since become the best of friends. Otto was a groomsman and Catherine was a bridesmaid. Admiral Simpson stood in for my father and Captain Bearing was the best man. I think Mo Mo has a crush on Captain Bearing, and it was all a bit awkward at the reception when he brought Kiki with him.

Mo Mo told Steve he was off the hook concerning Truc's passing away while under his care. For some reason Steve seemed most relieved by this reprieve. I know she misses her friend. There is sadness about her when we talk of our night with him at the restaurant.

The news of finding Palau Jr. could not have come at a better time. Steve had just finished the rough draft of a book regarding our amazing journey. Now we are holding off on publishing it until we return from this adventure. The end is yet to be discovered.

The Vonstreeps had returned to finish their attempt to circumnavigate the globe and were almost to Papua New Guinea when we contacted them in regard to Palau Jr. They sailed to the small island on which Palau. resided and confirmed that he looked and sounded exactly like his father. As a matter of a fact, so did his son and his grandson. The story behind his adventure to find another life and another island is a most amazing story but I will put that down another day.

We then contacted Truc's brother's grandchildren in the Marshall Islands. It did not take much to convince them to meet us.

It took us a week to fly to the nearest location in which the Vonstreeps could pick us up. With Palau Jr. on board along with his son, grandson and the children of Truc's brother, we embarked on the mission to find the island upon where Amelia spent her last days. For the family however, it is the place that Truc buried his beloved Mila.

From Palau's description and by calculating a three thousand mile radius from the Marshall Islands, we located the remote three-island chain Amelia described in her journal.

As I said, Truc junior has been a wealth of information on the topic of how his parents survived. It seems they were most resourceful. We know now Truc had intended his trip to bring Amelia home since the day she passed away. Palau described how his father worked on ways his plans to build the Electra and how his mother invented the cording used to support her wing. We discovered that the binding lines had been the Achilles heel on the first attempt which fatally injured Amelia.

It seems Mila would spend nearly a month making a ten-foot section, by first cooking the fibers to break them down. She would then reconstitute them in a mesh made from homemade glue, then wind the mesh into small strands and then the strands into cord. The entire process sounded extremely difficult, but we know now, that in all honesty the Electra would have never sailed if not for the work of her hand. Mila is as responsible for Amelia's return as much as Truc. It took a team to build our Electra.

Palau Jr. also took time in explaining how his father and mother were deeply afraid of being discovered. It seems their experience in the Marshall Islands had been far more traumatic than even Amelia described. They feared the Japanese were personally looking for them due to the dramatic nature of their escape. This explains why his father asked him to sail alone and to look for a people he could trust. Moreover, it explains why Truc Jr kept the secret of their location. We must understand that Palau Jr.

never met Amelia. He did not know the world was looking for her.

Our Truc would have left long before if not for his love of Mila. The Japanese had abused her and this had a profound affect. Truc did tell his son of his plan to stay with his mother until one or the other passed. As we know now, Mila passed away first, leaving Truc, a very old man alone with a boat that he had spent most of his adult life building.

So here, we sit today, on a ledge overlooking the cove where Amelia lived and died. It is easy to imagine the day the Electra sailed away through the same inlet. It is one of the most beautiful and peaceful places I have witnessed.

You should have seen us packed aboard the skiff as we made our way up the inlet. We were far overloaded with Palau Jr. and his two sons aboard. They are not small men like Truc and everyone wanted to go ashore first.

My Steve was a sight to see with his black bandanna and a patch over his bad left eye. I could not help but fall in love with my pirate as he came ashore. He was so sexy. All he needed was a peg leg.

It did not take long for us to locate their home buried in the edge of the jungle. The structure was still standing and it was obvious Truc left quickly. I suppose he knew he would never return.

The structure in which they lived sits high off the ground, to protect its inhabitance from crabs and storms. Their home looks as close to the Swiss family Robinson as one could imagine. We spent two hours searching the place and listening to Palau Jr. as he told his son and grandson the story of his parents. The two nephews are the sweetest men you will ever meet and the resemblance to Truc is uncanny. To see them all together is most disconcerting. You cannot help but to see Truc at each stage of his life in all of them.

Otto, Steve and Palau Jr. returned a while later to the Sand Seeker to bring Truc's remains ashore. At first, the President wanted Truc buried at Arlington National

Cemetery next to Amelia. However, Admiral Simpson requested that Truc be returned to Hawaii and buried beneath the palm where we first met him. It seemed fitting to those of us who had known him and to our surprise the President agreed and a monument was nearly complete, when we discovered Palau Jr. Of course, that is why we are here today. No one could argue with a sons' decision to return his father to the side of his mother. The circle is now complete.

We brought Truc to the outcropping in which Captain Ayumu and Mila are buried. There we located an empty grave that must have contained Amelia. It seemed most appropriate to bury Truc in the same grave beside Mila and Captain Ayumu. It is a grave, in which I believe, he knew he would return to one day. The ceremony was simple and it could not have been a better day for such a farewell. Palau Jr sang a song Truc used on our journey often. My heart can still hear Truc singing it as he sailed the Electra.

I am writing this entry as a magnificent sunset falls across the cove, sitting with my Captain upon this ledge that I am sure Amelia and Truc spent time. I do not want to leave here and I can tell, neither does Steve. This place is as close to heaven on earth as one can imagine. Everything about this island embodies my friend Truc and I cannot help but feel his smile upon us.

As Amelia said in her journal, the wind always seems to blow upon this ledge. I believe I can hear Truc in the wind. He is telling me to relax. He is telling me, in his own quiet way, that all will be okeydokey. This is the place to tell Steve about our next adventure. A little adventure, who I believe will be arriving in about eight months.

Commander Clair Elizabeth Evans Channing
United States Coast Guard

The End